SHOW ME THE MURDER

CAROLYN MULFORD

SHOW ME THE MURDER

WORLDWIDE®

TORONTO • NEW YORK • LONDON
AMSTERDAM • PARIS • SYDNEY • HAMBURG
STOCKHOLM • ATHENS • TOKYO • MILAN
MADRID • WARSAW • BUDAPEST • AUCKLAND

Show Me the Murder

A Worldwide Mystery/June 2015

First published by Five Star Publishing.

ISBN-13: 978-0-373-26949-5

Printed in U.S.A.

Acknowledgments

A writer works in isolation while putting words on the screen, but not in gathering information and in rewriting the drafts. I extend a public thank-you to those who assisted me in those initial and final stages.

To find answers to countless questions about police work, I participated first in the Montgomery County, Maryland, Citizen Academy and then in the Columbia, Missouri, program. The training sessions revealed not only how officers work but also how they think. In both places, the officers' skills and commitment impressed me. Staff members of the Boone and Randolph County, Missouri, sheriff departments also enlightened me on routine duties and special problems.

Central Intelligence Agency operatives don't talk about their work so freely, but I drew on my observations in Vienna and on retired operatives' (censored) books and casual conversations for essential information and insights.

In portraying both police and CIA activities, I took advantage of the freedom of fiction to create the quirky possible rather than the highly probable. Any errors are mine.

Members of my Washington, DC–based critique group began as professional associates and became close friends. Maya Corrigan, Mary Nelson, Helen Schwartz and Sylvia Straub spent many hours dissecting this book's chapters. Missouri friends Blenda Marquardt and Charlene Schillie gave valued comments on the complete manuscript. One of my most trusted critics has been Joyce Campbell, my friend since our Peace Corps service and my first and last reader on all my fiction manuscripts.

ONE

MADE IT. I turned off the two-lane highway onto the residential street leading to safety and sympathy. A pothole jarred me. Pain erupted beneath my ribs. Pulling to the curb, I held my breath until the agony became an endurable ache. I reached over to my purse and fumbled for the oxycodone bottle beneath my Glock 27. The trick would be to placate my wound without fogging my brain. I swallowed half a pill and opened the window to cool off while I waited for it to work.

Freshly mowed grass scented the air. A bed of white and purple irises beautified a yard in front of one of the old white frame houses. My mother had loved irises. Did hers still bloom? They'd add to the house's curb appeal when I put it on the market.

Or when Annalynn did that for me. I'd looked forward to seeing her again through five long days of stop-and-go driving. I could tough it out the last two blocks. I pulled away from the curb and, a block later, turned right onto Franklin Street. Ahead, Annalynn's pinkish tile roof and gray limestone walls towered above my childhood home, now nothing but a vacant little brick house. A yellow Volkswagen Beetle sat in her driveway so I parked in mine.

Pots of white calla lilies lined her front porch wall.

Funeral flowers.

Not Annalynn. Surely not Annalynn.

A slender blonde woman in a snug turquoise dress

rushed out the front door and down the porch steps toward the Beetle. Connie Diamante—as blonde and as irredeemably perky as she'd been in high school. She always knew what was going on.

I waved.

She did a double take and scurried to me. "Phoenix! Thank God you're finally here!" She bent to kiss my cheek. "When you didn't show up two days ago, I called your brothers in California and your office in Vienna to get your cell number. You really—"

I couldn't stand more of her prattle. "Has something happened to Annalynn?"

Connie stepped back. "You don't know."

Obviously. "Is Annalynn okay?"

"No, she's not." Connie flicked away a tear. "Maybe it's better—kind of cathartic—for her to tell you about it herself."

Enough melodrama. "*You* tell me. Right now. The short version." I reined in my impatience and softened my tone. "Please, Connie."

"Okay, okay, Ms. Bossy." She threw her head back and closed her eyes. "Boom died five days ago." She opened her eyes and waited for my reaction.

I nodded, my concern for Annalynn rather than her husband. "Heart attack?"

"I wish." She glanced toward the house. "A maid found Boom and a young woman in a sleazy motel room. The police say he shot her and then himself."

"No! I can't believe he'd cheat on Annalynn." The thing I'd liked most about the handsome, extroverted jock was that he adored his wife.

"Then that makes you the second person in Laycock. In the whole state of Missouri. His staff at the sheriff's department, his son and daughter, his minister—everyone except Annalynn—says he did it. She insists someone set him up."

I shook my head to clear it. Connie still stood there looking little older than she had the last time I'd seen her, some twenty years ago. "You think Annalynn's wrong."

Connie leaned down to my window as though to hide her words. "Yes, but I haven't had the nerve to tell her why, and I don't have time to tell you now. I'm singing at a big hundredth-birthday party and I'm running late." She straightened, a single worry line on her forehead. "She's alone. Her kids and their families left town a couple of hours ago, right after the funeral. They couldn't deal with their father's death, or with her reaction. She's been waiting for *you,* Phoenix. She's counting on you."

And I'd never been less capable. How could Annalynn—the perfectionist, the judge's daughter, the town's chief do-gooder—cope with her husband's death and public betrayal? "What can I say to comfort her? What does she need to hear?"

"You'll know what to say. You always do." Connie patted my shoulder. "But before you go in, fix your face. Your skin is the color of cement."

"Gee, thanks." Same old Connie. She'd always envied my bond with Annalynn. And that I stood four inches taller than Connie's five foot two.

She hurried toward her car in three-inch heels. "See you in church tomorrow."

Not likely. I hadn't gone into a church except as a tourist for decades. I flipped down the visor mirror. Bloody hell! If Annalynn saw me looking like this, she would freak out, call a doctor, and destroy my cover story. I retrieved my makeup kit and spent two minutes approximating my normal light-tan complexion. I ran a hand through my short black hair to plump it up. And to pull out a rare gray strand. Ready.

I eased out of the car, clung to it until the world quit moving, and walked slowly across the driveways and Annalynn's lawn and up the porch steps to her front door. After ringing the bell twice, I called, "Annalynn, it's Phoenix."

Quick steps sounded in the hall, and Annalynn opened the door. "At last! I've been so worried about you." She'd never been a hugger, but she drew me into the house and enveloped me in a painful embrace. "You shouldn't have driven all the way from Washington so soon after you left the hospital."

"I'm fine." She didn't notice the lie. "I'm so sorry not to be here for you."

Her welcoming smile vanished. She stepped back. "You've heard about Boom."

Connie had called it right. Annalynn needed to tell me the story of her husband's death. "I heard he died Tuesday." To reconnect, I put my hands on her shoulders. "You know I'll do anything I can to help you through this."

"I'm so thankful you're here." She drew back. "I'll pour us the last of Father's whiskey and tell you what I know."

"None for me," I said with regret. "No alcohol until I go off my pain pills."

"You're still on medication? Trudy had gallbladder surgery on a Thursday and came to church on Sunday."

I willed away a wave of dizziness. "She probably had laparoscopic surgery. Turkish hospitals still use the scalpel, or at least they did on me."

Annalynn frowned. "I thought you had surgery in Vienna."

Damn! An amateur's mistake. I revised my cover story. "I went to Istanbul to buy a Kayseri wool carpet for my spare bedroom. My medical evacuation to DC was from Istanbul." Via a military hospital in Germany.

Annalynn nodded absently and went through the open double pocket doors into the dining room and to the Queen Anne liquor cabinet.

I marveled at her composure. Near the end of a ghastly day, she remained elegant in a royal-blue sheath dress and pearls that surely came from elderly oysters. Her subtle makeup showed no smudges, and not a strand of her chestnut-highlighted brown hair had escaped from an intricate French roll. She wore her public face, the mask of serenity she used to conceal strong emotion.

She poured an undiluted double. "Would you like something to eat? People brought in mounds of food. I put aside some deviled eggs for you."

"No, thanks. Maybe later." My digestive system hadn't quite adjusted to solid food. Did I dare eat the deviled eggs? "Let's sit in the window seat."

She led the way down the wide central hall past the staircase to our old favorite spot and stepped out of her low-heeled pumps. She curled her legs up under her the way she had as a girl.

Moving gingerly, I assumed my old cross-legged pose facing her and leaned against the wall. I'd rarely felt so inadequate. "If it's too hard for you to talk about…"

"No, I want you to hear the truth." She sipped her whiskey. "Monday night I had a committee meeting. Boom went to dinner with a football buddy passing through. Bob or Bill or Bert. I can't remember. I came home a little before ten. Boom came in five minutes later and fixed some popcorn. We watched the ten-o'clock news together. Then I went upstairs to bed and he went downstairs to his office. I fell asleep."

Her businesslike tone and precise words told me two things: She had repeated this story many times, and she held her grief in a steely grasp that even she couldn't maintain. I reached out to take her free hand.

She breathed deeply and exhaled. "About two I missed him and came downstairs. He'd left a note on the dining-room table saying he'd gone out on a call." Her voice wavered. She took another sip of whiskey.

I squeezed her hand.

She stared out the window into the backyard. "I got up at seven and phoned the sheriff's department. No one knew anything about a call. About eight o'clock George Brendan, Boom's chief deputy, came by." She blinked several times. "I thought he was going to cry. He said—he said that they had found Boom at Sweet Nights Motel with a bullet hole behind his right ear. A woman named Maria Lopez—I'd never heard of her—was with him, and she'd been shot, too." Body rigid, she stared into my eyes. The public mask no longer hid her anguish.

She needed me to accept her denial of his betrayal. I weighed my response. The police had ruled it a homicide-suicide, but Annalynn hadn't. Honor her feelings. Respect her judgment. I made my tone curious, nonjudgmental. "Who shot them?"

Her shoulders relaxed. "I don't know. The sheriff's department claims Boom shot her and then himself. They refuse to investigate any further." She hesitated, gripping my hand as if it were a lifeline. "Even our kids believe he was having an affair and—and went crazy." She waited expectantly.

"I see." My brain went into a stall. I couldn't say they were wrong. I mustn't say they were right.

Annalynn set the whiskey on the windowsill, leaned forward, and clasped both my hands. "He *couldn't*—he *wouldn't* have betrayed me. Someone set him up." She lowered her gaze and her face contorted. When she looked up, her eyes held no tears. Her grip on my hands tightened. "I can't let people brand Boom an adulterer and a murderer. Phoenix, I have no one else to turn to. Please, *please,* help me find Boom's killer."

TWO

ANNALYNN'S PLEA MADE me shiver. The last thing I wanted to do was find information that would destroy her faith in her husband. I hedged: "Of course I'll do whatever I can, but I know how to analyze economic data, not investigate murder."

"If I don't look for the killer, no one will." She clenched her lips, fighting for control. "I can't do it alone, and we've always been a terrific team."

A cramp in my left calf made me gasp. I jerked my hands away, jumped up, and stomped my foot. She crumpled. I'd have to go along. "Sorry, a charley horse. How do you plan to prove Boom's innocence?"

Relief shone on her face. "I don't have a plan. I've been waiting for you."

She had no idea what to do. Neither did I, but she'd refused to consider that. "We'll work on it together." Act confident, matter of fact. Where to start? "We need the known facts, beginning with the police report."

She nodded. "Of course. Then what?"

Think. Be logical. "A list of the cases he was working on."

"None. He managed the department. He left the field work to his staff."

I scrambled for another suggestion. "A list of his enemies, people angry at the sheriff's department, or even at the dealership when he was selling cars."

"No one. He treated everyone he met like his best friend. Everyone loved Boom."

Then why would someone kill him? "That's wonderful," I said. She raised an eyebrow. The magic pill had diminished my ample capacity for deception. "I'm sorry, Annalynn. I'm too tired to think. Maybe a cup of tea and a deviled egg will revive me."

"Of course. We'll have a light supper and let you rest." She slipped on her shoes. "People brought so much food. I gave away as much as I could without offending anyone, but the freezer and the refrigerator are both packed."

Following her through the dining room into the spacious kitchen with a granite-topped island, I thought about what I would have done if an asset had died under suspicious circumstances. "We should check his schedule—what he was working on, who he saw, where he went."

She turned around to smile at me. "I told Connie you would know what to do. Boom kept a calendar on his iPhone. I'll look for it after we eat."

"Good." I switched to a safe topic. "I wish I'd come in time to see Walt and Gracie and meet your three grandchildren. Does Lynette still look exactly like you?"

"Boom thinks so." Annalynn gasped and covered her face with her hands. "I can't believe he's gone. I keep waiting to wake up from this terrible nightmare."

I patted her on the shoulder. "Go ahead and cry. Let yourself grieve."

"I don't dare let myself go until we find out who did this." She went to the large stainless-steel refrigerator. "Connie and I made up the bed in my old room so you'll have your own bath."

Anxious to deal with my fragility in private, I fished for a plausible reason to stay next door in my childhood home. Annalynn had told me my "house sitter" had left a bed and some other furniture when she moved to an assisted-living facility.

Annalynn rested her forehead on the shiny door. "I couldn't face the nights with no one else in the house."

No way I could leave after hearing that. "I'll put on the tea kettle while you pry dinner—supper—from the refrigerator."

BY THE TIME we gave up finding Boom's cell phone, my medication had moved into its sleep-demanding stage. Annalynn noticed and insisted I go to bed.

The grandfather's clock chimed nine as I climbed into the canopied nineteenth-century four-poster bed. When the Carrs bought it for Annalynn, I'd called it the umbrella bed. My four-year-old brain had reasoned the canopy was to protect Annalynn if the roof leaked. Despite exhaustion and an excellent mattress, I had to use every relaxation technique I knew to block out my concern for Annalynn enough to fall asleep.

At three o'clock the clock's chime woke me. Across the hall moonlight outlined Annalynn's slim figure, head bent, pacing back and forth in her bedroom. Her arms were folded tightly across her chest. Was she holding in her anguish? Pretending Boom's arms held her? Attempting to comfort herself? Her knees bent, her shoulders pitched forward, and she buried her face in clenched fists. I had to go to her. As I reached to push back my sheet, she straightened and took two long steps toward me. She closed her door.

I froze, every muscle taut. Was it cowardice or intuition chaining me to my bed? My muscles relaxed. Love and happiness we share. Grief we carry into a dark cave. Tears stung my eyes. I'd leave her alone in the dark tonight, but somehow I'd pull her out of that cave.

What if our search for the truth—an overrated concept—ended in more anguish for Annalynn? I'd have to stay far enough ahead of her to hide signs of Boom's betrayal. Better for Annalynn to blame me for failure than her beloved husband for infidelity. I'd never forget my desolation when I caught Russ cheating on me.

For the umpteenth time, I wondered why a woman of Annalynn's intelligence and ambition loved a good ol' boy who touched, but never grasped, the brass ring. An outstanding college athlete, he'd lasted only one year in the NFL and four years as a community college coach. The young couple moved into her newly widowed father's home with their two small children. Boom sold cars until the judge died. Annalynn invested—and lost—a chunk of her inheritance in a dealership. After diddling around for months, Boom ran for sheriff.

I remembered something else. Mom ended each report of Boom's failures with, "But he's such a good father, and he and Annalynn still touch each other like newlyweds." I had to remain open to the possibility that Annalynn could be right.

"PHOENIX. PHOENIX! WAKE UP!"

I ROUSED myself from a deep sleep to see Annalynn standing over me.

"Are you okay? You're whiter than the sheets!"

"I'm fine." I took in her beige-trimmed black dress and gold necklace and earrings. Church clothes. "I'm awake. Just give me a minute."

She smiled. "You can't fool *me* with that line." She sobered. "Please come to church with me. I can't walk in alone."

I closed my eyes. The only thing I wanted to do less than go to church was to get out of bed. "No one's expecting you to go to church today."

"I have to." Her voice trembled. "I have to show them that—that I know Boom didn't do anything wrong."

She knew these people well. Better to face them down than hide. I stretched, testing whether I could move without flinching. Twinges rather than jabs. I *could* go to church, but that would advertise my arrival in Laycock. "Can't Connie go with you?"

"No. She directs the choir." She turned her face away. "I can't ask any of our married friends. They're avoiding me because they don't know what to say."

That left me. No real reason for me to hide. My CIA Operations contact—furious that I'd jeopardized twenty-five years of deep cover by getting shot during a free-lance courier mission—didn't care what I did as long as I stayed in the States and kept my mouth shut. I sat up. "Fix some toast while I find something Methodist to wear. I warn you: I brought nothing but knockabout clothes."

She tousled my hair. "Try on the burnt-orange silk blouse that I put in your closet. It's perfect for your Mediterranean complexion. I'll start the coffee."

When Annalynn left, I swallowed a fourth of a pill, donned the blouse and black slacks, and applied makeup. After a moment's hesitation, I left the Glock in my purse. I'd rarely carried anything recognizable as a weapon while undercover, but now I broke into a sweat if I went out without my new gun.

Annalynn frowned as I came into the dining room. "The blouse is a little loose." Her eyes widened. "You've lost too much weight, and you're moving as though you're in pain. Oh, Phoenix, I'm so sorry I woke you."

"Don't worry. I'm fine." To prove it, I moved to my seat at the table more quickly than my body preferred. "Apple butter! I've missed that."

"With a glass of milk." Annalynn stepped into the kitchen and came back a minute later with the toast. "I looked in the SUV for Boom's iPhone. It's not there."

I heard her effort to remain calm. Annalynn wouldn't rest until she had answered her questions about Boom and the woman. "The police probably have it."

"No. George gave me Boom's things." She pressed her lips together a moment. "He never left home without that phone. His killer must have taken it to hide evidence."

Doubtful, but possible. Men devoted to their toys don't go anywhere without them, even to an assignation. But if someone took the iPhone, they would have destroyed it by now. "He probably kept a duplicate calendar on his computer."

"Yes, he did." The lines in her forehead smoothed out. "I was afraid you didn't believe me. Connie doesn't, even though she won't say so. No one else does either."

"That's good, actually." I'd have to turn lemons into lemonade for a while. "Anyone who could kill two people—and make it look like murder-suicide—is extremely dangerous. We'll accomplish more if we don't announce we're investigating." And Annalynn would look ridiculous if she accused anyone without evidence. "Don't mention the missing mobile—uh—cell phone. Don't criticize the detectives. If we find evidence, we'll need their help."

She stared at me, obviously assessing both my words and my attitude. "If you say so." After a moment she added firmly, "I won't pretend I think Boom killed himself or that young woman."

Too bad Annalynn was a congenital truth teller, a handicap I'd overcome. "You can say things like, 'He was a wonderful husband. There's been a terrible mistake.' Or maybe, 'I'm sure the police will find something to prove him innocent.' Be vague."

"I can do that." She clasped my hand. "Thank you so much. I would have run downstairs to the bomb shelter and screamed myself hoarse if you hadn't believed me."

WALKING WITH ANNALYNN down the church's center aisle to her second-row pew, I heard a low buzz and saw many eyes averted. To my relief, gray-haired women in their Sunday best and a few bald men in blazers nodded and smiled at us as they recognized Mary and Jack Smith's girl.

Before I sat down, I turned around to greet the last of my father's World War II buddies—and to scan the congregation. Most were casually dressed white, middle-aged parents with children too old for the toddlers' room and too young to sit in the back with the self-conscious teenagers. The church had added four well-dressed black families. What surprised me were two dozen or so Hispanics, both neatly dressed young families and men in their twenties and thirties. What job opportunities had brought Hispanics to Laycock, and what had attracted them to this old Methodist church? In a back pew on the aisle a young Hispanic man in a sparkling white shirt and styled hair met my gaze a moment and glanced away.

Trying to find something to say to drown out the whispers, I surveyed the familiar sanctuary's white walls, vaulted ceiling, and colored-glass windows. White lilies below and on both sides of the pulpit caught my attention. I pointed to them. "Has a florist joined the congregation?"

"I sent over some of the extra flowers," Annalynn murmured. "The new minister, Wesley Berry, likes flowers around the pulpit."

Of course. My gaffe alarmed me. I had to get off those pain pills.

When a lean young man who needed to trim both his brown hair and his mustache began his sermon, I put on my listening face and thought about preparing for sale the house I'd bought from Mom ten years ago to give her financial independence. Floors would have to be sanded, rooms painted, flowerbeds planted.

The choir interrupted my planning. Connie led middle-aged women and teenagers of both sexes in a spirited rendition of "This Little Light of Mine," a civil rights-era spiritual that Connie, Annalynn, and I had sung in our first appearance as a trio. Connie had fantasized about stardom. She'd expected to capture the musical comedy roles Debbie Reynolds had grown too old to play. Annalynn had envisioned herself Missouri's first female senator. I'd dreamed of spying on the Soviet Union.

When the service ended, several elderly members of the congregation intercepted Annalynn to say they were praying for her and to greet me. I linked my arm with hers and edged us through the social gauntlet toward the door.

Most people hurried away, but a strikingly blond young man built like a football player watched Annalynn from a pew halfway back. Unlike the other young men, he wore a business suit. As we drew near, he turned and walked to the side aisle.

Listening to tone more than words, I heard sadness and sympathy in most voices, but two women's polite condolences didn't disguise their relish of a proud woman's humiliation. Most of the men mumbled and didn't meet Annalynn's eyes.

No one mentioned Boom by name.

At the door, the boyish minister clasped Annalynn's hand and leaned forward to speak to her privately, prompting me to step aside.

A deep voice said, "You're Phoenix Smith, right?"

I turned to look up at a square head mounted on nearly neckless shoulders. "Yes."

"I'm George Brendan, the chief deputy. I'd like a word with you, ma'am."

"Of course." It was more command than request, but curiosity compelled me to comply. We walked down the steps and around the corner into the church parking lot. Facing him, I took in the tense posture, deep circles under blue eyes, almost invisible blond eyebrows, close-cropped blond hair with gray over the ears.

"Boom told me Annalynn respects you, takes your advice."

"We grew up together." Eyes cast down modestly, I noted the perfect shine on his big black shoes. His short-sleeved white shirt, black tie, and black pants resembled a uniform. Always on duty.

He waited until no one stood near enough to overhear. "I s'pose she's told you that Boom didn't shoot that woman or himself."

"She's finding it hard to accept." No point in denying the known.

He leaned close. "And, of course, she's upset about not getting the insurance money."

I amplified my genuine confusion. "I don't understand."

"She won't get it because he was—because he wasn't

killed in the line of duty. She may not even get his pathetic pension. I sure hope she won't lose her house."

Lose the house? Ridiculous. Judge Carr had amassed a fortune in stocks. He'd also taught Annalynn and me the art and science of investing as soon as we learned our multiplication tables. Annalynn had to be loaded. I sighed. "What can the poor woman do?" For a moment, I feared I'd overdone it.

The deputy's chest swelled, and the dominant male protector emerged. "I feel real sorry for her. I'll do my best to help her get his pension." He leaned closer. "But claiming Boom didn't kill that woman will only hurt her chances."

Why a warning about a paltry pension that Annalynn didn't need? "I'm sorry. I don't understand."

"Well, ma'am, if she keeps quiet, the board will let it slide through. Otherwise they'll poke around and find out Boom had been seeing that broad for months. My nephew saw them at a beer joint last February, and I found her initials on Boom's office schedule a half dozen times. Annalynn starts pushing, and all this dirt's gonna come out."

Some dirt he feared. "More humiliation for her, you mean."

"Yes, ma'am." He pulled a white handkerchief from his back pocket and dabbed his perspiring forehead. "You'd be doing her a real favor if you persuade her to, you know, let it alone. Accept what Boom did and move on."

THREE

THE DEPUTY'S WARNING gave credence to Annalynn's distrust of the department's findings. I concealed my antagonism with a polite smile. "Thank you for your advice, Deputy Brendan. If there's anything else Annalynn needs to know, please call me. I'll be in Laycock a while to sell my family home."

"Always glad to help, ma'am." He whirled around and marched to a beige Crown Victoria labeled Sheriff's Department. It had a Deputy 1 license plate, and the young blond man in the suit—his son?—stood leaning against it.

Connie trotted past me, calling over her shoulder, "Hi and bye. I'm off to sing for my water bill at the Montgomerys' sixtieth wedding anniversary."

Annalynn, her face white and tight, handed the keys to her silver Mercedes to me and hurried to the passenger side.

"What happened?" I eased under the wheel.

"That imbecile! He told me to ask God to help me forgive Boom!"

I tsked and made a mental note to grill the minister. I also decided to wait for a more opportune time to tell her what the deputy had said.

We rode the four blocks in silence. Her color returned, but she clutched the straps of her bag with white knuckles.

When I pulled into the drive and punched the garage-door opener, she sucked in her breath and said, "Boom always drove my car into the garage. He was afraid I'd scratch it." She covered her face with her hands. "I miss him every single minute."

I patted her shoulder, drove into the garage, and stepped cautiously out of the car. Discomfort, but no dizziness. I turned the subject to the distant past: "My first memories are converting our storm cellars into bomb shelters. Does the trapdoor to your shelter still work?"

"Yes. Boom reopened it when we updated our shelter after the September 11 attacks and turned it into his home office." She closed the garage door behind us. "Let's go look for the calendar on his computer."

We went into the house and through the kitchen into the narrow back hallway. Annalynn flicked a light switch and opened the basement door.

At the foot of the basement steps I glanced left at enough fitness equipment for a professional gym. It had crowded out much of Judge Carr's beloved wood shop.

She paused. "My first memory is of our fathers making your dining-room chairs." She went on through the big metal door leading from the basement into a cement-block hall and turned right into the Carrs' former storm cellar.

A glass-topped computer desk held nothing but a keyboard, a large monitor, and a Mont Blanc pen. Against the outer wall of the six-by-nine room a printer rested on a black two-drawer file cabinet. A four-shelf metal bookcase with piles of sports and hunting magazines, a few books, and some file folders stood against the wall across from the desk. The walls had been painted beige, and a patterned red-and-black carpet covered the cement floor.

Annalynn hung back. “You probably know more about computers than I do.”

Guaranteed. “I know my way around a spreadsheet.” I sat down in an ergonomic office chair that had cost more than everything else in the room. I tapped a key, and the screen came to life. Had Boom left it on? Maybe Walt or Gracie or their spouses had come down to check their e-mail. I found the calendar and opened it.

The faint sound of a phone ringing came from upstairs.

Annalynn hurried out. “Gracie said she would call right after church. I wish we’d put an extension down here.”

Expecting to find something damning on Boom’s calendar, I skimmed it from January 1 to June 1, two weeks after his death. His workdays looked as dull as mine.

A phone rang somewhere in the office. The second ring led me to the file cabinet. As I opened the top drawer, an old phone-answering machine clicked on and played the sound of a car revving up. The machine beeped, and a series of taps and scratches came over the line. Morse code. Who would use that these days? The caller ID displayed a number from the 580 area code but no name. When the caller hung up, I pushed the Rewind and then the Play buttons to listen to and decode the message.

“You have three messages,” a mechanical voice said.

The phone beeped. A woman screamed, gasped, and screamed and screamed.

I clapped my hands over my ears. I heard again the submachine gun firing, men and women screaming, the moans of the wounded. I smelled spices and blood and fear. My knees buckled. I collapsed into the chair.

"Monday, ten fifty-five p.m.," the mechanical voice intoned.

Head spinning, I clasped my right hand over where the bullet had sliced through my liver and took quick shallow breaths until I blocked out the Istanbul spice bazaar.

Nothing but Morse code came from the answering machine now.

"Sunday, twelve twenty-four p.m. That was your last message," the mechanical voice said.

Had I really heard screams of terror and pain coming from that tape? Or were they all inside my head? My uncertainty scared me. I'd learned long ago to meet my fears head on. I steadied myself enough to press Rewind and then Play.

For an interminable time screams of fear alternated with sobs of pain. Definitely not a flashback. So what in hell was going on?

"Monday, ten fifty-five p.m.," the mechanical voice intoned.

I wiped the sweat from my face with a tissue and put my brain in motion. The call had come in shortly before Boom died. He'd left the house when he heard those screams. A few hours later he and a woman, almost certainly that woman, had died. The call had lured Boom to his death. But how? He had to have known both who was screaming and where she was. Or received other calls—on the missing cell phone?

A setup. For a moment I exulted for Annalynn. Then it hit me that whoever had killed Boom might come after her.

No time for weakness, physical or mental. Get to it.

How? I'd paid no attention to the last two calls—both coded messages. I closed the office door and steeled myself to play the message tape again.

When the screams began, I checked the caller ID. No number. I decoded the second message: 5-1-8-6-a-m. May 18 at six a.m.? Day after tomorrow.

"Tuesday, six a.m.," the mechanical voice announced.

The call came from a public phone in a 915 area code shortly after Boom died.

The third message was identical. I went online to check the area codes: 915 was El Paso, 580 was southwestern Oklahoma.

A poorly concealed phone line. A familiar code. What on earth had Boom been hiding from Annalynn? An affair? Maybe, but the coded calls came from hundreds of miles away after his death. A police investigation? Annalynn had said Boom did no investigating. Criminal activity? Surely not a man who'd been an honest car salesman.

I had to tell Annalynn, but could she bear to hear that chilling tape? I'd always made decisions quickly, but now I didn't trust my judgment. I needed time to process what I'd heard. And I needed to check for any background noises on that tape.

She'd be back any second. I took out the message tape and replaced it with a fresh one from a box in the drawer. Closing the file drawer and opening the door, I returned to the computer and looked ahead to May 18 to see if Boom had noted a meeting early that morning. He had nothing on his schedule but a Chamber of Commerce lunch. I turned back to the previous Tuesday as I heard Annalynn's footsteps.

"My Daughter the Lawyer is preparing her first criminal case. She's so relieved that you're staying with me."

Annalynn leaned down to see the screen. "He checked his schedule last thing every night."

The schedule, broken into half-hour intervals, revealed little: 9:30—daily reports; 12—Little League lunch; 2—Rev. Berry; 5—dry cleaners.

I brought up Monday, Boom's last day alive. The schedule looked equally boring. "It goes back to January first."

Annalynn turned on the printer. "That's too much to check on the screen."

I hit Print and stood up. I needed to get out of here and think. "While you're finishing, I'll walk through the folks' house to get an idea how much work it needs."

She hovered over the printer. "The house needs nothing but cosmetic work—and cleaning out. Mrs. Hamilton couldn't take all her things with her, and you, Quintin, and Ulysses still have boxes of old things to go through in the basement and the garage." She picked up the first page from the printer with the tips of her fingers, as if it might be hot. "Don't be long. As soon as this prints, I'll put together lunch."

I went down the passage between the two houses. My family's storm cellar had been converted into a room with built-in bunks, but we'd used it mostly to store apples, potatoes, and home-canned tomatoes and peaches. The only times we'd actually slept there were during tornado warnings. Opening the unlocked door leading into my basement, I wove through cardboard boxes to the wooden steps.

I rarely thought about my childhood, but memories of our noisy, cluttered home invaded my mind. At the top of the stairs, I hesitated, dreading opening the door into silence. I hadn't realized how wrenching my first time in the house after my mother's death would be. Pushing my grief aside to give priority to the present, I stepped into the hall and turned left toward the front door and the undivided living and dining rooms. The midday sun lit the rooms, confirming that the walls needed painting. The living room contained nothing but a worn black leather couch, a kidney-shaped glass coffee table, and a floor lamp with a dingy white shade. The dining room housed only the console piano I had given my parents on their thirty-fifth anniversary. Music was one of the few passions I'd shared with Mom.

Playing the piano soothed my nerves and stimulated my thought processes. I slid onto the bench, opened the lid, and played a scale. Bloody awful. It hadn't been tuned since Mom died almost three years ago. I went on into the kitchen. The sturdy oak cabinets needed refinishing. I'd have to replace the drab countertops, the outdated olive-green appliances, and the faded green-and-gray linoleum.

I went back through the dining room to the hall. Ulysses and Quintin's empty bedroom needed repainting. So did my little corner bedroom, which contained two big boxes labeled B. Hamilton. I crossed the hall to my parents' bedroom. It held a single bed with a white chenille bedspread, Mrs. Hamilton's castoffs. Empty wire hangers hung in the bedroom and hall closets.

That left only the bathroom. The fixtures were well past their time. "Stop stalling, Phoenix," I scolded as I checked my face in the mirror over the dingy sink. Those screams indicated Boom didn't shoot the woman and himself. I had to tell Annalynn.

My resolve melted as I opened the door to the basement. I had no idea what had happened. I knew better than to leap to conclusions. Get the facts. Even the rumors. How? What sources could I tap? Connie. She knew something, and she would have heard any dirt on Boom from her cousin Trudy, a gossip magnet. Start there. Today.

AFTER PUSHING FOOD around on our plates and clearing the table, Annalynn and I spread out the calendar print-outs. Each day's entries appeared routine, but Boom had starred one day in the middle of each month.

Annalynn had no idea why. She shuffled the print-outs into neat piles. "I'll compare these to my calendar. Maybe I can figure out what the stars and the notes mean."

My chance to go talk to Connie alone, if I came up with a believable excuse. I chose my workaholic ways. "While you're doing that, I'll run out and buy a re-corder. I want to dictate notes for a report on investing in Hungarian high-tech start-ups."

"Good. You're in no condition to go through all those boxes."

I drove to Radio Shack and bought two microcassette recorders, a connecting link, and half a dozen tapes. I paid with my new P. D. Smith credit card, calculating that my initials and a suburban Maryland address would slow down anyone tracking me. Then I drove to the Dia-mante house and parked in the driveway next to Con-nie's VW. The bungalow had been painted a light blue, and a Japanese maple had replaced the long-dead elm. Yellow irises swayed gently in flowerbeds on each side of the front door. All in all, the place looked much as it had when I took piano lessons from Mrs. Diamante, a lively, lighthearted woman. I wished I could have told her how useful playing the piano had been to me as an undercover operative. She would have loved that.

Connie opened the door in a scarlet dress with

matching button earrings. "Come in. Thank goodness it's you. I was afraid that was Trudy's white Camry. She's a lot easier to take in small doses, and I've had a big dose of her these last few days."

A little of Trudy had always been more than enough. "Don't tell me Trudy and Annalynn are friends now."

"Heavens, no! Trudy volunteers at the church and considers it her duty to be underfoot when anyone in the congregation dies." Connie stepped back to look me up and down. "You look awful!"

I laughed. "Haven't you learned by now people don't want to hear the truth?" I appraised my old friend. Golden ringlets still circled the heart-shaped face. Even her theater-honed skill with makeup couldn't account for the lack of crow's feet and smile lines—and Connie smiled almost constantly. "You look terrific."

"I should. I used part of my divorce settlement to smooth out the biggest of the lifelines." She pirouetted, the full skirt swirling around dancer's legs. "But the body is my own handiwork."

She ushered me into the living room where a grand piano sat in front of the picture window. Giant floor pillows in rainbow colors provided the only seating.

I couldn't resist running my right hand down the keys. "Lovely tone."

"Except for my kids, it's my best souvenir of my marriage. Mom loved it." She blinked rapidly. "I don't keep anything comfortable in here because that encourages parents to stay and listen to their little darlings' efforts." She pirouetted again. "Come into the den. It's the way Mama left it."

A poster-size photo of first-grade Connie with Shirley Temple sausage curls dominated a photo gallery that featured her in various roles in community theaters and summer stock.

I touched the photo of our trio singing at the county fair. "I still play, but I spare the world my voice. I tried Mom's piano. It's badly out of tune."

"Never fear. The best piano tuner in town can be there at ten tomorrow morning."

"You tune pianos?"

"I'm the Jill of all musical trades—choir director, voice teacher, headliner at weddings and funerals." She curtsied. "And I directed *Annie Get Your Gun* at Laycock Community College last fall. A huge hit, if I say so myself." She patted a worn blue high-leg recliner. "Try this one. It has good back support, and you look like you could use it."

Swallowing a defensive reply, I took the chair. "Connie, I sneaked over here because I'm terribly worried about Annalynn. What is it you haven't told her?"

Connie plopped down on a plump sofa with a rose-bedecked slipcover. "I saw Boom twice with Maria Lopez, once huddled in a booth in a roadhouse near Jeff City and once in the back row of a movie theater in Kirksville."

Hmm. Both places were more than an hour's drive from Laycock, spots where Boom wouldn't expect to be recognized. He could have been meeting a lover or an informant. "Do you remember when you saw them?"

Connie fingered an earring, an old habit. "She's asked you to help her investigate, of course. Good luck." She closed her eyes and cocked her head. "I sang show tunes at a wedding reception in Jeff City the second Saturday in March."

Two months ago. Yet she'd said nothing. "And the other time?"

"April tenth. I'd taken two voice students to audition at Truman State University. That's what they call the college in Kirksville now. We went to a movie matinee after, and I saw Boom come in alone during the ads. A couple minutes later she came in, looked around, and sat down behind him. They left before the movie ended."

"Did he see you either time?"

"He only had eyes for her, as the song goes."

I hesitated to ask, but I needed a reaction to my theory. "Boom could have been working on a case. She could have been—uh—a stool pigeon."

"Boom doing undercover police work?" Connie laughed, an ascending trill. "The only thing Boom knew how to do was turn on a siren." She sobered. "Oh, he passed the department's required test on its handbook. Annalynn helped him study. He bet George Brendan, his deputy, she could pass it, too. She not only passed it, she made the best score in the last five years. Boom would never have won the election in the first place without her. And women voters. He could still set women's motors running."

The sobs and screams from the phone call reverberated in my brain. I tried another angle. "Could the young woman have gone to Boom for help? Could a jealous lover have staged a murder-suicide?"

"Is that what Annalynn thinks?" Connie sighed and shook her head. "That's really far-fetched, Phoenix. This gal had lived here only since January. Annalynn is going to have to accept the fact that Boom went bonkers when his mistress called it quits. He'd tied her to the bed, for God's sake. I hate to say this, but the sooner Annalynn admits that he went astray, the sooner she can get on with her life."

The voice of personal experience? "Maybe so, but she won't believe he was unfaithful without absolute proof."

Connie frowned. "Isn't that what I've just given you?"

"No, but it's a start. What else do you know about the woman?"

"Nothing much. She taught Spanish at the community college. Even Trudy doesn't know any dirt, and she vacuums the town for it." Connie retrieved a brown envelope from atop her stereo. "I kept all the articles from here and the Kansas City and St. Louis papers for you."

I rose, and my wound protested. I managed to smile instead of wince. "Thanks. I'll read these tonight." On the way to the door I noted the faded drapes on the picture window. Connie needed cash. Finally a problem I could handle. I made a small start. "I'd really appreciate your tuning my piano tomorrow."

DRESSED IN BROWN wool slacks and a light-blue cashmere sweater, Annalynn sat on the floor in front of the stone fireplace in the former billiards room. The printouts from Boom's calendar surrounded her.

"I miss the pool table." I gazed in disbelief at the huge television screen in the center of the long inner wall and, facing it, a two-ton blue-velvet sectional sofa that blocked the French doors. In summer Annalynn's sickly mother sometimes spent the entire day on a chaise longue by the open doors sketching birds and butterflies.

Perching on the edge of the sofa, I scanned the papers for the dates Connie had given me. Nowhere in sight. "Find anything?"

"Not really. I've color coded the entries." Annalynn's tone was calm, businesslike. "Red is for the ones I can't identify."

"I don't see many." A burst of heat along the bullet's

path told me that I'd be justified in taking more of the pill soon.

Annalynn handed me a spiral leather-bound calendar. "Help me check the red ones against my calendar, please."

In a few minutes we'd crossed off all the red marks. I had found no record of Boom's meeting the woman and no hint of what could be happening May 18.

I gasped as a hot poker twisted beneath my ribs.

Annalynn sprang to her feet. "Phoenix! Your face is gray! You need a doctor."

"No, no. I just need to lie down a little while." Teeth clenched, I toughed my way up the broad stairway, closed the bedroom door behind me, downed a fourth of a pill, and collapsed onto the bed. I'd definitely overdone it today.

My left hand fell on the plastic sack containing the news clips and tape recorders. Hurting too much to rest, I put the telephone tape in one of the recorders and plugged in the earphone. I turned up the volume. A television ad sounded behind the screams. Covering up the screams for other motel guests? A truck drove by during the second coded call. That caller hadn't known about Boom's death so probably wasn't involved.

Unless the coded calls were for someone else. For Annalynn.

FOUR

THE OXYCODONE HAD skewed my thinking. How could I suspect Annalynn of—of what? Killing her philandering husband? Playing games in Morse code? Nonsense.

Bloody hell! If Boom turned out to be a victim, the police wouldn't dismiss the possibility of her as the killer. The spouse goes at the top of the suspect list. So think like a cop. Most obvious scenario: Annalynn had discovered Boom was sneaking out to meet another woman. She followed him, confronted him, grabbed his gun, and shot him and the woman.

Impossible. Annalynn might have wanted to kill her husband—certainly I'd fantasized about killing Russ when I caught him with his paralegal—but Annalynn could never have staged a murder-suicide that would have fooled investigators.

But what if she'd hired a private detective to follow her husband? The detective had called her to come see for herself. Annalynn had shot the lovers, the detective had cleaned up the scene, and now he was blackmailing her with the coded phone calls. Feasible, but ridiculous to anyone who knew Annalynn. As a child she'd cried when captured lightning bugs went dark, and she still refused to kill mice.

The grandfather clock chimed seven times. I'd have to sabotage the clock to get a decent rest. Chimes woke me, or perhaps it was the figure looming over me.

"Go back to sleep," Annalynn said softly, spreading an afghan over me.

"No, no, I'm awake." I sat up. Eight o'clock. "I had a good nap."

Annalynn turned on the Tiffany lamp on the bedside table. "I'm worried about you, Phoenix. You're so pale and thin, and you always had more energy than three people. Please let me to call my internist and make an appointment for you tomorrow."

Involuntarily I put my hand over the long, sensitive scars I daren't show anyone. "Thanks, but I'm making progress every day. Really. Tomorrow I'll start walking to build up my endurance."

"If you're worried about your health insurance coverage in the States, I'll be glad to take care of your medical bills."

Touched and eager to seem well, I stood up. "It's sweet of you to offer, but I'm still on the company health plan." How could I have suspected her of anything nefarious? "I'll be down in five minutes."

She paused at the door. "*Still* on the company health plan? Phoenix, are you taking early retirement?"

Not voluntarily, although my day job had ceased to thrill. "I'm on extended medical leave. I'm thinking about going out on my own as a consultant."

"I'm so glad. You can move back home."

Moving to Laycock wasn't on my distressingly short list of options. "Laycock's not home to me anymore."

"It could be. Ask Connie. She never planned to move back, but after her divorce, she came to help her mother and stayed. She's made a new life for herself in the last two years." Annalynn paused. "You could teach economics at Laycock Community College, or work in the county's economic development office."

Appalled at the thought of either job, I marched into the bathroom. "You sound like my mother."

"I consider that a compliment." Annalynn's voice was tight. She left.

Feeling both put upon and guilty, I took my time brushing my hair and refreshing my makeup. When I stepped on the creaky step at the bottom of the stairs, Annalynn called from the entertainment room. She had put out a small cold buffet on the petrified-wood coffee table and set places on trays.

As soon as we filled our plates, I steered the conversation to safe grounds, Annalynn's daughter Grace and son Walt, both parents of preschool daughters, both pursuing promising careers, neither living in Missouri.

When Annalynn began describing Walt's new house in Omaha, I let my mind wander to Boom's calendar. I needed to check it myself.

"Enough about my kids," Annalynn said. "Did you go to Istanbul to see that charmer we had dinner with during the Salzburg music festival?"

"No, Jerry works in Ankara." As station chief.

"Of course. The embassy is in the capital." She smiled. "But that's not so far he couldn't meet you in Istanbul."

But he couldn't. He'd brought me in to do "a quickie freelance assignment" with no need to know. When I'd been shot, he'd made sure I was evacuated to the military hospital in Germany before the Turks discovered I wasn't Alicia Cramer, tourist and retired math teacher. He'd done nothing to spare me days of debriefing and a wide-ranging polygraph test after Operations transported me to a hospital in DC.

"Phoenix? What's wrong? What happened between you and Jerry?"

"He let me down. He'll never bounce on my bed again."

Annalynn frowned. "I didn't realize you were *that* close."

"We had a fling while I was getting over Russ. I didn't trust him, or myself, so I ended it." After leaving the Farm, we'd gone separate ways. "I ran into him again about five years ago. Still charming, still funny, still handsome. And twice divorced. We got together whenever he came through Vienna, and we had a great time in the Greek islands last summer." I smiled. "You know me. He's just one of a string of disasters d'amor." No self-pity. I'd made choices. I lightened my tone. "Remember when that guy I was so crazy about my junior year dumped me for a dumb blonde cheerleader?"

"Neil Jones. He married her. She died about four years ago. Cancer. He still lives by your grandparents' farm. He found a meth lab in one of their old hay sheds last summer." She smiled. "You should give him a call."

"After almost forty years? I don't think so. That reminds me, what happened to Connie's marriage?"

"When he gave up on breaking into show business, they developed separate lives, but they stayed together until Debbie and Vickie finished high school." Annalynn rose, grabbed our empty plates, and bolted toward the kitchen.

Concerned, I followed her.

She stood over the sink, her shoulders moving in suppressed sobs.

"Go ahead and cry." I rubbed her shoulders, hesitant to hug her but sure she needed to feel a sympathetic touch. "Let it out."

The sobs subsided. "No, if I let go, I'll never be able to stop. Oh, Lord, how am I going to make myself get up every morning knowing he won't be there?"

"You're a strong woman. You'll find a way."

Annalynn turned to gaze into my eyes. "Did you ever really love anyone? Ache to be with him every moment? Feel incomplete when he was out of your sight?"

"Three times, but Russ was the only one I married, and you know how that turned out." Too soon to talk about healing over time. "What you and Boom had was rare and precious. Cherish it."

"That's why I can't let people think he betrayed me." She straightened, her poise regained. "Tomorrow I'll ask George for the police report."

I had to tell her about the deputy's threat and those awful screams. Tomorrow morning. "You need to rest. Do you have anything to take?"

Annalynn picked up a small white sack from the work island. "The pharmacy sent over some sleeping pills. I didn't ask Dr. Murphy to prescribe anything, but I guess he knew I would need it. I'll take one now and go to bed as soon as I lock up and turn on the security system. If you want to go out before I get up tomorrow, just punch one-two-two-six—December twenty-sixth, our wedding day—into the box by the door." She reached out to hug me. "Thank you for being here."

In my bedroom, I opened Connie's file of newspaper clips. They told me little. The Sweet Nights Motel manager had called the police at seven ten a.m. Tuesday. Officers found the bodies of Sheriff Frederick "Boom" Keyser, fifty-eight, and Maria Lopez, twenty-six, a Spanish instructor at Laycock Community College. She'd been shot three times. He'd been shot once. No one had heard the shots. The coroner had ruled the deaths a homicide and suicide.

The rest of the coverage consisted of interviews with motel staff and townspeople who knew nothing about the crime. Obviously the police had stiffed the press. What were they hiding from the public? And from Analynn? I groaned. The medication had affected my judgment. I should have told her about the calls immediately. She had the right to know, and she might even know what they meant.

I got up and walked across the hall. She was sleeping. I closed her bedroom door, returned to my room, and opened my window for some fresh air. To counter the spring chill, I put on a long-sleeved navy T-shirt and running pants instead of my pajamas. I settled down, hoping for a healing rest to help me through the difficult day to come.

THE CLOCK CHIMED one and disturbed my light sleep. I moved into a more comfortable position. The sound of the French doors opening below me banished sleep. I reached for my Glock, stashed in the bedside table. Feet bare, I tiptoed through my half-open door.

Quick footsteps moved through the downstairs hall toward the front door—and the alarm box.

With the light from the hall window to guide me, I crept to the railing that edged the stairwell and looked over. A night-light cast a faint circle of light at the foot of the stairs. Someone blocked the light. I raised my weapon. The figure moved to the stairs, and the night-light shone on a man's shiny black shoes and dark trousers.

I aimed where the trunk of his body had to be.

He flicked on a small flashlight. The beam threw a distinctive shadow on the wall—the curved magazine of a submachine gun like the one I'd faced in Istanbul.

FIVE

FOR A NANOSECOND I thought the shooter had trailed me from Istanbul to Laycock.

The man swept his light slowly up the stairs.

I stepped back against the wall and knelt. The light stopped on Annalynn's bedroom door. He'd come after her, after Boom's widow. Finger on the trigger, I held my breath as the beam played on the closed door.

The bottom step creaked.

I flattened myself on the floor. The only way to even the odds of my nine-round semiautomatic against a gun that could spray thirty bullets was to kill him with one shot. I had to hit the sweet spot. Which I couldn't see without exposing myself.

The light beam dropped and disappeared. I counted off thirty seconds of silence. The step creaked again and footsteps moved into the dining room. A moment later the basement door opened.

Time to move. I crept to Annalynn's room, slowly opened the door enough to slip through, and closed it. The white telephone's keys glowed on the nightstand. Did Laycock have 9-1-1? I tiptoed over and dialed.

"Police, Fire, and Rescue," a woman said. "How can I help you?"

I cupped my hand around the mouthpiece. "An armed man has broken into five twelve Franklin. We need police cars with sirens blaring as soon as possible."

"Mrs. Keyser? Is that you, Mrs. Keyser?"

"No, Phoenix Smith, her houseguest. I heard him break in and saw a *big* gun." Probably an MP5, but the operator wouldn't expect me to know that.

"I'm calling all hands, ma'am. Stay on the line." A minute of unintelligible murmurs. "We'll have officers there in two or three minutes. Where are you?"

"Upstairs in Mrs. Keyser's bedroom—back southwest corner. I'm going to stop talking in case he comes upstairs." I put down the receiver, located a straight chair, and wedged it under the door handle. Better than a lock.

Annalynn hadn't moved. The bed wasn't safe, but I didn't dare risk drawing the intruder's attention by waking her from a deep sleep. An intruder, not a burglar. He'd held the weapon like a pro, but he'd been relaxed. He'd known the alarm code, and he'd expected Annalynn to be sleeping soundly. Deputy George Brendan?

My wound was pulsing, but adrenaline overrode the pain. More important, my brain was ticking: If he'd gone to listen to the message tape, he'd think Annalynn had it and come back upstairs. I crouched to the right of the door. If he broke in, I had a good chance of taking him out.

My flabby leg muscles cramped. I gritted my teeth and flexed my muscles. I didn't dare shift to a position that wouldn't let me shoot and roll out of the line of fire.

The sweet sound of a distant siren. And another. The duo grew louder and louder. Could the gunman hear them through the thick bomb-shelter walls?

A crash downstairs answered that question. The French doors banged.

I pushed myself up and stumbled to the window. A black figure disappeared into the orchard at the back of the yard.

As the sirens burped to a stop, I rushed to the phone.

"They're here. Tell them he ran out the back." I slammed down the receiver and yanked the chair away from the bedroom door.

By the time I switched on the light to the stairway, an officer was pounding on the front door and shouting, "Laycock Police. Open up!"

"Coming," I called. I darted into my room, put my gun back in the drawer, and hurried down the stairs to open the door. "He ran out the back."

A burly young man in a beige uniform sprinted around the corner of the house.

A middle-aged man wearing a dark-blue uniform pushed past me with his service revolver at the ready. "You sure there was only one, ma'am?"

"I saw and heard only one." I hit switches to light the chandelier in the dining room and recessed lighting in the formal living room. The officer's shiny black cop shoes caught my eye. "He came in through the French doors in the back and went through the hall toward the dining room."

"Some druggie after the silver," the officer said. Advancing slowly into the dining room, he stepped over a silver fruit bowl, one of Boom's trophies. He glanced into the kitchen and came back to head toward the entertainment room. "Were their antique candlesticks on the table?"

"Yes." Apparently everyone in town knew about the candlesticks. Good items to steal, but a petty thief would get more for an MP5 than for eighteenth-century French silver.

"Stay back, ma'am." He flicked on the light in the entertainment room. "He left in such a hurry, he didn't take time to close the doors on the way out." He glanced down at the hall night-light. "Where were you when you saw him?"

"By the top of the stairs."

"See his face? His clothes?"

"A big man in black." The cop sounded competent, but I'd keep my suspicions to myself for now.

He looked up the stairs. "Where's Mrs. Keyser?"

"Still asleep. She took a sleeping pill that really knocked her out." Much more than it should have. "Oh, my God!"

I rushed up to the bedroom and turned on the lamp by the bed. Annalynn was breathing naturally, and her color was good. "Annalynn! Wake up!"

The officer reached for her wrist. "The pulse is strong, regular. You think she may have overdosed?"

"No. She took only one Dalmane."

"Was she drinking tonight?"

"She had a drink about two hours before she took the pill." Which she hadn't requested.

"Better verify how many pills she took," he said, his voice kind. "Aren't you Quintin Smith's big sister?"

"Yes." I hurried downstairs to the kitchen.

He followed. "I'm Jim Falstaff. I remember how you beat the heck out of Quint, Uly, and me target shooting."

I tried to connect the heavy man with graying stubble to the skinny, peach-faced kid. The pills were still on the kitchen island. I opened the plastic container and shook out the pills. Nine. The prescription on the side said ten. "She took one."

He checked the prescription. "I took these once. One's enough to knock you out. She'll be okay, maybe a little groggy tomorrow morning." He smiled reassuringly. Suddenly his face reddened and he stared at the floor.

I remembered the boy who'd blushed apple red when

he saw me sunning in a bathing suit in the backyard. I folded my arms over my braless breasts. Good time to test the waters. "She's convinced someone killed Boom. Could she be right?"

"That's wishful thinking. I was the first officer on the scene. I'll never forget it." He covered his eyes for a moment with his right hand. "Every officer in the county came. Nobody doubts he shot the Lopez girl—woman—and then himself."

"Why are you so certain?"

"I'm no expert, but the bodies, the gun, the blood spatters, everything in that room yelled homicide-suicide." He hesitated. "This is confidential, but I think you should know: He had powder residue on one hand and strands of her pubic hair in the other."

"I see. Thank you for telling me." If someone had set Boom up, they'd done a good job.

"I'd like for you to stay with Annalynn while I search the house."

Adrenaline spent, I dragged myself back upstairs. Annalynn had turned onto her right side, and her long hair spread over the pillow just as it had on childhood sleepovers. She moaned, but she showed no sign of waking. I put my fingers on the carotid artery and counted the pulse. A comforting seventy.

Someone pounded on the front door. "Police! Open up!"

Not wanting Annalynn to wake, I turned off the light and hurried downstairs.

Deputy George Brendan stood there in tan slacks, a blue chambray shirt, and white sneakers. "The dispatcher called me. Is Annalynn okay?"

"Yes, she's resting." When he didn't move, I added, "Please come in."

Before I could close the door, the officer who'd run around back came to the porch steps and held up two candlesticks in gloved hands. "These belong here?"

"Yes," I said. "I'll take them."

"Sorry, but they're evidence. Tell Jim I got to go on another call."

"I'll give him a hand. Get going," Brendan said. He peered into the dining room. "Did the burglar get much?"

Certain now he'd been the intruder, I let my body sag and spoke in a weak voice. "I really don't know. Annalynn will have to go through things later."

Jim Falstaff stuck his head out of the billiards room. "Go on home, George. I've got it covered. I'll send you a copy of my report."

The deputy frowned. "I'll go home as soon as I find out what happened."

Jim stepped into the hall. "Some asshole thought he had easy pickings with Boom gone, I reckon. Phoenix heard him come in the French doors and called 9-1-1. The sirens scared him off before he had time to get much."

Brendan glanced toward the stairs. "Annalynn must have forgotten to turn on the security system. Lucky you were here. Can you describe the burglar?"

"No, except that he had really big feet." He didn't react. "They say that means another part of his anatomy is really small."

He yawned and covered his face with a big hand. "Never confront a burglar. Drug addicts can be vicious." He opened the door. "Tell Annalynn I'll be glad to sleep over for a day or two if she's afraid."

I looked the deputy in the eye and loaded my voice with sincerity: "That's a *very* kind offer. I'll be sure to tell Annalynn you came by."

SIX

A LITTLE AFTER TWO, Jim Falstaff gave up on finding the intruder's fingerprints and pushed the sofa back against the French doors. "If you remember anything else, call me."

I debated a moment. We needed an ally in law enforcement. Jim was no super cop, but he'd shown himself to be competent and decent. "I've been thinking about the gun. Some of the border police in Europe carry a gun like that. I could sketch it."

"That would be helpful."

I found a pad and pen by the hall phone and sketched the German-made MP5. To build rapport, I recalled the past. "Didn't you catch for the Thorns when Quint pitched?"

His face lit up. "That's right. You came to our big championship game." He stared at the sketch. "Jesus Christ! You sure about this?"

"Pretty sure. Who around here carries this kind of gun?"

"That's an MP5. The Highway Patrol and city SWAT teams use 'em. Not something you buy on the street. Man, am I glad we didn't walk into that!" A light dawned. "That's why you told the dispatcher we should come with sirens blaring. You wanted to scare him away so we wouldn't face that gun. You're still one damn cool gal, Phoenix." His face reddened. "Give Quint my best next time you talk to him. Tell him the wife and kids are fine." He strode to the front door. "Welcome back to Laycock."

As soon as his car pulled away, I headed for Boom's office and the phone. No message signal blinked. I opened the lid over the tapes. Both remained in place. I turned on the announcement tape. Silence. The box from which I'd taken the replacement tapes held two rather than four. Deputy Brendan had come for the tapes and grabbed the candlesticks to fake a burglary.

I dropped into the desk chair. He could have wanted the tapes to get rid of the screams or to listen to the coded messages. Or both. I rested my hand on the keyboard. Although I'd turned the computer off, the screen sprang to life. In the center flashed a request for a password for Quicken. So he'd wanted more than the tapes. Lacking my software to identify passwords, I resigned myself to waiting until Annalynn woke up.

So what had Brendan expected to find on the accounting program? Evidence of bribes? Dirt for blackmail? Whatever it was endangered Annalynn, and I could trust no one but myself to protect her.

I faced hard facts. I could barely take care of myself. A simple solution hit me: Get Annalynn out of Laycock. Her summer place near Branson? Too close to home. A visit to Walt or Gracie? Too obvious. Maybe drive the Lewis and Clark route, a trip we'd talked about as kids.

Too tired to think, I shut off the computer and turtled my way upstairs. I switched on Annalynn's bedside lamp to check on her. She lay quietly, but tears glistened on her face. I wiped them away with a corner of the silk sheet before going to my own bed and a light but restful sleep.

I WOKE CURSING the clock, but its hands showed nine forty-five and the ringing went on. Finally connecting the noise to the doorbell, I got up, grabbed my robe, and pulled it on as I went down the steps.

I peered through the peephole at an eye-blasting yellow-and-red sundress. Connie. I let her in.

"Oh, Phoenix. I woke you. I'm so sorry. You must have had an awful night. And you look—better!"

"Thanks, I think." I masked my irritation with a smile. "Make yourself at home"—she'd do that for sure—"while I check on Annalynn."

"Good morning, Connie," Annalynn called, leaning out of her bedroom door. "I'll be down as soon as I'm dressed."

"No wonder you overslept, after all that excitement last night."

I put out a hand to silence her.

Connie ignored it. "You must have been terrified!"

"What?" Annalynn ran down the stairs holding up the edge of a floor-length blue silk robe, her long hair tangled, the imprint of a wrinkled pillow on her right cheek.

Meeting her at the bottom of the stairs and guiding her into the undisturbed living room, I chose my words for both Annalynn and Connie. "Someone broke in through the French doors last night. I heard him and called 9-1-1. As far as I can tell, he took nothing but the candlesticks, and an officer found them." I led Annalynn to the sofa and sat down by her, a calming hand on her arm.

Connie sat on the other side of Annalynn. "Trudy heard he had a big gun."

Annalynn shook her head as though to gain her bearings, but her eyes were clear and her brow creased as she looked at me. "And you let me sleep through the whole thing! Tell me *exactly* what happened."

To avoid talking in front of Connie, I jumped up

and headed for the kitchen. “Of course, but it’s a long story and I’m starving. I’ll fix breakfast while you get dressed.”

“Phoenix! What are you hiding from me?”

One helluva lot. “I’ll tell you everything, but the city police will be coming by shortly to get a list of what’s missing. Wouldn’t you prefer to be dressed?”

Connie, her face red, patted Annalynn’s hand and stood up. “What Phoenix means is that she doesn’t intend to say anything while I’m here. I’ll go tune the piano.”

Annalynn grasped Connie’s hand. “Phoenix, you can talk in front of Connie.”

Footsteps sounded on the porch.

Annalynn rubbed her right temple. “Connie, since you’re the only one dressed, would you see who that is, please? If it’s an officer, tell him I’ll e-mail a list later.”

Peeking out the dining-room window, I saw a short, thin woman with frizzy gray hair and a frilly pink blouse best suited for a girl no older than three. Trudy. She’d come to the house with a casserole after my mother died and grilled me about my personal life. Now the busybody would want details of the burglary and my gallbladder surgery. I escaped into the kitchen as Connie opened the door.

“Hi,” Connie sang out. “Could you come back later? Annalynn’s busy right now.”

“I just need a moment,” a breathy voice said. “The sponsorship fee for the church’s baseball team is due today.”

“What does that have to do with Annalynn?”

“Boom promised to give Reverend Berry a check for it.”

Annalynn spoke up. “Come in, Trudy. I’ll give you the check. How much did Boom promise?”

“Five hundred dollars.”

I picked up the bottle of Dalmane and the cordless telephone and tiptoed down the back hall to the laundry room. Closing the door, I dialed the doctor’s number.

After six rings, a woman answered, “Dr. Murphy’s office.”

“Good morning. I’m calling for Mrs. Keyser about a prescription for Dalmane.”

“Are you sure she wants that? The doctor usually prefers to prescribe Ambien.”

So he hadn’t sent the sleeping pills. “She thinks she took Dalmane a couple of years ago. Could you check?”

“Of course. Our new computer system is wonderful. Do you have her medical record number?”

I read it from the bottle.

“I see no record of a Dalmane prescription. Shall I request one?”

“No, thanks. I’ll check with her first. Bye.” I went back into the kitchen.

Connie had put the kettle on the stove. She took a teapot and tea bags out of a cupboard.

“I’m sorry, Connie,” I said softly, putting the bottle on the work island, “but I didn’t want to talk about this in front of anyone before telling Annalynn what happened.”

Connie kept her back to me and took cups and saucers from a cabinet. “How on earth could she sleep through all that?” She, too, kept her voice low. She sat the dishes on the island and picked up the bottle. “Sleeping pills? She shouldn’t be taking these. Her system overreacts to any medication. You know that.” She closed her eyes a moment. “Annalynn and I have become very close since I came back. She’s been wonderful. She’s helped me deal with—a lot. Now she needs me. I won't let you shut me out this time."

This time? Old wounds hadn't healed. "I'm sorry. I didn't mean to shut you out. Ever." Connie knew better than that. "I agree that Annalynn needs both of us." I could trust Connie, but she had no expertise. I opened the refrigerator and searched in vain for the lemon. "We can talk about ways to help her while you're tuning the piano."

Connie reached around me and picked up a small round plastic container with a lemon in it. She closed the refrigerator door, brushing my nose with it, and took a paring knife out of a drawer. She pointed it at me. "We're a trio, not a duet."

The front door closed.

Connie sliced the half lemon into three pieces.

Annalynn joined us. "Stop stalling, Phoenix. What did this burglary have to do with Boom's death?"

Connie's eyes widened. "Oh, Annalynn! You're overreacting! The burglary had nothing to do with Boom. Trudy said it was some drug fiend."

I could stand it no longer. "Trudy knows shit!" I took a shallow breath as my wound reminded me I still needed the pain medication. "Annalynn, please check to see if anything else is missing. Connie, please fix something easy to digest. I have to take my meds before we talk."

Not waiting for their reactions, I hurried to my bedroom. Hand on the bottle, I glanced in the mirror. I really did look much better. Could I tough it out? No time to scramble my brain. Lightning flashed through my midriff. I couldn't afford to curl up helpless either. I took a fourth of a pill. From my bag, I pulled out some clean underclothes. From a dresser drawer, I pulled out the jeans and T-shirt I'd worn Saturday. I took care pulling off my long-sleeved top and winced as I reached back to fasten my bra.

"My God, Phoenix! Those scars are enormous." Annalynn stood in the doorway. "No wonder you're—let me help you."

"I can dress myself, thank you." I twisted to hide the scars. Big mistake. The move set in motion a tidal wave of pain. I collapsed onto the steamer trunk at the foot of the bed.

Annalynn whirled and went into her own bedroom. In a moment she was back carrying a short-sleeved white blouse. "This will be easier to get on than a T-shirt."

The wave subsided. I managed not to flinch as I accepted the blouse. "Thanks. I'm okay." I would be soon.

"You don't look it. Lie down while I get dressed."

Instead I washed my face and, behind a closed door, slipped on the blouse. The soft cotton felt—and looked—good. My color had returned. I heard muted voices from Annalynn's room and opened my door to see her and Connie with their heads together.

They stepped apart, and Connie said, "I cut up bananas in yogurt. Will that do?"

"Thanks. That sounds—edible." I much preferred berries to bananas with yogurt.

"You two go ahead. I'll be down as soon as I put my hair up," Annalynn said.

"I'll tie it back for you," Connie offered. "Get me your Hermes scarf."

The scene echoed their teenage years. Connie had always worn her curly hair short and loved experimenting with Annalynn's long, straight hair.

"Déjà vu, you two." I went to the kitchen and added granola to my bowl.

Annalynn and Connie took their places at the table, Connie with nothing but tea and Annalynn with a bowl of flakes topped with banana slices.

"The silver service is still locked in the cabinet," Connie said.

I plunged in. "That's because it wasn't a burglary."

"I suspected that," Annalynn said.

Connie scowled. "Phoenix, this is no time for your stupid jokes."

I glared at her. "Before I say anything else, promise you'll keep this to yourself. Annalynn's life may depend on it."

Connie, silent for once, crossed her heart.

Where to start? "The guy was a pro. He evaded the security system, and he carried an MP5."

"A what? Speak English." Connie glared at me.

"It's a submachine gun you can set to shoot one bullet at a time or in short or long bursts. SWAT teams use them."

"My Lord!" Annalynn gripped my wrist. "What was he after?"

"I can't be sure," I hedged, unwilling to mention the message tape in front of Connie, "but he went downstairs and tried to open a password-protected file in Boom's computer."

Annalynn pushed back her chair. "This proves Boom was innocent! He has evidence against his killer on his computer. Let's go!"

"Hold it!" Connie pointed her teaspoon at me. "What did the police say about this?"

A surprisingly apt question. "I didn't know about the computer until after Jim Falstaff left."

"But you suspected," Annalynn said, "or you wouldn't have gone down to check. Why didn't you tell Jim?"

I dealt my trump card. "Because Mr. MP5 was wearing cop shoes. And he knew his way around the house and your security system." I let that sink in. "I wanted to tell you before saying anything to Jim. We have to be sure what we tell him won't get back to the 'burglar.'"

Annalynn nodded. "We won't tell anyone anything until we find the evidence."

I stirred the glop in my bowl. "Even if we can't figure out *what* the evidence is, we have a good idea *who* is involved. Let everyone think it's drug addicts."

Connie leaned back in her chair, arms folded. "You think you know who it is and what to do."

"Yes." She was going to fight me. Nothing new in that. "If we can find evidence on the computer, we give it to the Highway Patrol. Then we get out of town until they've made an arrest."

Annalynn rubbed her forehead. "And if we can't find anything?"

"Then the three of us leave immediately on a nice long trip." Remembering Connie's financial state, I added, "My treat."

Connie threw up her hands. "I assumed you'd outgrown all those conspiracy theories by now."

The doorbell rang.

Connie went to the window. "It's George Brendan."

What rotten timing. "Tell him nothing! Absolutely nothing!"

"Please, Connie," Annalynn added.

Connie raised a skeptical eyebrow, answered the door, and invited Brendan in.

He wore a beige uniform and shiny black shoes. From the hall he said, "I came by to make sure you're okay, Annalynn."

Public face in place, she rose and walked toward him. "I'm fine. Thank you, George."

He shuffled his feet. "I'll get on along, then. Call me if you need anything."

"Could you please get me a copy of the official report on Boom's murder?"

He stared at his shoes. "Sorry, but I can't release the report until the case is officially closed."

I jumped in before Annalynn could challenge him: "When will that be?"

He shrugged. "It could be months. We sent the—uh—physical evidence to the Highway Patrol lab. I don't expect a full report before August."

"That's ridiculous!" Annalynn's fists clenched. "Sorry. I know it's not your fault. I'll call the governor and see if he can speed up the lab work."

"I can't do anything, the way things are. If the county commission appoints me acting sheriff"—he paused and looked at me—"I can make things happen."

"I understand," Annalynn said.

Connie tapped on her watch. "Phoenix, I need to start on your piano now. I have a voice lesson at twelve thirty."

I took a spare key from Annalynn's key drawer and handed it to Connie.

"I gotta go, too." Brendan followed Connie out.

I watched them stop to talk on the lawn. "Does Connie know him?"

"Of course. His wife sings in the choir." Annalynn sat down abruptly. "Surely you don't think George was the burglar."

"Who else would know your security code, where to go, what to take to make it seem like a burglary?"

"But he's been Boom's right-hand man from the

beginning. They fly to football games together, play poker together. George would never hurt Boom."

"Does he know who your doctor is?"

"I suppose. Why?"

"Because someone pretending to be from his office called in that prescription. Someone with access to your medical record number. Not many could get that."

Annalynn hid her face in her hands. "It can't be George."

I had to tell her about the phone calls. I could say George had taken the tapes and spare her hearing those terrified screams.

The phone rang.

Annalynn didn't move.

I hurried into the kitchen to answer it. "Keyser residence."

"I just got a call from Trudy," Connie said, her musical voice off-key. "Annalynn's check bounced."

SEVEN

PUZZLED BUT NOT ALARMED, I stepped from the kitchen into the laundry room and closed the door. “Relax, Connie. The bank probably froze a joint account.”

“Annalynn wrote the check on her personal account. The teller called Dickie Rothway, the bank’s emperor. He told Trudy to bring the check back tomorrow.”

“It’s obviously just a technical glitch,” I said. Or maybe not. Brendan had said Annalynn could lose her house. I should have taken that more seriously.

“Trudy has to turn in the money by noon. She hates to bother Annalynn, but—”

Call waiting buzzed. “Hang on a sec,” I said. “Keyser residence.”

“This is Richard Rothway. I’m so sorry to trouble you at this terrible time, Annalynn, but we have a problem here that requires your immediate attention.” He paused. “Could you come to the bank right away, please?” His tone conveyed both an unctuous plea and an urgent command.

“Hi, Dickie. This is Phoenix Smith. What’s the problem?”

“Phoenix! I didn’t realize you’re back in town. I know how close you and Annalynn are, but I can’t talk to you about Annalynn’s financial affairs.”

He’d been a crybaby in grade school and a suck-up snob in high school. “If she’s overdrawn her checking account, surely you can shift money from another account.”

"I can discuss this only with Annalynn."

Something serious. "I'll tell her you called." The jerk was looking forward to delivering his bad news personally. If he had any class, he'd have come to the house.

He cleared his throat. "I've cleared a few minutes for her at one o'clock."

"How thoughtful of you to handle this personally," I said sweetly, my disgust and unease growing. "I'll see if Annalynn has time to come down. Bye."

I punched back to Connie. "That was Dickie, as big an ass as ever." How could I keep Trudy from telling everyone in town Annalynn was broke? "Annalynn has to take care of some paperwork at the bank this afternoon, but I have plenty of cash on hand. I'll bring over the money. Please give it to Trudy and get the check back. Be there in five."

I hung up and went back to the dining room. Annalynn hadn't moved. In profile, her face looked unperturbed, but her eyes had a dullness that tore at my heart. I'd seen this reaction after a violent death before. Sometimes taking action speeded the healing. I said, "Could you hunt for the Quicken password while I go pay Connie?"

Annalynn stood up. "I'll do that right now."

"Then take your cereal with you. You need food to counteract the Dalmane."

"A lot of people know that I go to Dr. Murphy. Every time I have an appointment the waiting room is full."

"His other patients don't have access to your insurance number."

Annalynn shrugged. "The pharmacy has those on file. The clerk probably didn't even ask for them. You're wrong to suspect George."

I squelched a reply about how careful pharmacies are.

"Dickie Rothway called. He wants you to come by the bank at one o'clock to—to straighten out your accounts."

She didn't react. It really was a paperwork problem. Still, just in case: "If you don't mind, I'll come with you to cash a cashier's check."

"Of course." She picked up her cereal bowl. "Boom has been taking care of our finances the last few years. I hope I can figure out his record system."

She went to the basement. I went to my car to take money from the hidden panel in my trunk lid to pay Connie and to give Trudy.

Connie stilled the tuning fork as I came in the door. "It makes my ears itch, but I can fix most of the problems. I'm surprised you still play."

I grinned. "I've been the life of many a communist party." My repertoire of American show tunes, folk songs, country, and rag had provided great cover and earned me invaluable invitations to international social gatherings.

"Hard to imagine you at a communist party. You used to rant about the Red threat and how we let down the Hungarian freedom fighters in 1956."

"Speaking as a capitalist, please don't mention to Trudy that I provided the cash. She'll have the whole town thinking Annalynn is broke."

"I'm worried that she could be right." Connie played a discordant chord. "Boom's salary was fairly good for Laycock, but I'll bet it didn't pay their bills."

To reassure Connie and me, I said, "I wouldn't worry. Annalynn probably inherited a couple of million. How could anyone spend that much in Laycock?"

Connie laughed. "I'd love to try." She sobered. "The judge left a lot of his money to Walt and Gracie, and Boom lost a mint on that dealership. Trudy says

Annalynn and Boom cut their pledge to the church in half this year. Wesley Berry has had to look elsewhere for money to run the church's immigrant outreach program."

I couldn't believe my ears. "Since when has Laycock had enough immigrants for an outreach program?"

"The last five years or so. A couple of hundred Mexicans live in Laycock, and a lot more come here to buy groceries and stuff. Hundreds work at meat-processing plants in old half-dead towns. I heard that half the kids in Milan's schools speak Spanish. We have a great Mexican restaurant." She chuckled. "You left to see the world, and while you were gone, it immigrated to northern Missouri. Sometimes legally."

A car pulled into the drive. I glanced out the window. "Damn. It's Trudy."

Connie flipped through the money. "You gave me a hundred and fifty too much."

"That's yours for tuning the piano." I dashed to the basement door and down the steps and through the passage.

Annalynn stood by Boom's printer. "I figured out the password and skimmed the records, but nothing seems out of the ordinary. I'm printing everything."

"Notice anything out of place in the office?"

"No, but the files on the shelves are in such a mess that I can't tell whether someone disturbed them." She picked up the printouts and tossed them on the computer table. "I'm going to call the governor and tell him Boom was murdered while conducting an investigation."

A dangerous move. He wouldn't believe her, and word of the call would reach Deputy Brendan fast. "Let's find some evidence before we tip our hand."

"But I—you're sure it's someone in the sheriff's department, aren't you?"

"As sure as I can be with what little we know." Retreat when you've won. "We need to figure out how he outsmarted the security system."

Annalynn picked up the papers and followed me. "We have a motion-sensor camera out back. Boom disconnected the sensor on the French doors because they moved in the wind and set off false alarms."

"I know a little about security systems." A huge understatement. "I'll take a look outside while you go over the printouts."

I peeked out to make sure Trudy had left before stepping onto the front porch. A large bamboo basket overflowing with white New Guinea impatiens hung at each end. When I'd called to say I'd be driving to Laycock, Annalynn had said the flowers were a Mother's Day gift from Boom—along with white-diamond earrings. Not the gift of someone insolvent.

I walked along the north side of the house. A dozen variegated hostas were coming up in a yard-wide strip running from the porch to the big stone chimney. The five high and heavy windows would be harder to break into than the French doors at the back. At the corner of the house I stopped to inspect the deep, well-kept backyard. The buds had fallen from the cherry, pear, and apple trees at the back of Annalynn's double lot.

I shifted my attention to my much smaller backyard. The light-purple irises that marked the boundary line between the Smith and Keyser properties stood proud. Two red peonies, my mother's treasures, bloomed on each side of the back porch steps. My father had enclosed the porch so we could put a washing machine and freezer there.

Although neat and mowed, the yard looked abandoned without the doghouse and the small garden devoted mostly to tomatoes, green beans, and radishes. My mouth watered at the thought of biting into a ripe, red tomato holding the sun's heat.

The chiming of the clock carried outside. Noon. Time to get back to business. I walked across the stone-paved patio to the French doors. They showed no signs of forced entry, but I could have picked the lock in about two seconds. The motion sensor, mounted about eight feet high on an old city gaslight, should have set off the alarm. I stood under it to gauge what its view would encompass. The sensor pointed at the side lawn, not the French doors. Someone must have changed the line of view when the system was turned off. A tall man like George Brendan could have adjusted it without a ladder.

I USUALLY WORE an expensive suit and one of my heavier pieces of gold jewelry—my collection was my professional trademark—when I went to talk to a banker. I had neither, so I wore my jeans and Annalynn's white blouse.

She stayed in her room until ten to one. She emerged in a stunning dark-blue two-piece dress. She'd put her hair up and her public face on. She handed me a set of car and house keys. "These are to add to your key ring. Would you mind backing out the Mercedes while I check the mail? The code for the garage door opener is twelve twenty-six."

"Certainly." I smiled as I went to the car. My jeans and her designer dress echoed our childhood attire. So did Trudy as a nosy nuisance. Some things hadn't changed.

When Annalynn got into the car, I told her about Dickie asking Trudy to bring the check back tomorrow.

Annalynn frowned. "That's odd. She needed the money today."

"I had cash on hand so I gave it to her."

"You shouldn't have done that, but thank you. I'll pay you back when we get this straightened out."

We reached the Laycock First National Bank right at one. Built from the same limestone as Annalynn's house, the exterior looked much as it always had, but the modernized lobby had all the charm of a chain motel. An olive-skinned young woman in black slacks and red blazer rushed from behind a desk next to the line of tellers' windows to usher us to a faux-leather couch. Through a glass wall we could see Dickie, a small balding man with a pencil-thin mustache, looking at a computer screen.

"Mr. Rothway will be with you as soon as he finishes—uh—something," the woman said, going back to her desk.

"I don't like this—this waiting," Annalynn whispered. "Come in with me."

"I'll bet you a dollar the pissant is playing solitaire." I picked up a day-old *Wall Street Journal* from an end table. "Hmm. Kupfer-Collins is splitting again. Remember how excited we were when your father helped us buy our first shares?"

"We each paid thirty-three dollars. He bought me a share for my birthday for years. I had to talk Boom out of selling them to buy stock in a Japanese conglomerate. Dickie—he prefers Richard now—also urged Boom to put a hundred thousand into Enron. I said no to that."

Excellent decision. "I hadn't realized Boom followed the market."

"Yes. In fact, I turned the portfolio over to him. He made good money day-trading before the tech bubble burst. He tried it again after the dealership went under, but no one except Warren Buffett was making money by then."

I'd done quite well myself. "Why did Boom decide to run for sheriff?"

"He'd been interested in police work a long time. He took a training course years ago, but we couldn't afford for him to work on a police officer's salary. Then the meth epidemic hit. High school football players were stealing fertilizer—anhydrous ammonia—from farms to cook meth, and the sheriff couldn't stop it. Boom was so upset he couldn't sleep."

The young woman came over from her desk, her body telegraphing embarrassment. "Mrs. Keyser, Mr. Rothway can give you five minutes now."

Boiling at his gall, I smiled politely at the messenger.

He opened the door and buttoned his British-tweed jacket. "Annalynn, thanks for coming down. Phoenix, you haven't changed a bit."

The obvious lie told me how ill I looked.

As I accompanied Annalynn into his office, his official smile wavered. "I appreciate your maintaining an account here, Phoenix. Since we don't mail statements overseas, perhaps you'd like to review your account with Ms. Cordero."

"Thank you, Dickie," I said, taking a chair. "Perhaps later. I'm here now as Annalynn's financial adviser."

"Actually, I'd like to speak to you alone, Annalynn." He opened a folder on his desk. "It's not our policy to share our clients' confidential information with anyone else."

I smiled pleasantly. "I completely understand. No reputable banker would violate confidentiality. Having worked for years with venture capitalists, I know the legal problems bankers incur if regulators have the smallest hint of legal or ethical violations." I let my warning sink in a moment. "Why don't you give Annalynn the folder? She can show me whatever she wants me to see."

Annalynn, sitting ramrod straight, held out her hand for the folder.

His pulled it out of reach. "It's quite complex. I think it would be better if I summarize the major points for you, if you don't mind Phoenix listening."

"Please proceed." Annalynn's voice was polite but firm.

"You already know that your personal account is overdrawn."

"I've never been overdrawn in my life. My balance should be approximately two thousand dollars."

He fingered a printout. "The balance is three hundred ninety-five dollars and twenty-three cents. It's been an awful week. You probably forgot to record some checks."

Annalynn stared at him, disbelief on her face. "I doubt that. In any case, all you need to do is transfer money from the joint account."

Avoiding her eyes, he flipped to another printout. "That has a balance of ninety dollars." He looked up. "There was an automatic credit-card payment of two thousand three hundred dollars on Friday, and the cost of the funeral, of course."

Annalynn closed her eyes for a moment. "He would have transferred money from our savings account today." She said to me, "Our dividends and interest go directly into that account, and Boom distributes them from there."

The banker didn't need to look at the next total: "That balance is one thousand two hundred dollars. Shall I transfer it to your personal account?"

Annalynn's face flushed. "That can't be right!" She reached for the folder.

I assessed our former classmate. Too cowardly to break the law, too greedy not to go to the brink. "Okay, Dickie. This isn't a nineteenth-century melodrama of villainous banker versus helpless widow. I've caught financial juggling you couldn't even imagine. We'll need a printout of *all* activity on *all* of the Keyser accounts for the last three years."

He squared his narrow shoulders. "Naturally we'll be glad to provide a complete record, but it will take my small staff a few days to get to it."

Definitely hiding something. "No problem, Dickie," I said, keeping my tone casual. "I have plenty of time. I'll be delighted to go into your computer system and extract the figures myself." I sharpened my tone. "I even have time to go through the bank auditors' reports for the last five years."

He threw up his hands like a shield. "It's not my fault. Boom insisted on handling it this way. It's not my fault!"

EIGHT

THE BANKER'S CLAIM of innocence convinced me Annalynn had serious financial problems, and he had contributed to them. "What's not your fault, Dickie?"

He pouted like a spoiled brat. "Boom insisted on those sales."

Annalynn stared at the last page in the folder.

He picked up his phone. "Elena, please compile the records of the Keysers' investments and accounts for the last three—no—last five years."

I smelled disaster. "Dickie, have you been acting as Boom's broker?"

"No, of course not." He avoided my eyes. "Boom occasionally asked me to help him with some buying and selling. As his good friend, I did that." Beads of sweat glistened on his forehead. "I never took a commission or profited in any way."

Face pale but composed, Annalynn held up a sheet with the Kupfer-Collins logo. "I need copies of all authorizations to sell or buy, please."

Her calm request confirmed my fears.

"Of course, of course," Dickie assured her. "You'll receive absolutely everything." He pulled another folder out of his desk drawer. "I've found a solution for you, a home-equity loan that will give you sufficient cash until you—until you have a chance to straighten out your financial affairs."

My brain dinged: Brendan had known about this.

Connie had heard rumors of financial problems. Had Annalynn been the only one who didn't know Boom had run through her inheritance? Heartsick and furious, I said, "Dickie, why don't you explain this great opportunity you're giving her to lose her house while I check *my* account." I leaned over and whispered to Annalynn, "Sign nothing. We'll handle it another way."

I went to the young woman's desk. The nameplate said Elena Cordero.

She sprang up. "Is Mrs. Keyser okay? I feel so awful for her. First her husband's death, and then this."

So everyone knew. At least this woman wasn't gloating. I smiled. "Thank you, Elena. I'm glad to meet a human here. I'm Phoenix Smith. Could you help me cash a cashier's check, please?"

"Yes, certainly." She motioned me to a chair beside her desk. "Mr. Rothway said you'd want an account statement. I have that here."

I handed her the check and glanced at the balance: $2,232.16. Correct.

"You want this deposited to your account?"

"No, I keep this account open only to pay utilities and taxes. I do my banking elsewhere." In offshore accounts mostly. "I'll take cash."

"Oh, Ms. Smith," Elena said softly, "carrying so much cash is not safe."

The check was for $9,800, under the $10,000 that sometimes triggered questions. I projected my voice so all would hear: "What's not safe is putting money in this bank."

Elena gulped, and two customers waiting for a teller glanced my way.

Confident the remark would travel around town in hours, I lowered my voice. "I won't cart away all of it. I owe Annalynn for taking care of my house. Could you make out a deposit slip for her personal account, please? I'll take it to her to sign."

"Certainly." Elena looked up the account number and filled in a deposit slip. She handed it to me. "I'll give our chief teller your cashier's check."

I took a ballpoint from the desk and walked back into the office. Giving Annalynn money would hurt her pride, but being insolvent would humiliate her even more.

She watched the banker as though fascinated by his words. Connie had coached her in putting on that expression during junior high health class.

I put the deposit slip and ballpoint on the folder in Annalynn's lap. "Sign this. I'm depositing what I owe you for the new water heater and the yard work."

Annalynn looked up at me absently. "I don't remember how much it is, Phoenix. I'll look it up when we get home."

"I don't want to come back. I'll estimate. Sign here, please."

Annalynn signed, and I returned to Elena's desk and wrote in $5,000.

Elena glanced at the slip and smiled. "We'll go into the back office to do this."

"Excellent." She'd realized my deposit was calculated to cover Annalynn's immediate cash needs, and she approved. "If anything comes through causing an overdraft for any of Mrs. Keyser's accounts, I'd greatly appreciate your calling me immediately."

Elena's smile broadened. "She told me her best friend was coming to visit. Living in Vienna must be wonderful. What kind of work do you do?"

We walked through a door behind Elena's desk. "I

analyze investment opportunities in Hungary, Poland, and the Czech Republic."

"Wow! How exciting!"

"It used to be. A lot of the challenge has disappeared since those countries have become integrated into Western Europe's economy."

A teller and Elena both counted out the money in hundred-dollar bills and placed it in an envelope that I stuffed into my purse.

As I went back into Dickie's office, he held out a paper to Annalynn. "If you sign this, I'll make sure no more checks bounce."

Annalynn had tuned out him, and possibly the world.

I grabbed the paper, ripped it in pieces, and threw those on his desk. "Are the investment records ready?"

He gathered the scraps. "I'll drop everything by the house this evening." He glanced to see if anyone was watching us through his glass wall. They were. He cleared his throat. "A home-equity line really is the best solution, Phoenix."

"The hell it is." I tossed the deposit slip into Annalynn's open folder.

Face impassive, she closed the folder, rose, and strolled toward the front door.

Elena hurried over to hand her a thick brown envelope. "I got this ready this morning after—you know." She caught my eye. "You'll find it—informative."

Annalynn smiled politely. "Thank you, Elena."

"Thank you very much," I added. Elena may have risked Dickie's anger in giving Annalynn the records so promptly. Why? Hatred for Dickie? Sympathy for Annalynn? Self-protection? Perhaps merely competence.

As soon as I started the motor, Annalynn turned on

the radio and punched up the volume. A Herb Alpert trumpet solo filled the car.

I reached over to turn it down.

Annalynn pushed away my hand. “Drive, please!”

“Where? Back home?” I stopped at the parking lot exit.

Annalynn clenched her fists and screamed.

Afraid people could hear her cries over the trumpet, I stepped on the gas and went right, away from downtown. She pummeled her knees and screamed for a long, long block.

She stopped screaming and turned off the radio. “Sorry. I’ve never been so angry in my life.” Her voice shook. “It was scream or grab your gun and shoot that bastard in—in the nether region.”

Her mother had used that euphemism. “How did you know I had a gun?”

“I opened your bag to drop in the keys while you were outside this morning.”

Hmm. “I carried it for protection while I was driving out.” That didn’t explain why I still had it. “Anything in particular that made you so angry?”

“I know Dickie had talked Boom into some bad investments, but I had no idea he’d sold off so much of our Kupfer-Collins stock.”

Bloody hell! “Shall we go see a lawyer, or the prosecuting attorney?”

Annalynn closed her eyes and leaned back against the seat. “If I do that, everyone will say that Boom mismanaged our finances. I won’t blacken his reputation that way.” She moaned. “Oh, God! Trudy will tell everyone about the bounced check.”

“Maybe not. Connie told her it was a banking error.” That wouldn’t stop the talk. “You should flash some cash to show you're not worried about money." Not reassuring. "We'll get your finances straightened out in a day or two."

"Yes, of course. Even if the investments are as bad as Dickie claims, I can sell the place in Branson." She took a deep breath. "Everything will work out. We're almost to the country club. Let's have lunch there." She smiled. "Laycock's second biggest gossip will probably be there."

I pulled up to the 1950s-era clubhouse with its Tara-style front.

Annalynn got out of the car wearing her public face. "We'll go to the bar. The omelets are delicious, and huge. We can split one."

The lobby looked more like a senior recreation center than a Southern mansion. We turned right into the bar, a spacious, pleasant room with light streaming through the front windows onto polished square wood tables.

Annalynn greeted two women sipping white wine and led the way to a table looking out onto a large wrought-iron birdbath.

A waiter brought iced water the instant we sat down.

"Thanks, Eddie," Annalynn said. "Could Sarah make one of her wonderful western omelets for us to share, please?"

"Sure. What would you like to drink?"

"Just water, thanks," I said quickly, not wanting Annalynn to order a drink under the dual handicaps of the sleeping pill and Dickie's news.

A tall, broad-shouldered bottle blonde in golf clothes came in a side door and strode toward us. "Annalynn, how are you? George told me you had a break-in."

"Hello, Lois. The burglar didn't have time to take much, thanks to Phoenix."

The woman stuck out her hand. “I thought you must be the famous Phoenix. I’m Deputy Brendan’s wife.”

I shook hands. The woman had said George “told” her about the break-in, not that he’d jumped out of bed to go check on it.

“How thoughtless of me,” Annalynn said. “I forgot you two hadn’t met.”

Lois Brendan focused on me. “Connie said you used to be quite an athlete. You play golf? I need a fourth tomorrow afternoon.”

I regretted I couldn’t yet swing a club. The golf course offered an excellent opportunity to pry information from people. “Sorry. I’m limiting my sports to shopping this month. In fact, Annalynn and I are planning a major shopping expedition.” Message: We’re going to spend money.

Lois didn’t react. “I understand you’re fixing up your house to sell. George’s nephew picks up extra cash painting and sanding floors and such. He’s handy with tools, and strong as an ox.”

I didn’t want to deal with laborers now. “Ask him to call me next week.”

The waiter brought the omelet and plates. Slices of orange and honeydew melon surrounded the omelet. He divided it for us, serving half on each plate.

Lois snorted. “They never give *me* that much fruit. Well, gotta run.”

I dug into the omelet, pleased that my appetite had returned and that a dull ache under my ribs didn’t prevent me from eating.

“I don’t think you should hire that boy,” Annalynn said. “Boom said he’s not reliable. He lost a football scholarship at MU because of some infraction. Last fall he almost flunked out of LCC, but Lois managed to get him put on academic probation. She teaches golf and tennis there. George worries about him all the time."

"Why is he George's problem?"

"His parents—they're both career military—sent Sean here for his senior year in high school. Apparently he got too friendly with a colonel's daughter."

I had no interest in strangers' problems. "Speaking of repairs, we need to put a much better lock on your French doors."

"We'll go by Strosmeyer's Hardware on the way home. I—and you—need lawn fertilizer. Boom didn't have time—" Annalynn caught her breath. "I'm so glad you're here."

"And I really do need to go shopping."

We chatted about shopping malls in Columbia, St. Louis, and Kansas City until we finished eating. To spread word of Annalynn's solvency, I passed her a hundred-dollar bill to pay for the omelet.

By the time I parked in front of Strosmeyer's display of tomato plants and flowers, spasms under my ribs warned me to keep the shopping short. Inside, row on row of farm, home, and gardening products stretched back into a building with all the decorative charm of a warehouse. On the far wall hung straw hats and overalls meant to be worn on a tractor rather than a runway. Up front, red and yellow plastic hummingbird feeders provided color.

Annalynn took a cart and started down the center aisle past rolls of wallpaper. "Look!" She pointed at a sample of white wallpaper with imprints of lavender irises. "This is exactly like the paper in your hallway when we were kids. We have to get it, Phoenix. It will make your house home again for you."

"I'll think about it." Not in the cards.

"We should get it now. If they run out, we'll never find it again." Annalynn tugged at a box. "Will these three rolls be enough?"

I couldn't disappoint her. "More than enough."

Annalynn eased the box into her cart. "Look who just came in."

I shifted around enough to see a tall, slender man with salt-and-pepper hair standing by a display of vegetable seeds. He laughed at something a young blonde woman said and swept his right hand back over his hair. Neil Jones. Better-looking than in high school. And still with a weakness for blondes. They walked out, his hand touching her back to guide her out the door ahead of him.

Annalynn smiled. "You still find him attractive."

"You're imagining things." Would that were true. "I'll get the locks while you tell the clerk what lawn fertilizer we need."

I found twelve-inch-long lever bolts and got in line with Annalynn.

A woman behind us said, "I'd paint rather than put on wallpaper. Paint's a lot less work."

The man ahead of us spoke up. "Hire you some of them beaners that hang out at Harry's Hideaway. They work cheap, and the sober ones do pretty good work."

"Who are the Beaners?"

"Mexicans. There's always a half dozen or so looking for work."

Disgusted at the ethnic pejorative but not wanting to make a scene, I held my tongue. A hot poker twisted under my ribs, and the world began to waver. I clung to the cart until it stood still.

"Let me help you to the car," Annalynn said softly.

The poker had cooled. "No, thanks. But I will go sit down while you finish up here." I handed her a hundred-dollar bill and strolled toward the car, relieved to reach it and collapse into the passenger seat. A young man came out with bags of fertilizer, and I pulled myself together enough to give him the key to open the trunk.

A minute later Annalynn slid under the wheel. “We’re going to the emergency room.”

“No!” I dared not explain my complicated injuries to anyone. “I’ve felt so much better today that I overdid it.”

“Don’t be stubborn. You obviously need medical care.”

“The doctors said it’s just a matter of time and rest now. I’ll take a pill and a nap.”

When Annalynn stopped the car in the driveway, I roused myself to go ahead and open the front door for her. As I punched in the code to turn off the alarm, the phone rang. I went to the hall phone. “Keyser residence.”

“Maria Lopez was good woman,” said a muffled woman’s voice with a strong Spanish accent. “She no Sheriff Boom’s lover. I no think he kill her.” The caller hung up.

NINE

I DIALED THE number on the caller ID as Annalynn came in the door. "Get to an extension. Quick!"

The phone rang five times before someone picked up. "Special Programs Office. Wesley Berry speaking."

Jesus Christ! "Good afternoon, Reverend Berry. Annalynn Keyser just missed a call from this number. Could you tell me who was calling, please?"

"Sorry, I came in only a moment ago, but I'll ask around."

Lot of good that would do. "If you'll tell me who's there, maybe we can figure out who called."

"Our English conversation classes for Spanish speakers are meeting. We have about ten students and their fifteen children here. Does that help?"

Not a bit. "Could you possibly read the class lists to me, please?"

A long silence. "I'm sorry, but we don't give out the names of our students."

I'd aroused suspicion. Move fast. "I understand. Thank you." Hanging up, I started for the front door. "Let's go. A woman with a Spanish accent said Boom didn't kill Maria Lopez."

I rushed to get behind the wheel, having more faith in my driving than in Annalynn's. My body objected to being rushed, but I kept going. Every second counted.

As soon as Annalynn closed the car door, I hit the accelerator. As I drove, I repeated the caller's exact words.

"I knew it," Annalynn said.

A van and half a dozen cars and aging pickups sat in the church parking lot.

"I don't recognize anything but the church van," Annalynn said. "Boom volunteered at the classes sometimes, but I never have. What's your plan?"

"Walk in casually. Look for familiar faces. Watch for reactions."

I couldn't keep up as Annalynn hurried in the front door and turned right to go downstairs to the church's education rooms. Children's high-pitched voices and laughter came from a room at the far end of the hall. Annalynn opened the door labeled Special Programs.

A card table in the closet-sized office held a telephone. Two beige metal folding chairs and a battered black four-drawer filing cabinet completed the furnishings. Anyone could have slipped in, made the call, and slipped out again.

I rushed to a large window in a room just down the hall. The young minister sat on a folding chair, and five women perched on small red, blue, and yellow plastic chairs. All were short brunettes in their twenties wearing T-shirts and jeans.

Annalynn whispered, "I've never seen any of these women before."

My crisis-evoked energy ebbed. The caller had eluded us.

Wesley Berry rose and opened the door. "Annalynn, I asked around, but no one here called you." He smiled at me. "I understand you've lived abroad, Ms. Smith. Would you consider working with one of our conversation groups on Tuesday evenings?"

Ms. Smith. That meant I looked old. "Sorry, but I

don't speak Spanish." The women whispered among themselves. None paid any attention to Annalynn.

"I didn't know you found time to teach a class, Wes," Annalynn said.

"Usually I don't." He stared down the hallway. "We're a teacher short. I have to get back to the class." He closed the door and stood with his back to us.

"He's hiding something," I whispered. "We'll corner him later."

He turned around and opened the door again. "Forgive me, Annalynn. I forgot to thank you for your contribution to the baseball team. That was very generous of you."

Annalynn nodded graciously as he closed the door again. "I can't believe Trudy didn't tell him—and everyone else in town—that my check bounced," she whispered.

"Connie must have something on her." I moved to the next room. The furnishings and the students looked much the same. I recognized the teacher: Elena Cordero.

Annalynn joined me. "I didn't realize Elena volunteers here. She's not a member of the congregation."

The young banking assistant rose from her child-sized red chair and came to the open door with a warm smile. "Would you like to join our conversation group? It's good for them to hear different voices."

"Not today," I said. She seemed far more at ease than the minister had. "Someone called Annalynn from the office. Did you see anyone come from there?"

"No, but I got here only a couple of minutes ago. You might check in the sanctuary. Some kids are up there rehearsing for a recital."

"Connie's students. I forgot about that," Annalynn said. "We'll check with them."

Although I had known identifying the caller was a long shot, the failure intensified my discomfort. I held my upper body rigid in hopes of delaying the pain sure to come as I followed Annalynn up the steps.

She rushed ahead and called over her shoulder, "You go on to the car before someone mistakes you for an unholy ghost."

Walking slowly to the Mercedes, I noted vehicles' makes, colors, and license numbers. Just in case. Someone inside had probably made the call. Maybe Connie could get her hands on the class lists, or persuade Trudy to. The caller wanted to give us information. Confronted alone, she might talk.

Or the call was a hoax. Someone who had heard that Annalynn didn't believe the murder-suicide story and hoped to sell her "information."

This whole thing was getting too damned complicated.

FOR MANY YEARS I'd slept with one ear open, but my flirtation with that final sleep had dulled my edge. A little after seven o'clock I woke from a nap refreshed and ravenous, feelings I hadn't had for almost seven weeks.

I ran a brush through my hair and went downstairs in my cotton robe. Annalynn and Connie stood in front of the French doors admiring the lever locks they'd put on.

Connie saw me first. "It walks. Does it talk?"

"It eats. Have you had dinner yet?"

"Yes, your *supper* is on the table," Connie said. "Turkey on whole wheat." She motioned with her head for me to follow her and led the way to the dining room.

I sat down. "Thanks. It looks wonderful."

Connie sat in Annalynn's chair at the end of the table and leaned forward to whisper, "Do you think that call was for real, or just somebody trying to get some money out of Annalynn?"

Her suspicion earned her a modicum of my respect. "We'll know soon. When people throw out bait, they hurry back to see if the victim has taken it."

Connie snorted. "And how would you know that?"

Careful. "Life experience."

"I found out which teacher the minister replaced." Dramatic pause. "Maria Lopez."

Was that what he'd been hiding? "Did he tell you?"

"No. Trudy found out today from the church's secretary. The rev has been keeping the details of his Special Programs on the high QT. He's afraid he'll draw attention to illegals. I haven't told Annalynn about Maria Lopez yet."

I looked over my shoulder to make sure Annalynn wasn't near enough to hear. "This whole thing scares me. We have to talk Annalynn into leaving town."

"Fat chance."

The phone rang, and Connie stood up. "I'm the answering machine. That's the fourth call since I got here."

"Phoenix, come join me, please," Annalynn called from the ladies' parlor, the long narrow room between the entertainment and living rooms.

I picked up my plate and went in. Bookcases filled with books and knickknacks still lined the wall against the living room. A carved Indian wood screen with mother-of-pearl inlay, my twenty-fifth anniversary gift, blocked my view of the back third and Annalynn. The front part contained an antique love seat covered with white-flecked blue silk, a matching stuffed chair and hassock, a small beige leather recliner, and a rectangular coffee table that matched the screen.

Annalynn came from behind the screen holding the

deposit receipt. "Make yourself comfortable. We're going to be here a while."

Her father's disciplinary voice, one that had cowed me far more than my gentle father's or busy mother's. Not good. I chose the stuffed chair, slipped off my sandals, and put my feet on the ottoman. I took a bite of my sandwich and savored it.

Annalynn perched on the love seat and leaned toward me. "You seem to know more about my financial affairs than I do. How is that?"

I must have missed something. "Annalynn, you asked me to see Dickie with you."

"But I didn't ask you to give Trudy five hundred dollars or to put five thousand dollars into my account."

I said nothing. How could I defend myself against a charge of generosity?

"Did you look at those printouts of Boom's accounts this morning?"

"No, I didn't." More's the pity. "Annalynn, I didn't know—I don't know—the state of your finances." Sometimes the simple truth works best. "I have spare cash. You need it." I risked wounding her pride to reassure her. "I won't let you lose this house. It's like a member of the family to you."

Annalynn ducked her head.

We'd never talked about our affection for one another. Our families didn't talk about love, nor did the people we grew up with. But Annalynn had lost so much in the last few days that she needed to know what she had left. "You're closer than my family to me, Annalynn. We've always been there for each other. I'm here for you now."

Tears glistened in Annalynn's eyes for a moment. "I know. That's why I can't accept your money."

"That's ridiculous!" The rejection stung. "I'll buy the house myself, if need be!"

Connie cleared her throat in the doorway. "That's lovely, Phoenix, but do you have any idea how much this house is worth today?"

"Do you have any idea how much *I'm* worth today?" Idiot! I'd revealed both my current wealth and my memory of the time when they, not I, had plenty of money.

Annalynn laughed bitterly. "The real question is: Does anyone have any idea what I'm worth? I certainly don't." She folded the deposit slip. "Thank you for the loan. It will give me time to get my finances straightened out." She turned to Connie. "Would you please see if you can find the dill pickles? Phoenix likes them with her sandwiches."

"Of course." Connie wheeled around and marched down the hall.

Annalynn waited until Connie's heels sounded on the kitchen's tile floor. "*You* are not getting out of here until you answer *all* my questions. It's time—long past time—that you stop being so secretive. I want your spit-in-the-eye oath that you'll tell me the truth, the *complete* truth."

I hadn't told the complete truth for so long I doubted I could. "Of course." I settled into the chair again.

Annalynn leaned forward and whispered, "Phoenix, I don't believe this nonsense about gallbladder surgery. You've been shot!" She took a deep breath. "I know you're with the CIA. Are you hiding out? Are you on the run?"

TEN

ASTONISHED, I FELL back on literal truth: "I'm not with the CIA. I did lose my gallbladder." Plus part of my liver. "I'm not—on the lam."

"Oh, Phoenix! You promised to tell the truth."

"I did." Hold it. Playing word games now was counterproductive. "I left the CIA years ago." She'd seen the wound. Denying it would only raise more questions. "I got in the way of a bullet while I was on a tour in Istanbul. I'm not hiding out." I couldn't get over her knowing about my secret life. "How did you find out I was CIA?"

"Father told me when he had his first heart attack. Your dad told him because—well, someone had to know."

Mom would have worried herself sick and my brothers might have criticized my career choice publicly. "Why didn't you tell me you knew?"

"I hoped you would tell me."

"I couldn't." True. "I'm relieved that you know, but we can't tell anyone else. If word got out, people I worked with, or simply knew, might be put in danger."

"Connie's coming. Later." Annalynn raised her voice. "Phoenix, it's all over town that you took a lot of cash from the bank. You're asking for another burglary."

Connie brought in a tray holding a pickle, a glass of milk, and a triangle of Camembert. "Annalynn's right. It's not like when we were growing up. Meth has doubled the crime rate here in the last ten years. Users steal anything they can get their hands on. Forgive me for saying so, but you look like an easy target."

Annalynn nodded. "She has a point. Meth not only makes people ill. It makes them paranoid. They hallucinate and lose all judgment."

"And their teeth. And skin off their face. Like lepers." Connie shuddered. "The stuff's really awful."

Annalynn lifted my feet to one side of the ottoman and sat down on it facing me. "We'll put the cash in Father's safe. Right now we have other priorities." Her eyes bored into mine. "You went down to Boom's office after Jim left because you knew the intruder had looked for something there. How did you know that?"

I chewed slowly as I debated whether to tell her about the calls in front of Connie. Obviously Boom had secrets, but the tipster's call—added to the screams—reinforced the possibility he was working an informant, not having an affair.

Annalynn threw up her hands. "For God's sake, Phoenix, stop stalling! Tell me what's going on. I have a right to know."

Out of long practice, I evaded the question. "Simple logic. Why else would he go to the basement?" Not fair to her. No more delay. "Plus something I found there. And yes, you have the right—the need—to hear what I know. And what Connie knows."

Annalynn spun around, almost knocking my milk off the tray. "Connie? What have you been keeping from me?"

Connie stepped back as though struck. A blush moved up her neck.

I dabbed at the spilt milk with my napkin. "Connie wanted to protect you, just as I did. We were both wrong, and we're both sorry. Let's move on." Get the facts on the table and face the repercussions. "I'll start."

Annalynn moved to the love seat, and Connie sat opposite her in the recliner.

I plunged in. "When you went upstairs to take Gracie's call Sunday, a phone rang in Boom's office, in his file cabinet. Someone left a message in Morse code. It surprised me, so I played the tape to decode it."

Shoulders straight, Annalynn clasped her hands together so tightly her knuckles turned white. She cleared her throat twice. "What was the message?"

"Tomorrow at six a.m. I assume the time for a meeting." When she didn't react, I went on. "Someone had left the same message earlier—right after Boom's death." How could I play the tape with those screams? How could I not?

Annalynn exhaled. "And you assumed the burglar came after that tape? Why?"

"Burglars don't carry MP5s or steal tapes from an answering machine." If I said nothing more, I could spare Annalynn hearing those screams.

Annalynn pointed at me. "But you already had taken the tape out to play in your new tape recorder. Let's hear it."

"In a little bit." I turned to Connie. "Tell her what you found out about Maria Lopez tonight."

Connie leaned forward, eager to share this information. "She'd been teaching language classes at the church."

"With Elena. She made that call." Annalynn's face lit up. "She would know that woman wasn't having an affair with Boom. And she could fake the accent."

I assessed the likelihood. "She was awfully relaxed,

but she knew by then no one had seen her. And that you took the message seriously. It must have been Elena."

Connie frowned. "But why would she make an anonymous call to Annalynn? Why wouldn't she tell the police?"

Annalynn clapped her hands together. "Because she doesn't trust the police."

A point for Annalynn. "And she may be afraid that whoever killed Maria and Boom will come after her." Quite rightly. Another person to exfiltrate as soon as possible. "Annalynn, I have a strong hunch that Boom was investigating on his own because someone in the sheriff's department—almost certainly George Brendan—is involved in heavy-duty criminal activity."

"That has to be it!" Annalynn's face glowed. Then she frowned. "But it's not George. How do we prove it, Phoenix?"

"We leave proof to the Highway Patrol, but we need something to convince them to investigate. Maybe whatever the burglar wanted from Boom's computer."

Annalynn sighed. "I didn't see anything on the spreadsheet that would interest anyone but me."

Connie stood up. "Phoenix, I want to hear that tape you've been hiding."

I couldn't resist sniping back: "I'll get it while you tell Annalynn about seeing Boom with Maria Lopez."

Annalynn glared at Connie. "Is everyone holding out on me?"

I skipped out and rewound the tape to start with the Morse code. If they didn't hear the code first, they'd never get beyond the chilling screams.

Connie wiped away a tear as I returned. "I'm sorry, Annalynn. I should have told you before." She paused. "I told Phoenix. Sunday."

Annalynn tipped her head back and closed her eyes. "I know you both meant to protect me, but you must stop it. From now on, I'm counting on you to tell me everything. I want your word, Connie."

"You got it." She sniffed. "And you two can't keep anything from me either."

Annalynn pointed to the recorder. "Let's hear the tape."

No promise from Annalynn. What was she hiding? I put the recorder on the coffee table and turned up the volume. "You'll have to listen carefully." I pushed Play and watched for any sign of recognition.

Connie spoke first: "I hear a pattern, but it ain't got rhythm."

"Boom used to tap out 'I love you' at dull dinner parties," Annalynn said. "I couldn't make out a thing, but obviously Phoenix did. Enlighten us."

"The message is 5-1-8-6-a-m—May eighteenth, six a.m. I think it was one caller using public phones in El Paso and southern Oklahoma. Does that mean anything to you?"

"No." Annalynn shoulders sagged. "Almost everyone has a cell phone these days. The only reason to use public phones would be to make the caller impossible to trace."

I envisioned a map. "El Paso's right on the Mexican border. Could someone be tracking methamphetamines coming from Mexico?"

"Possibly," Annalynn said. "Boom said crystal meth has replaced much of the homemade meth. Cooks can't find ingredients so easily now that farmers lock up their anhydrous ammonia and pharmacies restrict sales of tablets with pseudoephedrine."

Connie wrinkled her nose. "I've heard the do-it-yourselfers' labs stink like a cat's litter box."

"Boom said they smell like ammonia," Annalynn said.

Connie, never able to remain still long, kicked off her heels and rose to pace. "Kids in my *Annie Get Your Gun* cast called the Mexican stuff ice or glass and the homemade stuff crank."

Annalynn reached for the tape recorder. "This message could be about timing a drug bust." She hit the rewind button.

I lunged forward to grab the tape recorder, and the beast beneath my ribs stirred. I released my grip. I couldn't conceal those screams any longer. "You haven't heard the first call on the tape." Remembering that I'd turned up the volume, I reached for the recorder again.

Annalynn pulled it back. "You promised the complete truth."

"You'll get it, but please turn down the volume before you play it."

Annalynn pushed Play, and fear and agony surrounded us.

Connie ran from the room with her hands over her ears.

Annalynn threw the recorder onto the floor and pushed back against the love seat, but the screams went on. At last the mechanical voice announced, "Monday, ten fifty-five p.m."

"Oh, God! Oh, God!" Annalynn dropped to her knees on the floor to search for the tape recorder. When she found it, she clutched it in both hands and, still on her knees, rewound the tape. Eyes wide and face pale, she played the screams again.

As they ended, she twisted around to look at me. "He

rushed out to save her." She staggered to her feet and leaned against the door frame. "He must have located her through the caller ID."

"There wasn't any," I said. Shock hadn't slowed Annalynn's thinking.

Connie came in with a bottle of scotch and two glasses. "That tape's the most terrifying thing I ever heard." She poured generous sedatives into each glass.

Annalynn accepted the scotch. "Then he knew where she was. He must have records of their meetings. That's what the intruder was looking for on the computer."

An argument for leaving town. "By now he knows he took a blank tape, which means you've heard the real one, and something he wants to hide is still on the computer, where you could find it." My pulse rate quickened. I had to get her out of here. "Annalynn, he's going to come after you. Turn the tape over to the Highway Patrol and let them handle it while you get out of the line of fire."

Annalynn rewound the tape and hit Play. Connie and I covered our ears until the screams stopped, but Annalynn listened intently. "This proves nothing. I'm staying right here." She glared at me. "You tampered with evidence, Phoenix, and now we can't even prove Boom heard this message."

I clenched my teeth to keep from pointing out that removing the tape had preserved it. But I'd been foolish not to tell her about it immediately. Better to accept blame and get on with it. "I'm sorry. A dumb mistake."

Connie frowned. "I've heard of voiceprints, but I doubt anyone could identify the person screaming. Not even if you had a recording of Maria Lopez's voice for comparison." She sipped her scotch. "Those screams scared the shit out of me. I vote you pack a bag and go stay with one of your kids."

The tape recorder played the last message, and Annalynn turned it off. "Go home, Connie. This isn't a safe place."

Connie didn't budge. "If you won't leave town, at least stay at my house tonight."

"I'm not leaving." Annalynn's tone allowed no argument. "Phoenix can go with you." Without looking at either of us, she rose and left the room.

Connie sipped her scotch and stared at the tape recorder.

Not needing to agonize over whether to stay or go, I bit into my sandwich. It tasted better than it could possibly be. I luxuriated in eating solid food without my stomach debating whether to digest it.

Connie removed an earring, a miniature dream catcher, and tossed it on the table. "You're awfully quiet."

"I said what I had to say." I took another bite.

"You're staying, of course." Connie's musical voice sounded raw.

"Yes." I sipped my milk.

Connie slammed down her glass. "You're as stupidly brave as when you were a kid. I think you're actually relishing this—this adventure!"

"God, no! I came back to Laycock for the boredom."

"Well, you just missed months and months of it." She took off the other earring. "Okay, I'm in. Whatever happens, I'm in. I guess we better tell Annalynn and start figuring out what we're going to do."

"Do?"

"Well, we can't just sit around and wait for the bad guys to kill her. We have to figure out who done it and get them behind bars. Geez, I sound like a character in one of those old B movies." She winked. "Come on."

She walked to the front door and called, "Good night, Annalynn. See you tomorrow." She opened the door, held it for a moment, and slammed it shut.

Annalynn strolled out of the kitchen. "That old trick hasn't worked since the third grade." She hurried across the dining room and drew us together in a giant hug. "You have to promise me you won't take any chances."

I marveled at her naïveté in thinking we could do anything else.

Connie stepped back. "Maybe I should stay here tonight and help stand guard."

The doorbell rang. We all jumped.

I darted for the stairs to retrieve my gun even as I realized I was overreacting. I had to slow down about halfway up, but at least I'd moved fast for a moment.

"It's Jim Falstaff," Annalynn called.

I took off my robe and slipped on my jeans and the borrowed blouse before picking up my gun-laden purse.

Falstaff glanced up and saluted as I came down the steps. "I'll patrol close by from midnight until dawn. If you keep your exterior and downstairs lights on, I can spot anyone who comes near the house."

"Thank you, Jim," Annalynn said. "I can't tell you how much I appreciate that." She turned to Connie. "Thanks for coming by. I'll call you tomorrow."

"I left my earrings somewhere," Connie said. "Phoenix, will you help me find them?"

They were on the coffee table, but Connie knew that. "Let's look in the—what do you call the ladies' parlor now?"

"The den," Connie said, following me there and pointing to the tape recorder.

"Up to Annalynn," I whispered, "but I want a copy of the tape." I stuck the recorder in my purse and raised my voice. "They must be upstairs."

Connie palmed the earrings on her way out.

Once upstairs, I said, "Keep talking and moving around." I connected the two recorders and copied the tape soundlessly.

Connie opened my closet. "Good grief! Is this all you brought? It looks like you went into Walmart for ten minutes and bought the most nondescript blue, black, and beige stuff you saw."

That was exactly what I'd done. "I brought clothes for cleaning house." And for being inconspicuous. "I didn't anticipate such major social events as your students' recital." I checked the tape's counter. Done. "What a shame I'll have to miss it."

When we came downstairs, Annalynn emerged from the den to escort Connie to the door while I joined Jim.

"You sure about that gun you drew?" He kept his voice low.

"Positive." I waited to see whether he'd reach the same conclusion I had.

He leaned forward. "The only people who could get their hands on an MP5 *and* her health insurance numbers would be in the sheriff's department."

Bingo.

Annalynn spoke from the door: "That's Phoenix's theory, too. Surely there's another explanation. What does the chief think?"

Jim didn't meet her eyes. "I didn't mention that to him. If we're right, we got to keep it quiet until I got more to go on. Any idea who would break in? Or why?"

Annalynn looked at me, her eyes questioning.

I wished Jim had more experience handling major

crime. But he'd been smart enough to figure out the break-in wasn't a standard burglary and to keep his mouth shut. I nodded for Annalynn to go ahead.

"He came to destroy evidence that Boom had collected."

Face neutral, Jim took out a pad and pen. "What kind of evidence, ma'am?"

He'd gone from friend to cop. I took over. "We don't know, but he turned on Boom's computer and was trying to get into password-protected files."

"Oh, hell!" Jim chewed on the pen. "I'm gonna have to report this to the chief. He can take it to the Highway Patrol."

"Not yet," I objected. "A leak would be a disaster. Give us time to search the files for a specific person or crime."

Annalynn perched on the edge of the love seat. "I think Boom was investigating a major meth operation. You can take anything we find straight to the Highway Patrol or the Drug Enforcement Administration."

Jim squirmed. "I heard Boom never worked cases."

Maybe this cop was too honest to work with safely. "One reason for him to do that would be because he suspected someone in the department."

"Then he may have been working with someone on the M-squad, the regional major case squad." Jim rubbed his stubble. "Boy, I sure don't like this. You're really putting me on the spot."

An image of the officer as a boy flitted into my mind. He'd driven Quint crazy because he took so long to make up his mind. "Why don't you think about it tonight and come by before you go off duty tomorrow morning?"

"Yes," Annalynn chimed in. "Maybe by then we'll

have found something to prove Boom was murdered to keep him quiet."

He stared at her a moment. "I guess it can wait until morning." He closed his notebook. "Phoenix, I'd like you to show me that motion sensor out back again."

I despaired at his transparent ruse to get me alone. "Of course."

We went through the back hallway door and toward the old gaslight, which now operated on electricity.

I pointed at the camera. "Somebody set it so it doesn't face the French doors."

He walked around the light. "Had to use a ladder, or be a pretty tall guy."

"The intruder was tall." Don't mention Brendan. Let Jim come up with the name himself. A hint might help. "Another thing: Annalynn wants to see the police report and the crime-scene photos. The sheriff's department won't give them to her. Could you get her copies?"

He grimaced. "You need to talk her out of that, Phoenix. She's hanging on by denying Boom cheated on her. Those pictures would break her heart."

ELEVEN

JIM'S CERTAINTY THAT Boom had killed the woman and himself shook me. "You don't think it's possible he was working a case?"

"No way." He shifted to put his back to the house. "I've always liked Annalynn. She's never put on airs. She's nice to everybody. And she's smart. When she was president of the school board, the superintendent died. She held the school system together." He shuffled his feet. "I liked Boom, too. Can't say I had much respect for him as a sheriff. His only experience was as a reserve officer doing traffic or crowd control. Even so, he knew enough to never go anywhere without calling for backup."

I thought of the missing cell phone. We needed the call records. "So you saw no signs that the killings were staged?"

He met my eyes. "None."

His certainty didn't mean he was right. The KGB had faked murder-suicide quite well. The combo got rid of people while humiliating and silencing their families. But you needed skill to fool a batch of police officers. Amateurs wouldn't think to lure a man with screams either. "If Boom was having an affair and killed his lover, why would a heavily armed man break into the house to get to his computer?"

"Makes no sense to me. I see that MP5 in my nightmares. My wife says it's time for me to take a desk job."

His eyes swept the area. "With that orchard, it'd be pretty easy to sneak in here. Wouldn't hurt to leave the outside and inside lights on at your house. Lots of folks know about that tunnel."

"Annalynn's tunnel door would be hard to break through." Once we locked it. "The judge thought we'd have to keep the mobs out."

Jim walked toward my backyard. "Does your pole light work?"

I took my keys from my purse. "I'll check it now. The switch is on the back porch." I should have done that already. What else was I missing?

I unlocked the useless lock on the porch door and reached in to turn on the light. It illuminated my backyard up to the neighbor's fence and the area behind my garage.

"That helps," Jim said. "I remember watching you train some mutt out here. Maybe you ought to get a watchdog. I'd rather have a good dog than a security system. The darn things go off if the wind blows."

His suggestion and the sweet odor of the cool spring evening brought back images of my father sitting on the back steps and coaching me in training a collie-plus "You're thinking of Tricksy, the smartest dog we ever had." Everyone had loved that dog. Except Annalynn. She claimed Tricksy's bad breath made her sick. "I'll go through the house and turn on the lights. Thanks, Jim."

"Sure." He rubbed his chin. "I'll check around, see if I can find out the right person to talk to about this." He took a card from his shirt pocket. "Call me on my cell if you find anything. Annalynn got a gun?"

Stay close to the truth. "I don't know, but I bought one to carry on the drive out."

He nodded. "If you have to shoot, aim at the chest

and keep pulling the trigger. I don't care how good you are at target shooting, about nine out of ten shots miss when it's for real. See ya."

I stepped into the porch. The washing machine and dryer I bought for Mom years ago were still there. Several cardboard boxes sat on the floor. I opened the closest. It held part of a set of old dishes. Not my mother's, so they had belonged to the elderly woman I'd invited to house-sit.

I unlocked the sturdy wood door into the house. Uly and I had installed a good dead bolt on it after Dad died. A pro could get in fast, but the lock would stop, or at least slow down, a marauding teenager. I flicked on the dim hall light. The grandkids had painted the hall a soft peach years ago.

None of the interior doors had locks. I stepped into my old room and turned on the light. Anyone could come through those windows. I flicked on lights in every room and at the front steps. As I locked the front door, Jim backed a white police car out of the driveway.

Annalynn, standing on her porch, watched me cross the lawn and come up the steps. "You're moving much more naturally than you were this afternoon." She closed the door behind us and set the security system. "Would you like some pie before we start on the printouts?"

Ever the gracious hostess. "Thanks. Let's eat as we work. I feel great right now, but my brain may go mushy in a couple of hours."

"I thought you'd want to start. I've put everything on the dining-room table."

"Rhubarb pie!" My mouth watered in anticipation. "Who brought this?"

Annalynn smiled. "When you told me you were coming, I went to the farmers' market for fresh rhubarb. I made two pies and froze them. Your mother always did that."

"Umm. Delicious. This tastes just like hers. Thank you."

"I cheated and used commercial crust." Annalynn pushed her piece away and leaned toward me. "What did Jim tell you?"

I told her as little as I dared: "He's having nightmares, and he thinks you shouldn't see the photos or read the report." I took a bite of pie.

"Damn it! Nothing can be worse than not knowing." She touched my hand, forcing me to look at her. "Is that all?"

"He suggested we get a watchdog."

She wrinkled her nose. "Men never notice that you have furniture you don't want an animal slobbering over, shedding on, or scratching." Her jaw muscles tightened. "Did you tell him about the tape? Or the phone call this afternoon?"

"No. That's your decision. Unfortunately, I don't think he would know what to do with either." I remembered another problem. "And we can't mention the anonymous call until I can talk to Elena Cordero. I'll contact her tomorrow."

Annalynn squeezed my hand. "Thank you for believing me. Connie still thinks I'm deluding myself."

"The sooner we prove her wrong"—or right—"the better."

"Amen to that." She relaxed her jaw and handed me several sheets of paper. "I printed a set for you. What are we looking for?"

"Anything that doesn't fit. An odd heading. Numbers that conflict with what you know." Boom's deception wouldn't be complex or esoteric. "A dollar amount that could be a phone or an account number. We may have to go through several times to find it." I scanned the top page. Pretty straightforward-looking. "And maybe we'll be wasting our time. Whatever the person wanted may not be here."

"And if it isn't?" Her tight voice belied her calm face.

"Then we'll check everything else on the computer." I looked at the monthly headings under Expenses: Airplane, Cars, Charity, Church, Entertainment, Household, Insurance, Medical, Miscellaneous, Taxes, Utilities. Only the totals under Entertainment and Miscellaneous varied much, ranging from $500 to $2,500 over the last year. I estimated that the Keysers' monthly expenses averaged $2,000 more than Boom earned as sheriff. No wonder the check bounced.

Annalynn put a calculator, the thick envelope from the bank, and a folder on the table between us.

I resisted tearing into them. "I didn't know you own an airplane."

"With four other people, Boom's poker buddies. Dick Rothway and George Brendan have pilot licenses. They fly to ball games and hunts and Las Vegas. It burns money. My share should be worth around thirty thousand dollars."

Dickie again. With friends like him… "I don't see anything that looks like code. Do the figures look accurate?"

"Pretty much. I brought in the credit-card statements to check on the Miscellaneous and Entertainment items." Annalynn sighed. "Boom threw receipts in a cardboard box and pulled them out at tax time. I nagged him to keep monthly totals."

Not revealing ones. "Who does your taxes?"

"One of the bank's accountants. I looked for our IRS

forms for the last three years but didn't find them. I may have to get a copy from the bank."

Score another one for Dickie. I skimmed the numbers for the three previous years. All the expenses, but particularly Miscellaneous and Entertainment, had jumped two years before and never come back down. "What happened in August two years ago?"

Annalynn sucked in her breath. "How can you tell something happened?"

"Your total spending jumped about fifteen percent."

"That has nothing to do with this." She gave a page rapt attention. "I'll tell you about it another time."

Something bad. I focused on the Medical column. The bills for August, September, and October two years ago were $600 to $800 higher than during earlier months. I'd come back to that later. "What does Entertainment encompass?"

"Vacations, season tickets to the Chiefs' games, tickets to all sorts of pro sports, a lot of political and networking events, and things like that humongous television." She picked up another sheet. "You won't believe the money we spent on the campaign for sheriff. We sold some of our best stocks then." Her shoulders slumped. "We can focus on my financial problems later. Right now let's look for what the burglar wanted."

"I don't see anything here, but this is only expenses. We need to check the income file." I ate my last bite of pie. "Let's go down to Boom's office. I'll see what else is—and has been—on his computer while you look for his receipts or a ledger that will help with the breakdown of expenses. He could have been concealing payouts for an informant in, say, Miscellaneous."

"Good, and I'll watch for his files on our investments at the same time." Annalynn left her untouched pie in the kitchen on our way to the basement. "Tell me how you got shot and what Jerry had to do with it."

"It's a long story." One I couldn't tell. "We have work to do tonight. I'll give the high points at breakfast. Which I will cook. I promise."

"Are you being sneaky again? Do you promise to *tell* or to *cook?*"

I chuckled and didn't answer. Annalynn was going to be hard to evade.

I went straight to the phone to check the answering machine. No light blinked. "You need to ask the phone company for a record of local calls." I turned on the computer. "Did anyone else use this?"

"No, only Boom. The computer was one of those Miscellaneous expenses." She pulled a pile of magazines from the top shelf. "I'll get the recycling bin for these."

"Don't throw anything away until we've gone through it thoroughly," I said, absorbed in checking the computer. "Shake them for any loose paper and look through them for handwritten notes."

"I would never have thought of that. Thank goodness you know about investigating. We really don't need the police."

Her words alarmed me. "Yes, we do. I know where and how institutions hide financial records, but my tradecraft doesn't cover criminal investigations. We'd be foolish to try to handle this ourselves. We just need something to get a criminal investigator started."

"But surely as an undercover agent—"

"Not agent. Operative, a NOC, to be specific."

"A knock? Oh, that's N-O-C, nonprotected operative cover. You mean the government would deny you were an operative if you got caught?"

"Yes." I wanted to tell Annalynn what living a double

life had been like, of the emotional and physical difficulties of coordinating my day job and undercover work. To brag a little, to elicit sympathy, to share triumphs. No way. Not now, not ever. "Let's get to it and find something to give Jim tomorrow morning."

She shook inserts out of a magazine. "But Jerry was the one who brought you to Istanbul. Was it his fault you got shot? Did he make a mistake?"

I'd asked myself, and my debriefers, the same questions but received no answers. "Sometimes things go wrong."

"I've noticed."

I let her wry comment pass and concentrated on verifying that the computer contained no hidden files. Boom probably had used it mostly for playing Grand Theft Auto. "I've checked everything but the Quicken file. I need the password."

"Try F-K-three-seven-thirteen, his initials and his lucky numbers."

F for Frederick. I ran routine searches for hidden or false entries. Nothing. Having seen Expenses, I studied the Income headings: Salary, Winnings, Interest, Dividends. I'd guessed a little high on the salary. The other columns totaled approximately $2,000 a month. The Keysers were operating at a deficit.

"Annalynn, what does Winnings refer to?"

"Golf, poker, football pools, that sort of thing. He won forty or fifty dollars a month."

Wrong. He'd won around $500 a month since January. He surely had a file breaking down the winnings and the portfolio earnings somewhere. "Have you seen any CD disks or flash drives? Or anything resembling a ledger?"

Annalynn's whole body slumped. "We're not going to find it, are we?"

"Of course we are, but not on this computer."

"Could the burglar have deleted a file?"

"No." I looked at the jumble of paper still on the shelves. "It's probably where he could find it easily. Check under the shelves to see if he's taped anything there." I checked under the computer keyboard.

Annalynn ran her hand under each shelf. "Nothing." She went to the file cabinet and checked the drawers. Then she lifted the printer. "Nothing."

"I know it's here. I can smell it." A loose block in the wall? None. The inkjet printer caught my eye. We'd printed out quite a few pages, but the paper container remained half full. "Did you put paper in the printer?"

"No. Why?"

"Check the paper."

She lifted the sheets out. "There's something odd in the middle!" She threw the top and bottom sheets on the floor and held up lined notebook paper filled with figures. "Thank God! Thank God!" Her excitement faded. "This is a breakdown of our interest and dividend income." She turned to the next page. Then the next. "These figures can't be right. We don't even own Hi-T-Data."

The stock sounded vaguely familiar. "Maybe it's from Boom's day-trading."

"He sold all of those stocks years ago." Eyebrows furrowed, she handed me the pages. "I'll go get the papers from the bank. Maybe those will explain some of this."

When she left, I speed-read the figures. Boom had identified all the sources this time. Across the top of the most current page he had listed twelve stocks and the dividends from each for the last two years. Kupfer-Collins led the list, but the earnings fell far below what I'd expected. My brain retrieved Hi-T-Data. It had been one of those spectacular start-ups that fell into oblivion somewhere between 2002 and 2004. Yet Boom had entered earnings of $1,200 to $1,600 a month for the last eighteen months.

Bloody hell. Boom had hidden the records of whatever he was doing by mislabeling the sources of unearned income. I saw only one plausible explanation: Sheriff Boom Keyser had lost big money on speculative investments, sold off prime stock to cover debts, and replaced lost dividends with payoffs. Annalynn's beloved husband had been on the take.

TWELVE

WHO IN VANDIVER County had money and reasons to pay off the sheriff? A nursing home hiring illegal immigrants? A developer building with unsafe materials? A gambling operation? Whatever it was, the deputy must be in on it. If George Brendan hadn't killed Boom, he knew who had.

Annalynn interrupted my speculation. "You're turning gray again."

A reprieve. "I feel a little gray. Going through these papers is going to take hours, and we need to be up early in case something is coming off at six a.m. Let's call it quits."

Her frown lines disappeared. "Good idea."

So she had qualms about what we would discover, too. To divert her, I said, "I used to photograph papers with a camera concealed in a compact or a ring or a zipper pull or some such." Every kid knew about such spy toys. "After the Berlin Wall came down, I rarely did that. All I needed was an asset—an inside person, an informant—to tell me what to look for in published documents or send me disguised flash drives." I turned off the computer. "Most of it made no sense to anyone but an economist anyway."

"I don't understand what information you were after." Annalynn led the way into her basement and, at my suggestion, locked the heavy door to the tunnel.

"Everything from the real gross national product

to budgets for specific weapons and infrastructure—mostly information we publish here. During the Cold War all the Iron Curtain countries falsified their economic data to conceal their failures and intentions from us and from their own people. Russia, among others, still does."

"How did you find the assets?"

"Sophisticated networking." Usually at academic conferences, business meetings, social gatherings. "If I'm outed, it could pose major problems for casual acquaintances as well as those who passed me information either on purpose or unwittingly."

"I see." She went up the steps ahead of me. "Were the companies you worked for CIA fronts?"

"No, but they would come under suspicion for hiring me. I worked full-time for real companies and I wrote research papers for real peer-reviewed journals." Those articles gave me credibility and enabled me to ask questions I couldn't have otherwise without arousing suspicion. If my being shot masquerading as Alicia Cramer came out, it would discredit my research and make me a pariah. "How about pancakes for breakfast? Do you have any frozen blueberries?"

Annalynn laughed. "Now I know you're going to be okay."

I INTENDED TO get up when the clock chimed five. Instead, Mom called me to get ready for school. I opened my eyes. Annalynn, dressed in black slacks and a black turtleneck, stood by the bed holding my gun. "Why are you aiming at the clock?"

"I was afraid you'd grab the gun and shoot me." She put it back on the bedside table. "Jim just made a circuit around the house and left. How do you feel?"

I stretched cautiously. Only an inconsequential twinge. "Good."

"It's almost five thirty. What should we do?

"We'll stay up here with the lights off. You watch the front of the house, and I'll take the back." The way trouble would come.

"I took Father's revolver out of the safe, but I don't know how to use it."

"Put it away. It would probably misfire." I got up and reached for the black clothes I'd laid out the night before. "Don't let your mind wander even for a second. Watch for anything that moves."

The minutes dragged by. The trees beyond the reach of the outdoor lights went from dark blobs to sharp outlines. When the clock chimed six, I could see the leaves dancing in a brisk breeze. I waited fifteen more minutes before walking down the hall to find Annalynn peering through the curtains in her father's office.

"Relax, Annalynn. The meeting isn't here. It probably isn't anywhere."

She wriggled her shoulders and stretched her arms. "We can find out one thing." She hurried down the hall to the phone in her bedroom and hit one number. She listened a long time before hanging up.

"Who were you calling?"

"George Brendan. On the department hotline in his home office. It's next door to his bedroom. I let it ring nine times."

Interesting. "He could be in the shower."

"It's a few feet from the phone." She grabbed her purse off the dresser. "We're going to his house to find out if he went to a six o'clock meeting."

I envisioned the MP5. "We'll go, but we'll do it my way. Do you have binoculars?"

Annalynn opened her closet and rummaged through a shelf. "Boom used these to hunt longhorn sheep."

I brushed my hair with a few quick strokes and grabbed my purse, the Glock's spare magazine, and my black rain jacket. I planned the operation as we went out the door. "We'll take my car. He's less likely to recognize it. Where does he live?"

"In the Kent Gardens development at the north edge of town. Go down to Monroe and take a left. It's about a mile from there."

I hadn't been that way in years. "Where can we pull off the street to be out of sight?"

"The old Kelsey's Market. It's empty now."

"Good. We're going to do a quick ID change. Get a baseball cap, a scarf, and two pairs of glasses from the glove compartment. When I pull off the road, stuff your hair into the baseball cap and put on the big glasses. Then take the cloth dice from the pouch in the seat behind you and hang them from the rearview mirror."

Annalynn opened the glove compartment. "Are you serious?"

"Extremely." Instant simple changes worked better than long complex ones.

As we neared the market, I slowed to let a car ahead of us turn the corner and leave the street clear. The pothole-filled parking lot woke my wound, but I couldn't risk taking a pill now. Behind the building, I released the trunk lid and spun out the door. I extracted two magnetized Ohio license plates from the secret compartment, slapped one over each of my Maryland plates, and returned to the car.

Annalynn handed me the scarf. "Do you always carry fake plates?"

"They come in handy. Cops love to run plates on their

squad-car computers." I tied on the scarf pirate style. "Does he park in his garage or outside?"

"Outside. A Lionel train set takes up most of his garage."

Planes and trains. Expensive hobbies.

"He lives on a corner," Annalynn added. "We can see whether his car is there from the street that runs along the side of the house."

The sun had risen enough that I had a good view of big new houses on small lawns. So different from the Laycock I remembered. People had money to build big houses now. Too bad they didn't have the aesthetic sense to put them in a proportionate setting. "Where do I turn?"

"Just ahead. Between those fake marble columns with the real English ivy. The Brendans live two blocks down." She put the glasses on. "What are we going to do?"

"We'll decide when we see whether his car is there. Keep your chin down until it's time to look." I turned in slowly and studied the street ahead. No one was out, and newspapers still lay on the lawns. "Is there a stop sign at the corner?"

Annalynn took a deep breath, her only sign of nervousness since we'd left the house. "I don't think so."

"Then I won't slow down. Put your hand up to your face and look as we go by."

"It's the two-story brick on our right."

A waist-high brick wall ran along the front lawn and rose some six feet high along the side, blocking our view of the house the moment we crossed the intersection.

"The deputy car is there but the SUV isn't," Annalynn reported.

We passed a grove of oak and locust trees with picnic tables among them.

I slowed the car. “Is that a public park or private property?”

“A public park. We made the developer put it in.”

On our left were four houses under construction. I swung into a dirt driveway and turned around. “We’ll look for hummingbirds around the locust blossoms before the construction crews get here.”

Annalynn nodded. “I think the park has room for three or four cars at the back.”

I turned into the park’s drive and stopped behind a lilac bush. As we got out of the car, I said softly, “What type of hummingbird lives around here?”

“The ruby-throated. They’re much more plentiful than they used to be.” Annalynn walked into the trees toward the Brendan house some thirty yards away and raised her binoculars. “I can see the back of the house through here,” she whispered.

We both froze at the sound of a car. A few seconds later the motor went silent and a car door closed.

I grabbed Annalynn’s arm and pulled her down behind a brick barbecue.

I peeked over it, trying to find a clear spot in the greenery.

George Brendan came around the side of the house. He wore black slacks and turtleneck and carried a black jacket in his left hand and a large white-and-purple carryout cup in his right. He dropped it into an open trash can.

Annalynn raised the binoculars. She gasped and handed them to me. “Under the jacket.”

Brendan’s body blocked the jacket as he unlocked the back door and went inside.

I whispered, "What did you see?"

"A curved piece of metal."

I handed Annalynn the binoculars, retrieved a piece of paper and a pen, and made a quick sketch. "Did it look like this?"

Annalynn sank to the dirt and leaned against the barbecue. "Yes."

My heartbeat accelerated. "That's an MP5 magazine."

THIRTEEN

"SO GEORGE *is* the one who broke in, and he must have kept that appointment." Annalynn leaned against the barbecue, a line of white around her lips. "If he and Boom were setting up a drug bust, all he had to do was tell me he needed to look for information." She lunged to her feet. "Let's confront him right now. Find out what's going on."

"No! Not while he's armed like that!" Knees weak at the thought of facing the MP5, I pulled her down beside me. "We need to have some idea what he's up to before we give him any hint that we're suspicious." I checked my watch. Six thirty-five. "He didn't have time to drive far. The meeting must have been close by. Could you tell where his cup came from?"

"A service station south of town, the only one open all night. He could have gone south, east, or west from there."

I pulled myself up. "Let's get out of here before someone spots us."

We drove away from Brendan's house through rows of beige townhouses with postage-stamp yards. "Good grief! They should call this Vinyl Village, not Kent Gardens."

Annalynn didn't appear to hear me.

When we came to a sprawling new brick school, I turned into the parking lot behind the building. "I'll get the plates. You take care of the dice." I yanked off the scarf and tossed it into Annalynn's lap as I jumped out of the car.

When I got back in, Annalynn had pulled her hair into a ponytail and tied the scarf around it. She said, "Jim may come back and notice your car is gone."

"Right. I've got to clear away enough boxes to get my car into the garage so no one knows whether I'm there." No one was in sight as we pulled out into the street. "Where can we find blueberry pancakes?"

Annalynn smiled. "You're not going to get me into a restaurant where you can't talk about your secret life. We'll go by Dogwood Diner and get your pancakes to go."

I drove toward the square on an old street lined with white one- and two-story houses in spacious, well-kept yards. "Uly, Quint, and I used to race our bikes along here."

"Your house was a three-ring circus—with you and your brothers competing for attention in separate rings. I loved eating supper with your family."

I stopped at the light leading to the square, a lively place in my childhood and now an unused stage set. Of all of the businesses I remembered as a child, only the Dogwood Diner remained. Cars filled the parking spaces in front. I parked across the street by the Vandiver County Courthouse.

"You go in," Annalynn said. "I'm not up to being in public."

I scanned the cars and pickups. None familiar. I went in the diner and saw no familiar faces. Why would I after all these years? I gave my order to the cashier and sat on a counter stool patched with duct tape. Booths had lined the walls when I left for college. Four remained along the back wall, but Formica-topped tables dominated.

I tried to figure out what Boom and his deputy could have been doing for payoffs. The calls from the Southwest. Drugs? Not Annalynn's husband. Illegals? Surely not.

Two men in suits took a table behind me. One said, "Isn't that Boom's wife sitting in that car across the street?"

"Annalynn Carr Keyser in a dirty three-year-old Camry? I doubt it."

"I feel sorry for her. They always came across as the ideal couple. Now everybody in town—hell, everybody in the state—knows he was cheating on her."

"I wasn't surprised. She's always seemed like a cold fish to me. Not half enough woman for a macho guy like Boom."

Idiots, but Annalynn's poise had always made insecure boys defensive.

"Did you know he had a hot tamale?" The man had lowered his voice.

"No, but I'm not surprised. I hear he hung out at Harry's Hideaway a lot the last few months. You don't go out there for the food."

"I thought he was hustling the truckers and the beaners playing pool."

I couldn't hear the reply, but I heard both men snicker.

"Here's your pancakes, honey," the cashier called.

I slid off the stool and addressed the two men with a stranger's diffidence: "Do you have the time?"

"Five to seven," said the one who'd been sympathetic to Annalynn.

I stared at the jerk. "You look familiar. Are you Ken Kelso?"

He straightened his tie. "No, Cary Callaway. Callaway Insurance Agency." He handed me a business card.

The name clicked. “Oh, yes. You handle my home insurance. You’ll be hearing from me soon.” A cancellation. I nodded to the other man and paid for my order with my P. D. Smith credit card. I walked across the street and, as I opened the car door, looked back. The men watched me with their noses inches from the window. I waved.

Words tumbled from Annalynn. “I called Jim to let him know where we are and ask him to say nothing until the county commissioners appoint an acting sheriff. He says they’re meeting this morning. Phoenix, if George Brendan becomes acting sheriff for the next thirteen weeks, I won’t find out anything.”

I handed her the carryout. “If you don’t want him appointed, you have to put forward a better candidate.”

“I know.” She clenched her fist in frustration.

“Maybe someone who recently retired in a neighboring county?”

“I can’t think of anyone.” She opened her fist. “Why were you on a CIA mission years after you retired?”

A lie would only drive her to push harder. “I got a little—a lot—bored. I let a select few know that I was available for occasional short-term contracts.”

Annalynn looked up. “Like your vacation in the Greek islands last summer. Was that a real mission or a junket with Jerry?”

How did she guess that had been an assignment? Jerry and I had masqueraded as a couple celebrating their twenty-fifth wedding anniversary. “I couldn’t tell you if I wanted to. The CIA operates strictly on a ‘need to know’ basis.”

“What does that mean?”

“You receive only the information you need to do

your part of the job. That way you can't accidentally reveal anything." In a bar or in bed or under torture.

"What happened in Istanbul?"

"I was in the right place at the wrong time." And no one would tell me who shot me or why. The operation had been off from the short notice Jerry had given me to come to Istanbul disguised as a retired math teacher from Maryland.

"You know I'll never tell anyone. I never even told Boom you were an operative."

I checked the car behind me. It went straight as I turned left.

"For God sake's, Phoenix. Don't you trust me?"

"More than anyone in the world, but I can't talk about it." The hurt in her eyes told me she didn't understand. I'd have to tell her something that would tell her nothing. "Istanbul is a fascinating city. I went shopping in the spice bazaar." Impersonating a German-speaking tourist. "It's an old covered souk with dozens of small stalls. Most sell spices, of course, but some sell souvenirs and odds and ends. The souk smells heavenly some places and like a sewer in others. It's a warren. The aisles intersect, and some lead to exits and some to dead ends." I'd memorized the layout, making sure I knew how to reach every exit.

"A great place to meet someone. I understand."

Did she? My debriefers hadn't. But I hadn't told them my stupid pride had pushed me to proceed with what seemed a poorly planned operation. "I bought a lovely book of sketches of Istanbul in 1915." It had slowed down the bullet just enough to save my life.

"What else did you do at the bazaar?" Annalynn prompted.

I'd done everything right, chatting with members of

a tour group, checking for tails, strolling past the stall where I was to receive the drop. "I bought some apple tea and that scarf you're wearing." My only souvenir of the trip. I pulled into the driveway.

"Don't keep me hanging," Annalynn said, making no move to get out.

I had gone over this part of my story again and again, telling it to CIA debriefers, rerunning it in my head, dreaming about it. "I bought some cardamom, and all hell broke loose." When the vendor handed it to me, a bearded man had pulled an MP5 out from under a long brown coat. "I don't remember much of what happened. One of the tourists was a retired surgeon. He kept me from bleeding to death right there."

"My God, Phoenix! You came so close—" Annalynn took a deep breath and turned her face away. "I guess the Lord still has plans for you."

Unlikely. The Lord hadn't been my shepherd for a long time.

Annalynn undid her seat belt. "Did the police catch the—the assassin?"

"I don't know." That rankled. Jerry could have told me that at least.

"Did he shoot anyone else?"

"I think so." I hadn't wanted to know more than I'd guessed. "The Turkish doctors did a good job. Did you know that the liver regenerates? Mine will be back to normal soon. My blood and immune systems are almost there, too. I'm gaining strength every day."

Annalynn untied the scarf and studied the inch-wide black border and the series of sienna, orange, green, and beige geometric patterns that led to large, elaborate black swirls filled with more green, orange, and beige patterns. "It's quite pretty."

"You see that pattern in the tiles in some mosques and woven into carpets."

"How long were you in the hospital in Istanbul?"

"I'm not sure. I was unconscious or sedated the whole time." It took Uncle Sam's reps a while to figure out I would live and that they had to get Alicia Cramer out of there before the Turks realized it was a false identity.

"You must be a big hero in the CIA."

Bile rose in my throat. "Hardly. I committed the dual sins of getting shot and quite possibly of blowing my cover for all those years as a NOC." I fought to control the hurt and anger I couldn't share with anyone except Annalynn. "I'm persona non grata with the CIA and, if my cover is blown, with my employer and the ninety percent of my friends in Vienna who despise the CIA." My bitterness exploded. "That bullet wiped out my life."

FOURTEEN

I SLAMMED THE car door and strode across the lawn, ashamed and alarmed that, after decades of secrecy, I'd spilled my guts—just the way I had when we were kids.

Annalynn caught up with me at the steps. "I'm sorry nearly getting killed spoiled your career, but I'm immensely relieved that it's over. You can build a new life for yourself right here in Laycock."

No way. "And die of boredom."

"Kansas City or St. Louis, then. Even Columbia. You could teach economics." Annalynn unlocked the door.

"Teach! Are you trying to ruin my appetite?" I stalked into the kitchen and took plates from the cupboard.

Annalynn followed me. "What *are* you going to do?"

"I honestly don't know." A big reason for coming to Laycock had been for Annalynn's help in figuring that out. "I'm not going back to Adderly International. That's over."

"Why didn't you quit your job there when you retired from the CIA?"

"It might have aroused suspicion. Other intelligence agencies knew the CIA had a NOC who acted as a troubleshooter. Then I took on a special project and got a big promotion. I couldn't walk away." And I didn't have anywhere better to go.

She took the plates from me. "You're turning gray. Sit down and rest."

I eased into my chair at the dining-room table. "I'm

tired of resting. I'm sick of being sick. I'm used to burning the candle at both ends. Now neither end is lit." Bloody hell! I had become the kind of self-absorbed idiot I detested. "Sorry. I'm cranky because I'm hungry."

"And because you hate not having a goal, a focus."

She knew me very well.

Annalynn brought in the settings, two glasses of milk, and a little brown jug of maple syrup. "Of course! Of course! It's perfect!"

She didn't mean breakfast. I slid the pancakes onto the plates. "What's perfect?"

"I'll give the county commission a better candidate for sheriff than George: you. You can find out who really killed Boom."

A dangerous idea. "I appreciate the vote of confidence, but on paper and in fact, I'm not qualified. The commissioners wouldn't appoint me, and if they did, the law enforcement community wouldn't trust me."

Annalynn's face crumpled. "I was grasping at straws."

Find her another straw. "Could the police chief do double duty?"

"No. He should have retired years ago when meth brought in serious crime. I think that's why Jim didn't tell him about our suspicious burglary."

"The county coroner?"

"He wouldn't want the responsibility."

"Okay. Nobody obvious." I knew no names, but I knew types. "What about someone with political ambitions? Maybe a lawyer who would love to make a name investigating a sensational case others have flubbed."

Her frown vanished. "Nancy Kallenbach, the head county commissioner, plans to run for the state senate." She shook her head. "She'd never give up the commission for a thirteen-week appointment."

"You know local politics. Who would she like to see in the job?"

She pursed her lips. "Interesting thought. Excuse me, Phoenix, but I have to make some calls." She picked up her plate and hurried toward the den.

I finished breakfast and took the dishes into the kitchen just as the doorbell rang. Who came around so early? I grabbed my purse and went to look through the front-door peephole.

George Brendan's nephew. Instead of the business suit that he'd worn in church, he wore sharply creased beige slacks and a blue Laycock Community College T-shirt. A blue-and-white bandanna tied off like a bandage encircled his left wrist. That fashion statement hadn't reached Vienna.

"Mrs. Keyser, it's Sean O'Reilly," he called. "Is your neighbor here?"

I opened the door. "Good morning. I'm Phoenix Smith."

"Morning, ma'am. My aunt, Lois Brendan, said you need help fixing up your house."

An eager beaver. "In a week or two. If you'll give me your number, I'll call you."

He cracked his knuckles. "I sure could use a little work today—mop floors, carry stuff to your basement, spade your flowerbeds, whatever."

I glanced at the classic red Ford Mustang convertible parked behind my three-year-old Camry sedan. "Your car insurance must be due."

He grinned. "You got it."

I didn't want anyone in my house, but I needed my car out of sight. "You could clear out my garage." What did you pay here? "I'd guess a half hour's to an hour's work. How does twenty-five dollars sound?"

"Good."

I took the keys from my purse as we walked to the garage and found the one to unlock the padlock on the swing-out doors. Sean pulled the doors open to reveal a score of large and small cardboard boxes. I opened the closest, a collection of old but usable towels. The next held blankets. I pulled out an old green blanket that Mom and I had used for picnics. "Is there a homeless shelter here?"

"Reverend Berry gives stuff to the illegals."

"Good. Take these boxes to my back door, please." I unlocked my car and tossed the picnic blanket on the front seat.

In the next fifteen minutes Sean carried to the curb a dozen boxes of outdated college textbooks for trash pickup. I had him carry three big scruffy boxes holding my brothers' and my childhood memorabilia to the back door. I didn't dare toss those without going through them. That cleared enough room for my car. I inspected the jumble of old tools and gardening equipment in the garage's storage area. A snow shovel almost covered a small box. With the multipurpose tool on my key ring, I slit the tape holding the box closed. The Keysers' IRS returns. Boom had hidden them here. A bad sign.

Sean's shadow alerted me to his return.

"That's enough for today," I said. "Let's put the boxes out back in the house."

I unlocked the porch and back doors and had him place the towels and blankets by the washing machine and the treasures in my bedroom. I turned off the lights I'd left burning overnight, moving cautiously now to avoid stirring the slumbering beast.

Sean followed me down the hall. "How's Mrs. Keyser doing?"

"She's hanging in."

"Uncle George says she's in denial. Says she thinks somebody else killed the sheriff and that tramp with the father fixation."

Father fixation? Of course. Boom had seemed ancient to him. I turned off the floor lamp and the dining-room light. "Your uncle said you'd seen Boom with Maria Lopez. Where was that?"

"In a bar in Moberly. After a basketball game. I saw them somewhere else, too, but I don't remember where." He patted the dining-room wall above the piano. "I could paint these rooms for you."

Had he come looking for work, or had George Brendan sent the young man over to tell me he'd seen Boom with the woman? "Did you know Ms. Lopez well?"

"Not really. I took her Intermediate Spanish class. She made us read comic books and learn kids' songs in Spanish."

Good ways to learn basic vocabulary and idioms. I led him outside, locking the back doors behind us. "Did you like her?"

He shrugged his broad shoulders. "She was a teacher."

Only four or five years older than he was. We walked back toward my garage.

Annalynn came toward us dressed in a blue blazer and beige slacks. She had put up her hair and lightened the dark circles under her eyes. "There you are, Phoenix. I left you something to read in the den. I have to go"—she nodded to Sean—"to a meeting." She opened her garage door and stepped in with a wave.

I took thirty dollars from my purse and handed it to Sean. "Thank you." As I turned to pick up the box of tax returns, a rocket zoomed through my midriff.

"You okay, ma'am?"

The rocket disappeared and my capacity to breathe returned. "I'm fine. I had surgery recently, and I didn't take a pain pill this morning."

"You gotta be careful with painkillers. One of those idiot basketball players died from chewing a bunch of OxyContin."

A brand of oxycodone. My Lorelei. Could he see the medication in my eyes? I had to go cold turkey. As soon as possible. "I'll call you at your uncle's next week."

"I got my own place." He went to his car, an athlete's arrogance in his walk. "I'll give you a call."

Right. People who don't give you a number don't call. He'd verified my suspicion that his uncle had sent him to give—and to get—information.

I drove my car into the garage and then carried the box to the den. Annalynn had left a stack of financial records on the coffee table. No way I could spread everything out there, but the judge's big mahogany desk upstairs had nothing on it except his marble paperweight and a telephone.

Putting all the records in the box, I carried everything upstairs to the judge's office, forbidden territory in our childhood. I recognized no changes. Barristers' bookcases holding big, dark law books still sat beneath the two front and two side windows. A cluster of smaller books occupied a bottom shelf behind the desk: old and new books on the CIA. The judge and Annalynn had read up on my employer.

I put the box on the desk and looked out at my family's house. It had been a happier place than the castle. Annalynn's mother's bad health, and prefeminist attitudes, had darkened her daughter's childhood. Maybe that's why the outgoing, optimistic Boom had appealed to Annalynn. Or maybe it had been pure physical chemistry. Although reserved, she was a sensual woman.

I opened the box and spread out the papers for a quick review of the figures, child's play compared to what I analyzed at work. A decade-long slide toward financial disaster became obvious in minutes. The car dealership alone had cost Annalynn at least $500,000. Boom had lost more than he made on day-trading. Worse, as the dealership went deeper in debt, he'd sold solid stock to speculate and suffered major losses. By the time the market started to recover, he'd depleted their once-stellar portfolio. The records continued to show a steady drop in total value of stocks and bonds and in dividends and interest. Worth $1.5 million in 2000, their stocks' value fell to under $100,000 in 2010, half of it Kupfer-Collins. How could Boom have hidden such losses from Annalynn? The only possible answer sickened me: He'd taken payoffs in order to maintain their lifestyle. I'd be able to spot those. Subtle bribing of civil servants was one of my specialties.

No wonder Dickie had recommended a home-equity loan. It would take time for Annalynn to sell the airplane and the summer home. The wolf wouldn't be at the door, but he'd be prowling nearby. She'd never had to live modestly, or to earn a living.

The doorbell interrupted my thoughts. Going to the window, I saw Connie's yellow Beetle in the driveway and started for the front door. Before I reached the stairs, the door opened.

She sang, "Anything you can do," from a song of that name in the musical *Annie Get Your Gun* as she tapped in the security code.

A challenge to me?

She jumped when she saw me at the top of the stairs.

"I thought you were with Annalynn. She asked me to drop by."

"I'll be down shortly."

I took my time putting the papers away. Connie and I hadn't been in contact, even by e-mail, in years. Neither of us had felt the loss. She had been a lively, fun-loving kid who always wore the latest styles and starred in the school musicals and plays. She considered Bs good enough. Annalynn always helped her cram for history tests to keep the B from sliding to a C. The three of us had good times, but without Annalynn, Connie and I would have ignored each other. My return threatened to loosen the close ties they'd renewed in the last two years. Much as I wanted to brush off Connie again, that could only harm Annalynn. Connie would be here after I left. Time to act like an adult and mend fences.

I reached the bottom step as Connie opened the door for Annalynn.

Her cheeks were flushed and her eyes sparkled. "Let's go into the den."

My antennae went up. Annalynn had done something rash.

In the den, Connie took the recliner and I the overstuffed chair. Annalynn stood in front of the love seat, her hands cupping a small object.

"Tell us," Connie prompted.

Annalynn sucked in her lower lip, a sign of uncertainty I hadn't seen in years. "I got a job this morning. I start tomorrow." She opened her hands to reveal a bronze star.

FIFTEEN

CONNIE SQUINTED AND leaned forward. "That's Boom's badge."

Annalynn held the badge over her heart. "No, it's my badge. For thirteen weeks."

Bloody hell! She'd placed herself in even more peril. I rose and extended my hand. "Congratulations. You found the best person for the job."

Annalynn's eyes probed mine. "You don't think I made a mistake?"

Acting takes you just so far when someone knows you well. She'd recognize a bald-faced lie. "In your position, I'd have done the same thing." Never. Maybe. Quite possibly. I added, "Access to information is key in any operation."

Connie jumped up. "Operation, smoperation. It's insane! What were you thinking?"

"I was thinking that it's my best—maybe my *only*—chance to find out who killed Boom and why."

Connie threw up her hands. "Phoenix, don't just sit there grinning like the Cheshire cat. Talk some sense into her before she gets herself killed!"

"Calm down," Annalynn said soothingly. "If someone is coming after me, I'm safer as sheriff than as a civilian."

Not necessarily. "It's a done deal, Connie," I said. "Let's figure out how to make the most out of Annalynn's—opportunity."

Connie flopped down into the recliner and flicked the neon-pink fingernails that matched her sleeveless blouse.

Annalynn turned back to me. “I’d like you to be my assistant.”

Connie bounced up again. “That’s crazy, Annalynn. She knows even less about sheriffing than you do.”

“I wouldn’t be any help,” I agreed, “but you shouldn’t go into the department without someone to back you up.” Who could it be? “What about Jim Falstaff?”

Connie fingered a dangling earring. “He’s no Columbo.”

Annalynn ignored her. “Jim worked for the sheriff’s department before he worked for the city police. He knows the ropes.” She sighed. “I can’t ask him to take a job for three months.”

“No, of course not,” I agreed. But she needed him—badly. “Maybe you can get him seconded from the city police. If that won’t work, ask him to take a leave of absence. If need be, I’ll pay his salary.”

“Good grief, Phoenix,” Connie said. “Did you hit oil in your backyard?”

“No, I’ve worked hard for what I have.” I glared at her, remembering the many times I’d watched Connie and Annalynn buy things I couldn’t afford.

“Stop it, you two. We don’t have time for this nonsense.” Annalynn dropped the star on the table and marched out of the room.

Connie picked it up and toyed with it. “You can’t put this heavy thing on a blouse. She’ll have to wear it on one of those ugly tan uniforms.”

Still a deep thinker. And I still needed to make peace. “I’m sorry for—being testy. Let’s not jab at each other. We’re both worried about Annalynn, and you and I are her first line of defense.”

"How can you say that? You're so weak you can barely lift a gallon of milk."

Annalynn came back in. "Jim said no thanks, so I asked him to come listen to the tape. I think we should tell him what we saw this morning, too."

Connie tossed the star onto the table. "What did you see?"

I resisted my instinct to brush Connie off. If we kept her in the dark, she'd never get over it. "We saw George Brendan come home a little after six thirty with a gun like the one our burglar had."

Color drained from Connie's cheeks. "I can't believe it. He's a lousy baritone, but people say he's a great cop. Does he know you saw him?"

"No," I said, "we hid behind a barbecue."

Connie raised her eyes to the ceiling. "Geez, Phoenix. This is no time for you to indulge in your childish spy fantasies."

Annalynn burst into laughter. She collapsed onto the love seat, holding her sides as peals of laughter continued to fill the room.

"She's hysterical," I said. "I'll get her some water." And throw it on her. She'd tip Connie off.

"I'll get it." Connie rushed from the room.

"Get a grip, Annalynn," I whispered. "I'd love to tell her, but we can't."

Annalynn gasped for air and wiped away tears of mirth. "Sorry."

Connie rushed back in with a glass of water.

Annalynn waved it away and burst into laughter again.

Connie put the glass on the coffee table. "I've got to go give a piano lesson."

Still laughing, Annalynn motioned for Connie to go.

After the front door closed, Annalynn sobered. "It's just as well she's gone. You have to teach me to shoot a service revolver this afternoon. The commissioners decided passing a shooting range test would give me 'credibility,' which means give them cover for appointing me. I have to hit the standard target twenty-five times from seven yards or they won't appoint me. And I've never fired a gun in my life."

"Piece of cake." I lied without guilt.

"I have to do it in three minutes," Annalynn added.

More like pie in the sky. "That's not so bad. You can empty a fifteen-round magazine in a few seconds." If you're used to shooting or don't care what you hit.

The doorbell rang.

Annalynn went toward the door. "That must be Jim."

"You'll come across as stronger if you handle this alone. I'll go fix some lunch."

I went on into the kitchen. I took a container of homemade vegetable soup from the freezer. As it thawed in the microwave, I weighed the odds of Annalynn qualifying. She was coordinated and had good eyesight, though she now used reading glasses. If she didn't panic, she might do it.

Annalynn called from the hall. "Phoenix, where's the tape?"

"In my bedside table. I'll go get it."

"No, no. You shouldn't be running up and down those stairs. I'll get it."

A few seconds later, Jim Falstaff appeared at my elbow. "I find it pretty damn hard to believe that anybody faked that killing. What makes you think so?"

"Two things: the answering-machine tape and the mock burglary to get it."

I accompanied him back to the den, where Annalynn joined us. She turned the tape recorder on.

The officer's eyes grew big as the screams began. They ended and the voice gave the time. "Jesus Christ! Right before Boom died!"

Annalynn stopped the tape. "We're assuming someone tortured Maria Lopez and used her as bait to get Boom to the motel. We don't know whether the screams have anything to do with the other two calls." She turned the recorder back on.

The taps and scratches played.

Jim cocked his head and closed his eyes as he listened. "What *is* that?"

I answered. "Morse code for 'meet me Tuesday morning,' and George Brendan went somewhere with an MP5 this morning."

Jim's mouth dropped open.

Annalynn jumped in: "The calls came from Texas and Oklahoma. I think the meeting had something to do with setting up a drug bust. I can't believe George would kill Boom, but I can't trust him. That's why I need you in the sheriff's office."

Jim regained his professional demeanor. "I've heard nothing about a big drug bust, and everybody works on those." He scratched his freshly shaved cheek. "I think you're right that it's Maria Lopez screaming. How did Boom know where she was?"

I cheered silently. He had a logical mind, and he was hooked. "My best guess is that she was an informant—maybe drug dealers at the college—and she was meeting Boom or someone else at the motel. The caller ID didn't give the number, so Boom either knew where she was or received another call on his missing mobile—cell phone."

Jim jiggled his keys and stared at the floor. "Doesn't give us much to go on." He scratched his chin. "George runs the department like he was still in the army, but he's always been an honest cop, and he hates drugs. He's seen what they do to people." He jiggled his keys some more. "Tell you what, Annalynn. I'll meet you at the shooting range at ten tonight to see what you can do. You qualify and pull the right strings to get me transferred, and you got yourself a tired, overweight assistant."

Annalynn let him out and returned to the kitchen. "I need a scotch."

"No alcohol. Never drink and shoot." My body demanded nourishment. I dished up the soup. "How on earth did you talk the commissioners into appointing you?"

"I pointed out I've already passed the department's test on its handbook."

I waited, not bothering to hide my skepticism.

She grimaced. "I talked to Nancy before the meeting and promised not to run against her for state senate."

A shrewd move, and a major sacrifice. "That's one vote. And the other two?"

"I agreed to study whether it would be profitable to build a jail housing two hundred prisoners. We had to board prisoners in Sullivan County last summer. It wrecked our budget. The warden has been pushing for a new building big enough to board other jurisdictions' overflow, but a lot of people think it would be more trouble than it's worth. The commission wants someone to take the heat. I'm it."

Prisons as economic development. Not a happy thought, but a pragmatic one. "Determining the economic feasibility is simple. I can pull together figures for you."

Annalynn smiled. "I'm counting on that. If I can shoot well enough to qualify."

"It's easy to hit a big target at that distance." At a shooting range. "But you can't wait until tonight to practice. Is there a civilian range in Laycock?"

"At the country club in the old duckpin alley. They converted it when Missouri passed the law allowing concealed carry."

"That's too public." To be a credible candidate, Annalynn had to look like she knew what she was doing. "We'll do a dry run here before we go over. You better trim your nails so you won't break them when you put bullets in the magazine." And pray you don't have to reload during that three minutes.

Annalynn read my thoughts. "I can load magazines. Boom bet me I couldn't get all fifteen bullets in, so I learned to do it."

WHEN ANNALYNN COULD pop a magazine into my Glock, grip the gun properly, and sight down the barrel, we drove to the country club and parked in front of the pro shop by Sean O'Reilly's Mustang.

"Mrs. Keyser, good to see you." A bald man lolling behind the counter shot to attention.

"We'd like to sign up for target practice and rent the Glock model the sheriff's department uses. And we'll need bullets, please."

"Yes, ma'am." He put the gun and a box of bullets into a cardboard box and added two sets of ear protectors and two goggles. "I guess that break-in the other night made you a little nervous." He rang up the charges. "My sympathies."

"Thank you," Annalynn said. "I won't rest until I find out who killed my husband and—his friend."

He ducked his head. "No, no, of course not."

Annalynn handed him her American Express card and signed in for the range.

When we walked out, she said, "According to the sign-in sheet, Dickie Rothway just left, and Sean has been down there almost an hour."

I tensed. Sean's uncle would know about Annalynn's deal with the commission by now. "I'd rather no one watch you practice."

"They must be about done." She led the way past the bar, along a hall, and down stairs. I heard two guns firing, and a flashback of the spice market stopped me short. I hadn't expected that. I forced myself to move on, but my hand closed around the Glock in my purse.

Sean, standing behind a glass wall in the first lane, turned his head to nod to us. He jammed in a fresh magazine and emptied it in a few seconds.

I moved to see Sean's target. Every shot had gone into the head of the cardboard silhouette suspended in his lane. I rapped on the glass and gave him a thumb's up.

He stepped out and dropped the ear protectors to his neck. "Hi. Getting ready to practice for becoming sheriff, Mrs. Keyser?" His tone was curious, not antagonistic.

I replied, "Yes, she hasn't been target shooting for some time." He held a Glock 24, a pricey competitor's model. "Is that one of your uncle's guns?"

"No, ma'am. This is mine." He stroked it the way he would a cat. "A present from my parents on my twenty-first birthday. I'm studying criminal justice."

"Your uncle must be pleased that you want to follow in his footsteps."

He stiffened and his mouth settled into a horizontal line.

Intrigued, I prolonged the conversation. "What classes have you taken?"

"Forensics and crime-scene evidence." He put the ear protectors back on, went back to his lane, and reloaded.

A gangly young man with a large nose and a matching Adam's apple stepped out of the second cubicle, nodded at us, and stood behind Sean.

Annalynn and I went into the third cubicle. Hoping the boys would leave, I dawdled in suspending Annalynn's target and jockeying it into place via pulleys. Sean's friend left, but Sean continued to shoot.

Annalynn loaded twelve rounds into the magazine quickly and struggled to push the last three into place.

Sean finished a magazine.

I raised my voice. "Let's see what you can do, Annalynn." As soon as Sean began firing, I took the gun from her and fired rapidly, forming an X over the target's heart. I handed the gun back to her. "Good job."

As I'd hoped, Sean left while Annalynn reloaded.

She hit the target somewhere with ten of her first fifteen shots. Soon she could hit the torso thirteen out of fifteen shots. The problem became cutting her reloading time.

"Could I rest a while?" Annalynn pulled off the goggles and ear protectors. "My wrists are aching."

"I'll fire off a few to show how well you shoot, and we'll go get a snack." I fired a series of patterns on a fresh target.

"That was so much easier than I expected," Annalynn said as we walked to the bar. "I actually enjoyed it. Let's share a banana split the way we used to. The bartender can bring it in from the restaurant." Without waiting for an answer, she placed the order.

Amused at Annalynn's pleasure in her prowess, I

went to the table we had occupied the day before. Sitting felt wonderful after an hour on my feet.

Lois Brendan zoomed into the parking lot in a black SUV. She parked next to Annalynn's Mercedes and strode toward the clubhouse with a scowl darkening her face. Slamming the door, she marched down the hall without looking in the bar.

I guessed Sean had reported on Annalynn's target practice. "Lois Brendan just came in. If you don't want a public scene, we'd better leave now."

Annalynn squared her shoulders. "I may as well get it over with. Besides, if I goad her a little, she may say something."

Lois charged into the bar. "How much did you pay those stupid commissioners? You've got a hell of a lot of nerve to steal George's job."

Annalynn leaned back in her chair, her face placid. "If George wants to be sheriff, he can file as a candidate."

"He doesn't have a rich wife to buy votes for him." Spittle flew from her contorted mouth. "Boom got him so deep in debt that it will take us years to get out. At least my husband doesn't run after whores."

Annalynn didn't move, but her eyes darkened with anger. "And is he home all night every night, your faithful George?" Her right hand balled into a fist. "Was he in your bed the night Boom died? Was he in your bed last night? And the night before?"

"Bitch!" Lois whirled around, ran to her vehicle, and roared out of the parking lot.

I smiled. "I'd say you struck a nerve. Two or three, in fact."

Annalynn gripped the edge of the table. “I’ll never be able to find out who killed Boom if George controls the investigation. I have to qualify, Phoenix. I have to.”

SIXTEEN

I CALLED A halt to the practice when Annalynn put forty-five bullets in a row into the torso.

On the way home, she said, "You haven't told me what you found in Boom's financial records today."

Dreading my role as messenger, I summarized her financial situation in the impersonal voice I used with clients. I omitted my view that he'd been on the take.

Halfway through, Annalynn, her jaw clenched, turned her face away. When I finished, she said, "I didn't realize we'd lost that much. I know you think I was an idiot, but I turned our finances over to Boom to bolster his confidence. He was devastated when the car dealership—didn't work out." Her voice trembled. "That was my fault. I should never have pushed him into it. He loved selling cars, but he hated running a business."

She wouldn't—couldn't—believe he had done anything wrong. To hide my cynicism, I stayed in business mode. "I suggest you sell your share of the airplane to cover your ongoing expenses. If you can get a good price for the summer place, you can invest and earn enough to cover basic expenses." Barely. "Do you owe anything on it?"

"No. We paid that off when Father died. I'll contact a realtor in Branson."

We passed two Hispanic men loading a lawnmower onto a trailer.

Annalynn gasped. "Oh, my God! What if Maria

Lopez had information about the bank cheating Hispanics—maybe stealing money they were sending to their families?"

A flimsy straw to grasp. "Dickie wouldn't have the nerve to steal."

"Wes Berry says the immigrants are ideal victims." Annalynn's voice rose with excitement. "Boom went to talk to a car dealer who was selling them cars that had been wrecked. Most of them are good, hardworking people who came here to give their families a better life. Even the legal immigrants are afraid to call the police or challenge people who take advantage of them."

Worth thinking about. "Damn! I should have called Elena Cordero this morning. When I talk to her about that phone call, I'll ask about Dickie's financial shenanigans, too." I pulled into the driveway and on into the garage.

"Wait until she goes home from the bank and can talk freely."

Annalynn said nothing more until we closed the front door behind us. "It's time we go from defense to offense. We need a playbook."

I hated sports analogies. Before Boom's death, I would have said so. "Let's work on one."

We went into the den and she fetched two yellow legal pads and two ballpoints. "Where do we start?"

My body ached and my brain begged for the magic pill and a long nap. I forced myself to focus. "We start at the beginning—what brought Boom and Maria together—and work toward the middle—the murders. That will lead us to the ending—identifying the killers."

"Killers? Not one person?" She clenched and unclenched her hands. "It was so—so personal, so vengeful, so calculated. Death didn't satisfy the killer. He wanted to humiliate Boom. And her. Maybe me."

I considered her disquieting analysis. "Agreed. Still, Boom was a strong, armed man expecting trouble. One person couldn't have handled him and staged a murder-suicide. That takes two or three people, a gang. Maybe organized crime."

"Laycock doesn't have organized crime. Our major problem is meth, and most users cook their own. They're too spaced out to be organized."

"Then let's find out what Maria Lopez could have been involved in. Surely Elena can help there." I chose nonaccusatory words. "And we have to look for anything unusual Boom did, any diversion from his regular pattern."

"He'd been awfully quiet lately, but I thought that—" She dropped her eyes.

"This is no time for secrets. What was Boom worried about?" Besides money. I remembered the jump in medical expenses some time before. "Was he ill?"

Annalynn closed her eyes for several seconds. "He had diabetes. He controlled it pretty well with diet and exercise. He kept it secret because he was afraid it would hurt him with voters." She looked at me. "He loved that job. He was so proud of his March on Meth. He worked with the social service agencies and the churches to set up special programs for the children of meth abusers. He won a state award for that."

So he wasn't just a glad-handing, self-indulgent jock. But then Annalynn wouldn't have loved a man with no substance. "Let's go over the week before he died. Where he went, what he did. Unusual phone calls."

"I've thought about all that." She rested her chin on her hand. "He mentioned a meth fire at the Hollywood

Trailer Court. He went over there and came home depressed because the cook was a woman he'd helped get treatment twice." Annalynn's face brightened. "Maybe she gave him a tip on a meth dealer. I'll have Jim look into that." She made a note. "Wednesday night Boom played poker. Thursday night we drove to Rocheport to a bistro that makes its own wine. We had a lovely evening."

Missouri wine? I didn't mind not being able to drink that. "And Friday?"

"He took a nap while I revised the Garden Club bylaws. Then he went out to Harry's Hideaway. It's a sports bar on the east edge of town. Truckers stop there, and people come from all around on Friday and Saturday nights. Harry calls Boom whenever the place gets a little rowdy."

Truckers could have called Boom from Texas and Oklahoma. "Could it be a drop-off place for illegal aliens, or a distribution place for Mexican drugs?"

"No, no, of course not!" Annalynn's shocked denial turned into uncertainty. "How would I know? Boom never hinted at suspecting that."

I put it on my mental list of places to check. "Elena should be home soon. Where's the phone book?"

"I'll get it." Annalynn went behind the screen and came back flipping through the pages. "She lives in an apartment at three forty Washington Street." She wrote the phone number on her pad. "The minister knew Maria Lopez, too. Connie can talk to him at choir practice tomorrow night."

"Maybe she could find out something from the college students or faculty members she worked with on the show." I slapped my forehead. "We haven't done the obvious—look up Maria Lopez online."

We moved to the computer and I typed "Maria Lopez" and "Laycock, MO" in the Google search line. Ten items popped up, all on her death.

"I've seen these articles," I said. "They just say she's survived by her parents and several siblings in southern Missouri and graduated from a little Catholic college." The next page of listings provided a link to the faculty page at www.Laycock.edu. I clicked on it. "Maria Lopez teaches Beginning and Intermediate Spanish and advises Spanish-speaking students. She also teaches Conversational English for Adults in LCC's Continuing Education Program."

Annalynn flipped through the phone book. "She lived at three forty Washington, where Elena does. It's an apartment building."

"Then Elena may have vital information. For her and your safety, no one should see you together. Any idea where I could meet her?"

"What about the library? It's empty after supper. But I don't see how you can meet her either. Everyone associates you with me."

"Of course. Everyone knows everyone else here." I could deal with that. "We'll worry about that later. I'll use the hall phone, and you can listen here."

I dialed the number.

"*Hola*!"

Obviously Elena had been expecting a call from someone else. "*Hola,* Elena. We appreciated your call yesterday afternoon, but we need more information—for your safety as well as ours."

Silence. "Who is this?"

"You cashed my check yesterday. We have to talk—where no one will notice us. Please meet me at eight tonight in the library." Where? "By the magazines."

A long silence. "I really don't know much about—the subject."

"Anything will help." Offer money? No. Self-interest hadn't motivated this young woman. "Please."

More silence. Finally she said, "I'll think about it." She hung up.

I gave Annalynn a thumb's-up. "She'll be there." It felt good to be back in the game.

SEVENTEEN

"IT'S TOO DANGEROUS," Annalynn argued. "You can't go alone."

"I'll find out more without you there. I've had hundreds of meetings like this. I know what I'm doing." I might as well apply my tradecraft. "I'll use the clothes Mrs. Hamilton left behind to disguise myself as an old woman. She had chemotherapy last year. Maybe she left a wig, too."

Annalynn pulled me into a hug. "If you need a disguise, it's too dangerous. I couldn't bear to lose you too. Just talk to her on the phone. Please."

I patted her back. "I have to see her face, her body language. Don't worry. No one will recognize me."

Annalynn drew back. "You've been fooling strangers, not people who've known you since you cracked walnuts on the railroad tracks."

"Most of those people are dead." Shouldn't have mentioned that. "I'll make a deal with you. Connie will be here soon. If she recognizes me, we'll all go to meet Elena."

"Deal. You'll never fool Connie."

Doing so would be a pleasure. "I'll go see what's in those boxes."

The telephone rang, and Annalynn checked the caller ID. "It's the church." She lifted the receiver. "Hello." She listened for a moment. "I'm fine, Wes." She motioned for me to go.

I picked up a flashlight in the kitchen on my way to the basement. In the passage outside Boom's office, I shone the light on the ceiling. Two recessed fans provided ventilation. Between them was the manhole-sized trapdoor.

I wondered whether Boom had put his office here rather than upstairs in order to be able to sneak out. Another possibility struck me: Annalynn had made Judge Carr's pleasant office a shrine. Boom had made the bomb shelter his own. He must have found being married to the judge's daughter difficult at times. Maybe Annalynn really had pushed him beyond his limits.

Disconcerted by feeling sympathy for Boom, I moved into my unfinished basement and swung the flashlight around. Cracks covered the cement floor. A big piece of plywood walled off the furnace from the storage area. I opened the top of a cardboard box: years of *National Geographic.*

I went on up the stairs and to my old bedroom. I'd loved having windows on the side and back walls, and so would a burglar. Warmed by the afternoon sun still streaming in, I rummaged through the castoffs until I found a dark-blue dress with a big white B on the bodice, a white cloth belt to tie around the waist, and a high collar that would cover my neck. I added a light-blue cardigan. To my delight, a box held a passable gray wig. Another contained low-heeled black shoes. I tried them on. Tight, but I could stand them for an hour or so. I bundled up my finds and went back to my bedroom in Annalynn's house.

Annalynn tapped on my door. "Connie called. She'll be here in twenty minutes. Can I help with your—costume?"

"It's going to be pretty crude. Do you have a small pillow and two long belts?"

"I'll find something."

I hesitated a moment before shedding my slacks and shirt, but Annalynn had already seen the scar. She came in to help me belt on the pillow and pull a T-shirt down and elastic-waist shorts up over it.

Annalynn stood back to inspect the effect. "You're much too lumpy. Anyone can see you're wearing padding. Connie will laugh her head off."

"I'd prefer a body mold, but this will have to do. Help me get the blue dress over my head, please."

That done, I tied the belt and stood in front of the mirror on the closet door. "It is lumpy. I'll have to wear the sweater over it." I opened my makeup kit. "You go on down. If Connie gets here before I'm ready, tell her Mrs. Hamilton's sister"—had to be a B name—"Barbara came by."

"This won't work."

"Go, ye of little faith."

"That reminds me. Wes is coming over to discuss a memorial for Boom."

"That's nice." When Annalynn left, I pulled the wig on and brushed some of the faux hair over my forehead. Anyone who looked closely could tell it was a wig, but few would pay any attention.

I worked in age lines, brushed gray into my eyebrows, and added liver spots to the backs of my hands. Crude, but it would have to do. A pair of reading glasses planted halfway down my nose completed my disguise. Carrying the shoes and sweater, I went downstairs.

Annalynn came from the den. Dismay flitted across her face. "Better than I expected. The wig helps. You just made it. I heard Connie pull into the driveway."

I trotted into the living room, put on the tight shoes and ample sweater, and perched on the edge of a Windsor chair so Connie would have to sit at least five feet away. I made my whole body sag and curled my fingers as though they were arthritic.

Annalynn opened the door. “Come in. I have a guest.” She gestured toward the living room. “Mrs. Hamilton’s sister Barbara—umm—Cartland.”

“Oh?” Connie glanced into the room. “I don’t think we’ve ever met.”

Annalynn covered her mouth with the fingers of her left hand. “I was about to make some tea. I’ll let you introduce yourself.”

“Of course.” Connie walked into the room. “Hello. I’m Connie Diamante.”

I leaned forward as though to rise, keeping my head down.

“You needn’t get up.” Connie sat down on the sofa. “How’s your sister doing?”

“Not too well,” I said softly, pitching my voice a half octave higher and tightening my throat. “She loved living in Mary’s little house.”

Annalynn clasped her head with both hands. “Connie! Look at her!”

I straightened my shoulders, uncurled my fingers, and waved.

Connie’s mouth formed an O. “Wow! You make a really believable old woman.” She came for a closer look. “You’re good! How did you make your skin so gray?”

“That’s *au naturel,* I’m afraid.”

Annalynn rushed over. “You weren’t that white a little bit ago. Do you want me to get your pills?”

I resisted the temptation. Better to hurt than to be stupid. “No, thanks, but I better take a nap before the meeting.”

"What you need is chocolate," Connie said. "I stashed a box of Godiva."

"I shouldn't have all that fat," I protested. I'd had no chocolate for two months. "What the hell! Bring it on."

AT QUARTER TO EIGHT I slipped into the Beetle's passenger seat. I'd wanted to go alone, but Annalynn had vetoed that.

Connie stopped at the library's door and ran around the car to help me inside. "No trouble at all," Connie said, raising her voice just enough that the white-haired woman at the circulation desk, the only person in sight, could hear. "You let me know when you're ready to go, and I'll be glad to drop you off at your sister's."

The librarian glanced up.

I recognized the Roman nose of my favorite high school teacher, Mrs. Roper.

"Good luck," Connie whispered, and ran back to her car.

I rounded my shoulders and limped over to the desk in the uncomfortable shoes. "Could you tell me, please, where to find *Consumer Reports*?"

Mrs. Roper pointed to the far corner. "The magazines are back behind the nonfiction books. If you'll wait until Connie parks, I'll help you find what you want."

I folded my arms over my padded stomach. I'd forgotten how helpful Missourians are. Mrs. Roper wouldn't be easy to fool. "Thank you, dear."

Connie hurried in.

"Connie," Mrs. Roper called, her voice authoritative. "Would you please watch the desk for me while I show your friend what she wants?" Without waiting for an answer, she came from behind the high counter and took my arm. "If you have a moment later, Connie, I'd love to hear about Phoenix."

Connie grinned. "She's changed a lot. You won't recognize her."

Mrs. Roper guided me to a conference table by the magazine racks. "Do you know what issue you want?"

"I want the one on interior paints." Might as well read something useful.

Elena Cordero came from between the shelves, glanced at me, and turned to go.

Couldn't lose her now. "*Hola*!" I called in my old lady voice.

Elena came slowly to the table. *"Hola."*

Mrs. Roper put two boxes in front of me. "The top one has the index. That will tell you which issue you need." She smiled at Elena and left.

I stayed in character. "You're that nice Spanish lady in the bank."

Elena stiffened. "I work in the bank, but I was born in Missouri." She turned to go.

"A friend sent me. Please take an *Economist* and sit down." I picked up the index.

Elena's eyes widened. "Yes, ma'am." She went to the magazine rack.

I opened the index to interior paints and then pawed through the box until I found the right issue.

Elena peered up the rows of books before sitting down across from me with a copy of *Fast Company.*

"My friend," I said *sotto voce*, "is afraid whoever killed Boom and Maria will come after you if they realize you know something."

Elena gasped. "But I don't!"

Confusion and fear, not deception. "You know enough to be suspicious. Were you and Maria close friends?"

"Not really. She moved into my building in January, and we'd both volunteered at the church since February." Tears filled Elena's eyes. "She was nice, *muy simpatica.*"

I turned to the article on paints. "Did you know she'd been meeting Boom?"

Elena leaned forward but kept her chin down to whisper, "I saw her talking to him after a class. I thought he was hitting on her. I teased her about it. She laughed and said, 'He's an old man. And he's very married.' " She turned a page in the magazine. "She told me she'd never met a man so crazy about his wife. She wanted that kind of marriage."

So Annalynn had been right. A jealous boyfriend perhaps? I took a pen and small notebook from my purse and wrote down the name of a paint. "Was she dating anyone?"

"No. She moved here from Kansas City partly because her boyfriend didn't want to get married. She went out with me and Frank and our friends three or four times." Elena stole a glance toward the shelves. "The last time we invited her to go to Harry's Hideaway with us, she said no. She said someone she didn't want to see might be there."

Harry's was a busy place. "Do you know who he is?" I brought my magazine up close to my eyes.

"No idea. Maybe one of her ESL students or somebody who works at the college."

Surely Elena knew something more. "Did she ever act afraid of anyone?"

"Before she died, I would have said no." She sniffed. "Then I remembered that she asked the building manager to put an extra lock on her door about two months ago. Twice at least someone followed her car home after night class and waited until she got inside." She wiped her nose with a tissue. "I can't understand it. She was such a good person. She wanted to help people. What kind of monster would kill her that way?"

"One who's willing to kill again," I said. "Have you noticed anyone following you or watching your apartment?"

Eyes enormous, Elena stared at me. "No. Nothing like that."

"Please be very careful. Avoid being out alone." Bloody hell! I'd caused the young woman to disobey my good advice.

"My boyfriend doesn't let me go anywhere alone since—since then." She dropped her eyes. "He's reading a newspaper up front, and I'm going to stay at his place."

"Good." Talking about the bank would be delicate. I'd have to slide into it. "Did Maria ever ask you anything odd?"

Elena picked up her magazine. "Like what?"

"Like working conditions at the slaughterhouses or meatpacking plants in nearby counties."

"Sure. Frank works as a manager at a meatpacking plant. Some of it's awful work, but believe me, people are grateful to get the jobs."

"Did she ever ask you about the bank? About how well it's serving immigrants?"

"Of course." She smiled. "Everybody knows you have to keep an eye on bankers."

"Including Richard Rothway?"

Elena frowned. "He's better than most. Sheriff Keyser saw to that. Mr. Rothway was really upset when the sheriff died. I don't think he likes Mrs. Keyser much."

He'd been crazy about her in junior high. I felt sweat trickle down my forehead. The wig was a heating pad. "Did Maria ever mention drugs at the college?"

Elena thought a moment. "Not that I remember."

Strike three. I dabbed my forehead with a tissue.

Head down, she turned another page. "Wait. A bunch of us were talking about meth one night at Harry's. Somebody said some entrepreneur—I remember he used that word—is bringing in crystal meth and that Maria would see it at LCC soon. She didn't say much, but she was really upset."

Maria sounded like an idealistic young woman, the kind of person willing to become an informant. So hot I felt faint, I had to finish up. "If you think of anything or anyone who could have wanted her dead, or if you need any help, call Phoenix Smith. If you can't say why you're calling, mention venture capital." Afraid I would pass out and blow my cover, I put my hands on the table to push up my old woman's body. "Stay here ten minutes."

I hobbled toward the library entrance. I hadn't learned much, but I had stilled my doubts. Persons unknown had killed Boom Keyser and Maria Lopez.

EIGHTEEN

UNNERVED THAT I needed the arm Connie offered me, I steadied myself enough to note that the maroon Honda Civic parked next to Connie's car had a license plate with a 5-4-3 sequence. It had been parked at the church Monday evening. Elena's car.

I pulled off the wig as soon as Connie drove out of the parking lot.

"You look god-awful." Connie stepped on the gas. "I better get you back."

"Not yet. Go away from Annalynn's house." I struggled out of the sweater and kicked off the tight shoes. "I'll be okay as soon as I cool down."

Connie turned on the air-conditioning. "Trudy got over her surgery much faster than you are. Would you like for me to get her doctor's phone number for you?"

"No, thanks. I'm gaining strength every day, and most of the time I don't hurt."

"Was this masquerade tonight worth it? Did you find out anything?"

"Enough to convince me Maria was an informant rather than a mistress. I'll tell you and Annalynn together." I unbuttoned the dress and went to work on the belts holding the pillow in place. "I've got to get out of this stuff. Find a dark spot, pull over, and douse the lights."

Connie turned down an alley and stopped under a tree. I jumped out of the car long enough to slide out of the dress and get rid of the pillow. I tossed everything into the back and dropped into my seat. "Go!"

Connie's uncharacteristic silence warned me that I'd overdone the orders. "Sorry. I'm pretty uptight tonight."

"You've been wound up like a top since you got here. I know you don't want to worry Annalynn. I can keep a confidence. Is there anything you'd like to talk about?"

"Thanks, but—" Why not share a bit? Arouse a little sympathy to help repair our frayed friendship. "Okay. One of the reasons I came to Laycock is that I'm not going back to Vienna. I don't know where I'm going next."

"I know exactly what you're going through." Connie pulled out of the alley into a residential street. "Amazing, isn't it? All three of us have reached a life crisis. At least you don't have to worry about money."

The words reminded me that Connie, despite her carefree attitude, faced financial problems with no prospect of solution. "I guess we're all caught in the rain that must fall, but Annalynn got hit by lightning." Being shot had been a bolt out of the blue, too. Connie's dual crises of divorce and her mother's death had been less sudden but no less traumatic. "We'll help Annalynn through her storm, and then we'll work on ours." I checked my side mirror to make sure we weren't being followed before leaning back in the seat to placate my aching wound.

Connie roused me a little later. "Go on in the house. I'll gather up your stuff."

"Thanks." I stepped out of the car onto the cool concrete driveway in my bare feet. Walking across the grass reminded me of long summer evenings when Annalynn and I played hopscotch until dark and then chased lightning bugs.

Annalynn came out on the porch to meet me. "How did it go?"

Revived by the cool night air, I sat down in one of the wrought-iron chairs on the porch. "Good. Elena's sure Boom and Maria weren't having an affair but doesn't know why they were meeting."

Connie came up the steps carrying a bulging black garbage bag. "I thought I was going to have to carry Phoenix to the car. I think she has a fever. She needs a doctor."

"I'm fine," I insisted, annoyed that Connie had tattled.

Annalynn placed the back of her hand on my forehead. "You don't feel feverish. Tell me what Elena said."

I told them and added, "We should follow up on the possibility of drug dealing. Maybe check Maria's class rosters against arrests for meth possession."

"I'll put Jim on it," Annalynn said, her voice confident.

Connie handed the garbage bag to Annalynn. "Here's what's left of Barbara Cartland. See you tomorrow."

As Connie walked to her car, I realized that I was silhouetted against the dining-room window, an easy target for even a mediocre marksman. My rational self scoffed, but my instincts won. "Let's go in. I have to clean off this makeup." My eyes swept the street for anyone dawdling or sitting in a car.

Annalynn followed me in and closed the door. "Do you trust Elena?"

"Yes. She had nothing to gain, and she was smart enough to come to you rather than the police. Did you find out anything from Reverend Berry?"

Annalynn's face clouded. "I blew it. He made me so angry that I asked him to leave. To be precise, I demanded that he get out of my house."

For Annalynn to lose her temper was unusual. For her to be impolite to any guest was unthinkable. "What did he say?"

"He asked me not to take the appointment. He suggested I'm doing it to soothe my wounded pride." She pressed her temples with her forefingers. "Dickie put Wes up to it, I'm sure. They played golf with Lois this afternoon."

"They're all asses."

Annalynn led me into the den to our regular places. "Wes said that if I believed Boom was innocent, I should do something positive. I should create a memorial to him that helps Maria's people."

"Maria's *people?*" The condescension in the term irritated me almost as much as the boy minister's misreading of Annalynn.

She smiled wryly. "He wants a place where day laborers—code for undocumented immigrants—can wait for employers. He says people come, hoping to get work at the meat-processing plants, and end up in Laycock looking for handyman jobs. Apparently some people don't pay them the agreed amount."

"That's a genuine concern." Having given him credit due, I went to the point: "How much did he want you to give?"

Annalynn leaned back and stared at the ceiling. "He asked for the proceeds from the sale of the plane."

A clever way to finance a pet project. "You learned one thing: He doesn't know the state of your finances. Is the memorial suggestion why you asked him to leave?"

"No." Color had drained from her face. "I told him I couldn't think about anything else until I found out who killed Boom. The good reverend said that I might find out things I don't want to know." She covered her face with her hands. "I wanted to tear his heart out."

"Forget him, Annalynn. He's a foolish, self-righteous young man with no life experience."

"But he knows something about Maria and Boom. I should have stayed in control and wormed it out of him."

No point in denying that she had missed an opportunity. "We'll sic Connie on him. He's more likely to tell his choir director than you." I glanced at my watch. Nine fifteen. Only forty-five minutes until the shooting test. "I'm going to wash off Barbara Cartland and stretch out to relax for fifteen minutes." Would I be able to get up? I had to. "I want you to take some deep breaths—no scotch—and calm down."

JIM TOUCHED HIS cap in greeting as Annalynn and I got out of her SUV in the parking lot shared by the Laycock police and the Vandiver County sheriff's department. "I had to sign you up for the shooting range." He pointed to the Deputy 1 license plate. "You're going to have an audience."

"No problem," I said. "Does she need to load the second magazine during the three minutes?"

"No, she'll start with two full magazines."

Annalynn winked at me. "Piece of cake."

We went through a door between the sheriff's office and the county jail, down a flight of cement steps, and through a hall with walls of white cement blocks.

Jim hit a series of buttons to unlock a heavy door. It opened into a small room with a gun cabinet full of shotguns on one wall and a waist-high safe on the other.

George Brendan, in uniform, stood by the shotguns. A pudgy older man in LPD blues leaned against the wall.

"Good evening, Chief Rucker, George," Annalynn

said. "I appreciate your coming here so late." She took off her blazer. "Jim, do we have ear protectors for everyone?"

"I'm not sure, ma'am." He handed sets to her and to me. "We got plenty of earplugs." He passed those to the others and goggles to Annalynn.

Brendan said, "I already set up the target."

Jim walked to one of the two cubicles that fronted the target lanes and put his weapon and a spare magazine on the shooter's shelf. "She needs more ammunition."

Chief Rucker handed a box to Annalynn.

Walking to the shelf, she put on the ear protectors and goggles and picked up the gun. She adjusted her grip several times before she began firing at random intervals, studying the target between each shot.

George's lip curled into a sneer. Jim fidgeted.

Annalynn released the empty magazine. "Phoenix, take a look, please."

I joined her. All but two shots had hit the cardboard torso, but most fell near the edges. "Relax. You'll be fine. Remember to breathe. Don't hurry. Get the target in your sight every shot. Concentrate on your next shot, not where the last one hit."

When Annalynn had emptied two more magazines into the torso, I said, "She's warmed up. Let's have a fresh target and a timed run."

While Annalynn reloaded, Jim ducked under the shelf to clip a new silhouette in place. "You want to hold the stopwatch, Chief?"

"Sure. Tell me when you're ready, Annalynn."

George Brendan strode to the neighboring cubicle. "I'll count the hits."

"Ready." Annalynn said. She fired on a steady four

count. She released the empty magazine and slipped the next one in.

"Thirteen," Brendan said.

When Annalynn took several seconds to aim before resuming her measured pace, I knew she wouldn't be able to take all fifteen shots. She had to conquer her nerves and hit each one.

"Time," the chief called all too soon.

Annalynn laid down the gun.

Brendan walked into the lane to count the holes—twice. "Twenty-five."

The chief extended his hand. "Congratulations, Sheriff."

NINETEEN

GEORGE BRENDAN STALKED from the room, his blond eyebrows bright lines on his beet-red face.

Chief Rucker took out his earplugs. "Are you sure you want the job, Annalynn? George—and others—won't be easy to deal with."

Annalynn took a deep breath and exhaled. "I don't expect it to be easy, but no group could be more difficult than the school board."

He laughed. "That's for sure." He extended his hand. "If I can help, call me."

Annalynn took his hand and held it. "Lend me Jim Falstaff."

The chief shook his head. "I can't spare my best officer for thirteen weeks."

"I realize that you rely on him." She let the implication that the chief couldn't get along without the officer hang in the air. "Let me have him for a month, starting tomorrow. Surely you can you manage without him that long."

He stared at the ceiling and rocked on his heels. "I can manage if your department responds to all night 9-1-1 calls."

"Fair enough," Annalynn said.

"Let me remind you, Sheriff, you aren't a trained officer, so the state doesn't allow you to go out after the bad guys. You're limited to supervision and administration." He opened the hall door. "Good luck. Jim, you lock up before you start your shift."

"Sure," Jim answered. As soon as the door closed, he said, "You want me to start tomorrow?"

Annalynn picked up her blazer. "I don't expect you to come off a night shift to a day shift, but please do three things: Find me a gun and holster, get Phoenix a concealed-weapon permit, and copy the files on the city's meth arrests in the last year."

"The permit's a problem. You have to be a legal resident."

"Laycock is my legal residence," I pointed out. "I vote here." Absentee. "I've paid property taxes here for ten years."

He jiggled his keys. "I'm not sure that will do it. Sheriff, you can name her a reserve deputy. A deputy can carry a weapon."

"Sold," I said. "She needs protection constantly."

He frowned. "You found out something else?"

"Nothing to take to court," I admitted, unwilling to mention Elena even to Jim. "It's looking more and more like it involves meth, but we can't close out other possibilities." The fatigue that had been hovering over me pounced.

"You don't look so good, Phoenix," Jim said.

Probably better than I felt. "Anytime Annalynn leaves the station for anything, stick with her. On red alert. The killers thought they were pretty smart when they faked that murder-suicide. They didn't just shoot and run. They covered their tracks in a particularly nasty way. We have to assume they're still around, still operating, still ready to kill."

He digested that, the lines in his round face deepening. "I'll make sure we both get new Kevlar vests." He rubbed his chin. "Crystal meth from Mexico has moved into northern Missouri and southern Iowa. If that's involved, we gotta get help with this. No way we can take on a big crystal-meth operation."

Annalynn checked to make sure no one stood outside the door. "You think the killers are outsiders?"

"Locals got to be involved, probably as distributors. I'd bet their suppliers are part of a regional or even a national operation. Those guys are vicious, and they're armed to the teeth." He thrust his gun into his holster. "The local cooks make crank mostly for themselves and a few buddies. Some even use food coloring at holidays. You know, red and green for Christmas. They get real mean, but they're pretty damn pathetic, too."

He handed me the half-empty box of bullets. "I was in on four different busts where the houses were filthy and little kids had nothing to eat." He knelt to close the safe. "We were lucky with crack. That stayed in the cities. Meth hit us first, and now Kansas City and St. Louis are crying, too. I'd hoped these guys running the crystal meth up from Mexico would figure out they can make a lot more in the cities and leave us alone. The problem is, they already got a lot of addicts to sell to here."

They said good night, and I marshaled my energy to beat Annalynn to the outside door. Hand in my purse, I checked the parking lot before stepping outside.

"Phoenix, you're not my bodyguard," Annalynn said as we walked to the SUV.

"I have a lot more experience with sneaking around and looking for trouble than you do." I dreaded stepping up into the high vehicle, but the wound didn't protest this time. "Educate me a little about meth. Do people snort it like cocaine? Inject it like heroin? Swallow it?"

"All of the above. I think the people who make their

own swallow or snort mostly. I don't know the preferred way to kill yourself with crystal meth."

I WOKE FEELING rested and eager for action as the clock chimed seven. While I showered, I planned my day. First, go online for any messages from my staff in Vienna and my few remaining CIA contacts. Then check details on the Keysers' financial records and prepare to question Dickie.

When I opened my closet, I added another priority: laundry. Did Laycock have a decent clothing store? I needed some good clothes to accompany Annalynn to social and official events.

"Phoenix," Annalynn called through the door, "what should I wear today?"

"Something understated but businesslike." I put on my robe and opened the door. "Slacks and blazer maybe. With a tuck-in top that won't interfere with a holster."

Annalynn still wore her blue silk robe. Her skin, much envied in high school, lacked its usual glow, and dark blotches shadowed her eyes. She touched my cheek. "Your color is good this morning. You must have slept well."

"I'm starving again. Do you mind if we eat right now?"

Annalynn smiled. "You thrive on excitement. Go on and eat. I'm going to prepare a little speech to the staff this morning."

I pulled on my robe and went to the kitchen to toast some sourdough bread to eat with apple butter, two foods I'd missed in Vienna. I turned on the kitchen radio.

"We have big news this morning, folks," a man's voice said. "The county commission has appointed Annalynn Carr Keyser acting sheriff. Reliable sources, namely my wife and my mother, tell me Sheriff Boom Keyser's widow refuses to believe he killed himself and a young woman last week. Looks like Laycock has its very own soap opera. And here comes more breaking news: Today's menu at the middle school features macaroni with hamburger."

I turned the radio off. When the telephone rang, I ignored it. After the fourth ring, the answering machine went on. I didn't catch the person's name, but I heard *Kansas City Star.* Two St. Louis television stations called right after that. Damned troublemakers.

Annalynn came down wearing a chocolate-brown linen pants suit, a cream-colored silk blouse, and low-heeled pumps in time to hear the last message. A tiny frown reminded me of her taut control before geometry tests. "I hadn't thought about the press. Boom always handled reporters himself. I suppose I'll have to. Any advice?"

"Say as little as possible, and be boring."

She pursed her lips in thought. "When we had that ruckus on the school board, the broadcast reporters lost interest quickly, but the newspaper people kept demanding interviews. I finally held a press conference. I don't want to this time." She smiled. "I'll ask Nancy Kallenbach to do it. She'll be glad to stand in the limelight."

"That's absolutely brilliant." I sat down at the dining-room table and she joined me.

She poured us each a cup of tea. "And if we hold the press conference at five o'clock this afternoon, the television stations may not bother to send anyone. They like to tape early and have time to edit before the evening news."

I tried to look at Annalynn as if she were a stranger. She remained an attractive woman with great poise and presence, and she'd always been photogenic. She spoke well in a pleasant, low-pitched voice. She'd come across on camera only too well. Putting on a badge to prove her husband's faithfulness could become big news. "If you give them even a crumb, they'll come after you. They're going to want to know what evidence you have and why the sheriff's department didn't find it."

"The same things the staff wants to know." She rubbed her temples. "I'll tell them both the same thing."

"Which is?"

"That I'll investigate his murder and recommend what to do about a new jail." She went into the kitchen to fix a bowl of Cheerios. "Anything about creating jobs or raising taxes gets the public's attention. It would help if you could come up with some preliminary figures on the cost efficiency of a correctional facility housing a hundred prisoners versus one housing two hundred or more."

I relaxed. I needn't worry about Annalynn handling the press. "You realize that I can't come up with precise figures by five o'clock."

"Think like a politician, not an economist. I need rounded-off guesstimates, not final figures. And you won't have to start from scratch. Nancy sent over a box of files last night. They're by my desk in the den."

"Okay. I'll e-mail some figures to you." No long nap today. "What are you going to do about Brendan?"

Annalynn rubbed her eyes. "That kept me awake. I can tell him to take a long vacation, or I can ask him to carry on. What do you think?"

"Tough call." I thought aloud: "You don't want him to know we suspect he's involved in Boom's death. Can you cut him off from the investigation? With such a small staff, that may be impossible."

She brought her cereal to the table. "I'll wait to see what play George calls."

I cringed at the sports metaphor. "Are you going to ask for help from outside?"

"I may request a major case squad. That's a team of specialists—detectives, crime-scene investigators, et cetera—drawn from several jurisdictions. Usually you request the M-squad immediately. It may be too late now."

The doorbell rang.

Annalynn stood. "That's Jim. Wish me luck."

I PUT MY laundry in the washer and went to work on the files. They yielded more data than I'd expected. The commission had hired a consultant to gather facts, but lacked the political will to act. I soon saw why. Although the county had gained new population and businesses in the last five years, building even the smaller facility meant long-term debt and pinched budgets. Borrowing a few extra million to build facilities to board other jurisdictions' prisoners made sense—if other jurisdictions faced a long-term shortage of jail cells. From what I'd heard about the meth epidemic, cell shortages seemed likely. If other counties weren't planning to make crime pay by overbuilding and renting out cells. I needed to update the research, an easy job but not one I could complete today.

I put my laundry in the dryer, typed a report on Annalynn's computer, and logged onto her account. A message from the sheriff's department gave her e-mail address and a terse message: "SFSG." I puzzled over it a moment before recognizing "So far so good." I transmitted the report.

My fingers lingered on the keyboard. I hadn't checked my e-mail accounts since a Starbucks in Indiana. I went on to my office account and answered messages from friends and professional acquaintances. No fake spam from my one reliable contact at CIA headquarters. Jerry and I had orders not to communicate with each other. He'd be under fire for organizing a disastrous drop. Seven weeks ago. Surely by now they'd figured out who shot me. Almost every group bragged to someone.

For the tenth time I evaluated the only other alternative: The shooting had been personal rather than professional. Jerry could have set me up. But why? I'd done three insignificant jobs for him, one checking the after-hours activities of a Kurdish man attending a meeting in Vienna, another carrying cash to a Turkish agent in Munich, and the last helping a Syrian scientist elude a tail and board a plane to Rio. The biggest assignment had been our "vacation" in Corfu. He'd told me nothing about the operation, but he obviously was recruiting a Turkish intelligence officer. I'd kept the man's wife occupied by playing the piano as she sang country music learned by listening to CDs. Could the Turkish officer have spotted me and retaliated? Unlikely.

I checked the time: almost eleven thirty. I went into the hall and found the number for the First National Bank of Laycock. A real person answered. I identified myself as a bank examiner and asked for the manager.

"Richard Rothway. How may I assist you?"

"Hi, Dickie. We need to talk. Today. Two o'clock would be good."

He sighed. "I'm extremely busy."

"You talk to me today, or you'll be talking to a real bank examiner tomorrow."

"Very well. But not here. I'll take a late lunch and meet you at the country club."

"No, thanks." Too public. "The bandstand in Memorial Park at two." I hung up.

Hungry again, I ate some soup and returned to the computer. My CIA contacts in embassies communicated with me on blogs unrelated to the CIA. Following a circuitous route through various e-mail providers to an Australian account, I signed on to the blog maintained by a fan of Emily Dickinson's poetry. Nothing.

Frustrated, I shut off the computer. How could I hope to solve a murder in Laycock when I couldn't figure out who'd shot me in Istanbul? "Let it go," I muttered. "Whoever shot me is thousands of miles away. Whoever killed Boom and Maria Lopez is right around the corner."

TWENTY

A GRAY SKY THREATENED, so I wore my rain jacket and put my gun in the special pocket before leaving to meet Dickie. Sprinkles fell as I drove around the square block of Laycock's largest park. When I was six, my brothers and I had gone over after Sunday dinner and mingled with families holding reunions. Quint and I focused on the desserts—chocolate cakes with fudge icing, peach pies topped by hand-turned vanilla ice cream, slices of red watermelon with seeds for spitting contests. Uly had sampled everything. He'd so overloaded his stomach one afternoon that he threw up the undigested mish-mash in our backyard. Mom had glanced at the unfamiliar menu, made him clean it up, and forbade us to go to any more reunions.

I parked on a side street with a view of the bandstand. Raindrops splashed on my windshield. A young Hispanic woman grabbed a blond toddler and hurried away from the swings. Three Hispanic men in baggy jeans and red T-shirts rose from naps atop tables in the shelter and ran through the light rain toward a battered black pickup. When two o'clock came, the park stood empty.

A gray Lincoln parked close to the bandstand. Dickie turned off the motor but didn't get out.

I pulled up the jacket's hood and stepped out of the car. The banker, looking into the park, didn't see me until I rapped on his front fender.

He scowled and rolled down his window. "Let's talk in my car."

Getting in someone else's car—and their control—was a bad idea. "You won't melt in the rain. Come to the bandstand."

Finally he opened the door, put up an umbrella, and hurried through the rain carrying a black leather briefcase. He placed it on the picnic table in the center of the bandstand, brushed off the bench, and sat down. "I resent your attitude. Boom was my very good friend. I wouldn't be here if I weren't concerned about Annalynn."

Or scared. I sat down across from him. "Then you won't mind explaining some irregularities in the Keysers' accounts."

He opened his briefcase. "There are *no* irregularities."

"He sold, without her signature, investments that he and Annalynn owned jointly."

He kept his eyes down. "That was his business."

"You helped him do it. Ten times, by a quick count. That should be enough to lose your bank's charter and send you to jail."

"I just did what he wanted!" His face paled, and he loosened his gray tie. "He did it for her. She had to have her shopping trips to New York and drive a new Mercedes. He would have worked it out in two or three years." He reached in his suit pocket, brought out a small pill bottle, and fumbled with the lid.

I took the bottle from his trembling hands and opened it for him. Nitroglycerin. A heart attack wouldn't help. "Calm down. I'm not here to skewer you." Was he foolish enough to believe that? "I came to find out what happened and"—big stretch—"get your help. It's up to you whether Annalynn takes you to court."

He put a pill under his tongue. "It would hurt Boom's reputation. You know Annalynn wouldn't want that."

True. "What she wants is the truth. The whole truth."

"I doubt that." He smirked. "She won't believe he fell for another woman."

"Did he tell you that?"

"No, but I knew he was seeing her. My son saw them in a bar in Moberly." He took bottled water from the briefcase and drank deeply. "George Brendan didn't know about her, but the Methodist minister did."

Interesting. "Did you ask Boom about her?"

"No! Men don't ask even close friends about things like that."

The hell they don't. "My only concern is the financial situation. I've been able to reconstruct most of it from the account statements and the tax returns."

"This is absolutely everything I have from the last ten years." He handed me a big manila envelope from the briefcase.

"I'll need to study this and talk to you again. Why don't you give me an overview of the investments, and tell me why he sold off premium stock."

"If you can't figure that out, you're not the financial genius you claim to be."

True. "Do you want to tell me your side of the story? Or do you want me to draw my conclusions only from the figures?"

"Okay, okay." He leaned forward, eager to talk. "It started years ago when Annalynn insisted they buy that car dealership. A huge mistake. He never did much more than break even. He could see that everyone else was making forty or fifty percent in the market on those high-tech start-ups, so he sold the blue chips to buy high-tech stocks."

"And you recommended Enron, WorldCom, Cisco."

He drew back. "Only Enron. Ken Lay was a preacher's kid from Missouri. I lost money, too." He sipped his water. "Boom panicked when he realized he'd lost most of her sainted father's money. He had to sell the stocks to keep from going under."

"Even the ones he had no right to sell."

His eyebrows met over downcast eyes. "His name was on everything he sold."

And so was Annalynn's. I let it go, for now. "But why did he sell off a winner like Kupfer-Collins? She owns only twenty percent of what she did seven years ago."

"He sold it to give her the money she's used to spending." He wagged his finger at me. "He sold stock so she could visit you in Vienna."

Four years ago. "What about the last three years?"

"Well, he needed money for the campaign and the plane. Annalynn wanted him to buy that."

I'd had enough of his blaming Annalynn. "And she insisted on the huge SUV? And the fifty-yard-line season tickets? And the hunting trips to Canada?"

He sulked the way he had in high school. "She could see he wasn't happy the last couple of years. If he wanted anything, she said to buy it. She knew his salary didn't cover everything."

About the time those medical bills surged. Something more than diabetes. "What about Boom's outside income?"

His eyes darted left and right. "What do you mean?"

I handed him a spreadsheet showing what Boom had attributed to winnings and the dead stock each month for sixteen months. "I mean these. The amounts correspond to deposits. You must know where they came from."

He ignored the sheet. "I *don't* know."

But he'd wondered. "Give me an educated guess."

He leaned back, a smug smile beneath his thin mustache. "This is really bugging you, isn't it?" He ran his finger down the Winnings column. "This could be from sports bets, I suppose. Not poker. He lost at poker. He cleaned up during football season. He won a few dollars playing pool. Maybe he was gambling on sports online, too. It could have added up to as much as five hundred dollars a month."

Could have. "And the other column?" I hoped he'd continue to show off.

He chewed on his lower lip. "I can't even guess where this came from. He always made the deposits in hundred-dollar bills."

The currency of payoffs. An unexpected revelation from the cautious banker. Why? "And you never asked him about it?"

He raised his eyes to meet mine. "He said he helped a group with security." He waited for my reaction.

I got the point: Dickie thought he could use the possible payoffs to ward off legal action from Annalynn. I shifted gears. "Who filled out his tax forms?"

He dropped his eyes. "I did it myself this year."

He hadn't signed the form. "How did you account for this twenty thousand dollars?"

"I don't remember. You'll have to look at his forms." He swallowed and said with false bravado, "It would be hard for Annalynn to come up with a big tax payment."

He'd been frightened enough to fight back. And he had ammunition. I shrugged. "She can sell the summer home."

The muscles in his face relaxed, and he raised his hand to hide a smile. "The bank holds a mortgage for the full value." He closed his briefcase. "You see, Phoenix,

I've been a good friend. I can demand full payment anytime. I offered Annalynn that home-equity loan on the castle because it's her best way out."

Thunder rumbled and rain poured. He picked up his umbrella. "We're finished."

I rose, standing on tiptoe so he couldn't look down on me. "Thanks, Dickie." I made sure my smile included my eyes. "You've been—*enlightening.*"

His jaw dropped, and he hurried toward his car without even a good-bye.

I tucked the papers under my arm inside my jacket and ran toward my car. A sharp pain brought me to a full stop. The pain left as suddenly as it had come. "But I *ran,*" I exulted, walking on.

My spirits fell. Annalynn had to be told about Boom's payoffs. Or did she? Cash could signal under-the-table payment for services—tax evasion—rather than a bribe. Could he have been a consultant? Not unless it was in name only. No legitimate company would pay in cash.

TWENTY-ONE

THE CLOCK CHIMED three as I reached my bedroom.

"Call me at four," I told it. I exchanged my damp clothes for a robe, wrapped up in the afghan, and stretched out on the bed.

A burst of thunder awakened me. Or footsteps on the stairs. My gun was in the jacket pocket. I thrashed around to free myself from the afghan.

"Are you okay?" Connie turned on the light.

"I'm trapped. I feel like the filling in a burrito."

Connie laughed as she grabbed a corner of the afghan and tugged it loose.

I sat up, feeling ravenous. A good sign. "Let's go raid the fridge." I glanced outside. "I remember the magnificent spring storms."

"I waited until the lightning stopped, and I'm glad I did. I heard some interesting stuff at the student union." She paused, giving me time to wonder what. "Someone left a red rose on Maria Lopez's windshield several times."

"Who?"

"They said it must have been that *elderly* sheriff. And we *know* that's wrong." She led the way downstairs.

I didn't. By the time we reached the kitchen, I gave up. "How do we know that?"

"Boom was allergic to roses." Connie went to the refrigerator. "Apple?"

"Sounds good. What else did the students say?"

"Not much. They'd teased her about having a secret admirer, but she refused to talk about it. A security guard followed her home whenever she had night classes."

The car Elena had seen. "The guard must know who her stalker was."

"Nope. I asked the head of security."

Damn! "It's almost time for Annalynn's press conference. Let's go see if anyone covers it."

We took our apples into the TV room, each claiming an end of the long sofa.

"You haven't heard all my findings," Connie said. "An admirer left presents for her—inside her locked car. Apparently that's what scared her."

"It would scare me." Getting into a locked car without damaging it took about half a minute with the right tool. "What presents?"

"One kid saw her open a box with diamond earrings in it. She wasn't happy."

I groaned. "Boom gave Annalynn diamond earrings for Mother's Day."

Connie grinned. "But he never gave her an iPod with Mexican love songs on it. I doubt if Boom knew how to download to an iPod."

"Good work, Connie. I'll bet the police don't know that. Hmmm. Both sound like expensive gifts for a student. Maybe the stalker was a staff member."

"I think Maria met Boom at the church and asked him to discourage the stalker."

Another point for Connie. "Could be. Since you're off to such a good start, I've got a job for you tonight at choir rehearsal. Ask the minister why Boom's buddies think Boom was having an affair."

Connie chuckled. "If you ask me, they had typical

male fantasies about beautiful young women finding paunchy older men attractive." She turned on the television.

A breaking news sign came on, and an earnest-faced young man spoke. "KTVO brings you exclusive live coverage from Laycock. The Vandiver County Commission has called a press conference related to the alleged murder-suicide last week of Sheriff Frederick 'Boom' Keyser and college instructor Maria Lopez."

I was puzzled. "Why would the Kirksville-Ottumwa station cover this?"

"Boom's death was big news all over the area."

A thirty-something woman in a red suit stood at a lectern with three microphones mounted on it. "I'm Commissioner Nancy Kallenbach. Thank you for coming. The county commission has appointed Annalynn Carr Keyser interim sheriff. She will serve thirteen weeks. At that time the county will hold a special election to fill the office until the next general election. Sheriff Keyser will make a brief statement, and we will take your questions." She stepped to one side and Annalynn took her place.

Connie's mouth fell open. "My God! She's wearing a gun!"

Smart. "She's showing she means business."

"Good afternoon." Annalynn looked straight into the camera. "I've accepted this appointment for three reasons. One: To clear my husband's name and bring his killers to justice. Two: To continue his Youth Explorer program, which will train volunteers aged fourteen to twenty-one to assist us at public events. Three: To complete a study and recommend to Vandiver County's citizens the size of a new county correctional facility."

She stepped out of the picture, and Nancy Kallenbach

stepped forward. "I've distributed to the press Sheriff Keyser's preliminary statement on the study. The new correctional facility is no small question. Her initial estimates indicate that even the most modest facility would cost every resident approximately one thousand one hundred dollars."

The young man's face reappeared. "That's the dramatic development here. Sheriff Annalynn Keyser has promised to prove her late husband was a murder victim rather than a murderer. She told us earlier that she will give no interviews until the investigation is completed and arrests are made. This is Arlen Jayson reporting live from Laycock."

Connie changed stations. "Annalynn was fantastic! I hope she does as well handling the questions."

"She'll leave that to the commissioner. Too bad she couldn't get a uniform to wear before the press conference."

"Lucky, I'd say. That mushroom brown isn't her color at all." Connie channel-hopped for five minutes, but no one else was covering the conference live. After watching a bit of *I Love Lucy,* she turned off the TV. "What did you find out from the Turd today?"

"The turd?"

"That's what we called him in kindergarten. The first day he announced that his name was Richard Rothway the Turd. I'll never forget it."

I laughed until my wound ached. Finally I got out, "He didn't tell me anything related to the murders."

Connie cocked her head. "Did you expect him to? I thought you were trying to straighten out Annalynn's finances. How bad are they?"

Telling Connie was up to Annalynn. "My estimate the other day may have been overly optimistic."

"I thought so. I hope to God he had private life insurance. I checked on the Web. If he died on duty, she gets twenty thousand dollars."

Annalynn certainly hadn't mentioned private life insurance.

Connie pulled off an earring, a three-inch chain of golden circles. "I'm really worried about her. She's never held a paying job in her life." She stared at me. "It's that bad, isn't it? She's going to have to find work."

"I just did," Annalynn said. She leaned against the door frame. "Don't tell me you missed the press conference."

Connie jumped up. "You were great!"

Annalynn handed me a card and a paper bag. "Here's your ID as a reserve deputy and a regulation holster."

AFTER WE EXCHANGED accounts of the day's events over a pickup supper, Connie left for choir practice.

I carried our plates and silverware to the dishwasher. "Did it really go that smoothly with the staff?"

"No. I wanted Connie to be able to report—truthfully—to Trudy that it did. Actually it went better than I expected, thanks largely to George taking leave today. The rest were standoffish and awkward but not antagonistic. Diana, Boom's admin assistant, was coming round by the end of the day. That will help tremendously." Annalynn poured herself another cup of coffee. "What I didn't expect was the huge pile of paperwork—the officers' daily road reports, requisitions for equipment, paper, paper, paper."

I remembered Boom's light schedule. Maybe he hadn't put the routine paperwork on his to-do list. "What about the crime-scene report?"

Annalynn closed her eyes and pressed her lips together, struggling for control. "Diana copied it for me. She, and only she, thinks I'm right. Unfortunately she knows no more than we do about what Boom was working on." Her voice was strained and her face pale. "She made me a CD of the digital photos taken at the motel."

My whole body went leaden. How could Annalynn bear to see Boom covered with blood? "Maybe we should go through the reports first."

"I have to look at the photos right now. Before I lose my nerve." Annalynn reached for my hand and clung to it as we walked to the den.

I thought of the first day of kindergarten. Neither the judge nor Mrs. Carr had been able to take Annalynn, so the Smiths had sent us off together. Tonight no nurturing teacher would be there to tell us how brave we were. Tonight I had to be the nurturer. I had assured hundreds of people they wouldn't get caught "sharing" information. In disguise, I'd assured a dozen assets on the run that they would reach safety. Those experiences had not prepared me for this.

Annalynn let go of my hand to open a black leather briefcase and extract a thin, unmarked folder. She removed an unlabeled CD. "Put it in for me, please. I'll bring a chair from the dining room."

Stay calm, matter of fact. We were doing research. But I'd better look at the photos before she did. I inserted the CD and opened it. A string of slides came up, too small to see more than that many showed two people on a bed. Annalynn brought in a chair and motioned for me to move over so she could look at the screen head-on.

She settled in her chair and intertwined the fingers of her right hand with those of my left hand. "Let's do it."

I clicked on the first photo to expand it.

Annalynn moaned as it erupted onto the dark screen,

but she didn't look away at the sight of Boom, his upper body on its side across the legs of a dark-haired young woman with her wrists bound in something white and tied to a light fixture over the bed. The photo didn't show his face or the lower half of his body. Blood had clotted around his ear and in streams that had run down his neck. Her eyes and mouth were open and her face contorted. Blood covered her white blouse from above her breasts to where the hem met the bare skin just above the pubic hair.

After a moment of shock, I began to dissect the scene, starting with Boom's wound. "He died instantly. If he hadn't, we'd see a lot more blood."

Annalynn wiped away a tear and cleared her throat. "Then he didn't suffer."

"But Maria Lopez did." She'd bled a lot, apparently from three wounds. "Do you have the medical examiner's report?"

"Only the summary is there. I haven't looked at it. Go to the next photo, please."

It showed the bodies from the other side of the bed. Boom's lower body was twisted so that his bare buttocks showed. His pants were nowhere in sight. White boxer shorts covered his ankles. His left arm was under his body. The right arm stretched out in front of him. The gun lay on the bed under his right hand.

Annalynn pointed at the photo. "This proves they staged it!"

To me, everything screamed rejection, bondage, and murder. "What do you mean?"

"Boom *always* took his shirt off first. *Always.* It was part of foreplay, and he'd needed more and more foreplay since the diabetes."

A reason for her certainty in Boom's fidelity hit me. "He was impotent?"

"No, no, of course not. Just not as—not as quick as before."

He was impotent. Had he looked to a young woman for a cure? "Did you try Viagra or one of those other pills?"

"Two of them, and he had awful reactions." Annalynn stood and picked up her chair. "I've seen the photo I absolutely had to see. Would you mind checking the rest? I'll look at any that you think I should. Right now I'm going to pour myself a stiff whiskey."

"Of course." Curiosity whetted and shock banished, I scanned dozens of photos quickly before studying them one by one. The white bond around the woman's wrists was a pillow slip tied in a simple knot. Would it have held anyone who struggled? But with a gun on her, Maria Lopez wouldn't have struggled.

I spent a long time on the photo of Boom's outstretched hand over the gun. Sudden death usually causes cadaver spasm—making people clutch whatever they held. But maybe not for seven hours. I went to a broader shot. His body didn't look natural, but death never looks natural. The last in the series showed the rest of the room. Everything but the bed looked neat and clean. Far too clean. No reading material. No water glasses. No ice bucket. No list of channels on the small television set. Nothing on the cheap pressed-wood dresser.

The killers had cleaned the room. Before Boom got there? They surely would have left immediately after firing the shots. Maybe they had put a silencer on Boom's gun. I'd heard a TV behind the screams. How noisy would the motel have been late at night?

"I've got to see a room at the motel," I muttered.

"What did you say?" Annalynn put a cup of tea by the computer, carefully not looking at the screen.

"Look at this furniture. Does anything seem odd to you?"

Annalynn peered over my shoulder. "No, but you've always been more observant than I. What am I missing?"

"What's not there that should be." I turned off the monitor and rose. "Let's go through the reports. Maybe they'll answer my questions."

"I doubt it. It's a lot of useless detail." Annalynn went around the screen and sat down on the love seat. She handed me a folder from the coffee table.

Jim's report, a single sheet. "This tells us almost nothing we couldn't see in the photos. Less, in fact. Hmm. He responded to a call at seven twenty. The guest must have said he would vacate the room early, or the maid wouldn't have found the bodies so soon." Or perhaps that room rented by the hour. I leafed through the folder. "This doesn't include interview notes. Someone must have talked to the motel manager and the guests."

"I asked Jim to come over about eight thirty. Maybe he'll know." She sipped her drink. "I didn't want to ask you in front of Connie. What did you find out from Dickie today? Did you ask about the summer house?"

"Mortgaged for full value. By the way, did Boom have a private life-insurance policy?"

"No. He canceled it when the kids finished college." She answered absently, her eyes looking into space. "Did Dickie tell you where Boom got the money he listed under that dead company?"

"No." Give her the bad news while she'd hardly notice. "Boom didn't declare it."

Again she didn't seem to hear. "He must have been

gambling much more than he admitted. I asked him to stop, but he was always so sure he would win, and he usually did, particularly on football games." She frowned. "Don't look so judgmental."

"He lost almost everything." I regretted my bluntness immediately.

Annalynn bridled. "He would never have made those bad investments if Dickie hadn't given him terrible advice."

Which Boom took in spite of her warning. "Dickie admits that."

Annalynn covered her face with her hands. "If only we hadn't bought that dealership!" She turned away and rocked herself. "Oh, God, Phoenix, sometimes I'm so angry at Boom that it frightens me."

"You mean for losing your inheritance?"

"No, that was partly my fault." She rocked even harder. "I can't forgive him for going to that motel alone and letting someone kill him."

I sat down beside Annalynn and put my arms around her. "Anger is part of grieving. Just let it out."

"I don't dare. I don't know how I could hold myself together without you."

"I'm always here. I think it's incredible how strong you've been. Your father would be so proud of you."

Annalynn pulled away. "I'm not as big a fool as you think. I kept the Kupfer-Collins stock I had before we got married in my name. It won't last long if I have to live on it, but I can't worry about that now." She picked up her scotch. "I checked the answering machine. Someone named Miguel said Wes told him you need work done on your house. And Uly called to ask how you're feeling. You should call your big brother right now."

I chuckled and went to the computer. "He's not going

to believe that you're sheriff. I'll e-mail him." That way, he couldn't question me. I typed in Uly's address. "Maybe I better not tell him yet. Let's see: 'Uly, I'm staying with Annalynn, and we're taking care of each other. Too much going on to tell you about now. I'll call in a few days. P.' "

"Can't you at least end with 'Love'?"

"You want him to think I'm dying? You know my brothers and I never say anything nice to each other." That sounded awful. "That doesn't mean we don't love each other."

"Then say so. It's time for the Smiths to stop acting like battling brats. After all, you almost lost your chance to tell Ulysses and Quintin you love them."

"Thank you for your input. I will take the matter under consideration."

"Have you ever done anything I've suggested?"

"Why should I listen to *your* advice?" I had said that to Annalynn many times as we grew up.

A hint of a smile smoothed her forehead. "It feels as though you never left. I hadn't realized how terribly I've missed you. I can be myself with you the way I can't be with anyone else."

"Don't say that in front of Connie. She's feeling left out."

"I'm sorry about that. I love Connie, but, well, she expects me to be perfect."

"You certainly can't complain about that with me," I joked, relieved at the return to our old candor.

The doorbell rang three times.

"That's Jim," Annalynn said. She went to open the door and show him in.

I returned to the stuffed chair.

"Evening, Phoenix." He wore jeans, a blue chambray shirt, and loafers.

"Hi, Jim." I motioned him to the recliner. "We've looked at the report, but it doesn't tell us much. Did you interview people at the motel?"

"I started to. Then George took over." He pulled a small notebook from his shirt pocket. "It's an old one-story motel with twenty rooms. I went to every one. Two truck drivers had gone. I contacted both of them, and one remembered hearing a car pull in real fast a little after eleven o'clock. He didn't hear any shots, but he said there was a vanload of Mexicans drinking and playing loud music most of the evening. Around ten he told the manager to quiet them down or he'd call the police. They quieted some, but they were still partying when he fell asleep."

I had engineered such diversions. "They could have been paid to make noise."

"Yeah, but I get called out there four or five times a month for noisy guests."

Annalynn leaned forward, her eyes bright. "Did you talk to those men?"

"Nope. They were gone. Left a heckuva lot of beer bottles. The manager said they paid cash the night before and took off early. I couldn't read the name on the form, but I could tell the license number was a fake. So was the address, it turned out. We're never gonna find them guys."

"No," I agreed. Classic cover with witting or unwitting confederates. I couldn't say that in front of Jim. "What about the other guests? What did they hear?"

"A couple in room nineteen said their dogs got real upset when another dog threw a fit. They remembered because it drowned out the weather forecast on the ten-o'clock news. But that's before Boom left here."

I glanced down at the papers for a vital piece of information. Not there. "Jim, who registered for room thirteen?"

He rubbed his freshly shaved cheek. "The manager said a tall middle-aged guy—broad shouldered, athletic-looking—came in about seven wearing big dark glasses and a baseball cap pulled down over his face. The manager isn't sure, but he thought he was wearing a dark-blue short-sleeved shirt."

Annalynn sighed. "Like Boom was wearing."

Jim looked apologetically at Annalynn. "Yeah. He fit Boom's description, and Boom left the country club right around seven. Everybody figured it was him. The guy asked for a single on the back. He paid cash."

Annalynn chewed her lower lip, her face anxious. "What about the car? The license number?"

"The manager didn't remember the car, and the license number on the registration form was smeared like he'd spilled water on it."

I nodded. Standard tactic. "What name did he use?"

Jim grinned. "Smith. What else would it be?" He riffled through his notebook. "P. D. Smith."

TWENTY-TWO

A CHILL RAN through me. "He signed in using my initials?"

"I didn't realize," Jim said, eyes wide. "It could be a coincidence."

I shook my head. "No. The odds must be ten thousand to one against a coincidence. But why? And who would even know my middle initial?"

Annalynn jumped up. "Dickie!" She sank down. "And a dozen others. I told friends at the country club you were coming, and Boom told the story about your mother hating being Mary Smith, how she gave her children distinctive first names and initials as middle names: Phoenix D., Quintin K., and Ulysses L."

I envisioned George Brendan. Tall, middle-aged, athletic. A cap and glasses could have obscured his striking blondness. "Did anyone besides the motel clerk see this P. D. Smith?"

"Nobody I talked to," Jim said. "Everybody, including me, assumed it was Boom." He flipped through his notebook. "He told some guys at the country club bar he was going home about seven. What did he tell you?"

Annalynn rubbed her forehead. "He said he and a friend talked football over dinner. He ate a big bowl of popcorn during the news."

I could see why the police officers had assumed Boom had lied to Annalynn. "Jim, where did Maria spend the evening?"

"She taught a class from seven to nine thirty. Nobody saw her at the motel. Her car was parked a block away."

I digested this. "Hypothesis: Boom met the person using my name around seven, and Maria Lopez went to meet him in room thirteen around ten. Agreed so far?"

"Agreed," Annalynn said.

Jim thought it over. "Sounds likely."

"Now it gets tricky." I struggled to fit pieces together. "If Maria Lopez was an informant, the most likely target was meth dealers. So Smith would have been an undercover cop—maybe from the regional task force or the DEA."

Annalynn frowned. "But why wouldn't he come forward?"

Jim answered, "Because he's dead. Killing three carries no more penalty than killing two." He shook his head. "Nope. Can't be. We haven't had any reports of dead or missing officers, or of unidentified bodies."

"Good point," I admitted.

Annalynn thought a moment. "I think it's worthwhile to find out whether someone is investigating drug dealers. I'll go through Boom's task force reports for any mention of it. I'm going to the task force's meeting in Kirksville Friday morning, so I may find out more there. Jim, I want you to comb through the county files for any drug connection to one of our officers. Boom was being secretive for a reason."

Jim stood up. "Digging out that kind of information usually means a long, hard slog, but I'll get a start on it. Anything else?"

I flipped through the folder again. "I don't see any lab reports here."

Jim closed his notebook. "I don't know what George requested, but I can tell you the Highway Patrol lab takes months. He may have sent some stuff to the Criminalistics Lab at Kirksville."

"I'll have Diana find out," Annalynn said. "What are we looking for, Phoenix?"

"I'm no expert, but I'd say DNA on that pillow slip around her wrists. Boom wasn't wearing gloves, so if he tied her up, his DNA would be on the pillow."

"Damn smart," Jim said. "I'll bet nobody's ordered that. It costs maybe five hundred dollars, and it can take a year or so. DNA labs are backed up something awful."

But we could get other answers right away. "The medical examiner's report says the bullet in Maria Lopez's heart was the fatal one. Do you suppose he could tell from the organs or the bleeding if all the bullets were fired at the same time?"

Jim stifled a yawn. "You got me."

"That's enough for tonight," Annalynn said. "Go on home, Jim." She took him to the front door and returned rubbing her eyes. "Phoenix, why do you want to know about the bullets?"

"Curiosity." Know thy enemy. Did someone shoot Maria Lopez so as to prolong her death? If so, why? To punish her? To make her talk? To make Boom talk?

I GOT UP shortly after the clock chimed six. Rested and almost pain free, I showered and dressed. No excuse for even a fourth of a pill. The enticing aroma of coffee drew me to the kitchen. I settled for half a cup with milk. "Annalynn? Where are you?"

"At the computer."

I went into the den.

Annalynn still wore her robe. "I've been looking at the photos." She turned the monitor off. "The room does look like it's been swept clean. I wonder if they took everything that Mr. Smith might have touched."

"Good thinking, Sheriff."

"Do you know how to copy this CD? I'd like to leave this one here and take one with me to the Criminalistics Lab at Truman State tomorrow."

"I'll make a copy for you." I massaged Annalynn's tense shoulders. "Did you sleep last night?"

"Yes. Nature took over, I guess. Nightmares woke me this morning." She studied my face. "Your color is better, and your eyes look—clearer. What are you going to do today?"

"Plan the repairs on my house." And go by the motel to look at room thirteen.

I MADE DETAILED notes to give to a contractor and then treated myself to an hour at the piano. With the morning almost gone, I went into the backyard to enjoy the soothing sun and the exuberant spring greens. I remembered how much I loved May on my grandparents' farm. Where someone had built a meth lab near the creek where I'd waded and raced miniature bark canoes. What did a meth lab look like? Why not take a picnic lunch and find out? I fixed a turkey sandwich and put it, an apple, a water bottle, and my gun into my day pack.

I drove down Franklin and onto Monroe, the route Annalynn and I had walked to the Ben Franklin Elementary School. The front yards on Monroe were narrow because Laycock had widened the street to allow more traffic. I turned onto a blacktop road and drove past neat rows of ankle-high corn. The first farmhouse looked prosperous and well kept, as did the big red barn and smaller outbuildings. The next turn in the road took me past an empty foundation and a sagging, unpainted barn.

I tensed, dreading to see my grandparents' white farmhouse gone or, even worse, falling down. Coming over a small hill I was relieved to see giant maples alongside a freshly painted house. I stopped the car. The tall lilac bushes had disappeared, and a three-car garage stood where the barn had been. Obviously the current owners weren't farmers. I drove on, soon coming to a newish brick ranch home with two sizeable white barns and several smaller outbuildings. Turning left onto the narrow rock road that ran by the side of the house, I paused to admire an iron horse set on a frame between two sturdy posts. The flowing lines gave the feel of joyous movement. Below the horse was a rough board with "Neil Jones, Horse Doctor, 556-2002" burnt into it. Neil had prospered. No wonder he could still attract young blondes.

A quarter of a mile down the road, a plank bridge crossed the creek. I pulled over, leaving room for a car or tractor to pass, and got out. A dirt road between the creek and an untilled field led back to an old shed. I slipped on the day pack and walked to the bridge. The water was less than a foot deep, but hillocks of grass and rocks blocked its path here and there, their diversion lending melody to the running water.

I lifted my face to the sun. How had I endured all those years in an office? Never again. Feeling light and free, I walked along the dirt road, avoiding puddles from yesterday's rain. Small trees and bushes—brush, Mom had called it—lined the creek's banks, which sloped five or six feet to the water.

A whimper came from nearby. I stopped and listened. It came again, a dog in pain. Had someone put out traps for coons and caught a dog?

"Where are you?" I called, going to the creek bank. "Talk to me."

Another whimper.

I saw a break in the brush and trampled grass. Holding onto a sapling, I edged down the bank.

A large fawn-colored dog—a German shepherd?—lay with its hindquarters in the creek. Dried and fresh blood covered the dog's head and ears, matted the hair on its neck, and stained a leather collar. Flies and gnats buzzed around.

"Oh, God!" I knelt by the animal. A heavy leash wrapped around a small tree held it in place. "Somebody brought you here to shoot you, didn't they?" I touched the warm, dry nose. "Some of us don't die so easily."

I brushed the bugs away and unsnapped the leash from the collar, searching for tags or an ID. Nothing.

The dog, a young male, tried to rise, but he lacked the strength.

"You're a Belgian Malinois. What are you doing so far from home?" I leaned over him, caught some creek water in my hand, and brought it to his mouth. It was only a few drops, but he licked it and looked up, pleading for more. "Geez! This creek water is probably full of fertilizer."

Sitting on the wet grass, I poured water from my bottle into my hand for him to lap up. Slowly we emptied the bottle. "Can you get up now?" I tugged on his collar. He tried to move but collapsed.

I took the sandwich from my day pack and put it by his head. "Eat this, if you feel like it." I'd never be able to drag him up the bank. Was there a 9-1-1 for dogs? I grabbed my cell phone and dialed Neil's number.

"Veterinary Services," a woman said.

"I have an emergency, a badly injured dog in the

creek right down from your office. Can someone come help me, please?"

"We don't make calls for dogs. You'll have to bring him in."

Scheisse! "Is Neil there?"

"Hold on, please."

A moment later. "Neil Jones."

"This is Phoenix Smith. I just found a wounded dog in Grandpa's creek. He's too heavy for me to carry out. Can you come, please?"

"Phoenix! I'll be darned! Sure. I'll be there in five minutes."

I put away the phone and waved my hand over the dog's bloody head in a futile attempt to brush away the determined flies. He had to be starving. I took the turkey from my sandwich and offered it to him.

He gulped it down and licked my hand.

"You'll be okay. Eating is a good sign." I gave him a piece of bread.

A tractor turned onto the dirt road and stopped. "Phoenix? Where are you?"

"In the ditch," I yelled. I stood up and waved. "Here!"

Seconds later Neil came down the bank toward me, his long legs encased in faded jeans and his feet in sturdy work boots. "Heard you were back. Good to see you. What's the problem?"

"A head wound. And the right ear." I scrambled out of the way. "I gave him some water and a sandwich."

The dog bared his teeth.

"It's okay." I crouched down to stroke the dog. "He's here to help."

Neil scooted closer. "Looks like somebody shot him last night. I can patch him up at my office, but getting him out of here is going to be a problem."

The dog inched toward me.

Neil climbed up the bank. "If you can hold his head, I'll give him a shot to sedate him."

I eased the dog's head onto my leg and crooned, "You'll be okay."

His eyes closed.

Neil returned and knelt for a few seconds before slipping in the needle. "He'll be out shortly. Any idea whose dog it is?"

"I couldn't find any ID, but I'll pay for his care."

He didn't seem to have heard. "I don't recognize this breed."

"He's a Belgian Malinois. Europeans use them as police dogs. He's a first cousin to the German shepherd."

"A lighter build and a lighter color." The vet stroked the dog's short-haired coat. "He's out. I'll carry him to the cart."

He went up the bank carefully with the dog limp in his arms. I—braced against a tree—placed a steadying hand on his back as he climbed the first two steep feet.

Anticipating punishment from my wound, I followed cautiously. Only a couple of twinges. I hesitated as he put the dog on the cart behind the tractor. Someone had tried to kill a valuable animal in an isolated spot at night. Why? "I'll walk along the creek a little way to see if I find anything else before I follow you."

He nodded. "I'll take him into my clinic behind the house."

I walked in the tall grass at the edge of the bank, sniffing for the odor of decomposition and watching for signs someone had gone down the bank. After a few yards the bank became less steep. I followed the track to a rickety three-sided, tin-roofed hay shed. Two huge bales of moldy hay stood against the back wall. The only other thing in the shed was a small circle of bricks that someone had used to build a campfire. The remains of the meth lab?

I drove to Neil's. The young blonde who'd been with him at the hardware store was climbing into a blue Dodge Ram pickup as I parked in front of the clinic.

The blonde lowered her window. "Dad's taken your dog into the examining room. Go on in. There's a bathroom off the waiting room. You can wash up there."

So she was Neil's daughter. The day was looking better. I wasn't. Mud and blood covered my hands and stained my jeans and T-shirt. My sparse wardrobe had become even sparser. I went through a small reception room straight to the bathroom. When I'd cleaned up as best I could and brushed my hair with my fingers, I knocked on the only other door.

"Come on in," Neil called, "unless you're squeamish."

I steeled myself and went in. The dog lay on a metal table with an IV in his front leg. With the blood washed away, I could see black ears, a black nose, a black mask around the eyes, and a delicate head. Black tipped the fawn hair on the hindquarters. A handsome animal. "Will he recover?"

"Yes, it's not as bad as it looked. The bullet creased the head deep enough to leave a nasty scar but did no permanent damage. I can stitch it up. I can patch the bullet wound in the ear, too, but it will always droop. He's dehydrated and needs antibiotics, but he should be okay." He grinned. "My assistant's gone to lunch. Think you can stomach handing me my tools?"

"Of course." I'd seen worse.

"Then let's suit up." He showed me how to scrub and put on skin-tight gloves. Then, whistling tunelessly, he stitched the wounds, sprayed antibiotics on them, and put a small bandage over the cut on the head.

"That's it." He stripped off his gloves. "He'll be out a few more minutes. I can offer you a roast beef sandwich while we wait."

I suspected he was grinning behind the mask, wondering if I felt more like vomiting than eating. "Sounds great."

"Good. We can eat in the reception room and leave the door open." He took off his surgical apron and left.

I stroked the dog's back until Neil had set up lunch on the coffee table in the reception room. We sat on the old church pew that provided seating and dug in.

I'd missed Midwest beef. "Delicious."

"Prime Angus from my own herd." He poured lemonade from a thermos into two blue glasses. "You won't find better beef anywhere."

I nodded agreement and glanced at the dog. "Do you have a kennel here?"

"Nope. You'll have to take him with you."

Annalynn wouldn't welcome any dog, let alone a big beat-up one. "Does Laycock have a kennel that could board him for a few days?"

"No, and the pound tends to euthanize any animal that needs much care."

No choice. "Then I'll take him with me."

By the time we finished the meal, the dog was whimpering and his legs were moving.

I stroked his back until he quieted. His eyes remained closed.

Neil put the leash and collar, now clean, back on. "He's coming around."

I kept one hand on the collar and stroked him with the other. "You're okay. Take it easy. You're okay."

He raised his head, and I scratched him under the chin. He licked my hand.

"He's yours, Phoenix," Neil said. "Obviously his owner didn't want him."

I didn't buy that. A Belgian Malinois was a big investment on this side of the pond. He'd been well cared for. He'd responded warmly to me. Someone had loved this dog. Someone who might not have dodged the bullets.

TWENTY-THREE

I DUCKED MY head to hide a surge of elation. The couple's dogs at the motel could have been responding to this one. A visit to the motel might verify that. "Come on, boy. Let's go."

His triangle-shaped left ear perked up. The tip of the injured right one didn't move. He scooted toward the end of the table and gathered himself.

"Hold on to his collar," Neil said, sliding his arms under the dog. He lifted him down and stepped back.

The dog tottered for a moment, steadied himself, and gave a satisfied bark.

I laughed. "I know exactly how you feel." I picked up the leash, and the dog walked out the door at my side.

"I'll call in prescriptions for antibiotics and a mild painkiller to put in his food," Neil said. "You can pick them up at Animal Cares—right across from the Hy-Vee."

I held out my hand. "I can't thank you enough. But I can pay you."

"I'll need to check him again. You can take care of it then." He looked out across the barnyard toward the horses. "The 4-H Club is having a barbecue here Sunday about four. Why don't you bring him out about three and stay to meet the neighbors?"

Was he asking me for a date? "I'd like that." I asked my mother's standard question: "What can I bring?"

"Nothing. You're my guest."

I opened the back door of my car, but the dog moved on to the front passenger side. When I opened that, he scrambled onto the blanket on the seat, his head extending onto my seat. "He's used to riding in a car. I don't think his owner shot him."

"Maybe not. I doubt the owner is local. I'll go online and see if any of my colleagues know of a missing Malinois."

"Thanks." He was still a nice guy. And still attractive.

The minute I got into the car the dog put his head in my lap. I had to reach under him to release the hand brake. By the time I was halfway to Laycock, he was asleep. I drove straight to Animal Cares and parked in the shade of an oak that grew beside the one-story glass-fronted building. I roused the dog so I could pull on the brake and rolled down all four windows. "Stay—umm—boy." Naming him constituted a commitment I wasn't willing to make.

He whined when I got out, but he remained silent and unseen as I went into the store. I spotted a pharmacy sign in back and headed toward it.

The big-nosed kid who'd been shooting with Sean leaned on the counter, his fingers drumming. He straightened and removed an earpiece. "Can I help you?"

He hadn't recognized me. Young men don't really see older women, even ones in filthy clothes. "Dr. Jones called in prescriptions for me. My name is Smith." The tag on his shirt said Tony Engel.

"They're ready. And I got a note about dog food." He stifled a yawn. "You want that, too?"

"Yes, please." I handed him the credit card.

"It comes to one seventy-five forty-three. Are you Mrs. P. D. Smith?"

"No, I am P. D. Smith."

He blinked. “Oh, yeah. Mrs. Keyser’s friend. My folks live just down the street from her orchard, but I guess you left Laycock before they moved there.” He gave me the medication and the slip to sign. “I’ll bring the dog food to your car.”

“Thanks.” A pleasant surprise. That was one outdated tradition I appreciated.

As I came out of the store, the dog popped up and stuck his head out the driver’s window. He barked once as though to remind me he was there.

“I see you,” I said on my way to open the trunk.

The dog growled as Tony came toward the car.

“Quiet,” I said. “He’s bringing your food.”

The young man hesitated. “He’s a big one. What happened to his head?”

No need to advertise he’d been shot. “He ran into a door.”

The young man stared at the blood on my clothes as though seeing it for the first time. He dropped two bags of dog food in my trunk and hurried back into the store.

The dog didn’t stop bristling until the clerk had disappeared.

“I know you have a headache, but those aren’t good manners,” I said, leaning close.

He licked my face.

“Yuk! Don’t try that with Annalynn.” I went to the trunk and got a bottle of water to wash my face.

He whined and stretched toward the bottle. I went back in to buy a water bowl, filled it, and held it outside the car window while he drank. As soon as I got in the car, his head was in my lap. I decided to go by the Walmart to replenish my wardrobe and then check the nearby motel on my way home.

As we neared the entrance to the parking lot, the dog raised his head, sniffed, and began to whine.

"What is it?"

His nose pointed at a McDonald's with a "Grand Opening" sign.

"Surely a hamburger won't hurt you. You must be pretty hungry." I ordered a Big Mac at the drive-through and used napkins to wipe everything off the meat. I held up a patty and he downed it in two bites. The other burger went down just as quickly. No wonder I'd needed two sacks of dog food.

And I needed clothes without bloodstains to wear to the motel. I pulled into the huge Walmart lot and pulled into a spot with no other cars around. "Stay," I ordered.

He stuck his head out the window and watched me go but didn't bark. I couldn't count on continued silence, so I hurried into the store and reached for a cart.

"Phoenix! So good to see you. What happened?" Trudy Diamante Lamb bustled over in a greeter's vest. "Is that blood on your clothes?"

Damn! The story would be all over town. "Yes, but it's not mine. Can you direct me to the clothing?"

Trudy's eyes, framed by pink spectacles, grew enormous. "Whose blood is it?"

"I found an injured animal, and I'm in a *terrible rush.* Please point me to the casual clothes."

Trudy took my arm. "I'll take you. Sally can handle the door for a minute."

"Thanks. And could I change clothes here?"

"I'll get a key while you find what you want."

I picked up a pair of jeans and a navy-blue T-shirt exactly like those I wore. Needing blouses to wear over a holster, I grabbed a short-sleeved denim shirt and a long-sleeved blue-and-white-striped Oxford blouse.

Trudy reappeared and opened a fitting room. "You can try them on in there."

I changed quickly and folded my dirty clothes. When I came out, Trudy was waiting.

"This way," Trudy said. "Gladys will check you out."

A minute later I headed back to the car. I could hear the dog barking even before I got out of the store.

A man with a fringe of white hair on his bald head had pulled in next to my car. "You oughta do something about that dog. I'm afraid to get out of the car," he groused.

Griping made some people happy. I denied him the pleasure of a nasty retort. "Sorry. He's got an awful headache." I tossed my dirty clothes into the trunk and drove toward the motel. Just past four. A reasonable time to check in.

The dog's hackles rose and he stuck his head out the window as I turned off the street and into the short drive leading to the office.

He knew this place! The verification of my guess fueled a euphoria the magic pill couldn't equal. I returned to earth as I smelled curry. What if he was responding to unfamiliar odors? I parked out of sight of the glass-walled office and debated whether to take the dog in and see if the manager recognized him. Not with those bandages on his head and his teeth bared. If he'd just stay quiet. "Quiet, boy!"

He looked at me with unblinking eyes.

He was accustomed to commands, but which ones? "Down, boy! Down!"

He obeyed, but he frowned.

"Good boy! Stay. Quiet." I grabbed my day pack and hurried into the office.

A round-faced Indian man came from a back room. "You wish a room?"

"Perhaps. What do you have available?"

"Very good rooms. Because you come early, I will give you a special price: fifty dollars."

I played the bargaining game he'd introduced. "I'd like a less expensive room. I only need a single."

"For a single, forty-five dollars. Smoking or nonsmoking?"

The room had contained no ashtrays, but that didn't mean much. "Nonsmoking, and I have a dog. My brother stayed here once with his dog."

He took a key from under the counter. A piece of wood a foot long ensured no one would carry it away by mistake. "Room nineteen for sixty dollars. It has a special floor for pets."

The floor in room thirteen had no carpet. "I'd like to look at it first, please." I took the key and drove to the room on the short part of the old L-shaped motel. It had ten rooms strung out on the long side of the L and ten rooms back-to-back on the short side.

The dog whimpered and moved restlessly on the seat as I parked in front of nineteen. The moment I opened the door he sprang over me and raced to the door at the end. He sniffed and whined, bouncing up and down in agitation.

I was right! I checked the number: twenty-one. But the motel had twenty rooms. The next door said fifteen. Unlucky thirteen had become twenty-one.

The dog loped from door to door, stopping to sniff at each. Then, nose to the ground, he went in ever larger circles around the parking area like a police dog. When he'd covered the area, he went back to room twenty-one and dropped down, panting heavily, his head on his paws. He'd searched for scent, almost certainly that of the other P. D. Smith.

I opened the door to nineteen. The walls and furniture looked exactly the same as those in the photos. Linoleum covered the floor, but dark scatter rugs fashioned from indoor-outdoor carpet were on each side of the bed. An ashtray sat on one nightstand. On the television rested a card listing the channels. The dresser hosted a menu for a pizza parlor and a flyer for Harry's Hideaway.

The dog pressed his shoulder against my leg. "I'm sorry, boy. I think you've been orphaned. We better get you to a safe house. You're our only witness."

TWENTY-FOUR

THE DOG REFUSED to get back in the car. Pulling against the leash, he forced his way back to the room formerly known as thirteen and planted his feet.

"I should be able to outsmart a dog," I muttered, unwilling to risk injury to him or me by using force. Food. I opened the trunk and used the blade on my key ring to slit open a bag of bacon-flavored dog biscuits. I took out three, opened the front passenger door wide, and sauntered over to the dog. I held out the biscuits.

He looked up and sniffed.

"Let's go." I took three steps back. He didn't move. I dropped a biscuit in front of room seventeen and kept going without looking back. Hearing no paw steps, I tossed a biscuit in the passenger seat and went to close the trunk. "Come. Let's go."

He watched me but didn't move.

Call his bluff. I got in the car and turned on the motor "Come."

Ignoring the biscuit, he staggered toward the car with his head down. His despair brought tears to my eyes. I helped him hoist himself in.

He had come to me for help and comfort just as Analynn had. He had become my responsibility. I crooned to him and stroked his back until he calmed down and accepted a biscuit.

I decided not to question the clerk. I left the key on the front desk and got out of there. My priority was to get the dog home before anybody else saw him. Jim could ask the questions.

Now that I had good reason to hide the dog, he wanted to put his head out the window. I closed it and coaxed him to put his head in my lap again. "Where have you been for the last nine days, boy? Somebody must have stashed you somewhere close by. Maybe they planned to sell you and decided you were too hot. Maybe Annalynn's appointment scared people sure they'd gotten away with murder."

It was the height of evening rush hour, so driving home took ten rather than nine minutes. That gave me time to plan to put him in my house. When I got out of the car, he came right after me. He stuck so close I could hardly walk to my front door. I let him in and closed the storm door to go back to the car for the dog food.

He howled like a child deserted by his mother.

"*Verdammt*!" I hurried back to let him out. He pressed against my left leg as I retrieved the blanket, bowl, and prescriptions and carried them into the kitchen. Dropping the blanket on the linoleum floor and placing the medicine on the Formica-topped cabinet counter, I filled the bowl with water. When he began to lap it up, I headed for the front door. He beat me there.

"This togetherness could get old fast," I told him as he accompanied me to the car. I didn't dare lift the bags of dog food, so I cut the large one open and put some food into a plastic bag.

Back in the house, I added water and pills. While he wolfed down the mixture, I dialed Annalynn's direct line from my landline.

"Sheriff Annalynn Keyser's office."

"This is Phoenix Smith. I need to speak to her right away."

After half a minute, Annalynn said, "Are you okay?"

"I've found a lead to—umm—the third man. I can't bring it to your office."

"I see. Is it urgent?"

"It can wait a little while. Bring Jim. Good-bye."

The dog had licked his bowl clean and waited expectantly.

"You can have more later. Now you need to rest." I took the blanket into the living room, folded it in quarters, and put it on the floor. Then I stretched out on the lumpy couch.

He lay down on the blanket and put his head on his paws.

A tongue licking my face woke me. The room was half dark. I went to the window and saw Annalynn and Jim getting out of separate cars.

I turned on the floor lamp and opened the door. "In here."

Jim came up the steps ahead of Annalynn. He stopped as the dog growled a warning. "You got yourself a guard dog?"

I grabbed the dog's collar. "Quiet, boy. Friend. Friend."

He quieted, but his body remained tense as I pulled him away from the door and over to the couch. I sat down and put one arm around his neck.

Jim ventured in. "He sure oughta scare people away."

Annalynn peeked through the door. "Why don't the *people* come to my house?"

"You two go on," I said. "I'll be there in a moment." I gave them time to walk to Annalynn's before releasing the dog and going to the door. He stuck to me, and when I opened the door, he pressed against me. "Stay, boy."

He whined and looked up at me with imploring eyes.

"You're going to howl and tell the whole block you're

here, aren't you?" I snapped on his leash and picked up the blanket. "You have to be quiet."

Checking to make sure the street was empty, I locked the door behind us. The dog ranged two feet ahead of me sniffing the ground. As we went up Annalynn's front steps, the sniffing became less random. When I opened the door, he trotted in, nose to the floor. I gave him his head. He went into the dining room and nosed a chair.

Annalynn watched silently from the hall.

The dog went past her to the TV room. He circled the room and stopped at a recliner. He whined and looked up at me.

"That's where Boom sat," Annalynn said from the doorway, her voice shaky. She turned on the light. "Whose dog is this?"

"The man who signed in at the motel as P. D. Smith."

Annalynn took a tentative step forward. "How do you know?"

The dog came to me. I sat down at the far end of the couch. "You and Jim better sit. I have a lot to tell you."

When I'd finished my story, I said, "I'd hope you would recognize him, Annalynn. A Belgian Malinois is rare here outside large police departments."

"I've heard of that breed somewhere." Annalynn went to the lone bookshelf, pulled out a photo album, and opened it. "Boom's Christmas cards from his football buddies are here." Face alternately anxious and eager, she turned page after page. "Here it is!" She turned the album around to show a photo of a man kneeling with his arm around a dog with a black face and fawn-colored hair. Behind them water fountains spouted.

Jim squinted. "Who is he?"

Annalynn bit her lower lip. "I don't know." She pulled the photo out and turned it over. "'I've replaced Ellen with a Belgian Malinois. He flunked out of K-nine training, but he's the smartest dog I ever saw. Happy Holidays, Bill.'" She looked up. "Achilles?"

The dog, lying at my feet, raised his head.

"Bingo! We're in business!" I felt a moment of pure triumph.

"Thank God! I'll get Boom's address book and look for Bills." Face white, Annalynn rushed out of the room.

Jim took the photo over to the lamp. "He probably lives around Kansas City. He's standing in front of the Milles fountain." He handed the photo to me. "She's had a rough day. The warden is being a jackass. Annalynn asked him about food costs, and he answered like she don't know a quarter from a penny." He grinned. "She sliced him down a size. Tomorrow's going to be nasty, too. Some of the task force members don't want her to take Boom's seat."

I appreciated his letting me know. "Did you tell her?"

"Naw. She's got enough to worry about. Besides, she's good. Guess running the school board toughened her up. Polite as the dickens, but she don't take no trash."

Quick steps sounded on the stairs. "I found a home number and an office number for Bill Graksi in Independence." She took a deep breath. "I'll call from my desk. Phoenix, you listen on this extension. Jim, you take the one in the hall."

Graksi's phone rang once and the answering machine picked up. "Hi. Leave your name, phone number, and a reason I should return your call."

"This is Annalynn Keyser. I have Achilles. Please call me." She gave the number, disconnected, and dialed the other number.

I hung up until Annalynn called, "It's ringing."

"Graksi. Leave a message. I'll get back to you as soon as I can."

"This is Annalynn Keyser in Laycock. Achilles has been hurt. I'll be out of town Friday. Please call me on my cell phone." She gave the number.

Jim and Annalynn returned to the TV room.

"If he's dead, no one will call back," she said.

"Somebody will, even if he's missing," Jim said. He hid a yawn. "Sorry. I'm still adjusting to day shift."

"Go on home," Annalynn told him. "If no one calls back tonight, Phoenix can contact his office while we're at the task force meeting."

The moment the door closed on Jim, I said, "I'm hungry. How about peanut butter sandwiches?"

"That sounds amazingly good, but I'll eat at my desk. I have several hours of reading for that meeting. I know those career people are going to challenge me, and I've got to be credible if I'm going to get their help in solving Boom's murder."

"How can I help?"

"I'd like for you to go through the meth-related newspaper clips to look for—I don't know what. You'll figure it out. Jim will follow up on anything you find."

I smiled grimly. "Let's hope we've found their Achilles' heel."

A few minutes later we settled down in the den, Annalynn in the recliner and I in the stuffed chair. We put our sandwiches and iced tea on the coffee table and three two-inch binder notebooks and a file box on the love seat.

Achilles dragged the old green blanket to my chair.

"You've certainly won him over. He's actually quite sweet," Annalynn said.

Progress. She had stopped drawing back when Achilles came near, but winced when he walked on the den's Persian carpet. I had to get them to bond. "Would you mind folding the blanket for him, please?"

She didn't move. "He wants you to do it."

"He needs to know you're his friend. Later you can give him a snack."

Slowly Annalynn reached over the arm of her chair and picked up a corner of the blanket. She pulled it up and folded it while Achilles watched. When she dropped it on the floor, he stretched out and closed his eyes.

We worked in silence for half an hour.

She took another folder out of the box. "This reminds me of doing homework in high school."

Achilles raised his head and growled.

"Quiet!" I grabbed my gun and went into the hall as he darted to the door, hackles up. I relaxed as I heard heels click on the porch. Connie. I grabbed Achilles' collar and opened the door.

"Hi, Phoenix. Are you okay? Trudy said you had blood all over your clothes." She spotted Achilles. "The source of the blood, I presume."

"Come in and shake hands with Achilles."

Achilles sat and offered his paw, and Connie bent to shake it.

"He didn't shake hands with me," Annalynn said.

Achilles trotted over to offer her his paw.

I laughed. "This is probably why he flunked out of the canine corps."

"Connie, don't tell anyone about him," Annalynn said. "We think he belonged to the man who registered for room thirteen."

Connie fingered a circular cloisonné earring. "I'm lost. What man?"

"We're not sure yet," Annalynn said. "Did you have a chance to talk to Wes?"

"Yes. He thought Maria Lopez was great. She told him she had a problem discouraging a well-connected man and didn't want to ask for a restraining order. Wes sent her to Boom and feels responsible for bringing them together." She paused before delivering her big line: "That man must have been the guy who left the roses, the stalker."

I nodded. " 'Well-connected.' That eliminates ESL students, and most others. He could be a faculty member."

"Dickie's on the LCC board of governors," Annalynn pointed out.

Connie and I exchanged skeptical glances.

Annalynn threw up her hands. "Whoever it is, asking questions about him is dangerous. Promise me you'll keep out of this, Connie."

"You both think the stalker could have killed Boom?"

I weighed the possibilities. "Not alone, but that would explain their knowing Maria Lopez was at the motel. Annalynn has a point. Hold off on this until we find out more about Achilles' owner." Seeing Connie's jaw jut in protest, I added, "And be extra careful. Don't go out alone. If anyone follows you, head for a public place and call 9-1-1."

"I hear you," Connie said. At the door she added, "See you at the recital. No playing hooky, Phoenix. Wear your new Walmart outfit."

Annalynn and I worked until ten, breaking only to take Achilles outside.

Annalynn had started upstairs when the phone rang. She hurried to the hall phone. "Maybe it's Bill Graksi." She picked up the receiver. "Hello." Short pause. "Thank you, Neil. I appreciate the kind thoughts." Longer pause. "Yes, she's right here." Annalynn handed me the phone with a wink.

To my chagrin, I felt a blush from my teenage years creep up my neck. "Hi, Neil."

"How's the patient?"

"Lethargic, but he's steady on his feet, and he's been eating well."

"Good. I posted a query about a missing Malinois when you left. No response."

"Thanks." No need for him to know we had a lead. "Annalynn will check it out officially. In fact, it's better not to mention him to anyone."

He didn't answer for a moment. "Okay. Sorry for disturbing you. Good night."

I recognized the tone. I'd heard it many times from men smart enough to suspect I wasn't telling them everything. "Thus ends a very short romantic revival."

I jumped when Annalynn said, "He asked you out today, didn't he?"

I made light of it. "Just to meet some of the neighbors Sunday afternoon when I take Achilles out for an exam."

Annalynn beamed. "Not wearing the clothes in your closet. We're going to Columbia to shop Saturday." She chuckled. "You've been home less than a week, and you've found a dog and a man. Phoenix, you belong in Laycock."

I SLEPT DEEPLY that night, sure that Achilles, inches from my bed, would announce any visitors. I woke when the clock chimed seven and stretched to test my body. I felt good. No Achilles. Had I dreamed him up? A bit of bacon biscuit on the carpet verified his existence.

I put on my robe and followed the aroma of coffee to the kitchen.

Achilles was gulping down dog food while Annalynn nibbled on toast.

"Good morning, Phoenix. I gave him the amount the package said a sixty-pound dog would eat. He acted like it was an appetizer."

"I doubt that he's had much to eat lately. Did you put the pills in his food?"

"Yes, and I took him over to *your* backyard about six thirty. He wanted to go for a run, and I mean a *run,* not a walk. I'll leave that for you. I have to get dressed and go."

I made oatmeal for breakfast and talked to an attentive Achilles while I ate. When I went up to dress, I shut the bedroom door on him. He sat outside and whined until I gave up and let him in. Tricksy had never shown that much separation anxiety.

As soon as Annalynn left for Kirksville, I went into the den to resume analysis of the articles on meth arrests and trials.

Achilles sat watching me two or three minutes. His patience exhausted, he whined and trotted back and forth from me to the front door.

On his fifth circuit, I gave up. "Bring me your leash."

He ran off, and I went upstairs to strap on my holster and put on the new long-sleeved blouse over my T-shirt. He was waiting at the front door when I came downstairs. "Let's go out back. I don't want to advertise your presence right now." I shut off the security system and snapped on his leash.

Achilles charged out the French doors as soon as I opened them, jerking the leash from my hand. He raced around the gaslight three times and headed for the orchard.

"Achilles, come!" To my relief, he ran back. I unsnapped the leash. "I'm not going to try to keep up with you."

He tore off across the grass, circled a cherry tree in the orchard, and loped back toward me, pausing only to inspect the hummingbird feeder.

My eyes swept the area. The evergreen trees that bordered both the Keyser and Smith properties blocked my view of the neighboring yards. I heard no one. I strolled toward the orchard, confident Achilles would tell me if anyone approached. Reaching the trees, I looked for places an intruder could hide. Many branches hung low, and the trunks of the pear trees provided cover. At night anyone could step off the sidewalk into the orchard and remain concealed until reaching the lawn.

Achilles trotted around the trees, pausing occasionally to leave his mark.

When he began to flag, I walked toward the house with him trotting in circles around me. At the French doors, he whined and trotted a few feet away.

The air was still cool, but I was comfortable. "Okay. I'll work out here." He went into the house with me and stayed at my side as I gathered up the notebooks and my laptop and brought them to the sunny side of a glass-top patio table. "You can play, but stay close."

He cocked his head, apparently expecting clearer instructions.

"Go. Play." I opened the binder with articles from the last two years and watched him crisscross the yard with his nose down, going closer and closer to the trees. When he reached them, I called, "Come."

He trotted back. I let him go again until he reached the trees. The third time I called him back he got the point not to go into the trees. The holster was rubbing my wound, so I took off the belt and put the holster on the table.

The night before, I'd flipped through the older notebooks reading headlines, captions, and opening paragraphs. Reading with more care, I was appalled at the destruction meth had wrought on my home state's rural communities. Numerous articles reported on cooks setting fires, often injuring themselves and their children. A score of articles told of neglected children being taken from their parents' custody. Again and again the news items on arrests mentioned prior convictions for petty theft, burglary, or armed robbery. Most of the cases involved homemade meth, but in the last six months, almost half of those arrested in surrounding counties had possessed imported crystal meth.

I focused on repeat offenders and gangs as the ones most likely to kill a sheriff.

Achilles came to rest on the warm patio stones by the table. He perked up his good ear at the sound of the phone ringing inside. The caller hung up without leaving a message before I reached the phone. The caller ID showed only zeros.

A few minutes later Achilles sprang up and touched my hand with his nose. Body poised for action, he faced the chimney side of the house.

I took my gun from the holster. "Quiet, Achilles."

A tall white man in a dark-blue suit strolled around the corner of the house. A holster peeped through his open jacket.

I raised my pistol in a two-handed grip.

Tail wagging, Achilles barked and ran toward the man.

"Achilles!" Ignoring the gun, the man knelt and ran

his right hand along the dog's back. "What big wounds you have."

I lowered the gun but kept my finger by the trigger. Could he be Bill Graksi? Could I have read the situation so wrong?

Grinning, the man looked up at me. Blue eyes twinkled in a long face with a prominent nose. "The DEA divisional office in St. Louis asked me to check out Annalynn's call to Bill Graksi." He stood up. "I would've known you anywhere, Phoenix. Remember me?"

A cocky crooked grin showed white, slightly uneven teeth. A full head of light-brown hair with strands falling over the high forehead. A little under six feet, but with broad shoulders that fit nicely in the off-the-rack suit. Mid-forties. I rated him a strong seven. I didn't recognize the face or the baritone voice with the slight mid-Missouri drawl. "Sorry. I can't place you."

He tapped his nose with his right hand as his left continued to stroke Achilles. "A schnoz like my mother's. You told me to be careful where I stuck it."

I'd seen that nose at the library. Mrs. Roper's son, Stuart. He'd be about forty-eight. "Is her phone number 556-1655?"

He laughed. "I can't believe you still remember it."

Achilles trotted back to put his head in my lap.

I relaxed but remained vigilant. "I called it at least once a week when I was president of the Math Club. I've been planning to call her."

He came toward me with hand outstretched.

I kept my hand on the Glock. Graksi lived in Independence, not St. Louis. "Sorry to be rude, but I'd like to see your DEA ID."

"You're certainly cautious today." He pulled back his suit jacket with his left hand and slowly reached into the inside pocket with his right. He took out a worn leather fold-over and tossed it on the table. "Here's my identification."

Genuine. "Thanks." I extended my hand. "Have a seat."

"What's going on? Why are you guarding Achilles? Where's Bill Graksi?"

TWENTY-FIVE

I stroked Achilles' shoulder. So his master's body hadn't been found. But then, Achilles had been shot only within the last thirty-six hours. "I don't know where Bill Graksi is, and if you don't, then it's urgent to put out an APB for him and his car."

"He left the Kansas City office at noon a week ago Monday to go on a week's fishing trip. What makes you think he's missing?"

"It's a good bet that meth dealers killed him and Boom Keyser and Ms. Lopez."

"You've jumped to conclusions." He sat down across from me. "He sent a text message to the office Monday saying he'd been delayed."

"That doesn't mean he sent it. Has anyone spoken to him?"

"No. That's why the agent checking his messages asked me to come by while I'm in town." Worry lines replaced laugh lines. "Why do you think Bill had anything to do with the deaths last week?"

A fed wouldn't take my theories seriously if I couldn't show credentials. "Sheriff Keyser has deputized me to help on this case. Here's the short version of what we know." Or assume. "Boom set up a meeting between a female informant and Graksi at Sweet Nights Motel about ten. Just before eleven Boom received a call that drew him to the motel. The police found him and the woman there and called it a murder-suicide. Annalynn knew better. Yesterday I found Achilles left for dead near an old meth lab. When I took him to the motel, he went nuts."

"Why would someone hold a dog for ten days and then shoot him?"

"Because Annalynn announced that her principal goal as sheriff would be to catch Boom's killers. Achilles became a hot dog."

Stuart didn't smile at my pun. "And Bill Graksi?"

An insight burst from my subconscious. "If the police had found his body at the same time they found Boom's, the spurned-lover fakery wouldn't have worked. Once the killers knew Annalynn was investigating Boom's death as murder, it didn't matter if someone found the bodies of the dog and his owner."

Stuart stared at me with cynical eyes. "How much of that can you prove?"

"Not nearly enough," I admitted. My credibility depended on honesty here. "We have no idea who the killers are—and it must have taken several men to handle Graksi, Boom, and Achilles—or how they knew about the meeting." He didn't look convinced, but he was listening. "And don't call in local help on this. If they'd been investigating, Annalynn wouldn't have pulled strings to get appointed sheriff. We suspect that Boom, who wasn't exactly a cop's cop, worked alone because he'd identified a dirty deputy."

Stuart opened a cell phone. "You're right. We need to check on Bill's whereabouts. Would you mind fixing some coffee while I make some calls?"

"Certainly." I strapped on the holster to accent my status as deputy and went—Achilles stuck to my leg like a burr—to the kitchen.

Stuart joined me as I poured the coffee. "The KC

office found 'BK' on Bill's calendar for that Monday night, and he never picked up the boat he'd rented. We're putting out an APB. Tell me *everything* you know or suspect."

For two hours I told and retold what we had discovered—omitting Boom's unexplained income, the Morse code messages, and the visit to George Brendan's house. Stuart told me little except that Graksi served on a team specializing in interstate meth trafficking. He and Stuart had worked undercover together in their early days with DEA, and their photos had circulated among drug traffickers.

When Stuart stopped to take and make more calls, I copied the section of the tape with the screams and the CD with the photos of the murder scene for him. As I came from the den, Achilles barked and trotted to the dining-room window.

I checked. Neil was walking up the sidewalk looking like Gary Cooper in *High Noon.* I opened the door. "Hi. Come to see your patient?"

Neil ran up the steps smiling. "I brought a sample of antibiotic spray for the wounds." He handed me a small bottle and knelt beside Achilles to inspect the wounds. "He's doing better than I expected. If you see any problems, call me. Otherwise spray him with this each morning and night. I'll see how the wounds look on Sunday." He stroked the dog. "Gotta cow waiting for me. Take it easy."

I scanned the street as Neil walked to his pickup. No one around.

"Not many vets make house calls on dogs," Stuart said from the end of the hall. "And not many economists investigate murder. We'll take over now. And, believe me, when one of our agents is missing, we go all out."

I'd heard similar speeches before. "You're telling me to butt out."

"This is no job for gifted amateurs, even ones with badges." He handed me a card. "I haven't been able to reach Sheriff Keyser. Here's my cell number. Call me if you see any sign of trouble—strangers watching the house, anything." He paused. "Do you really know how to handle that Glock?"

I'd kept my marksmanship a secret as a NOC, but I needed to emphasize my "manly" skills now. "My dad taught me and my brothers to shoot. In fact, I sold your mother a frozen turkey I won in a turkey shoot. After the September 11 attacks, living abroad became much less safe for Americans, so I took up target shooting again. Yes, I can handle my gun."

"Being able to hit a target isn't the same as shooting a person. For God's sake, don't take any chances. Just sit tight with Achilles until I get back."

I'd never responded well to orders. Mentally giving him the finger, I smiled humbly. "Of course."

"I mean it. Just taking care of Achilles could put you at risk, and plenty of people saw you with him yesterday." He pocketed his phone. "I'm in my own car, so as far as anyone knows, this was a social visit. Let's keep it that way for now."

"I understand." I opened the door.

He took my elbow and guided me out onto the porch. "A little camouflage." He leaned forward and kissed me on the cheek the way he might an aunt.

"Very little." Spying Trudy's white Camry coming down the street, I congratulated myself on buying a used car so common that the town gossip had one.

"You're right." He pulled me to him and kissed me thoroughly.

I put my arms around him and enjoyed it. When he lifted his mouth, I held him so he couldn't move away. "Does your wife know about your camouflage?"

He grinned. "Divorced for five years. One daughter seventeen, one son fifteen. Car paid off. Twenty-three years to go on the condo mortgage." He kissed the tip of my nose. "I'll be back later this afternoon, Dr. Smith. Mom loves it that you have a PhD."

Quick with words and a damned good actor. I'd have to be careful.

Achilles whined and nuzzled me.

I scratched under his chin and ushered him indoors. "Don't worry. He's not beating your time. Or are you afraid he's deserting you? Let's get something to eat." We went to the kitchen. "And when she got there, the cupboard was bare." No eggs. No milk. No meat. No fruit. I couldn't face tuna casserole.

Rummaging through cabinets, I found a can of vegetable soup to warm and gave Achilles the last half serving of dog food in the house. By the time I finished my soup, he was whining by his empty bowl.

"Still hungry? Okay, let's go get some food out of the car and see how you like piano music. Playing Mozart helps me think." I strapped on my holster, snapped on his leash, and found a plastic bag to put the dog food in.

Achilles went into my house willingly, but he hung back as I filled a melamine bowl from the cupboard with water. When he started lapping it up, I hurried out the front door, closed the storm door behind me, and ran to my car. His anguished howl followed me. I scooped some dog food into the bag and called, "I'm coming."

As I closed the trunk lid, I heard a car moving slowly down the street. People drove that slowly only when they were looking for something. I stepped to the front of my car, crouched behind it, drew my gun. Being paranoid is underrated.

A few seconds later a vehicle pulled in behind mine. A door opened, and someone stepped out.

Achilles' barks turned to ferocious growls.

I sprang up ready to fire.

A young Hispanic man in a black leather jacket held up his hands. "Hey, lady. I'm just here looking for work." He shouted to be heard over Achilles, and the accent was pure American.

He'd been in church Sunday. I aimed at his chest. "What kind of work?"

"I heard you want to get your house ready to sell. My company can do anything you want—painting, plumbing, electricity."

Late twenties. Expensive clothes. Hair styled, not just cut. A black Jeep Cherokee. Definitely not a day laborer. "Where did you hear I needed work done?"

"The Methodist minister."

The minister, not Reverend Berry. Not good, but a Miguel had called. "What's your name?"

"My friends call me Pancho." He glanced toward the house. "You pull a gun on me and your dog's acting crazy. What's going on?"

Too slick. "We had a burglary recently. I'm not interested in hiring a contractor right now, and you're upsetting my dog. I'd appreciate it if you would move on."

"Sure, lady. No problem." He hopped back in the car and backed out much more quickly than he'd turned in. As soon as the car was in the street, he gunned it.

I caught a glimpse of an out-of-state license plate and 65 as I ran to the house to calm the frantic dog.

He almost knocked me over bolting out the door. He raced down the street after the car.

"Come! Stay! Sit!" When he kept going, I ran into the street to take a shot, but the Cherokee slid around a corner two blocks away.

Achilles raced after the car for a block before slouching back toward me.

"Bloody hell! I blew it!" I punched in Stuart's number.

"Roper."

"Phoenix. I just had a suspicious visitor."

"What? Are you okay?"

"Fine." I gave a terse account, winding up by offering, "I saw him at church Sunday. I'll see if the minister knows who he is."

"What makes you think he's not just what he said?"

"Achilles. He's bared his teeth and growled, but he's never reacted like this."

He staggered up to me, his nose almost touching the sidewalk.

"Get inside the castle and stay there."

"We're going!" I cut him off.

I pulled Achilles inside, locked the front door, and went through the basement to Annalynn's house. How had [illegible] known Achilles was here? Maybe he hadn't. Plenty of people had seen the dog in a white Camry with Maryland plates. But someone had known my connection to Annalynn or he'd never have driven down this street. He hadn't expected any trouble from a woman my age, and he'd had a cover story ready.

The phone rang. I picked up the hall extension. "Keyser residence."

"Hi." Annalynn said over a blur of voices and laughter. "I just talked to Stuart's boss. They seem to have things well in hand there. I'm going to visit the Criminalistics Lab before coming home, so I'll be late. Go on to Connie's recital if I'm not there."

So the DEA had briefed her—up to Pancho. "Do you think Pancho will be there? Well-dressed Hispanic, American accent, about twenty-eight, drives a black Cherokee."

A long silence. "I don't know him."

No point in worrying her. "I'll tell you about him tonight. See you."

I put out food and water for Achilles. Head hanging, legs splayed, he ignored it. I led him into the den to his blanket and sat down beside him. I stroked him and crooned compliments about his bravery until he fell asleep.

Time to phone Reverend Berry. When I picked up the phone at Annalynn's desk, Achilles crawled over to put his nose on my foot.

"Wesley Berry. How may I help you?"

"Good afternoon, Reverend Berry. This is Phoenix Smith. A young man from the church came by looking for work. I've misplaced his number. I'm hoping you can help me find him."

"What's his name?" He sounded guarded.

"Pancho."

"I don't recall a Pancho." He paused. "I told Miguel Paloma to call you."

"That wasn't the name. I saw this man in the congregation last Sunday. About twenty-eight, five feet nine or so, great hair."

"Miguel's about fifty."

He'd become more forthcoming. Pursue it. "This man was sitting alone at the end of a back pew, to your left. He had on a white shirt, no tie."

"I remember a newcomer who didn't sing, but I don't know who he is."

The minister knew nothing, or he improvised well.

"Thanks. If you happen to find out who he is, please give me a call." I hung up and reached down to stroke Achilles. "That run took a lot out of you. And of me. It's one thirty. Let's grab a nap."

Upstairs, Achilles settled down on his blanket and I stretched out on the bed. I intended to think, but I awoke to the three-o'clock chimes and the sound of a gentle rain. Achilles followed me back to Annalynn's computer and rested his head on my knee while I checked my contact blogs. No messages.

His good ear went up. He barked and trotted out of the den as the doorbell rang.

Gun in hand, I went to the peephole. Stuart. I ran my hands through my bed hair before opening the door.

Raindrops glistened on his hair. "Find out anything from the minister?"

"No." I punched in the code. "Sunday was Pancho's first time at church."

He glanced at the gun. "Have you seen the mug shots the St. Louis office e-mailed to you?"

"E-mailed to me?" They were darned good if they'd found my e-mail address.

"To Annalynn."

"I'll check."

He followed Achilles and me into the den and watched as I downloaded six photos of young Hispanic men. "None of these is Pancho." I downloaded another group. "Nor these."

I went through six other batches without spotting Pancho.

"Don't worry," Stuart assured me. "They're throwing every possibility at you. Elimination helps."

Another message popped up, and I recognized an alias used by my only trustworthy contact at CIA headquarters. I flicked off the monitor. Why on earth was Jill using Annalynn's e-mail address? "Would you mind putting on some water for tea?"

"Glad to." He left.

I opened the message. "Hi, Daniel Edward Applebaum is asking everybody about you. Do you have a date with him? I haven't heard anything from your old boyfriend. Have you? Willie."

So the DEA was checking on me. Somebody was either suspicious or being incredibly thorough. I deleted the message and, with my new appendage, went to the kitchen. Stuart was ignoring a whistling teakettle and talking on his cell.

He closed his phone and rushed to turn off the burner. "We'll take Achilles over to the motel room and see what scents he can pick up."

It surely had been cleaned, but worth a try. "I'm ready when you are."

He shifted his feet. "I mean, uh, a dog handler will work with him. It would be better for you to stay here. Having two masters confuses a working dog."

I looked down at Achilles. He'd stuck to me like Velcro since Pancho's visit. "I'm not sure he'll go without me."

Stuart knelt and stretched his hand out to the dog. "You know me, boy. You'll go with me."

Achilles moved closer to me, his right front paw on my left foot.

Stuart rose. "This can't wait. Where's his leash?"

"It's on the chair. I'll put it on him."

"Thanks. It might be a good idea for you to walk us out to the car, too."

"Okay. Would you check for an umbrella in the hall closet? It's under the stairs."

I put the leash on Achilles and turned off the security system at the door.

Stuart handed me a black umbrella with pink poodles around the edges.

I smiled. "Annalynn's granddaughter must have a thing for pink poodles. Annalynn certainly doesn't." Umbrella up, I ran to Stuart's dark-blue Corolla and opened the front passenger door. "In you go, Achilles. You like the front seat."

He gazed up at me without moving, his brow in a frown.

Smart dog. "Okay, I'll sit here, and you can get in the back." I opened the back door and slid into the front seat.

Sixty pounds of damp fur landed on my lap.

Stuart grinned. "You sure outsmarted him." He reclined the driver's seat. "In the back, Achilles. Go on."

I pushed on the dog until he hopped in back. "Now what? Do you want me to come with you, or do you intend to drive across town with a howling dog?"

Stuart returned his seat to its position and got in. "He'll be okay. Just stay there a sec." He took off his damp jacket and his tie and handed them to me. "Keep my things until I get back, please. And pucker up."

"More camouflage?"

"He needs to understand we're coming back to you."

I doubted Achilles would draw that conclusion from a kiss. I puckered.

After a second long kiss, Achilles barked, a note of disapproval in his tone.

Stuart sat back and pulled on his seat belt. "Is he speaking on behalf of that vet?"

I smiled and opened the car door. Letting the rain cool me down, I ran for the porch. Achilles howled, but Stuart pulled out of the drive anyway.

A pleasant tingle running through me, I hung Stuart's jacket and tie over a dining-room chair and put the umbrella back in the closet. I savored the encounter a few seconds and then put the notebooks on the dining-room table and got to work. Every time I thought I had a likely suspect, I found he or she was incarcerated or dead.

"Here we go!" The last four arrests involved people under twenty-five possessing imported crystal meth. Four of the fifteen caught since early January were students at LCC who lived in adjoining counties. No one caught possessing crystal meth lived in Vandiver County. So what did this tell me? The stats were too small to be reliable, but it looked like the purveyors of crystal meth were staying away from Laycock. A dirty police officer might well keep the filth away from his own door. Or was the sheriff's department ignoring the importers?

At five thirty I looked up the number for the town's Chinese takeout and ordered enough food for three.

When it arrived, I was the only one there to eat it. I took my plate to the computer and wrote an innocuous comment on the Emily Dickinson blog to emphasize my desire for information on the Istanbul incident.

The phone rang at quarter to seven. "This is Stuart. The handler will work with Achilles until around eight. I'm going to take Mom to the student recital at the Methodist Church. Shall I come by for you?"

"No, thanks. I'll see you there." I went upstairs to put on the long-sleeved blouse to cover my holster. It was still raining, so I slipped on my rain jacket and picked up the pink poodle umbrella.

The street was empty when I backed out of the driveway, but a block later car lights appeared behind me. Despite the rain, I made out Elena Cordero's license plate.

She followed me into the church parking lot and parked at the end as I pulled in near the door, beside Trudy's matching Camry.

I opened the umbrella and ran the few feet to the steps, up them, and in the open doors. God, but it was good to move easily again.

Trudy stood just inside the doors in a candy-striped blouse and a dark-blue skirt. "You have an umbrella just like mine. Could I borrow it, please? My granddaughter left her music in my car."

"Certainly." I handed her the umbrella and wiped my shoes on the mat.

A car motor roared. Tires squealed. A woman screamed as metal met metal.

TWENTY-SIX

I REACHED THE steps in time to see Elena's car jump the curb and careen down the street. "Oh, God, no!" I raced into the parking lot.

Sticking out from between the two white Camrys was an ankle with a bare foot pointed the wrong direction. I whipped out my cell phone and dialed 9-1-1 as I ran to Trudy. She was sprawled between our cars. The driver had crushed my Camry's right-rear fender and Trudy's left. I maneuvered between the cars to reach her head. Blood oozed from her forehead. More ominous, she wasn't talking.

The dispatcher answered, and I barked, "We need an ambulance immediately to the First Methodist Church parking lot. A hit-and-run. Victim unconscious. Maroon Honda Civic. License number begins 5-4-3. Car owner Elena Cordero." I stuck the phone into my pocket and bent to check Trudy's pulse. A little weak, but there.

People were swarming around the cars now. I spotted Connie. "Get everybody out of here. I've already called for an ambulance."

Stuart pushed his way through. "Is she badly hurt?"

"I don't know. We can't do anything like this." I checked my crumpled fender. Nothing to keep me from moving my car. "You hold her to make sure she doesn't move. I'm going to back out so we have room to give CPR." I jumped into my car and backed out in a straight,

straight line. Once clear, I angled my car so the lights shone on Trudy.

Reverend Berry ran up carrying two umbrellas. "What can I do?"

"Get the kids inside and calm them down," I said, taking the umbrellas and holding them over Trudy and Connie, who knelt beside her with a cell phone to her ear.

Trudy moaned.

A faint police siren sounded louder and louder. An ambulance was coming from the opposite direction.

Trudy opened her eyes. "What happened? Oh, it hurts so much. He came right at me! Why would he do that?"

The ambulance pulled into the parking lot, and two men jumped from it.

Stuart took my arm and led me a few steps away. "Her car matches yours. He mistook her for you."

"Pretty da—doggone stupid. Trudy had the poodle umbrella, but her clothes are completely different."

A sheriff's department car slid into the lot and two doors slammed.

Annalynn enveloped me in a tight embrace. "Thank God! I thought you'd been hurt."

Jim Falstaff came up behind her. "Who got hit?"

"Trudy. By someone in Elena Cordero's car. It followed me here."

Annalynn turned to watch the paramedics preparing to lift Trudy onto a gurney. "Elena reported her car stolen a few minutes ago. We heard the call on the way in. You were right, Phoenix. The killers have connected Elena to Maria. Jim, get Elena into protective custody immediately."

He hesitated. "Hadn't I oughta secure the crime scene?"

"Let the city police handle that," Annalynn said firmly. "Elena can't wait."

Jim hurried back to the car and pulled out with siren wailing.

Stuart spoke softly into Annalynn's ear. "You and Phoenix should get out of here right now."

"In a moment." Annalynn put an arm around Connie's shoulder. "How is she?"

"Her ankle's broken, and they think she has a concussion." She wiped rain or tears from her face. "He drove right at her. If she hadn't jumped between the cars, he'd have killed her. I called her husband to go straight to the hospital."

As the ambulance pulled away, Annalynn's cell phone rang. "Hello." Pause. "Not yet." Pause. "Get somebody on it. Bye." She put the phone in her purse. "Jim just saw Elena's car on the lawn of an empty house near Franklin and Benton."

The minister ran up holding a red umbrella. "No one inside saw a thing. Shall I tell them to go home?"

"Yes, please," Annalynn said, "but have the adults put their names and phone numbers on a sheet as they go out."

Stuart opened my car door. "My sister will take Mom home. I'll follow you."

Chilled from the rain, I yanked off my wet jacket and threw it in the backseat. I shivered so hard that I had trouble putting the key in the ignition. I managed to turn on the motor just as Annalynn stepped into the car. "Did you find out anything in Kirksville?"

"Ice from Mexico is popping up everywhere, even among people who were making their own meth. A drug ring started a new distribution network early this year, and we're seeing the effects. We've been lucky here so far, but that won't last." She sighed. "I told the task force Boom was murdered because he'd found a lead, but I don't think they believed me."

"The DEA seems to." Pulling out of the parking lot, I checked for anyone sitting in the cars parked along the residential street. No one. I turned on the heat. "What did the forensics people say?"

"They couldn't tell anything from the photos. They did say that approximately eighty percent of all suicides using pistols put it in the mouth. Apparently to get any action, I'll have to pry the forensic evidence away from the Highway Patrol's overloaded lab and send it to the Kansas City Police lab."

I checked again. No one behind us. "It looks like the killers took Graksi's cell phone and used it to send that text message. They probably took Boom's, too."

The rain bucketed when we reached Annalynn's. Thoroughly chilled, I said, "We should've picked up your pink poodle umbrella that I lent Trudy."

"That's not mine. Someone left it at the house last week." She grabbed my arm. "You *were* the target. But why would they come after you? You weren't even in town when Boom died."

"Let's talk in the house. I need some hot tea." I put my jacket over my head and hurried toward the porch.

Annalynn unlocked the door. "Your teeth are chattering! Get into a hot shower while I make the tea. Then you're going straight to bed."

"Fine with me." With my weakened immune system, I dreaded catching a cold. I stayed in the shower until I felt warm. Dry clothes felt great. When I opened the bathroom door, Achilles greeted me, his tail raising a breeze. Nobody loves you like a dog. I praised and petted him until he settled down.

On the bedside table were a pot of tea, a teacup, and a note: “We’ve gone to talk to Elena at my office. Go to bed. Love, A.”

I poured a cup of tea, and Achilles nudged me. “I haven’t forgotten you.” I stroked his shoulders and marshaled my thoughts. Could there possibly be some connection between the attempt on my life tonight and the one in the spice market? Why had the DEA checked on me, a peripheral person? Until someone tried to run me down.

Achilles whined.

“I’m sorry, boy. You’re hungry, and you need your pills and your antibiotic spray.” I downed the lukewarm tea and went downstairs to meet his needs.

When he began to eat, I went to the computer in the den. I’d not hounded Jerry or Operations for information on what happened in Istanbul, but the hit-and-run made it urgent that I know if the assassin could possibly have followed me to Laycock. If so, my presence was endangering Annalynn and others. I logged on and checked for messages on my contact blogs and select e-mail addresses. Nothing. Jerry had a secure cell phone and I had an untraceable one. Calling him violated basic protocols. Operations would have a fit—if anyone found out. My career had ended. What could they do to me? Jerry and I were used to coded double-talk. The trick would be to give nothing away.

I went back upstairs and checked the charge on my international mobile. Enough for a short call, which was all I dared make. I stretched out on the bed to work out my strategy and then dialed.

The phone rang six times before he picked up. And said nothing.

“Hi, guy,” I said. “What’s new?”

"Who is this?" His voice sounded rough. It was the middle of the night in Ankara.

"A fan of apple martinis." We'd used that ridiculous code in Corfu.

"I can't talk right now."

"Fine. Tell me who served me that black Russian and I'll hang up."

He cleared his throat. "I can't believe you're asking."

"Give me the damned recipe." A hint of the group behind it was all I needed.

"Or you'll do what?" His voice was condescending, confident.

I lightened my tone to make my threat more ominous. "Or I'll ask the professor." That was Jerry's name for a senator who'd questioned operations in Turkey.

"You wouldn't!"

I'd stepped over the line. I had to explain my urgency. "Someone served me a similar drink tonight. I wonder if it's the same bartender."

"In Nowheresville?" His tone was incredulous.

So he'd kept track of me, or rather someone at Langley had.

He was quiet several seconds. "It's a different bartender. Be careful." He hung up.

Achilles put his head in my lap.

I stroked him. After two days, I could trust him more than a man I'd known thirty years. Jerry had sounded truthful, but being a convincing liar is a prerequisite for an operative. Truthful or not, he was right. A link between the bazaar and the bizarre wasn't credible. I had to look for answers here in Laycock.

TWENTY-SEVEN

I OPENED THE front door for Annalynn and Connie. "How's Trudy?"

"A broken ankle from the car hitting her, a concussion from her hitting a car, and a cracked collarbone from hitting the pavement," Connie said.

I was relieved it hadn't been much worse. "Want some hot tea?"

Connie went to the liquor cabinet. "To heck with the tea. I want whiskey."

"Straight," Annalynn agreed, punching in the code but leaving the door open.

Stuart came in wearing a blazer and no tie and carrying a plastic grocery bag. "You're looking chipper again, Phoenix. Have you thought of anything that would help us with the hit-and-run?"

"No. The whole thing's almost farcical. He hit the wrong person, but he had the smarts to have a pickup car waiting a few blocks away. Then he abandoned Elena's car where people would notice it."

"He may be a meth user," Annalynn said. "Their brains get addled. Will you join Connie and me in a whiskey, Stuart, or will you have tea with Phoenix?"

He smiled at me. "A drop of whiskey in your tea would help warm you."

"Doctor's orders," Connie said. "She had emergency gallbladder surgery in Istanbul, and they messed it up."

He raised an eyebrow. “In Istanbul?”

“I was on vacation there,” I said. Had to get him away from that. “What’s happening with Elena?”

Stuart glanced at Annalynn before answering. “We talked to her briefly, but since you suspect someone in the sheriff’s department, we’re taking her and her fiancé to St. Louis. She said you’d warned her to be careful.”

I wondered why they’d taken the boyfriend, too. “He works at some meatpacking plant. Did he say anything about drug use there?”

“He’s seen no sign of any drug other than alcohol,” Stuart said.

Annalynn added, “But he noticed one day that a Jaime Caballo wasn’t the same man who’d been Jaime Caballo the day before. His supervisor laughed at him and said half the beaners are cousins with the same names.”

Stuart shifted his feet. “That’s confidential, of course. We’ll pass it on to Immigration, but they’re too busy elsewhere to bother about a few illegal workers here.” He smiled at Annalynn. “Sheriff Keyser, I make a mean cup of cocoa.”

Connie put down the whiskey and went to find a pan. “Phoenix loves cocoa.”

He went into the kitchen and took a gallon of milk, a can of cocoa, sugar, and marshmallows from his bag.

I wondered if he was trying to distract us or thought Sheriff Keyser shouldn’t be drinking.

“I think you can relax now.” Stuart poured milk in the pan. “The bad guys clear out fast when they know the DEA is on their tails. They’ve got too much to lose and too little to win to risk coming after you again.”

A dangerous assumption. “We—all three of us—need to be more careful, not less.”

He raised his eyebrows in surprise. "Certainly you need to be careful, but why would someone come after all of you?"

"We've all been working on this investigation. I found Achilles, and that prompted Pancho's visit and the hit-and-run. Connie has been asking questions about Maria Lopez, and Annalynn told the world she's going after Boom's killers. The killers are afraid we're going to bring the strands together and identify them."

Only Annalynn nodded in agreement. Stuart pursed his lips and frowned. Connie put her right hand on her hip and cast her eyes at the ceiling.

"Connie, you should stay here tonight." I stopped. Telling her to do something was counterproductive. "None of us should go out alone until the killers are arrested."

Connie cocked her head at Stuart. "Does this sound as far-fetched to you as it does to me?"

Head down, he stirred the milk. "It's a good idea for all of you to hole up here."

Annalynn stiffened. "I didn't let the sheriff's department shut me out of the investigation, and I'll be on the phone to Washington if the DEA tries to."

"We'll keep you in the loop." He winked at me. "You and your cool-headed deputy."

"Be sure that you do," Sheriff Keyser said.

Stuart mouthed "help" to me and said, "Phoenix, have you shown them the mug shots? Maybe they've seen one of those creeps."

I led the way to the den and clicked open the sets of photos one by one. Neither Annalynn nor Connie recognized anyone.

Connie leaned over and sang softly in my ear: "Phoenix and Stuart sitting in a tree, K-I-S-S-I-N-G."

"Oh, for God's sake!" I protested. "Don't be so infantile."

A smile played on Annalynn's lips. "What are you keeping from me?"

Connie giggled. "Trudy saw them 'smooching' on the front porch this morning. She told at least half the people at the recital." She sobered. "She's good-hearted. She didn't deserve to be hurt."

"Here's the cocoa," Stuart announced, putting four mugs on the coffee table.

Connie took the recliner. Annalynn sat in the stuffed chair. That left the love seat for Stuart and me.

He sat down. "Please go over what happened tonight, starting with when you noticed the car following you." When I finished, he drummed his fingers on his cup and stared into space. "Did he have a clear shot as you went from the car into the church?"

"Not really. The umbrella blocked his view of my upper body."

His cell rang. "Excuse me." He rushed out of the den.

Connie tiptoed to the door and then came back. "Darn," she whispered. "My best date in the last two years has been an American-lit teacher. In less than two weeks you have two macho men on the string. It must be your exotic European air."

Annalynn raised an eyebrow. "Is flirting one of your strategies?"

I held a finger to my lips. Stuart was coming back.

He stopped at the door. "I've got to go. Do you want me to send over a guard?"

"No need," Annalynn said. "We have the alarm system and Achilles, and my deputy and I are both willing and able to shoot."

"Right." He ran his right hand down the front of his shirt. "Phoenix, where did you leave my tie?"

"It's hanging over the back of a dining-room chair." I went toward the dining room, Achilles at my side.

Stuart leaned over to look under the table. He picked up a long, tattered rag.

Achilles grinned.

"My favorite tie." Stuart shook his finger at the dog. "You were getting even with me, weren't you? Fair enough." He stuffed the tie in his pocket and strode to the door. "You have good taste in ties, Achilles." He stepped out onto the porch. "And in women." He closed the door.

"What a cornball line," Connie said. "I wish he'd said it to me."

I had no desire to relive high school. "Let it go, Connie. He's flirting as a distraction, a way to take his mind off the death of an old friend. It means nothing." But it certainly felt good. "If you'll excuse me, I'm going to bed."

Annalynn smiled knowingly. "Sweet dreams."

NINE HOURS LATER I woke refreshed but uneasy. Although the people bringing in the meth might cut their losses and run, the person who'd engineered the murder-suicide wouldn't. Killing Boom and Maria hadn't been enough. He'd disgraced them. What he'd done with Graksi, I couldn't guess.

The killers had to have known Boom personally to have his phone number and to guess how he would react to the screams. They also knew he went to his home office every night. Who but his deputy would know those things? I pulled on a pair of jeans and a blue T-shirt and wished for one of Connie's brazenly bright blouses.

When I went downstairs, Annalynn was eating cold cereal at the dining-room table while Stuart—dressed in black slacks and polo shirt—traced something on a map.

Heart in my mouth, I blurted, "Where's Connie?"

"Relax," Annalynn said. "She's at home, under guard, giving piano lessons."

"Good morning." Stuart half rose and treated me to his crooked smile.

"Good morning." He rated an eight today. "What's up?"

Annalynn leaned her forehead on her hand. "George called me late last night half drunk and apologized over and over for believing Boom was a murderer." She straightened. "Phoenix, George can't be the one."

"We can't discount the possibility." The set of her mouth told me she wouldn't change her mind, so I changed the subject. "Did Elena come up with anything else?"

Stuart shook his head. "Not yet, and I doubt that she will. She and her fiancé will stay at his sister's farm near Ottumwa until we're sure it's safe for them to come back."

Achilles barked behind me and greeted me with a doggy grin.

"Good boy. You didn't wake me up." After ample stroking and scratching, I got back to business. "I'll check any new mug shots before I eat." I went into the den, logged on to Annalynn's account, and opened a new set. Bingo! "Stuart! Here's Pancho!"

The agent came running. "You're sure?"

"Positive. He's younger here, and his hair is longer, but that's the guy." I sent a brief reply.

Stuart studied the photo. "I don't recognize him." His phone rang. He answered and pumped the air with his free hand. He strode out of the room giving the victory sign.

Annalynn peered over my shoulders. "I don't recognize any of them."

Stuart rushed back in, his face jubilant. "We've got him! Troopers pulled him over for speeding about three this morning just north of Dallas. They held him because he'd skipped bail on a drug charge. We're checking to see if he and Bill ever crossed paths."

"Thank God," Annalynn said. "What happens now?"

"We'll question him and trace every move he's made in the last two weeks."

I couldn't share his jubilation. "Pancho couldn't have driven the hit-and-run car and then driven as far as Dallas."

"You're right," Stuart agreed. "He's not working alone."

"We're going to get them. We really are," Annalynn said, her voice catching.

"And soon," Stuart assured her. "We better go monitor developments from the sheriff's department. It's our communication center."

"I'm ready," Annalynn said. "Phoenix, why don't you and Connie go shopping in Columbia this afternoon?"

"Why don't you all go?" Stuart said. "The action has moved away from here."

Annalynn and I exchanged glances. Obviously he considered us peripheral players.

Achilles dropped a tennis ball in my lap.

"I see somebody brought you a bribe." I scratched behind his good ear. "Stuart, I had an idea during the night: Do you ever use dogs in lineups?"

He grinned. "You mean have Achilles sniff out the killers?" He sobered as he saw I was serious. "I've known people to stage lineups with dogs, mainly to persuade somebody to talk, but you can't build a case on a dog's identification. Don't worry. We'll find these guys and the evidence to convict them."

"Don't forget this gang has a local connection."

"We'll get them all." His voice rang with conviction. His face softened. "You okay with being alone?"

I had heard that question from many men in both my professional and my personal life. I was tired of it. "Don't worry about me. I once shot a fly off an apple twenty feet away." That was when I could still see the wings on a fly at that distance.

"A fly's not the same as a man. You ever shoot a man?"

"No." He hadn't asked about a woman.

TO PROTECT BOTH Achilles and myself, I played ball with him in the basement. When he tired of the game, I skimmed the blogs and found no messages. I logged into my office in Vienna to check e-mail and files from projects I'd been supervising. My staff was doing just fine without me.

Connie strolled in about eleven thirty wearing shorts and a low-necked blouse. She glanced at the spreadsheet on the monitor and went to the recliner. "Checking to see how much you can afford to spend on clothes?"

I ignored the gibe. "I'll finish up here. Would you mind calling Annalynn to see if she plans to go?"

"Are you really rich?" Connie's voice was sober, not flippant.

"Rich is relative. I don't own mansions or television stations. I own stocks, and they're always unpredictable."

"Could you retire right now?"

Why lie? "Financially, yes. Psychologically, no. I've always worked hard, the equivalent of fifty years over the last thirty." Not nearly as hard since I left the CIA. "I like to work. I like to get things done. I like to see results." Even if seeing them sometimes took years. During the Cold War I'd courted one Polish economist for two years before I got the data I wanted.

"Your health improved as soon as you started helping Annalynn investigate," Connie said. "I'll go call her."

I finished my work and went offline, confident that neither my day job nor CIA work had anything to do with the hit-and-run.

Connie stuck her head around the screen. "Annalynn said she's doing nothing but waiting. She suggests leaving now and eating in Columbia."

"We'll have to take Achilles along."

"Your boy toy is taking him out to sniff old meth labs this afternoon."

I resigned myself to being out of the loop. "Okay, I'll be ready as soon as I put on my holster and a blouse to cover it." I was leaving her out of the loop. "Connie, if you could do anything you want for the next five years, what would you do?"

"*Mame, Hello Dolly, Sweeney Todd.* Preferably on Broadway, but I'd settle for a first-rate touring company."

Dreams don't die. Why should they? "You're twice the singer you were in high school. You'd be a great Auntie Mame."

Connie bowed, her face surprised. "Thank you, thank you very much." She chuckled. "Speaking of nonexistent careers, you're going to love this. Trudy told me that Wes asked her if you're an FBI agent."

Annoyed, I blurted out, "FBI? Why would anyone accuse me of that?"

"*Accuse* you? I thought you'd get a kick out of it. You wanted to be a spy when you were a kid."

No way could I explain to Connie the long enmity between the FBI and the CIA. I waved my hand dismissively. "That was kid stuff. But, seriously, what made him think I'm FBI?"

"He heard it somewhere. After all, nobody was investigating Boom's death until you got here. You have a police dog. You have a gun. You and Bill Graksi both go by P. D. Smith. Besides, it didn't take a genius to figure out that car was after you, not Trudy."

"I couldn't be with the FBI. I've lived in Europe for years."

Connie frowned. "Why aren't you laughing about this? Do you think the rumor made you a target?"

"It could be." Attacking an FBI agent and bringing the Bureau's wrath down on you was stupid, but reports said meth users' paranoia produced risky actions. And they'd killed a sheriff already.

Connie fiddled with her earring. "Before Annalynn gets here, I have to ask you for a favor."

"You need money?"

"Not me. Trudy. She's worrying about how they'll pay the hospital bill."

"Tell her to relax. I know a foundation that provides for the care of crime victims." I hadn't set it up to do that, but I could change the rules.

"Thanks so much." She rose and kissed me on the cheek.

"Just don't tell anyone else."

She cocked her head? "Not even Annalynn?"

"No."

Annalynn came in the door. "Phoenix, you promised me no more secrets."

Stuart followed her in, and Achilles glued himself to my left leg.

"It's a small personal matter between Connie and me," I said, reaching down to stroke my dog. Getting away from him wouldn't be easy. "Where's your ball?"

He darted away, picked it up, and raced back to me.

"Let's go play outside. Stuart wants to throw the ball for you." I strapped on my holster and grabbed my purse.

Annalynn went toward the stairs. "I'll get into my civvies. You can drive my Mercedes."

When we went through the French doors, I handed Achilles' leash to Stuart. "Let's check out the orchard first."

"We've got a man watching it," Stuart said. "I thought about your idea of a lineup for Achilles. Maybe the killers did, too."

Good. He'd listened to me. "Maybe they heard that ridiculous rumor that I'm with the FBI."

"I heard DEA." He threw the ball toward the orchard. His eyes bored into mine. "You act like you've had some law enforcement experience."

I smiled, relieved he'd guessed wrong. "Just self-defense training, but thank you."

"Maybe I should come with you today."

"No. Searching the meth labs is crucial, and Annalynn really needs this detour to normality. She's been incredibly strong, but I'm not sure how much more she can take."

"Okay, but put me on speed dial and call if you see *anything* suspicious."

I took out my cell phone and punched in his number.

He watched over my shoulder. "You must have a photographic memory."

"Only for numbers." Modesty is a virtue. "Achilles, bring me the ball."

He loped toward me, coming to the side away from Stuart.

I tossed the ball underhanded for Achilles several times, each time moving closer to the gap between the house and garage. Once in position, I handed the ball to Stuart. "He's all yours."

"Right." He threw the ball into the trees and pulled a plastic bag from his pocket. "I've got some treats." He jogged toward the trees to intercept Achilles.

I hurried toward the Mercedes. Annalynn and Connie had just stepped off the porch.

"Hurry," I urged, heading for the driver's seat. "We need to get out of here before he misses me."

Connie grinned. "Are you talking about the man or the dog?"

I ignored her. "Where's your gun, Annalynn?"

"In my purse, and it weighs a ton." She climbed into the front passenger seat.

I looked at the gas gauge. "We better fill up on the way out. Where's that place George Brendan got his coffee?"

"Speed-Well," Annalynn said absently, "where you turn off Jackson to go to Sixty-three."

I checked the street. No cars ahead or behind us. "Anything new?"

Annalynn sighed. "Pancho—Jesus Olviera—says he's never heard of Laycock. I don't think they'll get anything out of him any time soon. Everyone says he's the key."

We rode in silence as I turned onto Jackson.

"I heard something interesting," Connie offered. "Stuart's been divorced about three years."

I couldn't stand an incorrect number. "Five years."

Connie laughed. "Just seeing if you knew. Do you know why she divorced him?"

I scanned the street and driveways. "No, and I don't care." Connie wouldn't be able to resist telling me.

Annalynn smiled. "Please, Connie, tell us why Stuart got his divorce."

"His wife said he worked long hours and spent any spare time with the kids."

Annalynn tapped my knee. "He sounds like one of those people who works so hard he neglects his personal life. Does that remind you of anyone?"

A man waved frantically from an oncoming Lincoln. Dickie Rothway.

I stopped and lowered my window.

He leaned out of his. "Annalynn, I just wanted to say how sorry I am about how people got the wrong idea about Boom. I knew he'd never be unfaithful to you."

"Thank you for all your support," Annalynn said, her tone and face betraying nothing. "You can be sure I won't forget it."

"Uh—yes. Well, enjoy your shopping trip."

I went on full alert. "Hold it! How did you know we're going shopping?"

He shrugged. "Somebody at the bank mentioned it."

A car behind him beeped, and he pulled off.

I didn't move. "Did either of you tell anyone we're going to Columbia?"

"I told my staff and the DEA team," Annalynn said. "And, yes, George could have overheard."

"You didn't say it was a *secret,*" Connie said. "I mentioned it to Trudy."

If I'd been working with them on an operation, I'd have blasted them out of their shoes. I took a deep breath and reminded myself they were civilians.

Annalynn touched my arm. "Do you really think it's a problem? Should we go back home?"

A horn sounded behind us. Lois Brendan. I stepped on the gas. "Let me think about it."

I debated whether to go all the way to the service station. The whole town knowing where we were going posed a danger. Or had Istanbul made me overly cautious? We all needed a break. I pulled up to the only empty pump.

"Hi, Ms. Smith," Sean Brendan called from a self-service car wash. He put down the hose and came over. "I heard about what happened last night. I figured you'd be holed up with that big police dog today. You're one gutsy lady."

I smiled as though flattered. He'd meant *old* lady. I put the nozzle in the gas tank and slipped my credit card into the slot.

"You ready to have that work done on your house?"

I didn't want to get into that. "Not while it's serving as a doghouse."

He grinned. "Gotta keep that mean dog away from all Mrs. Keyser's antiques."

I nodded.

He went back to his hose. "Enjoy the beautiful day."

"You, too." I topped off the tank—for less than half of what I paid in Vienna—and got into the car. Go home and stew or try to ease the tension? We'd be on a busy state highway, and the mall would be full of people. I overrode my unease. "Let's go shopping."

"And singing," Connie added. "Maybe we can still

harmonize. Let's try something from the sixties. Remember 'Downtown'?"

"Petula Clark sang it," Annalynn said.

"Start us off, Connie." I pulled into the street. No one followed us. I watched constantly, but all was clear as we went onto 63 and into our imitation of the Supremes' "Stop! In the Name of Love." When we finished the song, the only vehicle behind us was a do-it-yourself moving truck. Ahead was a Ford pickup loaded with brush. Not wanting to risk being hit by an errant branch, I passed it.

Ahead both lanes were clear. A black Nissan sports car burning oil waited on a country road. It pulled out behind the pickup.

Annalynn had relaxed. "What was that song by the Temptations that we liked?"

Connie began to name songs.

The pickup turned off, and only the Nissan remained in sight on the long downhill behind us. It accelerated.

I was going seventy-five. I moved up to eighty, but the car continued to close the distance. "Annalynn, get your gun and my spare magazine out." I accelerated to eighty-five as I started up a long hill. The Nissan narrowed the gap.

A puff of dust flew up in the right shoulder. "Connie, get down! Annalynn, recline your seat until you can barely see out. Then get my phone and hit one."

Ninety-five, and the Nissan was closing. It had to be souped up to come up the hill that fast. A bullet whacked the back of the car.

Annalynn gasped. "Stuart. It's Annalynn. We're under fire north of Moberly. Notify the Highway Patrol."

I braked lightly and zigzagged between lanes. We flew over the top of the hill onto a flat stretch with a curve all too close. "Hold on tight! I'm going to do a bootlegger's turn." I lowered my window. "Be ready to shoot."

I yanked on the emergency brake with my right hand and spun the steering wheel to my left with every ounce of strength in my left arm. The back end of the car slid around and the car rocked like a rowboat at sea, banging my head against the door. I released the hand brake and grabbed the steering wheel to control the car.

Annalynn fired two shots through her open window as I pulled my gun from my holster. With no time to aim, I fired into the windshield of the oncoming car.

The Nissan fishtailed toward us.

Accelerating onto the shoulder to get out of the way, I fired my last bullet into the Nissan as it careened by.

"We got them! We got them!" Annalynn screamed.

I took a sharp left back onto the highway to follow the Nissan, but it flew off the right shoulder over a shallow ditch and into neat rows of young corn. It mowed down sprouts for some fifty yards before the muddy ground brought it to a halt.

I pulled onto the shoulder. "I need my spare magazine."

"Here." Annalynn put her hand down the front of her blouse and pulled it out. "You're bleeding!"

I slammed the loaded magazine into place. "Out! Out! Get behind the car. The engine block is our best protection." I half fell out of the car.

Connie burst out the back door and duckwalked around me to sit down with her back against the front tire.

Annalynn crawled across the seat and out of the car. "Do you think they're dead?"

"I don't know." I peeked over the hood. "I'm going to shoot the first thing that moves."

Annalynn crouched by Connie. "I have only two or three shots left. Should I put in my other magazine?"

"Yes, I have only eight rounds," I said.

Fingers appeared on the edge of the Nissan driver's windowless door. I fired, and a man screamed and jerked his hand inside.

Annalynn tugged on my blouse tail. "Get down!"

I ducked down but kept the car in sight. "I have to see to aim!"

"I'm sure we hit them both. Don't shoot anymore unless you see a gun," Annalynn ordered. "I'm an officer of the law. I should give them a chance to surrender."

Unconcerned with such niceties, I searched for another target.

Annalynn shouted, "This is Sheriff Keyser. You're under arrest. Throw out your weapons immediately."

"Help me," a man screamed. "Help me! I'm shot! I'm dying!"

"What a shame," I yelled. "We're so sorry. Now throw out your weapons and come out of the car with your hands up."

"I can't find it! Help me! For God's sake, help me!"

The moving truck rolled to a stop behind us.

I waved it on with my gun. "Move on! Get out of the line of fire!"

The driver took off with squealing tires as a flashing light appeared at the top of the distant hill.

My head hurt. I wanted this over. "Throw out your guns or we'll turn you into sieves."

A pistol dropped beside the Nissan. "I can't move. I think Binkie's dead."

"Binkie?" Connie slapped her cheeks and groaned.

"Some guy called Binkie tried to kill us? The crooks in *Guys and Dolls* had scarier names than that."

I remembered a newspaper story: "He was arrested for drug possession last year."

"There's our meth connection," Annalynn shouted to be heard over the advancing sirens. "Phoenix, we need these men alive for questioning."

A wave of dizziness clouded my vision. My head pounded. My legs turned to jelly. I had to sit down.

Annalynn grabbed me. "Phoenix? Phoenix? Phoenix!"

TWENTY-EIGHT

MY KNEES WOULDN'T hold me up, but I held on to consciousness and the hood. "I just need to sit a minute." I slid to the ground and put my head on my knees. My hand quickly found a lump above my left ear. My hair was sticky with blood. "Work with the troopers, Annalynn." I closed my eyes to concentrate on clearing my head as the first car pulled around us and the second blocked the road behind us. I kept my head down as the troopers came running. Good time to look out of it. I didn't want to explain how I knew to make that bootlegger's turn and come out of it shooting.

"She's hurt. Please get her to the median out of the line of fire," Annalynn said.

Arms lifted me, carried me across the road, and deposited me on the ground.

Connie knelt over me. "Are you in a lot of pain?" Her voice trembled.

"I'm okay," I whispered, opening my eyes. "This is Annalynn's moment. Tell everyone how she shot those guys after they shot at us."

Connie pulled back. "Why are you suddenly so modest?"

"Goddammit, Connie. Just do it. For Annalynn." I closed my eyes and listened to the troopers shout at the suspects and go into the field after one cried for help.

"Annalynn's covering them," Connie whispered. "You'd think she knows what's she's doing."

Excellent. The better Annalynn looked, the fewer questions I would have to answer. I relaxed. "They're sure those guys won't resist, or they wouldn't go out there."

A minute or two later Annalynn, her face taut, knelt by me. "Binkie is dead, and we hit the driver at least twice. It looks like they had only one gun, a twenty-two pistol." She handed me my Glock. "How bad is it? Tell me the truth."

"My head's throbbing, but the wooziness has passed." I shifted. "My left shoulder is a little stiff. I'll bet I've got a dandy bruise, but I don't need a doctor."

"Don't be an idiot," Connie said. "You—"

Annalynn cut her off. "You swear?"

"I swear. Be sure to tell the troopers and Stuart how *we* made the one-eighty turn and you emptied *your* magazine. You can give them the details later."

Annalynn opened her purse and pulled out her phone. "I'm calling Jim. Connie, please call Stuart."

Connie looked around. "He's probably still holding on. Where's Phoenix's phone?"

"Somewhere in the car." Annalynn flashed her star at a slow moving car in the northbound lanes and motioned for the driver to keep going.

Connie ducked down to scoot across the lanes to the Mercedes. She picked the phone up off the floor. "Stuart?" Pause. "We're all bruised, but Phoenix is the only one bleeding." Pause. "One's dead. An addict called Binkie." Pause. "See you soon."

She pranced over to me. "He's on the way to take you home."

It's hard to evade questions in a car. "He'll take *us* home. You can tell him, preferably at great length, that you didn't see anything because you were ducking bullets in the backseat."

Connie pouted. "Don't be so bossy. You still don't play well with others." She held out a supplicatory hand. "Sorry, Phoenix. I'm not used to getting shot at. You can't be comfortable on that damp ground. Let me help you into the car."

Didn't play well with others? I'd always had lots of friends as a kid. Well, enough. I'd always had Annalynn. The wet ground was chilling me. I raised myself on one elbow.

Connie extended both hands.

I took one and used my other hand to push myself up. My legs worked—barely. I took Connie's arm to walk to the car and ease myself into the backseat.

An ambulance stopped in the northbound lanes, and Connie directed the paramedics toward the field.

I covered my bloody hair with my hand until they had rushed by. Then I leaned back in the seat to think. Obviously the car had been waiting for us. Unfortunately everybody in town knew we were going to be on this road. Probably the drug traffickers' local chief had sent out Binkie and whoever. But with a .22. It could be deadly close-up, but no pro would carry one for a car chase.

The car door opened. Paws cut into my leg and a tongue licked my chin and my cheek. Achilles sniffed my hair.

I hugged him, partly to keep him away from my face and hair and partly because I needed to hug someone.

"I'm so sorry," Stuart said, pulling Achilles off me. "You had a better handle on this than any of us. I would've sworn they wouldn't come after you again." He bent for a close-up look. "Have the medics checked you?"

"No need," I assured him. "It's a shallow cut. It's stopped bleeding."

He brushed back my hair. "You've got a good-sized bump. You should be checked for a concussion." He strode away.

Achilles came at me again.

"Down, boy." I swung my legs out of the car and began the stroking/scratching ritual, trying to keep my face out of the reach of his tongue.

Stuart escorted a young woman with café-au-lait skin to the car and pulled Achilles away.

She inspected my bump and cut, shone a light in my eyes, and checked my blood pressure. "You look fine, but stay awake at least two hours. If you feel faint or have any pain, get to a doctor immediately. And take it easy for a day or two." She hurried away.

"They're having trouble getting the driver out of the car," Stuart said, "but they've got him stabilized. They found the finger someone shot off."

Excellent shooting at that distance. "Take Achilles down there and see if he recognizes them. Please."

"Of course. Come on, boy."

"Go with Stuart," I said firmly as Achilles pulled back. "Go." I picked up a water bottle from the floor of the car, took a sip, and then washed my face. "Go. I'll stay here."

"Annalynn has ruined her Ferragamo pumps," Connie reported.

My head throbbing, I leaned back and closed my eyes. At least I had a good excuse not to answer questions.

Connie touched my arm. "Achilles looks interested, but he's not going postal. He's bringing Stuart back."

Damn. The men in the car hadn't been at the motel. The guy who'd sent them would try again. But why had he sent two idiots armed with a .22? Did he send them to succeed or to fail?

Stuart interrupted my speculation. "I've cleaned the mud off his paws. Let's go."

Achilles at my side, I walked to the backseat of Stuart's car. Achilles sprawled across my lap as soon as I got in and wouldn't get off until the car was moving. Then he wriggled around until his head was in my lap.

Stuart looked at me in the rearview mirror before pulling out. "The driver is from Huntsville. He has a record."

I digested this. Huntsville was somewhere around Moberly, not in Vandiver County. "Did he say why they were shooting at us?"

"They wanted to scare off the undercover agent so they could get their supply of crystal meth. They were supposed to pick it up from a trash can in Macon tonight."

I sighed. "That's so stupid, it must be true."

Stuart turned left at a cut-through to reach the northbound lane and head back to Laycock. "He'll remember more when they slap an attempted-murder charge on him."

"I doubt it. These two were expendable know-nothings. The boss calculated they might get lucky and kill us, and if they got caught, they'd be blamed for Boom's death."

Stuart didn't say anything for several seconds. "You've been right so far."

Connie twisted around in the seat, her brow wrinkled with worry. "If these two didn't kill Boom and Maria Lopez, who did?"

"I don't know," I said. "Any ideas, Stuart?"

He blew his horn and flashed his badge at gawkers'

slow-moving cars, pulled around them on the shoulder, and stepped on the accelerator. "I know little more than you do. Maybe less. We're almost certain it's a gang of crystal-meth drug traffickers. Pancho's part of the operation, but these two—it's too early to say. We're working twenty-four/seven to track Pancho's movements and identify his associates."

"I'm interested in only one associate, the local honcho," I declared. "The road the Nissan pulled out of is coming up on the left."

Stuart slowed, turned into a cut-through, and stopped. He called in to report the road and pulled back onto 63. "Tell me exactly what happened when you left the house."

"Of course," Connie said. "Let's see. We met Richard Rothway. He said..."

I tuned out Connie's detailed recital and thought of the people who knew about the shopping trip: Trudy and her visitors, the sheriff's staff, Dickie, Sean, possibly his aunt, and unknown others.

"Phoenix!" Stuart said urgently. "Are you with us?"

"Sorry. I was thinking. Did you ask me something?"

"Yes. Who fired the shots into the Nissan?"

No lies. Too easy to catch. "Annalynn fired first. She was amazingly coolheaded."

Stuart nodded. "How many shots did you fire?"

"Nine. My magazine plus one in the chamber."

He said nothing for a moment. "Ballistics will show whose bullets hit."

I shrugged, making my shoulder ache. "It seems an awful waste of taxpayers' money. After all, it was obviously a clean shoot."

His eyes met mine in the rearview mirror. "No one's questioning that."

I stroked Achilles. "Did you find anything at the meth sites?"

"We barely got started. We'll take Achilles out later. As soon as you feel well enough, I want to go over this whole case with you." His voice held new respect.

I made a point: "*The sheriff* and I will be glad to do that."

"Of course." He glanced at Connie. "I need to ask you both about Boom."

I yawned. Had he discovered Boom's unexplained income? "I never knew him well." Annalynn had loved him. That's all I'd needed to know. Until now.

"He was an articulate jock," Connie said, speaking slowly rather than at her usual quick pace. "He could drink beer and play pool at Harry's Hideaway in his jeans and then put on a tux and comment on the wine at a charity ball. I'm so ashamed"—her voice broke—"that I thought he cheated on Annalynn."

Stuart turned onto the road leading to Laycock. "By the way, Phoenix, where were you the night Boom died?"

In a Cumberland, Maryland, motel feeling nervous enough to register as Rose Dowd, a well-established alias. "Some little B and B in western Maryland, or maybe it was eastern West Virginia. I didn't drive far that first day."

"She was so weak it took her five days to get here," Connie added.

"And yet today she made a bootlegger's turn and came out of it shooting. That was incredible! Where did you learn to do that, Phoenix?"

He'd read the skid marks. "A defensive-driving course for Americans working for international businesses. Ironic that I'd have to use that trick in Missouri."

"Really?" Connie's eyes widened. "I thought you were just a bad driver."

I gave her a silent cheer.

Her phone rang. "Hello." Pause. "She's no more incoherent than usual." She handed me the phone. "It's Annalynn."

I smiled to warm my voice. "I'm fine. What's happening?"

"George called. A woman who lives near where the driver ditched Elena's car saw an old Nissan parked there last night. George is convinced these two did the hit-and-run and killed Boom. Should I let him, and the public, think that?"

Great possibilities. Annalynn had always been sharp. "What's your reasoning?"

"For one thing, the killer will think he got away with it and stop trying to kill you. For another, the DEA will have time to track down the interstate drug traffickers while we look for the local connection."

"Go for it. I'll tell Connie and Stuart. What about the press?"

"Watch my press conference at four o'clock. What can I say about you?"

"Preferably nothing." I thought a moment. An idea began to form. "Try to drop in that Achilles has the biggest doghouse in town. I'll explain later."

"I'll try." She cleared her throat. "We'll get the monster behind this, won't we?"

"Yes, Annalynn. We'll get him."

TWENTY-NINE

WE PICKED UP lunch at the new McDonald's before going to Annalynn's house. I busied Achilles with a hamburger, but Stuart proved harder to distract. He peppered me with questions about my job in Vienna.

I had worked hard to keep professional jargon, British expressions, and acronyms out of my public vocabulary. Finally I responded with a stream of economic terms that left Stuart blinking.

Connie threw up her hands. "What language is that?"

His phone rang, and he went into the hall.

Connie leaned across the table to whisper, "You didn't learn to make that turn in some one-day course."

I leaned toward her. "It was a two-day course."

She curled her lip. "Smart ass." She raised her eyes to look behind me. "What do we do while the DEA does its thing?"

"Hole up in the castle," Stuart said. "Do you have another gun, Phoenix?"

"No. The only other gun in the house is an antique revolver. Why?"

"Because you and Annalynn have to turn in your guns for testing. Considering what's happened, you probably want another weapon."

An understatement. "I'd prefer another Glock 27."

"I'll see what I can do."

"I'd like one, too, please," Connie said. She acted like she was asking him to bring her a drink from the bar.

I warned Stuart off with a raised hand. "No, no. People who don't know how to use guns tend to shoot their friends."

Connie glared at me. "If you can teach Annalynn to shoot in one afternoon, you can teach me." She ducked her head and looked up at Stuart through her long eyelashes. "I shouldn't be defenseless."

"You're right," Stuart said, "but Phoenix is right, too."

Annoyed, I said, "You say 'You're right' to everyone."

"Mostly to you." He leaned over and kissed me on the cheek. "Down to business. We now know Bill called Boom's cell phone at eleven p.m. Monday. He was on the line only a few seconds."

"Hmm." I thought a moment. "That's six minutes after the screams, which Boom didn't hear immediately. The killers probably wanted to make sure Boom came." He'd been a fool to go alone. My head resumed throbbing. "I'm going to clean up." I went upstairs and closed the bedroom door before Achilles could slip in behind me.

The bathroom mirror showed me the cut was inconsequential. The throbbing came from an inch-long lump above my left ear. I took care not to touch it as I pulled off my grimy top. A palm-sized bruise adorned my left shoulder.

Feeling energized, I told my reflection, "I was damned good out there today."

Under the shower, I stopped congratulating myself. I'd put us at risk by ignoring my qualms about leaving Laycock. The gun battle had given me a rush, but I'd lost our best information source with that fatal shot. Hold it: no choice, no regrets.

I let warm water run onto my matted hair, but some blood clung. When I massaged shampoo into the sticky stuff, the cut stung and the lump hurt like hell. The magic pill called. I didn't dare answer. I had much bigger problems than these injuries. I couldn't wait for these guys to try again. I had to go after them.

Nice sentiment. No strategy. So come up with one.

Follow the meth. Buyers could lead us to the killers. Where would you go to hear who was selling? I had no idea. Where would Binkie have hung out? A pool hall? That den of iniquity had probably disappeared with typewriters. A park? The town had only two, and good neighborhoods surrounded both. Neighbors would call the police. A bar? People kept mentioning Harry's Hideaway. At least there I'd hear the reaction to the shoot-out and the investigation. Now to figure out how to slip away.

"Phoenix," Connie called through the door, "it's almost four. Are you okay?"

Achilles whined.

I reached for a towel. "I'll be out in a couple of minutes."

"I put one of Annalynn's fleece tops on the bed for you."

"I have broader shoulders and a bigger bra. Remember?"

"Just put it on. And a little makeup wouldn't hurt."

No makeup could compensate for a head of wet hair. Besides, I wanted to look like I needed an early night. A glance in the mirror told me I did.

The light-green fleece felt wonderful against my skin, and it was just snug enough to be interesting. I could still draw glances, at least from the post-forty contingent. I joined Connie and Stuart, sitting down between them on the huge couch where they were watching KTVO.

A young man in a blue blazer, white shirt, and red

tie faced a camera in the sheriff department's parking lot. "This is Arlen Jayson in Laycock, Missouri. Acting Sheriff Annalynn Keyser is about to announce developments in the investigation into the death of her late husband, Vandiver County Sheriff Boom Keyser."

The camera focused on Annalynn, face grim but composed, walking from the back door of the sheriff's department to a lectern holding three microphones. She wore the light-brown uniform with the shiny star over her heart. She held no notes.

"Good afternoon. I'm Acting Sheriff Annalynn Carr Keyser. At noon today I was traveling south on Highway 63 in my personal car. A black Nissan coupe approached at a high speed and the passenger began firing. Two bullets hit my car."

She lowered her head a moment and then gazed into the camera. "My deputy and I returned fire, wounding the driver and killing the passenger. Both have convictions for drug possession. We are investigating their possible connection to meth traffickers operating in northern Missouri and southern Iowa. We believe this group was responsible for the deaths of Frederick Keyser and Maria Lopez. I can't give you a full report of our ongoing investigation, but I'll take a few questions."

The KTVO reporter stepped forward. "Can you tell us the names of the two men who fired at you?"

"The deceased is Rudolph Andrews, twenty-seven, of LaPlata. We will release the other name after we've notified his relatives of his injuries."

"Ronnie Walters, KOMU-TV," an unseen woman said. "Who was the deputy, and which of you fired the fatal bullet?"

Annalynn hesitated a nanosecond. "We don't know.

When someone shoots at you, you fire back as fast as you can, but you have no idea what you hit."

She'd ignored the first question. The camera moved back to show Annalynn and three reporters.

"Vernon Kann, *Laycock Daily Advertiser,*" a silver-haired man said. "Bystanders reported that a man in street clothes took a big dog to the wrecked car. Who was the man, and why did he do that?"

"They saw a DEA agent and a dog belonging to a missing DEA agent. This dog has a keen sense of smell." Annalynn's lips hinted at a smile. "Dog lovers needn't worry. He's being well cared for in the biggest doghouse in town." She looked left. "Deputy Jim Falstaff has photos of the missing agent, William Graksi, for the press. We ask citizens to call Deputy Falstaff if you have seen Agent Graksi in the last two weeks."

Jim held up the photo of Graksi with Achilles.

"Thank you," Annalynn said. "We appreciate the media's assistance."

The KTVO reporter's face filled the screen. "We'll have more of this breaking story on News Three at six o'clock."

Connie turned off the television. "You'd think she'd been briefing the press for years. And that color isn't as bad for her as I thought."

"She was very cagey," Stuart said. "She didn't mention either of your names. Most people will assume Jim Falstaff was driving the car."

"She was protecting us." I gripped his knee as a chill ran through me. "People know you're the DEA agent with the dog. Your mother needs protection."

"Relax. I already sent her and my sister's family to stay in my place until this is over." He studied me. "You look fine, but I'll stay here if you want. The handler can take Achilles without me."

"That's not necessary," I assured him. Much easier to sneak out if he and Achilles weren't there. "But I must have a gun." And another car. That crumpled rear bumper made my car much too easy to identify.

"I'll make some calls." He rose and went out onto the porch.

The phone rang, and I hurried to the hall to answer it. "Keyser residence."

"Phoenix, we have to turn in our guns for testing," Annalynn said. "Do you want me to get you a department service weapon?"

"Yes, please." Never hurts to have a spare. "And I'm going to need to rent a car when I put mine in the shop. Is there a Hertz or Avis in town?"

"No, but you won't need a car. See you soon."

Stuart came back inside. "The handler wants to get going. Checking all those isolated meth labs could take us hours. I know you're a crack shot, but I don't like leaving you here alone."

"I'd be insulted if you took anyone off the case to guard me."

He frowned. "I guess you and Annalynn have proved you can handle yourselves, but I don't like it." He sighed. "Let's go, Achilles."

The dog didn't move, so I walked to Stuart's car and opened the back door. Achilles hopped in. Guilt flooded me as I closed the door.

Stuart jumped into the driver's seat and turned on the motor.

Achilles began to howl as I walked toward Annalynn's house.

I turned around to wave, and to check the street once

more. Down the block two boys about eight rode skateboards on a driveway. Across the street two houses down an older man dug in a flowerbed. I went inside and set the alarm.

Connie blocked my way, her hands on her hips and her arms akimbo. "Phoenix, you drive like a race car driver, you shoot like a cop, and you carry cash like a lobbyist. What have you really been doing the last thirty years?"

I laughed. "Bond. Jane Bond." I put on my earnest face. "When I first went abroad, being an American gave you a sense of security. Now companies give executives self-defense courses and tell them to use different routes to work every day."

"And I thought working for a financial consulting firm would be a dull job." Connie stepped aside and ran her right hand through her curls. "I'm really worried about Annalynn. She's put herself out there as the target. I know she's protecting us, but I'm afraid she doesn't care what happens to her."

I blinked, surprised and disturbed. "God, I hope not." I had to end this. Could I trust Connie to help me get out of the house? No choice. I walked to the window seat and motioned for her to join me, something she'd seen Annalynn do many times. "For Annalynn's sake, I can't wait around for the killers to make the next move."

"But what can *we* do?" Connie perched on the edge of the seat as I took my usual cross-legged position.

"*We* need to find out more about the meth scene, the kind of information people don't share with the police."

"Fat chance we have of finding anyone who'll tell us anything."

I wagged a finger at her. "Don't give up so fast. You know the town better than I do. Where do potential addicts congregate? They're not all teenagers, from what I read." The sun shining through the window was uncomfortably warm. I moved into the shade. "The paramedic told me to stay awake for two hours. I'm out of the woods, so I'm going to rest until Annalynn gets back. Think about it."

I went upstairs and stretched out on my bed to plan the evening. I awoke as someone came into the room. A whiff of Chanel 5 identified Annalynn.

"Hi," I said. My shoulder had stiffened. "The DEA made any progress?"

"Some." She walked to the other side of the bed and stretched out beside me. "The owner of Sweet Nights Motel recognized Pancho. He's stayed there several times, and he always paid cash. He wasn't registered that night, but it's possible he saw Bill Graksi there and didn't register." She rubbed her temples with the tips of her fingers. "Credit-card records show he's bought gas in Columbia twice a month for almost a year."

"Traveling I-70, no doubt. Have they checked other motels in the area that night?"

Connie leaned against the door frame, silent for once.

"I've asked sheriffs in the surrounding counties to do that. And we released his photo to the press." Annalynn closed her eyes. "We're making a map of abandoned buildings where someone might have taken Bill Graksi. Do you think he's alive?"

I'd avoided thinking about that. "No. I'd guess that they staged a one-car accident in some isolated place the same night they shot Achilles."

Annalynn opened her eyes. "Why a car accident?"

"His car was too hot to sell, and so was Achilles. A car accident is easy to fake, and they would want his 'accidental' death to be distant in time and place from Boom's so no one would connect them."

"I'll put out the word to check any wrecked or abandoned cars." She closed her eyes again. "Why do you suppose they're after you?"

Connie stepped into the room. "They think she's *P. D.* Smith, DEA or FBI agent, and knows something that could identify them."

That made sense, except for one thing: "What could I know?"

Annalynn rubbed her eyes. "Whatever Boom knew. You scared Dickie. Maybe he's been laundering drug money, and Boom found out."

Connie paced, arms folded, head down. "I think you're the target, Annalynn, not Phoenix. They're afraid you'll find Boom's notes."

Annalynn shook her head. "Any notes must have been on that missing cell phone. We've looked everywhere else."

"Even if Boom didn't hide evidence, the killers must be afraid he did," I pointed out. "That stunt today shows they're pretty desperate. Annalynn, you need more protection than Jim can give you."

"I won't be going anywhere without a DEA agent, and Stuart will spend the night here." Annalynn stood up and rubbed the back of her neck. "I'm taking your gun back with me, Phoenix. I put a department service weapon in the den."

"You have to eat before you go back, Annalynn," Connie said as she would to an adored child.

Annalynn nodded. "See what you can find in the refrigerator, please. I'll be down in a minute." She went into her bedroom.

I followed Connie downstairs but turned left to the

den to check the gun. Then I went online to rent a car to drive to Harry's Hideaway. No rental car companies in Laycock. Hotwiring a car was risky, but I might have to do it.

I joined Annalynn and Connie in the dining room.

Connie ladled vegetable soup into three bowls. "I need to go home for a couple of hours to get clothes and water my plants. Phoenix and her Glock can go with me."

"No," Annalynn said sharply. She took a deep breath. "I'm sorry. Of course you need to go home. A deputy is coming to watch the house at eight. He'll take you both over and guard you there."

Going to Connie's house put a serious crimp in my evening. "I have the alarm system and a gun. I'll stay here."

"You can play my grand," Connie said. "Come on, Phoenix. Be reasonable. It's not as though you have anything better to do." She nudged my foot under the table.

"Thanks for pointing that out." I glanced at Annalynn. She wore her calm public face, but tension radiated from her. "Fine, I'll go. I really miss my Steinway."

Annalynn took a bite of bread. She chewed on it forever.

"I'd like a glass of wine," Connie said. "Shall I pour one for you, Annalynn?"

"No, thanks. I can't drink before I go on duty. Excuse me." Annalynn picked up her bowl and went to the kitchen. "I'll take this to the office with me."

I followed her. "I'm so proud of you. You're handling this like a real pro."

Annalynn held her napkin to her mouth and spat out the bread. "My throat is so tight I can't swallow."

I enveloped her in a hug. "No one would guess it. Hang on a little longer. We're close now."

Annalynn clung to me for a moment. "Do you really believe that?"

"Yes. With the DEA and every police officer for miles working on it, the pieces of the puzzle will come together soon. I'm sure of it."

Annalynn drew back, a forced smile on her lips. "I can make it through another day. As long as I know you and Connie are safe." She reached into the cabinet for a plastic container. "I know I have to eat. And tonight I *have to* sleep. Whiskey doesn't work. Maybe I'll take half of one of those sleeping pills."

"Work until you're exhausted," I advised. The later the better. "The DEA will have a lot of information flowing in tonight."

Annalynn poured her soup into the container. "I'll be home around eleven. Promise me you two will be careful."

"We will." I walked Annalynn to the door and sat down to eat the soup. It had to fuel a long evening.

"I thought she was going to lose it," Connie said. "She's always been so self-disciplined, so controlled, but she's on the brink of the screaming meemies."

I buttered some bread and waited.

"Aren't you going to ask me what I've planned for our evening's entertainment?"

Wanting to scream that this wasn't a game, I said, "Please tell me."

"You remember how I used to climb out my bedroom window?"

I nodded.

"That's how we'll get out. We'll sneak back here and pick up my car."

My hopes for escape rose. "Where are we going?"

"Harry's Hideaway. It's really the only action around. Everybody goes there, and everybody will be talking about what happened today and about Boom."

I took a bite of bread. Connie had reached the same conclusion I had, but taking along an amateur was too risky. "Everyone knows you. They're not going to talk in front of Annalynn's friend."

Connie grinned. "But they'll talk to an old woman and her daughter from out of town. You fooled Mrs. Roper under bright lights. The Hideaway is almost dark. We can fool anybody."

A cocky novice. Sure disaster. "Performing a scripted role on stage is child's play compared to maintaining a character in a thrown-together disguise. People here don't know me. A simple disguise is all I need. I'll go in alone."

Connie's cheeks flamed. "God! Your ego is XXL! You think you're Superwoman and I'm a never-has-been who can't do anything right. Let me remind you that I'm the one who found out that Maria Lopez had a stalker. I can get those truckers and hustlers who play pool to brag about all the stuff they know."

"Long-distance truckers?" One could have made those coded calls to Boom.

"Sure. Boom played pool with them all the time. Come to think of it, you should wait in the car while *I* work the crowd."

Mend fences fast. "Connie, I'm sorry if I've seemed condescending about this, but I've had quite a bit of experience going to parties to pick up gossip on financial matters. It's a lot like improv. Have you ever done improv?"

"No, but I've prepared for roles by going out for a

day as my character." She frowned. "If I don't go, you don't go."

Stall. "Tell me your plan."

"I'm a country singer and you're my manager. Now, are you going to trust me? Or are you going up to bed early the way you're supposed to?"

I'd survived as a NOC by trusting no one but myself. I trusted Annalynn, and she had put herself out front to protect us. Now I needed Connie. I smiled and extended my hand. "Okay, partner, but we have to fill in lots of details, and we can't risk using your yellow VW or my banged-up Camry. Can you borrow a car from someone?"

"Not at this short notice, but I know a used-car dealer who rents clunkers on the side. We could pick it up from that Dairy Queen two blocks from my house."

"Ideal."

She sprang up. "I'll call him."

"Let me do it. We don't want him to have your name."

"You have to pay by credit card, and your name's all over town by now, including that P. D. Smith on your credit card."

I pretended to give that some thought. "I have a foundation credit card I can use." Move on before she thinks too much about that. "Do you have a good wig? And makeup that will work up close?"

"I've got everything we need in my theater stuff. I'll get the phone number."

I finished my soup and was still hungry. "Does Harry's serve food?"

"Great mesquite hamburgers, spicy chicken wings, and yummy steak fries. Here's the dealer's number."

I glanced at it. "I'll call from a cell phone." I hurried

upstairs to get one. To my dismay, Connie came right after me and listened as I dialed.

"Clunkers On Call. Ed Callaway speaking."

Callaway. The insurance man in the diner had been a Callaway. "Hi, there. Am I glad to get you." I raised the pitch and volume of my voice and added a little drawl to it. "My car's broke down and I can't get it fixed until Monday. Have you got anything under twenty-five dollars a day I can get right away?"

"Can you drive a manual?"

"Sweetie, I was changing gears before Yuppies discovered pickups."

He laughed. "In that case I've got a car you can have right now. What's your name and address?"

"Rose B. Dowd, twelve ten Silver Spring Street, Silver Spring, Maryland, two zero nine one zero. I'm out here visiting family."

"And your credit card number?"

I gave him the number from my Dowd card. "The person who told me about Clunkers said I could pick it up at the Dairy Queen. Is that right?"

"I can get it there in about forty-five minutes. Louise, the cashier, will have the papers and the key. Appreciate your business."

I hung up. "We have thirty-five minutes to get our stories straight and plan the disguises. Once we're in your house, we have to move fast."

Connie's eyes glittered with curiosity. "Who *are* you?"

"Rose Dowd, sweetie." I reached into a concealed pocket in my rain jacket. "I do some financial investigations under that name." I handed her the driver's license. "Here's my pitcher." I put my hands on her shoulders. "This is no game. You and I both came up with the same place to go listening tonight. The bad guys may do the same. If either of us slips, we could tip him—her—them off, and they're ready to kill."

Connie didn't blink. "Then you'd better be careful."

THIRTY

I RECOGNIZED THE burly young deputy who shepherded Connie and me as the officer who'd run after the intruder.

"Be sure to close all the curtains, ma'am," he said as Connie and I got out of the car at her house. "And stay away from the windows."

"We'll stay out of sight," I assured him. I scanned the street as Connie unlocked the front door.

Inside, she turned on the light in the den and closed the drapes. "To the closets."

I hurried to Mrs. Diamante's bedroom, virtually untouched a year after her death, and located the brown pants suit and dark-red blouse Connie had suggested. Her mother had been an inch shorter and thirty pounds heavier than I. Just about right. I changed clothes and looked around the room. A knitting bag with needles protruding struck me as a viable weapon. I carried it into Connie's bedroom.

She had put on black jeans and a white suede shirt decorated with red and blue beads. "Annie Oakley's shirt. Perfect for a country singer."

An amateur error. "On stage. Off stage you're too conspicuous, not to mention a great target if we have to run for it. Change your height by dumping your stilettos. Do you have cowboy boots and a black long-sleeved blouse?" Could this work?

"I *never* wear black tops." She sighed. "Okay. That

means I should tonight. My girls gave me a black silk blouse when Mom died." She went to the closet.

"For color, turn a scarf you never wear into a bandanna." That would save making up her neck. "You can take it off to signal trouble."

"Okay, Madame Director, choose one of my stage wigs." She switched blouses, opened a large makeup box on her vanity, and stuffed her blonde curls into a hairnet.

I selected a long brunette wig with bangs and stepped behind Connie to fit it from front to back. "This is a great fit. You won't need any adhesive." I brushed the bangs so that they fell down over the forehead and the sides so that they half covered Connie's cheeks. "Spread on a darker foundation while I find what I need to give you a scar."

She frowned and fussed with the hair. "Fake scars are too obvious close up."

"Not the way I do them. People feel it's rude to notice scars, so they'll avoid looking at yours. You're less likely to be recognized."

Connie watched in wonder as I created an inch-long scar on the left cheek. "You're really good!"

Thinking of no credible explanation for my skill, I said, "What you really need is a nose job."

"I've got a fake gold cap for my left incisor."

"Excellent!" I picked out the makeup I needed. Quality stuff. "God, the way I look tonight I'm not going to have to do much to add fifteen years."

"Wear my big Marian the Librarian glasses. Taking them off can be your signal to get the heck out of there."

My confidence increased as we finished our faces.

"Now your hair," Connie said. "Since you can't stand a wig, I'll give you a central part and spray on gray." She froze. "What if George or somebody else who knows you is there?"

"Cops are great observers. He could be a problem." I contemplated discovery. "If someone recognizes one of us, pretend we got a little drunk and dared each other the way we used to in high school."

"I hope you're a lot better actress now than you were then."

"I manage." I grayed my eyebrows while she grayed my hair. "I need a waist pack for my gun."

Connie found one that matched the red blouse.

We inspected ourselves in the vanity mirror, and we both nodded approval.

I looked at my watch. "It's eight thirty. Let's go."

"I'll put a student's rehearsal tape on the piano while you set the TV to turn on at nine thirty."

That done, I grabbed the knitting bag, opened the bedroom window, and pushed up the screen. I heard nothing outside but the distant thud of a basketball on cement. Bridal wreath bushes blocked my view, and blocked anyone else's view of me swinging my legs out the window and dropping to the ground.

Connie came right after me and lowered the window most of the way. She led me through her dark backyard to an unlit alley. We met no one there or on the sidewalk. As we approached the Dairy Queen, I slowed my pace and rounded my shoulders. Connie put a little extra swing in her walk.

Inside the old square white building, teenagers occupied most of the booths. A teenage girl slumped behind the counter. Her tag identified her as Louise.

"Evenin'," I said. "I'm Rose Dowd. I'm here to pick up a clunker."

"Sure." Louise reached under the counter. "Here's what you gotta sign. I need to see your driver's license."

I handed the girl my license. The photo showed different glasses and hairdo, but the hair in the photo was gray.

Holding the papers close to my eyes, I skimmed the agreement. Stinging me on insurance. "What's this twenty bucks for insurance?"

"You gotta pay it if you want the car." The girl examined her green fingernails.

"He didn't say nothin' about no insurance on the phone," I said, knowing she expected a protest. "Let me talk to your boss."

"It's Saturday night. He's not available. Do you want the car or not?"

I frowned. "You got me over a barrel, but believe me, sweetie, I'll be talking to him about this." I scrawled a signature with my left hand.

The girl gave me a key. "It's the green one with no hub caps out back."

"Thanks, hon," I said. As soon as we were out the door, I added, "Earlene, let me hear your 'Coal Miner's Daughter.'"

Connie had barely finished the song when we pulled into Harry's lot.

"We got an hour," I said in my Rose voice. "Mosey to the door at nine forty-five." The large gravel parking lot was half full of cars and pickups. Three big trucks stood along one side. I cruised the lot until I found a pull-through space that gave me a clear path to the road.

"The dinner crowd's gone," Connie said. "It'll be mostly drinkers and pool players. Jesus! I haven't had so many butterflies since I played Laurey in *Oklahoma!*"

I gritted my teeth. Connie wasn't in character. "You'll do swell, sweetie."

In our childhood, the brick building had housed a small grocery store and a large garage. Three of the four doors to the car bays remained. The fourth, in the middle of the building, had been turned into an entrance with glass double doors.

A young man in a red Harry's Hideaway T-shirt greeted us. "Come on in, ladies. Please seat yourselves. You can order food and any of fifty beers at the bar."

"Well, ain't this something," I said, using curiosity as an excuse for surveying the room. Three lifts for cars served as bases for pool tables. At the one nearest the wall on my left a dozen or so men watched a big man in a green polo shirt polish a cue. Beyond them in a dark corner stood an upright piano.

At the second table eight college-age men and three women mingled, paying little attention to the game.

Straight ahead a wide passageway led to the tables and, beyond them, the bar. I spotted an exit sign to the left of the bar. Over the bar a giant screen displayed a Cardinals game. Three football jerseys enclosed in heavy wood frames hung on one side of the screen, three baseball jerseys on the other.

On my right a dozen or so noisy teenage boys and girls surrounded the third pool table. Most were talking on cell phones. Behind them was an arched doorway with Tequila Junction painted over it. It had swinging doors like the bars in Westerns.

Dickie brushed by me with a hurried "Excuse me" and went to a table where Cary Callaway, my soon-to-be former insurance agent, and two other men sat.

"Let's take that table," I said, pointing to one right behind the banker. "I can see the screen from there."

Connie muttered, "If you say so." Detouring past the older men's pool table, she poked her head between two beefy shoulders to watch a man rack the balls. "You fellows wouldn't mind a girl watching, would you?"

"Anytime, honey," one of the men said. "You can have the front row."

I grabbed her arm. "Earlene, we're here to eat."

She made a face. "Later, guys."

I pulled my chair out from the table so my back was inches away from Dickie's and lowered myself into a chair.

"The whole thing sounds fishy to me," Callaway said. "I think Jim Falstaff shot those guys and Queen Keyser's taking the credit."

"The chief says Annalynn's a good shot," Dickie answered. "But I know she's a lousy driver."

I stared at the blackboard over the bar. "What kind of hamburger is that?"

"Mesquite? That's a wood they use to cook it. Want to split one, Ma?"

"I reckon. You go get it. And a beer."

Connie shook her finger at me. "No more sugar today. You'll have Diet Pepsi."

I heaved a sigh and opened my knitting bag.

Callaway said, "I bet she paid off people to make it look like Boom wasn't cheating on her, that he was a big hero."

A fist thudded on the table. "He was a hero!" Dickie pushed his chair back against mine. "You know how Boom felt about drugs. It makes me sick to my stomach that I ever believed he killed himself."

"I know Boom was your pal," another voice said, "but I'm reserving judgment."

"I won't listen to this," Dickie growled. "You better not let George hear you. He'd toss you into that brick wall." He stormed off.

Connie came back to the table. "You got all the money, Ma. Give me a twenty."

I dug into the waist pack for the cash. "I want it well done, you hear?"

Callaway and his friends left, and a young Hispanic man came to clear their table.

I swiveled in my chair. "I see you got a little bitty stage and a big piano over in the corner. Anybody singin' tonight?"

He looked blank.

"Any music?" I moved my hands as though playing the piano.

He shook his head. "No music. Television."

"Games don't last forever. Is the boss, the *jefe,* here?"

He pointed to a big man with a shaved head at the bar. "That Mr. Harry."

I put my knitting bag on the table and pushed myself up out of the chair. I hesitated as George Brendan, in uniform, strode toward the bar. He nodded toward the end of the bar, and Harry headed that way.

I shambled to within eavesdropping distance.

Harry wiped the bar. "Boom didn't just stop trouble. He drew customers. People like to hang out with a former pro football player."

"You don't have to pay me two hundred dollars. I'll do it for a hundred and fifty."

I gave myself a point for learning where some of Boom's undeclared winnings came from. Obviously Harry—with no waiters—was cheap. Yet he'd paid Boom as a glorified bouncer. And maybe to allow teenagers to play pool in a bar.

Harry gazed out over the room. "I can handle these guys myself. What I might need is someone who can quiet down the Mexicans when they guzzle too much tequila. They liked Boom. Hell, they practically genuflected whenever he walked in." He glanced at the busboy and then at me. "Got a lady waiting to see me. We'll meet in the poker room in fifteen minutes." He motioned for me to come over.

I hesitated a moment to let the deputy turn away. "Evenin'. I'm Rose Dowd. I noticed yuh got a stage. I got a country-western singer that'll pull in a crowd for yuh."

"Sorry, ma'am. We don't book any singers or bands here. I've tried several times, but my customers won't pay a cover charge for entertainers." He studied me. "I take it you're not from around here."

"No, passing through. We heard that Harry's Hideaway is worth a look." I gestured around. "Love what yuh've done with it. How're the acoustics?"

"Real good. I play a little jazz piano on slow nights."

Yikes! He was buying this crap, but backing off now would arouse suspicion. "Then yuh know the business. Could be yuh just haven't found the right attraction. Yuh go to hiring bands, that's a lot of money. A girl singer wouldn't set yuh back so much and would bring in the boys."

He rubbed his chin. "Who's the singer?"

I pointed to Connie, who was sashaying to the table with our hamburger. "Earlene Dowd. She's been singing backup in Nashville, and she's ready to go solo. We come through here three or four times a year. Earlene could do Friday and Saturday nights as we go through."

"What's she sing?"

"Classic country. None of that crossover pop garbage."

He glanced at his watch. "I'm busy for the next half hour. If you want to stick around, I'll listen to her."

I beamed. "Yuh're a man who recognizes opportunity." Unfortunately.

I went back to the table. "I got you an audition, Earlene, in half an hour."

"That's great!" Connie's delight was real. And out of character. She caught herself. "It may be a tough crowd. Everybody's talking about the sheriff who got killed."

"Yuh better sweet-talk them truckers into clapping mighty loud." The odor of mesquite-smoked meat made me salivate. Surely this hamburger wouldn't offend my digestive system. I took a bite. "Best burger I've had in years!" Not a huge compliment. The Viennese had never mastered hamburgers. Nor devil's food cake.

Connie stood up. "I can't eat right before I sing. I'm going to cruise." She bent to wipe a crumb from my jacket and whisper, "Wes just went into Tequila Junction."

She headed for the pool table in full sway.

I cataloged the patrons as I ate. Seven couples and three families were finishing dinner. Four older men nursed drinks on stools at the bar. Most of the men at the adult pool table wore jeans and long-sleeved casual shirts.

The cones of light over the pool tables showed no one with the lean look or the raw blemishes of meth users. Beer seemed the drug of choice. The college group drank beer and soft drinks, and the teenagers had soft drinks and juices.

I picked up my bottle of Diet Pepsi and strolled over to the display wall that separated Tequila Junction from the main room. It honored local high school and community college sports with photos, jerseys, and outdated equipment.

I heard a commotion, and George Brendan appeared in my peripheral vision.

"Goddammit, Sean!" He clutched his nephew's upper left arm. "If I ever hear you say anything like that about Boom again, I'll knock some sense into you. I mean it!"

Sean jerked away. "You're a fool! He was a dirty old man infatuated with a cold bitch. I'm ready to put on the gloves whenever you are." He strode back to the pool table.

I kept my head down until Brendan stomped away. I slipped through the swinging doors into a small, dark bar.

Not one table held a woman or a blond man. I eased into a chair by the door and put my bottle on a round pressed-wood table. Most of the men wore flannel shirts over T-shirts, and all focused on a soccer game on a giant TV mounted on the far wall. In spite of the bar's nickname, everyone was drinking beer, mostly Tecate or Corona. Stranger still, the men were quiet.

The Methodist minister sat with a group that had pushed three tables together, but his companions seemed unaware of him. He spoke to the man on his right but received no reply. After a moment he went to the bar and ordered. With a Tecate in hand, he spoke to two young men at a table in Spanish and received polite but dismissive smiles.

At least one of the men had been in church. I sipped my drink and pretended to watch the screen. The young minister came toward me. I held the bottle in front of my face as though ready for another sip.

"Good evening," he said. "You must be a soccer fan."

"I just came in to get away from the noise of those pool tables," I said. "I never seen such a quiet bunch. Is that a custom with these people?"

"No, they're usually pretty lively." He spoke more to himself than to me. "But at least they're here. Last Saturday night this room was empty."

"How come?"

He sat down across from me. "Fear. The sheriff and a young woman died in a motel room. The *vaqueros* were afraid townspeople would blame the wicked Latina woman, and their community."

The bastard had implied an affair. "So how come they're back?"

"There's a news report he was murdered while conducting a drug investigation. It didn't have anything to do with the undocumenteds."

Hold it! What did undocumenteds have to do with the murders? "You mean all these men are wetbacks?"

He smiled. "I haven't heard that term in a long time. I doubt anyone here tonight lacks—umm—papers."

He assumed I was too ignorant to understand his inferences. "The dead sheriff was investigating illegal aliens?"

He crossed his arms. "No, no, not at all. That's a federal matter. He respected the hard-working immigrants. He went after people who tried to cheat them."

Was this relevant? "What about the new sheriff? Will he protect these people?"

"I really don't know." He picked up his beer and pushed back his chair.

"I heard there's a poker game. Do you know where it is?"

Surprise crossed his face. "They play in a room behind this bar, but it's a private game. Good night."

I waited a minute before returning to the main room. A roar of laughter and a round of backslapping at the collegians' pool table drew my attention. Sean's big-nosed friend was waving his arms in the air and flashing victory signs.

Sean stepped from the mob surrounding the table and bellowed, "Harry, bring a case of beer and a carton of Coke for my victims!" He hoisted a petite brunette, possibly a Hispanic, up onto his shoulder. "And a drink with an umbrella in it for my biggest fan."

She struck a cheerleader's arms-up pose. Then she grabbed his ear and twisted it. He put her down and pushed people away to get back to the pool table.

I strolled back to my table. Connie bent over the adults' pool table as a man pointed to a pocket. No need to worry about her for the time being. These men had probably never seen her before. I glanced at the bar. Harry raised the barrier across it to let Dickie, Brendan, and the insurance man file through and into the back.

Surely they would talk about Boom and what or whom he'd been investigating. That back room must have a window. Closed, it would do me no good, but the only way to know was to find it.

I caught the busboy's eye. "Don't take my Pepsi, please. I'm going to the Ladies'. Where is it?"

He pointed to the rear exit sign.

I went down the hall and into the door labeled Cheerleaders. A middle-aged woman in a dirty white apron stood by the open window smoking a cigarette.

I inhaled deeply. "That smells so good. I haven't been able to sneak a smoke in days." I fumbled in my waist pack and pulled out a bill. "I'll give yuh five dollars for the rest of your pack and some matches."

The woman crushed out her stub on the sink. "I only got about four left. You can buy a pack at the bar."

"But my daughter would see me doing it."

The woman smiled. "I get it. Sure." She pulled a crumpled pack of Marlboros and a matchbook from a breast pocket under her apron.

"Is there somewhere outside to smoke?"

"Go out the door down this hall. You'll find plenty of butts out there." She stuffed the bill in her pants pocket and left.

I checked my appearance. I wouldn't want Dickie or George to see me in a bright light, but no one would ID me in a dim one. I walked my old woman self out the back door. No smokers there, and the only light came from the kitchen windows. I strolled past a reeking garbage bin. The kitchen door was right around the corner. I walked past it and paused just short of a window expelling cigar smoke. I shook a cigarette from the pack and tore a match from the matchbook.

"Let's drink a toast to Boom, the greatest guy I've ever known," Brendan said.

Glasses clinked and voices murmured.

"We've got to decide what to do about the airplane," Harry said. "Annalynn wants to sell Boom's share."

"I'd like to sell my share, too," Brendan said.

"We all miss him, George," Callaway said, "but that's no reason to lose a good thing. Let's buy Boom's share."

"I'm with George," Dickie said. "I'm ready to sell."

"Boom held us together, I guess," Harry said. "He was a great guy, a real man's man, but I never saw him as an investigator. What really happened, George?"

"I don't know." His voice was harsh, intense. "But I'll run down the sonofabitches that killed him if it's the last thing I do." Silence. "We knew him better than anybody. He must've told somebody something. For Christ's sake, think about it!"

"We all have, George," Callaway said. "If he didn't tell you, he sure wouldn't tell us. What did he tell Annalynn?"

Silence.

"He must have told her something," Harry said. "She's the only one who knew he wasn't nailing that woman."

"She couldn't believe he would be unfaithful to *her,*" Dickie sneered. "He didn't tell her lots of things. Phoenix is the one running the show. She's mean as a weasel."

A lovely compliment.

"I've had an offer for the plane," Harry said. "He'll give us what we paid."

"Take it," George said. "Who's the buyer?"

"A condition of the sale is that we don't reveal the buyer's name. We have to agree to that before I can tell you."

"Show of hands," George said. "All in favor of taking the offer?"

"That settles it. We sell," Harry said. "It's the Methodist minister, Wesley Berry."

"He makes less than a teacher," George said. "He's not got that kind of money."

"Yes, he has," Dickie said. "Let's take the money and run. Somebody go get him."

A door opened.

"George is going to have a heart attack if he doesn't calm down," Callaway said.

"It kills him that Boom didn't tell him what he was doing," Dickie said.

The kitchen door slammed.

George Brendan bore down on me.

THIRTY-ONE

I SCRATCHED THE match and lit my cigarette.

Brendan grabbed my wrists in his huge hands. "Who're you? What the hell are you doing out here?"

"Owww! Yuh're hurting me!" I blew smoke in his face and dropped the cigarette, making him jump back. "Since when is it against the law to smoke outdoors?"

"Funny place to smoke," Brendan snarled. "Why were you eavesdropping?"

"What're yuh talkin' about? I just now lit up." Strategy, not strength. I could handle this.

The woman who'd sold me the cigarettes came out the kitchen door. "She's smoking out here so her daughter won't see her."

Harry stuck his head out the window. "Let her go, George. That's Mrs. Dowd from Nashville. She doesn't give a damn about our plane."

Brendan released me. "Let's see your ID."

I'd have bruises to hide tomorrow. Keeping my head down, I handed him my Dowd driver's license.

"This is a Maryland license."

"That's right. I live there. My daughter lives in Nashville."

Harry blew a ring of cigar smoke. "Sorry, Mrs. Dowd. Everybody's pretty uptight right now. Tell your daughter to be ready in ten minutes."

"Thanks. I'll do that." I shuffled back the way I'd

come. Earlene would have to audition now. Bloody hell! Nothing riskier than becoming the center of attention.

Connie stood beside the table holding the knitting bag. Relief crossed her face, quickly replaced by annoyance. "Where have you been?"

I let the cigarette pack fall to the floor. "The toilet."

"You sneaked out for a smoke!"

"Earlene, you go on in five minutes. You want to warm up?"

"No, I been vocalizing a little for the boys. I'll be okay."

I watched a tall man in a Stetson and a petite ash blonde in a rose-colored sweater walk toward us. She looked up at him and laughed, and he put his hand in the small of her back to guide her to a table. This blonde definitely wasn't Neil's daughter.

It didn't hurt the way it had in high school. "Saturday is still date night."

Connie frowned. "What are you talking about?" She glanced at the couple.

Harry came from behind the bar. "Are you ready, ladies?"

Connie extended her hand. "Earlene Dowd. I'll sing 'Coal Miner's Daughter.' I hope you gotta decent sound system."

"Not bad. We use it karaoke nights. I'll introduce you in a couple minutes."

I leaned on Connie's arm as we walked toward the piano. "I wouldn't count on the sound system, Earlene, and this is a noisy bunch. Let me get their attention at the piano before you sing." I lowered my voice. "Stay in your lower range. Think Loretta. And keep the mike in front of your face. If I'm too fast or too slow, signal me with your right hand." I smiled. "Yuh're goin' to knock 'em dead, sweetie."

"Thanks, Ma."

Harry put a floor mike by the piano, turned a blue spotlight on center stage, and stepped into the light with a hand mike.

"Ladies and gentlemen, may I have your attention, please."

"Quiet down," one of the truckers yelled. "We got a special guest."

"Very special," Harry said. "An old friend of mine from Nashville agreed to sing one song for us tonight. Here's Earlene Dowd with 'Coal Miner's Daughter.'"

"Good evenin'," she said. "It's a pleasure to be here tonight to share one of my favorite songs."

I began a soft two-fingered version of "Chopsticks."

"Ma, what are you doin'?"

"Warmin' up." I moved into increasingly complex fortissimo passages. The amount of effort it took me to perform the familiar bit dismayed me.

"Ma! That's enough!"

I worked all the harder.

Connie walked over to the piano and grasped the lid.

I jerked back my hands. "I'm warm now." And so was the audience. I played the introductory chords to "Coal Miner's Daughter." Worried that people who had heard Connie sing at church would recognize her voice, I played a little too loudly. I needn't have worried. Connie's light-opera soprano had gone breathy country.

With the last note, the truckers applauded and yelled, "More! More! More!" Others took it up.

We'd agreed on one song to support our cover story, but she kept taking bows.

Brendan worked his way over to Harry and said something to him.

Harry stepped into the spotlight. "We've had a request for a song to honor our good friend Boom Keyser and his widow, Annalynn. Earlene, would you sing 'Stand by Your Man' for us?"

I relaxed. I'd learned the song in 1992 when Hillary Clinton said she wasn't Tammy Wynette standing by her man. I nodded to Earlene.

"I'd be mighty proud to do that," she said. "Folks were telling me their tragic story tonight. How he died doing his duty and his wife stood by him when no one else would. I'll be singing from the heart."

I'd always regarded the song as demeaning to women, but the words projected loyalty and courage as Connie sang them. When she wailed the final line, tears glistened on her false eyelashes.

For several seconds, the audience was completely silent. Then applause erupted.

Connie stood with her head down for a moment before bowing to acknowledge the applause. She lowered the mike as the applause continued.

Close scrutiny multiplied the odds of discovery. I took off my glasses and rose to show the crowd—and Connie—that we were done.

She waved, and the older pool players surrounded her.

Harry shouldered his way to me. "Let's talk business. What's her fee?"

I had no idea. "First time out, two hundred fifty for Friday, three hundred for Saturday, two forty-minute sets each night." He hadn't flinched. "Plus ten percent of your bar profits from her first set until closing."

"Ten percent of whatever's over the previous week's

take," he extended his hand, "providing you're at the piano making smart remarks."

Take it and get the hell out. "Agreed. I'll send yuh a contract next week." Too professional. "And I figure yuh owe us a little something for tonight."

He grinned. "I can see why you handle the business end." He reached into his back pocket. "Fair's fair." He handed me a fifty-dollar bill.

I palmed it. "I'd appreciate it if you'd get her away from her fans. We got a long drive tonight." I glanced at my watch. Past ten. Annalynn would be frantic if she found out we'd skipped.

Harry bulled his way toward Connie. "Ma says it's time to hit the road, Earlene. Don't worry, fellas. She'll be back in June to do two full shows a night."

"Thanks, guys," Earlene said. "I expect to see y'all here next time."

One of the truckers took her arm and broke a path for her.

"Ma, don't forget your knitting," Earlene said.

"I'll get it," a gray-haired man offered.

I shuffled toward the door, keeping away from the lighted pool tables.

The man with the knitting bag caught up with me outside. "I don't usually come here, but I been pretty lonely since the wife passed. I'm sure glad I came tonight. That was fine music. When will you be back?"

Touched by his words, I smiled at him. "I'm not sure, but Harry will announce it. Any requests?"

He thought a moment. "I'd sure like to hear Earlene sing 'Help Me Make It Through the Night.' "

"I'll put it on the list." I opened the car door. Fooling Brendan had been exhilarating. Fooling a grieving man depressed me. At least I could give him a moment. "I'll look for you then. Good night."

Humming "Stand by Your Man," Connie checked her cell. "Oh, God! Three messages from Annalynn."

"Tell her we'll come home when the program we're watching ends." No one pulled out behind us.

"Can't I just tell her where we are?"

"She'll worry. We'll fill her in when she can see we're safe."

"Hi, Annalynn." Pause. "We're fine. We're watching an old Judy Garland special. It's over at ten thirty. Bye." She hung up. "I don't think she bought it."

"Where can we leave the car?"

"The Bullocks, two houses down from me, are gone this weekend. We could park it in their driveway off the alley tonight."

When we pulled into the relative safety of the Bullocks' drive, adrenaline gave out and exhaustion took over. I wasn't sure I could move.

"All clear." Connie opened her door. "I'll lead the way."

I summoned the energy to follow Connie through the bushes. My wound ached at the thought of sliding across that windowsill. I whispered, "I can't pull myself up."

"Stay here. I'll get a step stool."

Connie opened the window, jumped, and wriggled through the window headfirst. A few seconds later she handed a three-step ladder out the window.

I climbed up and, with Connie's help, sat on the windowsill and swung my legs into the room.

Someone was pounding on the front door.

"Just a sec," Connie called. She jerked off her wig and hairnet and ran her hands through her curls. She flicked on the light on her way out.

"Hide the scar," I said. I closed and locked the window and went into Mrs. Diamante's bedroom to shed the pants suit.

At the front door, Connie said, "Sorry, Deputy, but I've been in the bathroom with Phoenix. She isn't feeling very well. We'll be out in five minutes."

Good girl. I dressed in my own clothes and went into Connie's room to remove the makeup.

She changed clothes at lightning speed. "Use my scarf for your hair."

"Don't forget the tooth," I cautioned, resisting the urge to lie down.

Connie rubbed off her scar. "Oh, Lord! You're turning gray. If you collapse, Annalynn will kill me."

The least of my worries. I tied the scarf over my hair and headed for the door. "Let's go while I can." I checked the street and neighboring yards for any movement before I let Connie step outside. Nothing. We walked to the car. "Sorry for giving you a boring evening, officer."

He said nothing, but he glared at us.

When the car pulled into Annalynn's drive, Stuart opened my door and pulled me out. "Where the hell have you been?" He slammed the car door and pinned me against it with his right arm. He leaned down and whispered, "What have you been up to, Alicia Cramer?"

Scheisse. He'd found the secret pocket in my suitcase and my fake driver's license. I went limp.

THIRTY-TWO

STUART GRABBED MY waist with both hands, and I cried out in genuine anguish.

Annalynn came running down the porch steps. "Is she hurt? Call Dr. Murphy!"

"No doctor," I said. "I just need to lie down."

Stuart picked me up as though I were a child and carried me into the house and up the stairs to my bed.

Annalynn pushed him aside. "Is it your head?" She pushed back the scarf.

"Look at that," Connie said. "She's so sick her hair has turned gray."

Despite the pain, I burst into laughter at the absurdity of her comment.

Connie joined in, flopping facedown on the end of the bed and punching the mattress with both fists as she tried to overcome near hysteria.

An avalanche of pain killed my laughter.

A smile played on Annalynn's lips. "Who did you question this time, Barbara?"

Stuart clapped a hand to his forehead. "Barbara?"

"She wasn't Barbara," Connie choked out between giggles. "May I tell them, Phoenix? Please, please!"

I concealed my pain by making a joke: "Connie and I went cruising tonight."

Stuart didn't laugh. "Explain yourself."

Not smart to joke with a man who'd just found your

fake identity, but I couldn't help grinning. It felt so good to have something to laugh about. "Tell them, Connie."

She sprang off the bed and turned my bedroom into her stage. "Oh, Annalynn! It was one of the best nights of my life. Better than sex—or at least any sex in the last ten years." She twirled around and posed in Earlene's vamp stance. "I was Earlene from Nashville, and she was Ma, my accompanist, and I've never in my life received such an ovation."

Stuart raged over me. "Are you crazy? After two attempts on your life, you went to some sleazy bar to perform?"

I couldn't resist a mock defensive answer: "It wasn't sleazy."

Stuart slapped his forehead again and mouthed obscenities.

Annalynn laughed. "You went to Harry's. What did you find out?"

My laughter vanished. "We worked different parts of the room and haven't had time to talk, but I didn't learn anything major." Something was missing from my room. "Where's Achilles?"

For the first time, Stuart smiled. "Your four-legged admirer fell asleep by his food bowl. He was as exhausted as you *seem* to be."

"As I *am*," I said. "I'll give you the highlights." I selected my facts. "I saw no indications of drug dealing. You need to run a background check on the Reverend Wesley Berry." I held up my hand to forestall questions. "Three reasons. First, the Hispanic patrons would barely speak to him. Second, he knows something about fraudulent papers for illegals."

Annalynn broke in: "The DEA is investigating

whether crystal meth is coming in through Mexican workers at the meatpacking plant. What's number three?"

"Berry is buying the airplane. That money can't have come from his salary."

Connie winced. "Not drug money. I can't believe that."

"We'll run a check on him," Stuart said. "What did you find out, Connie?"

"None of Boom's pool-playing pals knew anything—or so they said—about any crystal-meth operation. One of the truckers said Boom asked him what he heard along his routes, but he had nothing to tell him." She glanced at me. "I heard a lot of talk about the murders and the shoot-out this afternoon. They assumed Jim was the driver." She thought a moment. "I checked out the young crowd, including the teenagers. Nobody looked like they were on meth—no sores, no anorexic bodies. I agree with Phoenix that Harry's isn't a drug center."

Stuart had relaxed. "That's what our people reported. They picked up on the Hispanics' coldness to Berry, too. They're upset because he didn't defend Maria Lopez's honor when she died in that motel room. After all, she volunteered at his church." He beetled his eyebrows at me. "Tell me, hotshot, who were our agents?"

Hell. I hadn't spotted them. I guessed: "A petite brunette flirting with Sean?"

"You're right. She didn't spot either of you. She said the LCC students consider meth users white trash. One said somebody sells it in a fast-food parking lot in Moberly."

Humbling. The young woman had come up with important information. The other agent had to have been someone in Tequila Junction. "Connie, why don't you give them a detailed account of your evening? Stuart may pick up on something that ties in with the DEA agents' reports."

Annalynn rose. "We'll do it downstairs and let you sleep."

Stuart touched my hair. "How are you going to get that gray out?"

"In the shower." My head hurt. My shoulder hurt. My liver hurt. "In the morning." I kicked off my shoes, pulled down the cover, and stretched out fully clothed. "Turn off the light on your way out, please."

Annalynn pulled the sheet up over me. "Call me if you need anything."

I closed my eyes to rest them while I figured out my next move. I opened my eyes as the clock chimed seven. Lying still, I didn't hurt anywhere. I raised my left hand to feel the lump on my head through my lacquered hair. Smaller but still tender.

Achilles lay beside my bed on his blanket. He raised his head.

I reached down to stroke him. I had to be careful. I was getting uncomfortably fond of him. I got up and found clean underwear, jeans, and a blue T-shirt in the closet. Someone had done laundry. Undressing, I saw the bruise Brendan had made on my right wrist. He needed money badly. If he was dealing meth, he'd surely have money. Maybe not enough. I needed to find out whom he and Boom had been meeting, the most likely source of Boom's unexplained income. As I washed the gray out of my hair, I went through half a dozen scenarios of ways to get answers from Brendan. I decided to go with the simplest: Break into his house and go through his files.

When I emerged from the bathroom, Stuart stood in the bedroom door. He held a finger to his lips and motioned for me to follow him.

He led me to Annalynn's computer and turned on the monitor. "Read this while I finish breakfast."

The screen held a PDF of a State Department memo. Heart pounding, I read about the evacuation of American tourist Alicia Cramer, who had been severely wounded when a gunman opened fire in the spice bazaar. The Kurdish vendor, a German tourist, and a Turkish housewife had died. The gunman had escaped.

The evacuation of Alicia Cramer surely had tipped Stuart off that I'd been on a mission. Ironic. For more than twenty years I'd remained undercover so deep that not even people I'd trained with at the Farm knew I was a NOC. Keeping my status secret from other operatives had been critical to my longevity. Over the years I'd helped several out of jams either in disguise or through my personal networks. And now I'd been outed in my hometown. I had to convince Stuart to keep my secret.

I went to the dining room to face him with no idea what to expect.

He met me with two plates filled with blueberry pancakes and bacon. His eyes held mine as we took our places. "In my twenties I worked undercover on six operations. One lasted six months."

So he understood. The butterflies in my stomach folded their wings.

He handed me the maple syrup. "I've never done anything half as stressful or as exhausting. I still have nightmares about some close calls."

Confirm nothing. "I love blueberry pancakes."

He pointed to my wrist with his fork. "How did you get that bruise?"

A good diversion. "Brendan caught me eavesdropping at Harry's. He let the old woman sneaking a smoke go." I took a bite. Delicious. "He's hard up for money."

"With his income and expenses, he should be."

They'd already checked. "How much is he short every month?"

"Does it matter?" He'd gone on the alert.

I shrugged. "The more money people need, the more they'll do to get it." And people would do a lot for a little.

He sliced his pancakes into bite-sized squares. "The Brendans bought as much house as they could afford. Then he bought into the airplane, with all the extra expenses that entailed. And it's taking his twin daughters five years rather than four to finish their degrees. When he sells his share of the airplane, they should be okay. Barely."

Not from what Lois had said. "The down payment on the house must have eaten up their reserve. And I suppose his nephew's apartment and his car insurance cost the Brendans seven to ten thousand dollars a year."

"They don't pay for either, and Lois gets free tuition for him. His buddy told our agent that Sean bought the car with money he inherited. I know you suspect Brendan, but everything indicates he's clean." He leaned close. "What else happened last night?"

"Other than Connie's debut as a country singer, not much." I fast-forwarded through the evening. "Some say Annalynn engineered a cover-up, that Boom wasn't murdered."

He took a bite and chewed much longer than necessary. "You must know that Annalynn, as the wronged wife, topped everyone's suspect list."

He meant she'd been cleared. "Of course. Money should lead us to someone." Could be time for another chat with Dickie. "Have you checked Harry's finances? He runs the bar with minimum outgo, but he doesn't hesitate to spend money if he wants something."

"His brother-in-law is a software engineer. He tipped Harry off to a winner in the nineties. They sold out before the bust, and Harry used part of his killing to convert his dad's building into the bar. We don't think the ice is coming into or going out of there."

The phone rang once.

I scraped two slices of my bacon onto his plate. "Did Achilles seem familiar with any of the meth labs?"

"No, but he certainly knows the odor of meth. Annalynn has compiled a list of isolated labs in the neighboring counties. We'll visit those today."

Quick footsteps sounded on the stairs. Annalynn called, "They've found Bill Graksi in Forest Lake, north of Kirksville." She picked up the hall phone. "Go ahead." A long pause. "Thank you. I'm on my way." She hung up and faced us. "A boater saw the car late yesterday afternoon. It took a while to identify it because the license plates on it were stolen in Oklahoma. The Adair County sheriff said the body has no identification, no jewelry. It has been in the water at least a day."

Stuart opened his cell phone. "I'll notify the team. You can go with us."

"Thank you, but I prefer to go with Jim," Sheriff Keyser said. "Maybe you better bring Achilles. Phoenix, please call George and ask him to coordinate from the office until I get back. You stay with Connie. She insists on directing the choir this morning."

My opportunity for B and E. "I'll see that she gets to church safely."

WE HAD NO guard this morning, so I had Connie drive around the block to check for loiterers before pulling into her driveway to pick up her music.

"Phoenix, what are we going to do with the clunker? We can't leave it in my neighbors' driveway."

I'd been waiting for the question. "I'll drive it to the church and park it nearby." The picks on my key ring would get me into Brendan's house.

Connie cocked her head at me as she let us in her front door. "You're up to something. Spill it."

"I have an errand to run. I'll be back by the end of the service."

Her usual smile disappeared. "I thought you trusted me."

Telling her increased my—and her—risk, but I sensed that my answer would determine our relationship. Besides, she'd notice if I wasn't in the church. "I'll tell you—if you promise to tell *no one.*"

Eyes wide, she crossed her heart. "You're planning something illegal or dangerous."

"Something *necessary,* and during church is the only time I can do it."

She planted her feet as though to withstand my assault. "I'll come with you."

Bloody hell! She was really into this. "Thanks, but I need you at the church to throw people off. And if I'm caught, I need you to swear that I've been acting strangely since that bump on my head."

"I can certainly testify to that." She took her music sheets from the piano bench. "Before I promise anything, tell me what you're going to do."

Gambling that she'd approve, I told the truth: "I'm going to search George Brendan's home. At least I am if Lois is singing in the choir today."

Connie's mouth dropped open. Then she nodded. "She'll be there. I'll ask her to sing my solo. Where should I say you are?"

"I went to the pharmacy to get something for the lump on my head."

She nodded again. "And when do I start worrying about you?"

A natural conspirator. "Ten minutes after church. Stay there. If I don't show up, contact Annalynn and tell her where I went."

Red spots glowed on Connie's cheeks. "Are you going to use a disguise?"

Why not? "I could use a cap and a pair of sunglasses. And thin rubber gloves."

Connie disappeared and returned shortly with a billed yellow cap, a huge pair of sunglasses, and kitchen gloves. "For God's sake, Phoenix, don't take any chances. We've got that gig at Harry's coming up, and I really need the money."

Afraid she was serious, I said nothing. I tucked the cap under my arm and checked the street before we got into Connie's car.

Connie drove into the empty alley, stopping just beyond the driveway where we'd parked the clunker. No smile now. "I'll leave my phone on vibrate."

"Thanks. You be careful, too. Stay in a crowd." I sauntered to the car and got in. Putting on the hat and sunglasses, I drove half a block behind Connie to the church and double-parked until she went inside.

"Hi ho, hi ho, it's off to break in I go," I sang as I headed toward Kent Gardens. I met no one I knew until I turned into the subdivision. Sean's car zoomed out from between the entry pillars. He turned left without glancing my way.

Darned close. I envisioned the Brendans' house. I'd seen no cameras or any other sign of a security system.

I parked the car in the little park and got out to

inspect some wild strawberry vines, searching in vain for berries, wandering back and forth, edging closer and closer to the Brendans' backyard. Detecting no signs of occupants or curious neighbors, I stepped over the low wall and walked across the backyard. Keeping my gun hand free, I took the key ring and the gloves from my pocket. I grasped the doorknob with the gloves and turned it to get the feel of the locks. The door opened.

I froze. Even in a low-crime town like Laycock, would the Brendans be so careless as to leave their door unlocked? Maybe Sean had forgotten to lock up. I evaluated the silence a full minute before slipping inside. To my right was the kitchen. The doors on my left were closed. Using the gloves, I opened doors to a utility room and a closet. Nothing of interest in either. Three steps led up to a landing and more steps to the second floor. I tiptoed up and walked down the hall to the last room on the left where the door stood open. George Brendan's office, my first priority.

A built-in gun case filled with more than a dozen old rifles and shotguns covered one wall. A collector's treasures. No MP5 there.

Near the windows stood a metal computer desk. Floor-to-ceiling closets ran along the back wall. I opened the door to my left. A bathroom connected to the master bedroom—an alternate exit. I opened the other bathroom door and the bedroom door wide enough to slip through and went back into the office.

The computer was an old Dell. An ancient inkjet printer sat on a bottom shelf. I pulled on the gloves and touched a key. The monitor sprang to life. His accounting file. I scrolled through it quickly. Standard monthly bills took everything he earned. Lois's salary barely covered the daughters' education. He had a blank column labeled Moonlighting under income.

He'd already deleted any entries, and I didn't have the software or time to retrieve them. I checked and found the printer was on. Maybe he'd left a paper trail.

I slid back a closet door and opened the top drawer of a four-drawer file cabinet. Tax returns going back five years. In the second drawer hung neatly labeled files. The corner of a sheet of paper peeked out of a file labeled Utilities. I pulled it out. It was a chart with about forty Hispanic names—all but five of them male—on the left and monthly columns for January through June to the right. Through April, four to eight names had x's. I recognized two names: Miguel Paloma, the laborer Wes Berry had recommended, and Jaime Caballo. But who was Caballo? Not Pancho. His name was Jesus Olviera.

A door slammed downstairs.

I stuck the paper in my pocket and closed the file drawer and closet door. Drawing my gun, I crept to the bathroom door and waited to hear where the person was headed. Heavy feet came up the stairs and down the hall past the master bedroom. I ducked through the bathroom into the bedroom as those feet marched into the office.

The chair creaked. "Oh, hell," Brendan said. "I didn't close the file."

Now or never. I slipped into the hall and tiptoed down to the office door.

He swiveled in his chair as I raised the Glock.

"Hands on your head, Brendan."

Eyes bugging, he complied. "What in hell do *you* want?"

If only I knew. "I want to know why you killed Boom Keyser." The relief on his face told me I'd guessed wrong.

"You're nuts! I loved the man like a brother. Annalynn knows that. So does your fucking boyfriend. He's checked me out every which way."

Boyfriend? Stuart. "I know you're dirty, Brendan. I saw you break in with that MP5. What were you after?"

He glowered. "Boom's case notes."

"Don't give me that bullshit! You went to find out when the next rendezvous would be. That's why you took the tape out of the answering machine." Then I remembered where I'd heard of Jaime Caballo. Elena's boyfriend had seen one Jaime Caballo one day and another the next. "All those illegals using other peoples' papers really weren't all that grateful, it seems to me. That few hundred dollars a month won't begin to pay for your lawyer when you're hauled into federal court."

Blood flooded his face. "We helped poor people earn money for their families. What difference did it make that they rotated in and out?" He smirked. "Besides, you can't turn me in without turning in Boom, too. You think Annalynn's going to thank you for that? Anyway, it's over." He shifted his feet to point toward me.

"You try to rush me and you're dead. Face the computer."

He clamped his mouth shut and obeyed.

He wouldn't rush me—not because he feared me, but because he didn't. I'd goofed. I had to shame him into keeping quiet about Boom and about my B and E. "Boom was playing at sheriff, but you're an experienced officer with a reputation for integrity. Why on earth did you take bribes from low-life coyotes?"

"They weren't coyotes," he said, his tone defensive but his face blank.

I jeered, "If they walk like coyotes and they talk like coyotes—"

"You're not telling anybody else, so I'll tell you," he

said, and sneered. "Years ago a village in Mexico raised money for a dozen men to sneak in, get fake work papers, and send back money. The agreement was that they'd come back in a year and pass their fake papers on to twelve others. Some of them got real papers. About three years ago they landed jobs at a meatpacking plant near here." He stopped.

I finished for him. "And not everybody wanted to go back on schedule."

"Right. They had a brawl that almost exposed the whole thing. They asked—someone—to referee the changing of the guard, and he recruited Boom to make sure everybody complied with the contract, and nobody got hurt."

Why would either man facilitate such a scheme? Only one possible answer: "The Reverend Wesley Berry asked you to do it."

Brendan's left eye twitched. "He's a big advocate for the immigrants."

"And why didn't you perform this altruistic service for nothing?"

He tucked in his chin. "Lots of officers moonlight as security guards. You talked to Rothway. You know Boom needed the money bad. Annalynn's an expensive woman."

What crap. My arms ached from holding the gun steady. "What did they say when you met them Tuesday morning?"

"So you knew about that." He grimaced. "They asked where Boom was. They didn't kill him."

I lowered my gun but didn't holster it. "Where's the MP5?"

"Locked up in a safe in the basement." He put out his hands in supplication. "We want the same thing, to find whoever killed Boom. Annalynn thinks you're smarter than God. You got a way to smoke this guy out, I'm in."

Better to have an ally than an enemy. "I have one idea that would work better if you handled it—a special lineup so Achilles can identify the killers."

"A dog ID?" He snorted. "It might work, if we knew who to put in the lineup."

"If nothing else, we can eliminate some suspects. I'll give you my list, and you add to it."

"Okay. Better than doing nothing. I'll get on it." He stood up, a big, powerful man in a crisp uniform. "You've been asking me a lot of questions. I've got one that's been driving me crazy to ask you." His face contorted. He turned away and took a couple of seconds to regain control. "Why in God's name didn't Boom tell me what he was doing? Why didn't he call me instead of going to that damned motel alone?"

I had no answer.

THIRTY-THREE

I PARKED THE clunker on the street and slipped into a back pew as the congregation sang the final hymn. Only half a dozen Hispanics this week. The minister had lost credibility, or the DEA's attention had scared them away.

As soon as the service ended, Connie, still in her choir robe, wormed her way through the dispersing congregation to say, "Call Annalynn while I put my robe away."

Annalynn answered immediately. "Where are you?"

"At the church. I met with George. He's arranging a lineup for Achilles this afternoon. How is he?"

"He's okay. We didn't take him near the body. Hold on a moment." A long silence. "Stuart and I are driving back with Achilles."

"Phoenix," Stuart said, "if you don't stop going out on your own, I'm going to put you in protective custody."

In the background, Annalynn said, "Wrong tactic."

Stuart sighed. "Please, *please* go right back to Annalynn's house with Connie and stay there." He cut the connection.

At least he said please. I waited for Connie, and we walked out together.

The minister greeted her warmly. "The music was particularly lovely today."

He shook hands with me. "Ms. Smith, how are you feeling?"

"Rather rocky. I'm sorry to have come in so late." Push him a little. "I'd hoped to talk to Miguel Paloma."

He waved at a departing car. "Miguel went to his hometown for a funeral. I'll ask him to call you the next time I see him."

Right. He'd probably gone to a meatpacking plant in Nebraska.

Connie suppressed her curiosity until we got into her car. "What did you find out?"

"George Brendan didn't kill Boom. He's agreed to set up a lineup for Achilles."

Connie raised an eyebrow. "I can hardly wait to hear Achilles testify. Besides, you're supposed to take him to Neil's at three today."

"He's fine. His exam can wait a day."

Connie stopped the car half out of the space. "Are you avoiding Neil?"

"Maybe." Being dumped by Neil had been one of the low points of my teenage years. Connie knew that. "I admit I liked it when he seemed interested. I've always had a weakness for tall, handsome, soft-spoken, rugged men." Who didn't? "Seeing him walk in with a date last night hurt my pride a little. I'm over it."

"Good. Neil was always too bland for you. You'd have realized it if you'd dated him another week." She patted my knee. "Stuart's much more your type. I'll bet he's a tiger in bed."

I wouldn't mind testing Connie's theory, but not until my wound healed.

At Annalynn's house, I fixed an omelet and explained the lineup as we ate. "Even if Achilles doesn't identify a killer, the word will go all over town that he can."

"My God! You're using Achilles as bait." She shivered. "That's downright cold."

And necessary. "If you have a better plan, I'll be glad to listen."

Connie cocked her head. "Will you? You never used to listen to anybody. Your way was always the best way."

Damn. I was ready to declare a truce, and she was remembering old battles. "You're talking forty years ago. Teenagers never listen to anyone else."

"Ridiculous. Teenagers are conformists. They listen to everybody but their parents." She rubbed the back of her neck with her right hand. "Annalynn would never have dared take this on without you. You can't let her down. You can't be wrong."

I wished that were true. "Unfortunately, I can."

"I don't believe it. A flash of humility. You must have grown up."

Modesty had never been my best quality, but I'd certainly been humbled in the last two months. I picked up my half-full plate. "I have some work to finish before Annalynn gets back."

"Take it easy, Phoenix," Connie said, her voice gentle. "Don't try to lift more than you can carry. You proved Boom was innocent. Leave it to the professionals to find the killers." She followed me into the kitchen. "Annalynn needs you more as a friend than as a super cop. She's going to lose control and go to pieces soon, and she's going to need both of us to help her put herself back together."

We had a truce after all. "I know, and I really do have work to do." I hurried upstairs to the judge's office to match Brendan's monthly checklist of illegals to Boom's Hi-T-Data income. The number of names checked each month corresponded to Boom's totals if I allowed $250 for each. A pittance, but it added up to trouble.

Brendan had deleted the bribes from his file, but a computer whiz could recover the record. Apparently Boom stuck to pencil and paper. I'd destroy the printout to make sure Stuart didn't latch onto it, but I also needed a coded record. Something quick and easy—say a list of club members using the German equivalents of the Spanish names.

Connie stuck her head in the door. "Annalynn called. They'll be here in ten minutes."

Too soon. I needed help, and I needed to solidify our relationship. "You took Spanish in high school. Will you help me with something *no one* else can see? You don't want to know what it is. Really."

Her eyes sparkled. "Something from George's house. I'm in."

She gave me English equivalents to the Spanish names. I translated them into German and input the list onto my laptop as members of a jazz club. When we finished, I tore Brendan's list into little pieces and flushed it down the toilet.

"They're here," Connie warned. "I'll go down."

I put my laptop in the closet, slipped off my shoes, and stretched out on the bed. My pillow didn't feel right. I reached inside the pillow slip and pulled out my Alicia Cramer driver's license. Stuart had returned it.

A rush of paws sounded on the stairs.

I kept my eyes closed until licks covered my face. "Yuk! Down, Achilles, down." I washed my face and sat down on the bedroom floor to give him a canine massage and inspect his wounds. They were healing nicely, but his right ear still drooped. Probably it always would.

Stuart strolled in. "He's been pining for you all morning."

"He knows he's been orphaned." I wrapped my arms around him. "His whole world has disappeared." As had Annalynn's. And mine. And Connie's.

"He won't leave you again. You'll have to come with us for the lineup."

Annalynn spoke from the doorway: "Do you really think we'll find the killer in this lineup, or is this Step A setting up Step B?"

I shrugged. "It may work. If it doesn't, we'll go to Step B."

Stuart's body tensed. "What's Step B? How many people will it take?"

"I don't know yet. Why?"

"Because the DEA has pulled everyone but me out of Laycock."

"WAIT WHILE I back out the SUV," Annalynn said as we reached the garage. "Stuart and Phoenix can share the backseat with Achilles." She eased the tank out a few inches at a time. She'd rarely driven it because Boom used it as his official vehicle.

I stared at Stuart, daring him to say anything about women drivers. His eyes stayed on the street.

Achilles whined and pressed against my leg. He pulled back on his leash until all his people were in the SUV. Then he leapt onto my lap and barked at Stuart three times.

"Yes, we're all going this time," Stuart said.

I pulled out a cell phone. "I have to call Neil." I reached his answering machine and left a brief message saying I couldn't bring Achilles until tomorrow.

We pulled into the sheriff's parking space a little before three and went inside into a cement-block hall.

Brendan came to meet us. "Everybody complained, but they're coming. I've stashed the civilians in the break room. Here's your spot." He opened the barred door of a holding cell and grinned as Achilles and I stepped inside. "A dog and his bitch."

Stuart shoved Brendan against the bars and held him there with a full-body press. "What was that?"

Achilles growled.

"Sorry," Brendan said, his hands at his sides. "Punch line of an old joke."

"Let's get on with it," I said. "You're upsetting Achilles."

Stuart stepped away from Brendan and into the cell. "No problem."

Brendan closed the door. "We'll start with the prisoners and a couple of parolees I picked up for the occasion."

I sat on the steel bench attached to the wall. It was only about two feet wide, and when Stuart sat beside me, it was quite cozy. Achilles sat equally close on the other side.

A thin young man with sores on his face and arms stumbled down the hall. He stopped to stare at us. "What did they charge the dog with?"

Achilles sniffed and sneezed.

"Move on," Brendan said.

Six more men in their twenties and thirties and two women in their forties came by. Achilles showed less interest in each one.

Brendan came to the cell. "Not even a growl?" He looked down the hall. "Annalynn, you sure you want to go on with this? Dick Rothway threatened to sue."

"Bring him last," Annalynn said.

Brendan grinned. "I'll get them started."

Achilles stretched out on the floor with his head on my feet. He didn't raise his head as footsteps sounded in the hall.

"Hi, Stu. Never thought you'd end up behind bars."

The bar owner stuck his hand through the bars to me. "Hi, I'm Harry Prodski. I own Harry's Hideaway."

"Phoenix Smith." I rose to shake his hand. "I've heard about your place."

"Come on out and see it for yourself. We got a great new singer who'll be appearing on select weekends this summer."

"I wouldn't miss that," Stuart said, his lips twitching. "Thanks for coming."

Cary Callaway ambled down the hall, feigning nonchalance. He frowned at me. "I don't see what good this will do. You can't take a dog to court as a witness."

"If he identifies the killer, we'll find the evidence," Stuart said.

As the insurance man went on down the hall and out the door, I said, "He didn't want to sell the airplane. He may have more money than he should."

Achilles stood and sniffed.

A balding man in a brown suit, a light-blue shirt, and a red bow tie hurried up. "I don't have time for this nonsense." He stared at Achilles, who was still sniffing. "That's the first Belgian Malinois I've ever seen. I have a German shepherd myself." He reached into his pocket and pulled out a dog biscuit. "May I?"

A little poison would end the lineup. "Thank you, but we're restricting his diet."

"Of course." He hurried off.

I couldn't place the man. "Who was that?"

"Dr. Murphy, the one who didn't prescribe Dalmane. Jim added him."

Achilles stuck his head between the bars and looked down the hall toward Annalynn. He whined.

"Just a little longer," I said as quick steps sounded in the hall.

Achilles yawned.

"This is your doing," the banker snarled to me. "You'll hear from my lawyer about this."

I smiled. "Laundering drug money is a felony, Dickie. You pinpoint the drug traffickers' local contact and we'll help you out."

"You're crazy!" He rushed out as Achilles growled and bared his teeth.

"We've got one more," I said. "My current front-runner."

Stuart called, "Brendan, where's the other one?"

"He just got here. He'll be there in a minute."

Stuart took a firm grip on Achilles' leash. "You must know something that I don't. I wouldn't even have put him on the list."

Achilles pricked up his left ear as footsteps came down the hall.

"Good afternoon," Wesley Berry said. "What's this all about?"

Strike two. One more and I was out.

THIRTY-FOUR

"JUST ROUTINE, REVEREND BERRY," Stuart said, letting go of Achilles' collar. "We put some ringers in any lineup."

Brendan joined us and gave me a told-you-so look. "Thanks for coming in, Wes. Lois is serving homemade cookies in the lobby."

The minister reached through the bars to stroke Achilles. "Happy to help out." He strolled away.

Annalynn's shoulders drooped as she opened the cell door. "Now what?"

"First we eat a cookie. Then it's on to plan B." No faster way to spread rumors than to talk in front of Lois Brendan and Boom's buddies.

Several men waited in the lobby. Each held a cookie in one hand and a paper cup in the other. Lois stood behind a counter by a pot of coffee and a plate of cookies.

Harry leaned against the counter. "We've been talking, George. That dog must be the only witness. Can he really identify the killers?"

I answered. "He's already identified one. When the gang knows we can ID them, they may snitch on each other to get a better deal." I turned to Annalynn. "If you'll lend me Jim, I'll take Achilles all over town until we sniff them out."

Dickie laughed derisively. "You're going to have that dog smell fifteen thousand people?"

"No, Dickie, I'm going to start with what we know

about the local connection and target the most likely places." I smiled. "Such as your bank."

He shook his finger at me. "Watch your mouth, Phoenix." He tossed his paper cup in a trash can and hurried out the door.

Lois sidled up to Achilles and held out her hand for him to sniff. "I'd start at the college."

"Yes, the college seems a logical place," the minister said. "Maria was upset about something that happened at LCC. I suggested she talk to Boom about it."

Annalynn's body tensed, but her face remained calm. "The stalker. Did she say whether it was a student or teacher? Or another employee?"

"Sorry. I've told you everything I can remember." The minister brushed crumbs from his shirt and opened the door. "If you'll excuse me, I have other appointments."

Harry followed Berry, pausing at the door to say, "You're welcome to bring the dog to my place anytime."

"You rest, Phoenix," Annalynn said, taking Achilles' leash from me. "Stuart and I will take Achilles through the cells, offices, and lockers."

And give me a chance to hear what Lois had to say. "Go, Achilles."

Lois handed me a cookie on a napkin. "I always worried about George doing dangerous work. I never thought teaching could get you killed. Poor woman. If only she'd confided in George instead of Boom." She flushed. "I mean—well—George has a lot more experience than Boom." She unplugged the coffeepot, put the plate of cookies in a plastic bag, and walked toward the door. She stopped in front of me, the lines in her face seeming to have deepened. "Is Annalynn going to run for sheriff?"

"She hasn't mentioned it," I said, hiding my surprise. "Thanks for the cookies."

As the door closed behind Lois, I raised an inquiring eyebrow at Connie. She stood in front of a poster on baby car seats. "You're unusually quiet."

"Harry bragged about what a great singer he's discovered. Can't Ma send him a contract? That one gig would pay my plane fare to Seattle to see my grandkids."

I'd find a way to help her financially, but this wasn't it. "Connie, fooling people with a disguise more than once is difficult." But I'd done it a dozen times one winter in Budapest.

"We'd have time to do really good makeup," she argued.

She still dreamed of stardom.

WE WERE ALL quiet on the drive home. Achilles had reacted to no one at the jail. I'd have to flesh out the ghost of plan B. When we pulled into the garage, I asked a vital question: "Annalynn, where's the trapdoor?"

"In front of the SUV. Why?"

"Does it work?"

"I suppose so."

I scrambled to get out ahead of the others and scan the street for hidden gunmen. I kept Achilles, sure to be a prime target, at my side as Annalynn lowered the garage door. Stuart was being equally vigilant. "Stuart, how did—umm, your colleague—die?"

"We don't know yet." He took the street side as we walked toward the house. "No bullet holes. No stab wounds. No bindings. They put whiskey bottles in the car. I'm guessing they drugged him and pushed him in to drown."

"And the time of death?"

"More than twenty-four hours, less than five days. Drowning is tricky. We may not be able to narrow it down much more than that."

Annalynn unlocked the front door and turned off the security alarm. "It's well past four. Stuart and I both have calls to make. Let's meet at six to discuss our next move."

"Good," I said. "I need a little time." Maybe a lot.

Connie made a face. "What am I supposed to do until six?"

"Think about your country music repertoire," Stuart suggested, sitting down at the dining-room table. "Harry's going to be awfully disappointed if you don't show up."

"I've got a job for you, Connie," I said. What could it be? "We need a time line showing events and the people involved from Maria's first contact with Boom up until today. Annalynn, Connie will need to see the reports and notes." Again.

Annalynn nodded. "Of course. It will be good to have a fresh eye."

Connie perked up. "Do you want the time line on paper or the computer?"

I moved toward the stairs. "Computer, with plenty of space for notes. A hard copy for each of us." I bent to take the blanket trailing from Achilles' mouth and carry it upstairs for him. We both needed a nap.

I fell asleep almost instantly and woke to the sound of chiming. Six o'clock. But no evening sunlight streamed in. Through the window I could see dark clouds. Droplets covered the glass. Energy restored, I washed my face, ran a brush through my hair, and headed downstairs.

Stuart met me at the foot of the stairs, blocking me on

the final step so that I stood slightly above him. "You're looking much better." He ran the back of a finger down my cheek. "Or is that makeup?"

"No, it's—"

He pulled my face down and his lips cut off my words in a no-holds-barred kiss.

Puzzled but pleased, I closed my eyes and did my part. Until I sensed an audience.

Neil Jones watched us from the door of the TV room, the corners of his mouth curving up. "Evening. The barbecue got rained out, so I came by to check on Achilles."

"Thanks, Neil." I edged by Stuart. "That was very thoughtful. How is he?"

"He's done very well. I should check him again in a few days. I better get going."

I escorted Neil to the door and bade him good night with my best smile.

As soon as the door closed, Stuart stepped up and put his arm around my waist. "He couldn't measure up to you in high school, and he's nothing but an ego booster for you now. You'd get tired of that 'Aw, shucks' act fast."

Stuart had pegged me exactly. He could be dangerous. "It's none of your business."

"Maybe not, but the way you've been taking risks is." He shifted to face me. "You act as though your life doesn't matter to—to us. You have to stop going it alone."

"You're right," I said, throwing his favorite phrase back at him.

He grinned. "Glad to hear you say that. We set up in the TV room."

We joined the others. Annalynn and Connie sat on the floor by the coffee table. Stuart went to the far end of the huge couch.

Connie handed me two sheets of paper. "I started the time line in February with the stalker."

I sat in the middle of the couch and studied the top sheet: six known out-of-town meetings between Maria and Boom, the first in late February and the last in early May. "Other people came forward with sightings?"

"Right," Annalynn said. "The last one was an LCC student."

Connie tapped on her sheet with a pen. "Elena must know something else. It can't be a coincidence that they stole her car for the hit-and-run."

I'd recognized the tactic. "They stole her car to try to shift the blame. Just like what they did by staging a murder-suicide and by sending Binkie after us."

Annalynn pushed a tuna sandwich toward me. "Connie and I think Maria's stalker is the local dealer. That's why he had money for expensive gifts. He must have been stalking Maria when she went to the motel to meet Boom and the DEA agent."

I agreed. "It fits with what we know."

Stuart handed me a ballpoint. "I can add some times to our list. Bill Graksi received a call from Boom the Friday before the murders and left his house with Achilles around four Monday. A clerk at the McDonald's by the motel remembers a man with a big dog in the drive-through sometime between six and eight."

I studied the time line. "The laborers' party got noisy about nine and went on until almost midnight. It gave the killers a way to cover up any noise they made." Those chilling screams. "They didn't do anything when Graksi came back to the room with Boom. Either they weren't concerned, or taking on two cops at once was too risky. Maria showed up after her night class, at a little before ten, and Boom came on home."

Stuart leaned forward, elbows on his knees. "It seems significant that the gang didn't act until Maria arrived. They grabbed her and Graksi, and then they called Boom on Bill's phone to get him back there. Why?"

Annalynn shuddered, and Connie stroked her back.

I remembered the photos of the crime scene. "Of the three victims, Maria had the most painful death. Quite likely a prolonged death. I think the stalker followed her to the motel. He killed her as much for revenge as to protect himself." I couldn't get the idealistic young woman's face out of my mind. "Whoever killed them knew something about crime scenes. He must have law enforcement training."

Stuart shrugged. "These days anyone can learn the basics by watching TV crime shows." He pointed at the time line. "What about the Morse code messages? Where do they come in?"

"They don't." I embroidered the truth: "George and Boom were doing some confidential security work for a businessman who moved hazardous products once a month. He insisted on coded messages."

Annalynn reacted first, her face incredulous. "Why didn't Boom tell me?"

"Because it was dangerous, so dangerous that George took an MP5." I didn't look at Stuart, the one most likely to question my story. "George didn't tell Lois, either."

Stuart glanced at me and looked away. "You can fill me in on that later."

"We still haven't the slightest idea who to be afraid of," Connie said, her voice trembling.

"That's why we need Plan B." I decided to give them the extreme version so I'd have room to retreat. "Everybody leaves, and I wait alone in my house with Achilles."

"That's insane!" Stuart sprang up. "You're *not* facing those killers alone!"

"Of course not! But it has to look that way." I reached out a reassuring hand to Annalynn. "Let me explain what I have in mind. But first, we need to see whether we can use the trapdoor."

Stuart stopped gritting his teeth. "I checked it. It's easy to get through, but it's heavy to open."

Annalynn's face had turned china white. "Your plan has to be foolproof, Phoenix."

If only anything could be. "Here's how it works. Four people go into the garage. Achilles and I go next door. The car backs out. Four people drive away." I held up my hand to shush Stuart. "Two passengers are dummies. Two people go through the trapdoor and come through the passageway into my house. Dummies work better at night, but we can fix them up to pass during the day, too."

He leaned back and stared at the ceiling. "You figure they're watching us."

"If they aren't, they will be soon."

Connie had curled into a fetal position. "My God! You planned to make your house the trap and yourself part of the bait all along."

I answered Annalynn rather than Connie: "It's the quickest—and safest—way to get them."

Stuart's hand moved to his gun. "You're right, but *I'll* take Achilles next door. You'll leave with Annalynn."

Annalynn tossed the time line on the floor. "It's too risky. We'll put Achilles under guard and wait for the DEA to get answers from Pancho."

Connie looked at Stuart and then at me. "Do we dare wait?"

"No," I said, certain I was right. "We have to be ready by tomorrow morning."

Stuart nodded. "Here's what we'll do. Three agents come here. Three agents—you three masters of disguise—leave. I go next door with Achilles. The others go through the passage."

"An ideal solution," I agreed, "but what if you can't get three agents back here in time? Let's prepare to do it with dummies and deputies."

Connie hopped to her feet. "I'll work on the dummies. What can we use?"

A roll of basso thunder made me shiver. "We can put something round—say a soccer ball—into the hood of a jacket. Use a pillow for the body and a broad hanger to shape the shoulders and fasten onto the headrest."

"Strictly as a backup measure." Stuart got up and motioned for me to come with him. "I'd like a good look at your house before I call in the cavalry, Phoenix."

"Right. We'll go through the passage."

Annalynn gripped my shoulder. "I can't do this, Phoenix. I can't risk your life. I want you and Stuart to put Achilles in the car and go."

I patted her hand and said with much more bravado than I felt, "Since when have I done what you wanted me to do?"

"You're wasting your time, Annalynn," Connie said. "She'll do it her way." Her face now showed excitement rather than concern. "Where are the hoodies?"

Annalynn hesitated a moment. "I'll get them."

Achilles stayed close as Stuart and I went through the passage into my basement and up the stairs into my house.

I switched on the hall light and then the overhead light in the dining room. It left the living room in deep shadow. I turned on the floor lamp by the couch. "They'll come in through Annalynn's backyard. They can break the lock on my porch door with a hard shove. The dead bolt on the house door will hold them a couple of seconds."

"I see three doors on each side of the hall. Where does each lead?"

"Behind the dining room are the bathroom, a coat closet, and the only bedroom with a closet. Behind the living room and the basement stairs are two bedrooms."

Stuart walked down the hall toward the back door. "They'll shoot off the lock and keep shooting as they come through the door."

A shoot-out in my childhood home. Incredible. "The front door is right in the line of fire from the back door. If I were surprised, I'd head for the basement. Anyone coming through the basement door after me would be an easy target."

Stuart stepped into the big bedroom and turned on the light. "They'll count on Achilles rushing them. Let's record him barking and run the tape to convince them he's at the back door. With luck they'll empty their guns before they come in."

"I don't think so. They'll want to make sure they kill him this time."

"When they come in, I step out of the closet and get the drop on them from the back while the other agents cover them from the dining room and basement."

He was too confident. "Forget about covering them. Shoot to kill."

Instead of answering, he turned out the bedroom light and went back to the dining room. "Let's turn the piano around so that the back becomes an extension of the hall wall. One person can use the piano for cover."

He inspected the living room. "No shield here. A bullet would slice right through that couch."

Footsteps sounded on the basement stairs. Connie came into the hall carrying a flesh-colored Styrofoam head with eyes and lips painted on it and a marshmallow taped on for the nose. "How does this look?"

"You haven't captured the Roper nose," Stuart said, "but that should do under a hood. Could you help me move the piano, please?"

"Sure." Connie handed the head to me with a questioning look.

I nodded. I'd improve on it later.

They positioned the piano so the keyboard was in the dining room and the back to the living room.

When Connie left to add eyelashes, I sat down at the keyboard and ran my hands over the keys. "If you don't mind, I'll play a little while. It helps me think."

"Be my guest. I'll take a look at the basement."

I played a warm-up scale. Achilles sat listening, his left ear twitching. When Stuart came back upstairs, I stopped playing and closed the lid so Achilles couldn't drool on the keys. I shivered. "It's chilly tonight."

"It's raining. Let's go back to Annalynn's where it's warmer to make my calls."

His cell chirped. "What is it?" He pulled me close and shared the receiver.

Annalynn said, "The dispatcher called me about a fire in an abandoned house about five miles out on Route Y. A firefighter found a Kansas City Royals cap, like Bill Graksi's, on the ground outside."

Stuart stiffened. "We were there yesterday. We would've found the cap. They've baited a trap for *us*."

"That's my reading." Annalynn's voice was calm. "But here or there?"

I took charge. “Pretend to fall for it. Tell the dispatcher to radio George to meet you there. Then get a dummy into the car through the trapdoor. Stuart will come out of here, go into the garage, and come back here through the trapdoor.”

He pulled the phone away. “You’re going with Annalynn.”

“You don’t stand a chance alone. Together we can handle them.” I grabbed the phone. “Annalynn, call Jim to meet you at the church in his personal car. Have him call the closest backup on his cell and tell them to wait in the Franklin School parking lot. As soon as we have a hint of trouble, we’ll let you know by cell and you can send in the backup.”

“We’ll be no more than a minute away. Stuart, call my cell as soon as you’re in place.” She hung up.

Stuart took back his phone. “You and Achilles choose your spot in the basement while I help Connie get the dummy through the trapdoor.” He ran down the steps.

I led Achilles down the basement steps. “Stay, boy. Quiet.” I went back up, closed the door, and moved the floor lamp from the living room to the keyboard side of the piano, stretching the cord to its full length. I turned off the overhead light in the dining room and left on the lamp. They’d expect me to hide behind the piano or in the kitchen. The couch wouldn’t stop bullets, but I’d have a better chance of surprising them and getting off fatal shots from the floor behind it.

Stuart ran up the basement steps wearing a hooded sweatshirt. “You belong in the basement.”

“Don’t argue. They’ll expect me to be there. I’ll be behind the couch flat on the floor. Don’t aim low.”

He licked his lips. “You’re right. I’ll keep low, too.” He pulled the couch out from the wall a foot or so and dragged it to within an inch of the hall before hurrying out the front door with his hood up. "Back in a minute."

I locked the door and sat down at the piano to play the bold opening chords of Beethoven's *Ninth Symphony*. That would tell anyone lurking out back—and Achilles—I was there. I kept playing as Stuart came through the basement door and crept down the hall to the bedroom. Three minutes later I switched to *Eine Kleine Nachtmusik,* a soft piece that wouldn't drown out someone bursting in the back door.

"Phoenix!" Stuart called softly. "Your yard light just went out."

I finished the passage before sliding behind the couch feet first on my back with the Glock in my hand.

A thump at the back door announced the arrival. A second later a burst of bullets hit the back door. A couple thudded into the front door.

The MP5. The final pieces of the puzzle clicked in place. Bloody hell! He knew the house! I unplugged the lamp.

Achilles barked wildly as the back door burst open.

Bullets sprayed again, shattering glass.

A scream of pain in the bedroom. A shout of triumph in the hall.

Stuart had little chance of surviving that barrage. No time to grieve. I'd heard only one set of footsteps, only one gun. He'd come alone. Achilles and I had a chance.

The gunman fired a burst into the door of my brothers' bedroom, another into the hall closet, and another into the bathroom. He was looking for me.

Achilles growled like a grizzly on the basement steps. Outside a car took off with a screech of tires.

I'd get only one shot, and I had to take it as he got into position to fire through the basement door at Achilles.

A burst of bullets twanged piano wires and cracked the front windows. He'd almost emptied the magazine. He'd fire the rest through the basement door and come after me with his Glock 24.

Silence. He was listening for me.

Achilles howled. He was at the top of the steps in the line of fire.

I stuck the plug in the wall. As the killer fired toward the light, I propelled myself toward the hall with my feet and fired at the sweet spot just behind his ear.

He dropped like a log, his head a foot from mine and the MP5 still clutched in his hands.

I reached out with my left hand and jerked the MP5 away. I got to my knees and opened the basement door as far as the sprawling body would permit.

Achilles squeezed through.

"Guard him, Achilles!" A useless command. He'd died instantly. Just as Boom had. I stumbled over the body, ran into the bedroom, and switched on the light. Stuart's left leg stuck out the closet door. Blood covered it and the floor around it. Five bullet holes angled down the closet door from top to bottom.

"Stuart?" I tossed the MP5 on the bed and jerked the door open. He lay on his back, but I saw no blood except on his legs. Blood gushed from his right calf. I yanked the slip off the pillow and wound it around the leg above the wound. Grabbing his gun off the floor, I released the magazine and used it to tighten the tourniquet.

Annalynn's voice came from a cell phone on Stuart's chest. "Phoenix! Phoenix!"

I gave the tourniquet a final twist and grabbed the phone. "We need an ambulance *now.* Stuart is losing a lot of blood. I think he's going into shock."

"It's on the way. Are you okay?"

"Fine. So is Achilles."

"What about the killers?"

"The driver took off when the gunfire started, but I killed Sean."

"Sean? Sean O'Reilly? George's nephew?"

"Yes. That's why Boom didn't tell George about the investigation."

THIRTY-FIVE

I WOKE TO the unpleasantly familiar odor of a hospital. Had I dreamed my return to Laycock? I opened my eyes. Stuart lay in a bed four feet away. Of course. I'd fallen asleep on the other bed after his long surgery. I threw the blanket off and swung my legs—now in green scrubs—over the side of the bed to the floor.

Stuart remained pale in spite of the transfusion, but he didn't appear to be suffering. I leaned over and brushed the corner of his mouth with my lips.

He opened his eyes. "You can do a lot better than that."

I drew back. "Not until you're vertical again. How do you feel?"

"Lucky. Woozy. Confused. When I heard the submachine gun, I dropped flat, or at least all of me except my knees did. My legs caught on fire. Who shot me?"

"Sean O'Reilly, Deputy Brendan's nephew. He stole his uncle's MP5 yesterday, probably right after he heard they'd found Graksi's body. I should have suspected him. For a kid with no job, he had too much money—his own place, an expensive car, a fancy gun. I knew he was spying on Annalynn, but I thought he was doing it for his uncle."

"Was Sean the stalker?"

"Yes. His buddy—the kid who drove away when he heard the firing—confirmed that. Sean hated Maria because she refused to date him, and he hated Boom when he saw them together. Hell hath no fury like a man scorned, you know. Apparently his expensive gifts and his aggressive courting not only alarmed her but also aroused her suspicions, and she told Boom."

"I doubt if they had anything more than vague suspicions," Stuart said, his voice barely audible. "An experienced agent like Bill Graksi would have reported it before he came here. How did Sean, Pancho, and friends put Bill, Boom, and Maria together?"

"Pretty much the way we guessed. Pancho claims Sean freaked out and killed Boom and Maria and took Graksi and Achilles to kill later, but Sean couldn't have done it alone. His buddy, Tony Engel, can prove he was doing inventory at the pet store until midnight that night, so he's in the clear for the killings. He confessed to Annalynn that he was selling crystal meth for Sean."

Stuart digested this. "How did they know how to fake a murder-suicide?"

"Sean had just taken a forensics course, and he'd pumped his uncle about crime-scene investigations. I should've paid more attention when he bad-mouthed Boom and poor Maria Lopez." I'd missed another clue, too. "He was wearing a bandanna on his wrist the day he cleaned out my garage. I thought it was a fashion statement, but he was covering where Achilles bit him."

Stuart reached for my hand. "But you didn't know Achilles existed yet. It's always easier to see the clues after you know who done it."

"Good morning," Connie trilled from the door. She wore matching turquoise slacks and sleeveless top and carried a long white cane. "I brought you a visitor." She stepped aside, and Achilles darted to me.

I knelt to hug him, fending off his attempts to lick my face.

Achilles put his paws on Stuart's bed and licked his hand.

"We have to keep my *guide* dog quiet," Connie warned. "Stuart, you're looking—alive. How do you feel?"

"Terrible. I'm going to need weeks of tender loving care."

I laughed, relieved that he felt well enough to flirt. "I'm sure your mother will be delighted to give you that."

"Naturally," he said, "but my mother can't take care of all my needs."

Connie pretended to gag. "Actually, you look better than Phoenix does this morning." She turned on the TV suspended from the wall. "It's time for Annalynn's press conference. She'll give the expurgated version."

Annalynn, her uniform crisp, her face drawn, walked through the jail parking lot to a lectern holding a dozen television and radio microphones. "Good morning. I will summarize recent developments in the investigation into the murders of Boom Keyser, Maria Lopez, and William Graksi, but I can take no questions today."

"Come on, Sheriff Keyser. That's not fair," a reporter called.

Annalynn ignored him. "Yesterday morning the Adair County sheriff's department pulled a car containing the body of DEA Agent William Graksi from Forest Lake in Thousand Hills State Park. Agent Graksi came to Laycock two weeks ago to assist my late husband in investigating a crystal-meth operation. Saturday the DEA arrested an alleged member of that organization, but we had been unable to identify the local traffickers. Agent Graksi's dog was our only witness."

"God, but she's good," Connie said.

Annalynn sipped from a paper cup. "Last night

Sean Brendan O'Reilly, twenty-two, entered the house in which we were protecting the witness. Mr. O'Reilly opened fire. In the exchange of fire, he wounded a DEA agent and suffered a fatal wound."

Beautifully done. Everyone would assume Stuart killed Sean.

"An officer stopped a vehicle fleeing the scene. We will file charges against the driver, Tony Engel, twenty-one, later today."

Jim Falstaff touched her elbow, and they stepped away from the mikes.

"I can't place Tony Engel," Stuart said.

"The kid who told your agent at Harry's that Sean bought the car with inherited money. Tony works at the pet store where I took Achilles and paid with my P. D. Smith credit card, which is probably why they targeted me."

Annalynn returned to the microphone. "In conducting a search of Mr. O'Reilly's safe-deposit box at the First National Bank, we found"—she ducked her head and breathed deeply before continuing—"we found my husband's cell phone. It had one text message on it. 'Need help. Come alone.'" She raised the cup to her lips, obscuring the lower half of her face for several seconds. She put the cup down, revealing her public face. "Our investigation is continuing," she went on, her voice steady. "We will issue a more detailed statement within twenty-four hours." She walked away as reporters shouted questions.

I turned off the set and, seeing Stuart's clenched jaw, rang for a nurse. "You need something for the pain." Knowing a call didn't necessarily mean a response, I went into the hall and beckoned to a nurse at the station.

The woman nodded pleasantly. "Two minutes."

"We better get Achilles out of here before she comes," Connie said. "You'll have to go with me, Phoenix. He won't leave without you."

"Go ahead," Stuart said. "I don't want you to see me cry."

I kissed him on the lips, lingering this time. "I'll be back."

Connie put on her sunglasses and took my arm. "Lead me out." As soon as we left the room, she said, "Achilles whined all night. I found him curled up on your bed this morning. I don't know what the law says about ownership, but he's your dog."

I hadn't owned a dog since I left Laycock. I'd had to make too many quick trips and unexpected night runs to keep an animal. It was nice to be adored. I pressed the elevator button. "We have to return that clunker." No loose ends.

"I'll turn it in at the Dairy Queen and tell them Rose Dowd is a friend of mine. In fact, Earlene will stay at my house when she sings at Harry's Hideaway."

She wasn't going to give up on that.

Annalynn drove up in her SUV as we came outside. She jumped out for a quick group hug. "Thank you. You've both been wonderful."

Tears glistened on Connie's cheeks. She fluffed her curls. "And, unlike Phoenix, I'll be wonderful next week."

Annalynn laughed. One hand on my shoulder and one on Connie's, Annalynn said, "Phoenix is always wonderful, and so are you." She sobered and panic flitted across her face. "But next week won't be. How am I going to live without Boom?"

Achilles licked her hand.

"I know," Connie said. "You're going to hurt like hell

for a long time. But Phoenix has a marvelous idea for the three of us. She'll tell you about it later."

I smiled as if I knew what Connie was talking about.

Annalynn's eyes widened. "Give me a hint."

"I'm still in the conceptual stage."

"Please, Phoenix, don't be coy."

Not coy. Clueless. "I won't say a word until I've run some numbers and made some calls." I frowned at Connie. "You weren't supposed to say anything."

She giggled. "I couldn't resist."

Annalynn smiled. "Déjà vu, you two. I have to go back to the office. The reporters should have left by now." She stroked Achilles. "Does this marvelous idea involve Achilles, too?"

"Of course," Connie said. "By the way, how's George doing?"

Annalynn climbed into her SUV. "He's in shock. I told him to take whatever time he needs, but I expect him to be back on the job soon." She drove off with a wave.

Connie's smile disappeared. "Phoenix, why didn't Boom tell George about his psycho nephew?"

"Boom had suspicions, not proof. Besides, blood is blood, even when you don't get along. Maybe Sean started selling drugs partly as a way of thumbing his nose at his uncle." I pictured the strong young body sprawled on my hall floor and felt regret but no guilt. "I don't know why he became so vicious. He did. He had to be stopped."

"I suppose Sean hated Boom and Maria because he thought they were having an affair." Connie shivered. "I can't stand to think about it anymore. Let's go. You have to work on your marvelous idea."

"What on earth are you talking about?"

She pirouetted to her yellow Beetle. "You just promised Annalynn a reason to keep going without Boom. And you never let Annalynn down." She unlocked the car doors. "I can hardly wait to hear what you come up with."

"Neither can I." I let my dog into the backseat. "Whatever it is, you know that you and I can't solve Annalynn's problems for her. We each have to find our own solutions." I lifted my face to the optimistic spring sun. "I'll come up with something. It's like when we graduated from high school and went out into the wonderful unknown. We're going into our second adolescence."

* * * * *

ABOUT THE AUTHOR

CAROLYN MULFORD DEVELOPED a love for writing while growing up on a farm in northeast Missouri. After earning degrees in English and journalism, she served as a Peace Corps Volunteer in Ethiopia. There she became fascinated by other cultures. She has followed those interests by traveling on six continents and editing a United Nations magazine in Vienna, Austria, and a national service-learning magazine in Washington, DC. As a freelancer, she wrote hundreds of articles and several nonfiction books before changing her focus to fiction and returning to Missouri. Her first novel, *The Feedsack Dress,* became Missouri's Great Read at the 2009 National Book Festival. In *Show Me the Murder,* an ex-spy and two old friends deal with crime and personal crises in rural Missouri.